# Blood of the Labyrinth

by Aveline Hart

*Her blood can seal the world - or destroy it.*

First Edition: 2026

*For those who were told they were too much to be loved. May you find someone who chooses you anyway—especially if he has horns.*

# Table of Contents

# The Scent of Burning Ash

The dead town still smelled like wet ash and the copper sting of old blood.

I moved through it anyway, because the alternative was standing still, and standing still in places like Black Hollow had a way of becoming permanent.

The ruins were skeletal. Roof beams had collapsed inward like broken ribs, and whatever fires had eaten through this place had been thorough enough to strip the walls down to blackened stone. Charred timber jutted from the ground at odd angles. What had once been a market square was now a flat expanse of scorched earth and wind-scattered ash, still soft underfoot despite however many seasons had passed since the burning. Rain had come recently. The whole place smelled of it, that heavy mineral dampness pressing down from a sky the color of bruised iron, and underneath it, the ghost of something older. Older and worse.

I kept my hand near the longer of my two daggers and my eyes moving.

The grain shipment had passed through here six hours ago, according to the tracks. Three wagon wheels, two sets of horse hooves, and at least four men on foot, one of them dragging his left leg. I'd been following the trail since before dawn, cutting east through the Scorched Borderlands. My eyes stung with a gritty, dry heat from too little sleep, and a faint tremor worked its way through my fingers whenever I let my hand drift from my belt—the predictable tax of too much bitter coffee brewed over a fire too small to be safe.

The refugees at the Millhaven hollow needed that grain. They were down to root paste and rain-caught water, and while I had no particular interest in being anyone's savior, I had a very particular interest in the information their elder had promised in exchange for consistent supply runs. Information cost less than steel and lasted longer, and in my line of work, it was the only currency that never devalued.

So I tracked stolen grain through a dead town in the rain.

A fine life.

I paused at the edge of what had been a cooperage, pressing my back against the only standing wall and scanning the open stretch ahead. The tracks veered left here, toward the Whispering Thickets, which was a name given by someone with either a sense of poetry or a sense of humor, because there was nothing whimsical about that tree line. The Thickets were a narrow band of dense, gnarled forest that pressed up against the old border markers, the kind of place where sound behaved strangely, where a snapped twig echoed three seconds too late from the wrong direction, and your own voice felt flat and instantly muffled, as if the damp moss were actively swallowing the air before it could reach your ears, leaving you feeling slightly too thick in the lungs.

The kind of place you didn't follow tracks into without a very good reason.

I had several reasons. None of them felt good.

But I went.

The silence hit me the moment I crossed the tree line, and not the comfortable kind of silence that settles after a long night. This was the other kind, the kind that had weight and texture, the kind that meant every living thing in the area had already decided to be somewhere else. No insects. No birds stirring in the branches overhead. Even the wind had pulled back, leaving the leaves motionless despite the storm pressure still building in the sky above.

My heartbeat felt very loud.

I slowed. Put each foot down with deliberate care, testing for dry leaves and snapping twigs before committing my weight. The tracks were still visible, the dragging boot print distinct in the soft earth, but they had changed course twice in the last hundred meters in a way that no one transporting stolen grain would bother to do.

They were not leading me somewhere.

They were drawing me somewhere.

The realization arrived with cold clarity rather than panic, because panic was a luxury I had never been able to afford. I stopped moving entirely, crouched low beside a mossy boulder, and cataloged what I knew. Four men, minimum. Probably more positioned in the canopy or behind the larger formations of deadfall to my right. The dragging-foot print was deliberate, a detail designed to hold my attention on the trail and keep me from scanning the perimeter. Clever. Not clever enough, but clever.

They had positioned themselves well. I gave them that.

The first one came from my left, which was the direction I had already marked as secondary concern, which meant he had been patient enough to wait for me to dismiss him. That was the most dangerous kind of mercenary, the patient kind, and I moved before he finished clearing the undergrowth, dropping under the arc of his sword and driving my elbow into his throat with the full rotation of my shoulder behind it.

He went down hard and loud. So much for silence.

Two more broke from the right immediately, which told me they had been waiting for exactly that sound. I let the first one's momentum carry past me, catching his extended sword arm and redirecting rather than blocking, using his own forward drive to slam him into his partner. They tangled briefly. I opened a deep cut across the first man's forearm as he went down and turned to put the boulder at my back before the fourth one appeared.

He was bigger than the others, and he came in low, which meant he had done this before. I took a graze across my left ribs from his knife before

I caught his wrist, twisted, and felt the joint give with a sound that made even me wince. He screamed. I put my boot into his knee and moved.

Running was not retreat. Running was tactics.

I broke hard for the eastern edge of the Thickets, where the tree line thinned enough to give me speed and sight lines. My ribs burned where the knife had caught me, not deep, not dangerous, but insistent in the way minor wounds always were, demanding attention I couldn't spare. Behind me, I could hear the two I'd knocked down recovering, voices calling to each other in the mercenary shorthand of men who had worked together long enough to stop using names.

They were organized. More organized than grain thieves had any reason to be.

The thought arrived and lodged there like a splinter as I pushed through a wall of low-hanging branches and broke into the narrower corridor of trees near the border markers. Something about this was wrong in a way that went beyond ambush mechanics. The positioning had been too patient. The numbers were too deliberate. And none of them had shouted anything about cargo or payment or the usual noise that came with mercenary work. They had simply come for me with quiet, methodical violence.

“Alive,” one of the mercenaries barked somewhere behind me, close enough that I could hear the strain in his breathing. “The Catalyst has to be breathing.”

Catalyst.

The word hit harder than the knife had.

I nearly made it to the tree line.

Nearly.

The voice stopped me three steps from open ground.

"You always were expensive, niece."

I stopped.

The world did not stop with me. Rain had finally started, a thin, miserable drizzle that caught in my hair and ran cold down the back of my neck, and somewhere behind me the mercenaries were still moving, slower now, as though they had been told there was no longer any need to rush. The realization of what that meant hit my chest first, a sharp contraction that made it hard to draw a full breath, before it spread outward to numb my fingers and pool like lead in the bottom of my stomach, each second of understanding colder than the last.

Valerius Thorne stepped out from between two ancient oaks as though he had been waiting there for a pleasant afternoon, which, knowing him, he might have been. He looked exactly as I remembered him from the last time I'd had the misfortune of breathing the same air, which was to say he looked like a man who had spent too long pretending to be better than he was. The tattered finery. The thinning hair plastered to his temples from the rain. The watery blue eyes that had always known how to arrange themselves into an expression of wounded dignity whenever he needed someone to believe he had feelings worth respecting.

He was holding something.

A flat disc of silver, palm-sized, etched with symbols that made my eyes want to slide away from them. Labyrinthine. Recursive. The kind of geometry that looked like it had been designed to be looked at from somewhere other than here. Even at ten feet of distance, the metal had a quality to it, a faint wrongness in the air around it, the way lightning smells before it strikes.

My blood knew it before my mind did.

The sensation was visceral and immediate, a sharp, pulling ache deep in my sternum, as though something inside me was straining toward the artifact against my will. Or straining away. I couldn't tell which, and the ambiguity was more frightening than either option would have been alone.

"I should have slit your throat years ago," I said.

My voice came out steadier than I expected. I was grateful for small mercies.

Valerius smiled, and the smile had the same quality it always had, the one that had fooled me when I was young enough to still want an uncle who was worth the word. He let out a slow, practiced sigh, his lower lip twitching with the perfect imitation of a tremor. The expression of a man burdened by difficult choices made on behalf of people too foolish to appreciate them.

"Yes," he said, his tone carrying the particular softness of someone who had rehearsed this. "That was always your weakness. Hesitation."

He stepped forward and lifted one hand, touching my cheek with a gentleness so deliberate it made my skin crawl. I didn't move. My daggers were in my hands but the mercenaries were close enough behind me that drawing back meant walking into them, and the silver artifact in his other hand was doing something to my concentration, pulling at it, making the edges of my focus smear in ways I did not understand and did not like.

"How long?" I asked, because knowing mattered, and because if I kept him talking I had time to find the angle I was missing. There was always an angle.

"Months," he said, with the satisfied ease of a man who had looked forward to this conversation. "You are not as difficult to track as you believe, Elara. Not for someone who knows what to look for."

"And what exactly are you looking for?"

"Your blood," he said simply, as though that were a reasonable sentence. "Which is worth considerably more than you have ever understood. Than they allowed you to understand."

The artifact pulsed.

I felt it in my teeth. In the hollow of my throat. In the marrow of my forearms where old, half-healed breaks had left the bone slightly denser than it should have been. The pulling sensation sharpened from a dull ache into something with edges, and my blood responded to it in a way that was entirely involuntary and deeply alarming, a hot, surging pressure that moved beneath my skin like something trying to answer a call I had never consented to make.

"What is that?" I said, and I hated that the words came out rougher than I intended, hated the way my voice betrayed the fact that I was frightened, not of Valerius, never of Valerius, but of the thing in his hand and whatever it knew about me that I didn't.

"A key," he said. "Of sorts. Or a lock. The scholars disagree."

He tilted the disc slightly, and the symbols on its surface caught what little gray light filtered through the canopy and threw it back wrong, refracted into colors that had no names in any language I spoke.

"The people who want you," Valerius continued, his voice taking on the particular cadence he had always used when he wanted me to understand that he had already won, "are not people you negotiate with, my dear. They are people you serve. Or, more accurately, they are people whose purposes you fulfill, whether you consent to or not. I am simply the mechanism of delivery."

"You sold my family," I said. "You sold the village. And now you're selling me."

Something moved in his expression. Not guilt, exactly. Something thinner than guilt. The ghost of a man who might have felt guilty once, a long time ago, before he had practiced his justifications often enough that they had calcified into something he had mistaken for truth.

"I made impossible choices," he said, "so that one branch of this family might survive. You were always too headstrong to understand the larger picture."

"The larger picture," I repeated.

"Yes."

I lunged for him.

Not for the artifact. For his throat. Because there was a version of this that ended with Valerius Thorne bleeding out in the Whispering Thickets and the silver disc buried under six feet of scorched earth, and I wanted that version badly enough to stop calculating and simply move.

I almost reached him.

The artifact activated between one heartbeat and the next, not with light or sound or any of the dramatic warnings that magic in stories always provided. It simply happened, the way terrible things always happened, without ceremony and without mercy. The symbols flared, the wrongness in the air collapsed inward, and something cold closed around my throat.

Cold iron.

The collar snapped into existence against my skin with a sound like a lock finding its catch, and the effect was instantaneous and total. My knees hit the ground before I understood I was falling. The strength went out of my legs, then my arms, then my hands, and my daggers dropped into the wet earth without me feeling them leave my grip. The heightened awareness I had carried since childhood, the sharpness of instinct, the extra half-second of perception that had kept me alive through a dozen situations that should have killed me, compressed down to nothing, as though someone had pressed a cloth over a flame.

I was still conscious. That was the cruelest part. Fully, horribly conscious, aware of every detail with the dull, stripped-down senses of someone ordinary, someone without the extra layer of perception I had never even thought to name until it was gone. The rain on my face. The mud soaking through the knees of my trousers. The cold of the iron against my pulse point, not just cold in the way of metal left outdoors, but cold in the way of something designed to be cold, deliberately, specifically cold, the kind that had intent behind it.

Valerius crouched in front of me.

He looked genuinely sorry, which was the most infuriating expression a human face had ever arranged itself into in my presence, and I had seen a great many infuriating expressions in twenty-five years of being alive.

"It will pass," he said, with the gentle authority of someone who had no idea what he was talking about. "The disorientation. They told me it passes."

I tried to tell him what I thought of that.

What came out was not words.

The darkness arrived in stages. First at the edges of my vision, then from the center outward, which was the wrong direction for darkness to move, but nothing about this was behaving according to any rules I recognized. The iron at my throat pulsed with a cold that had migrated from my skin into the deeper tissue, into the blood itself, muffling something I had never known was there until the moment it was silenced.

Valerius said something else. I lost the words before they reached me.

The ground was wet and cold and smelled of ash and rain and old, old blood, and the last thing I registered clearly was the sound of the mercenaries moving around me with the unhurried efficiency of men who had already been paid and had nowhere else to be.

They hadn't been after the grain.

They had never been after the grain.

The Thickets swallowed the sound of my breathing, and the dark swallowed everything else.

# The Iron Collar

I awoke choking on iron and the certainty that I had already died.

The certainty faded, but the iron did not.

It pressed against my throat with a cold that had nothing to do with temperature and everything to do with intent, a suppression so thorough that even drawing breath felt like working against something that did not want me to function. My body cataloged damage in the mechanical way it always did after violence: bruised ribs, raw wrists, a deep ache in the back of my skull that pulsed in time with my heartbeat. The floor beneath me was hard, vibrating faintly with the rhythm of wheels over uneven ground.

Wheels.

I was moving. I opened my eyes.

The cage was iron, obviously. Reinforced bars as thick as my wrist, bolted to a heavy wooden frame that had been built for exactly this purpose. Not cargo. Not livestock. Something that would fight. The bolt pattern on the hinges told me that much before anything else did. I had been put inside by someone who understood that whatever they were transporting would eventually try to leave.

I sat up slowly, testing the collar's tolerance for even that much movement. The nausea rolled in immediately, a nauseating, grinding pressure behind my eyes that turned my vision briefly white at the edges, then receded to something manageable. Not gone. Just waiting.

Outside the cage, the world was wrong.

I had known, somewhere beneath the dark, that I was no longer in the world I knew. The knowing had arrived the way bad news always did, quietly and completely, before I had any defense against it. But knowing and seeing were different things entirely, and what I saw through the bars of the transport cage made me want to close my eyes again and decide none of it was real.

The sky was the wrong color. Not storm-gray, not the bruised purple of coming rain, but something deeper and stranger, a color that sat between blue and black and occasionally shimmered at the edges with faint luminescence, as though the atmosphere itself had a pulse. The sun, if that was what passed for a sun here, hung too large and slightly off-center, casting light that threw shadows in directions that did not correspond to where it sat.

The land was worse.

Massive formations of black stone jutted from the earth at angles that defied anything geology should have been capable of, twisted into shapes that were almost recognizable as something, almost faces or hands or open mouths, close enough to familiar that the brain kept trying to resolve them into sense and kept failing. Between the formations, things grew that were not plants, not exactly, clusters of pale growth that pulsed with faint bioluminescence in colors I had no names for. Soft blue. Sickened gold. A green so deep it bordered on black. They clung to the rock faces and spread across the ground in patterns that looked deliberate and geometric, as if something had arranged them rather than simply grown.

In the distance, horned silhouettes moved against the strange sky.

I looked away from those.

The road, if it could be called that, was pale stone worn smooth by centuries of use. The Bone Road. I had heard that name whispered by people who traded in dangerous information, always with the specific tone reserved for things that were real but better left unconfirmed. I had confirmed it now. I would have preferred not to.

The caravan was larger than I had initially registered. Three transport wagons ahead of mine, two behind, surrounded by mounted guards in mismatched armor that carried the particular quality of gear assembled from multiple sources rather than any single military tradition. Mercenaries. Professional enough to follow formation, sloppy enough that two of them were already sharing a flask in the late morning.

I counted exits. There were none worth counting.

The cage lock was a double-throw mechanism I might have managed with a pin and forty seconds of patience under normal circumstances. My circumstances were not normal. Every time I shifted toward the lock, the collar tightened its cold around my pulse point in a way that wasn't quite pain but was close enough to pain's cousin that my hands refused to cooperate. My fingers fumbled. My concentration slid sideways. The nausea returned with interest.

I tried anyway. Twice. Failed both times in ways that were humiliating in their completeness.

I sat back against the bars and breathed through my nose and tried not to let any of what I was feeling reach my face, because two of the guards nearest the cage were watching me with the casual attention of men who had transported difficult cargo before and knew better than to look away entirely.

Cargo.

The word settled in my chest like a coal.

Not a prisoner. Not captive. Not even a slave, which would have at least implied a transaction between people. Cargo implied I was a thing being moved from one location to another, that the question of whether or not I counted as a person had already been resolved, and the answer was irrelevant to the current logistics.

The rage that came with that was the cleanest feeling I'd had since I woke up.

I held onto it carefully, because clean feelings were useful and I couldn't afford to waste anything.

The two guards nearest me spoke quietly, not bothering to lower their voices. I kept my gaze on the unnatural sky and listened.

"The Court's buyers will be at the crossing before nightfall," the first one said. He had a voice like gravel in a cup, deep and slightly wet at the edges. "If we make the checkpoint by the third bell, we collect the full rate."

"Full rate." The second one let out a sound that wasn't quite a laugh. "Do you know what the Court pays for a breathing Catalyst? I'm retiring somewhere warm. Somewhere with a coast."

"If you live to retire."

"I'll live. The cargo's collared and caged. What's going to stop us?"

Catalyst.

The word again. I had heard it in the Thickets, right before the darkness, and hearing it a second time did not make it less alarming. It made it more alarming because repetition meant it was not an error; it was a category. They had put me in a category I had no knowledge of, and people who were put in categories by organizations powerful enough to hire this many mercenaries tended not to survive long enough to learn what the category meant.

I filed the information alongside everything else I could not use yet and kept my breathing even.

The attack came without warning.

One moment, the caravan was moving, the guards settling into the particular boredom of men who expected nothing to happen. The next, the world came apart at the edges with a violence so sudden and so absolute that my mind registered the noise before it registered the cause: a sound like thunder that had been compressed into something sharper, the wet crack of armor failing, and then screaming, which stopped faster than screaming usually did.

The cage lurched as the wagon horse panicked and the driver failed to hold it. I grabbed the bars and held on while the cage swung sideways, metal biting into my palms, and through the gaps I caught fragmented images of what was happening outside.

Not rescue. Nothing as hopeful as rescue.

The mercenaries were dying with the terrible efficiency of men who had encountered something they were not equipped to fight. I could see three of them down already, a fourth backing against his own horse with his sword raised in the posture of a man who understood he was going to die and was trying to decide whether to admit it. The attackers moved through the caravan like a coordinated tide, massive shapes that my collared instincts could only partially process, only partially warn me about.

Beast-folk. Minotaur war-band.

The knowledge landed with the particular coldness of understanding that a situation has gone from bad to worse by a margin I couldn't yet calculate.

It was over in less time than it should have been. The screaming stopped. The sound of combat resolved into the quieter sounds of aftermath, armor being searched, orders given in a language I didn't speak but whose cadence I recognized as command structure rather than chaos. These were not raiders. There was no looting frenzy, no celebration, no disorder. Someone was running this with the same precision the mercenaries had lacked.

The cage door was still locked when the silence settled.

Then the footsteps came.

I heard him before I saw him, not because he was loud but because everything else went quiet around him the way sound drained away from the center of something massive. A gravitational quiet. The kind that preceded things that could not be ignored.

He appeared at the edge of my vision first as a shape that my mind refused to accept as a single entity, too large, too dark, occupying space with the complete authority of something that had never in its life considered whether it was welcome somewhere. He moved with a silence that was wrong for his size, controlled and deliberate, and he stopped three feet from the cage door and looked at me.

Ivory horns etched with silver that caught the strange light. Soot-black fur across a frame that made the iron bars of my cage look decorative. Molten gold eyes that did not widen, did not soften, did not perform anything at all. Just looked.

The collar reacted.

Whatever the collar had been doing to me since it snapped closed, suppressing, pressing down, silencing, something about his proximity made it do something different. A sharp, pulling vibration moved through the iron against my throat, a resonance I felt in my teeth and behind my sternum, as though the metal recognized something in the air around him and was responding to it involuntarily. My blood moved with it. That same hot, surging pressure from the Thickets, the sensation of something inside me straining toward something outside, something I had not consented to and could not explain.

I locked my jaw and held still.

He studied me for a long moment. I did not look away, because looking away from a predator was a choice with predictable consequences and I was not interested in the consequences.

One of his warriors said something behind him. He responded without turning his head.

Then he looked back at me, and something in his expression shifted the way deep water shifted when something large moved beneath the surface, not visible, only felt.

"Touch me," I said, "and I'll gut you."

My voice came out steadier than I had any right to expect, given the nausea and the collar and the fact that my hands were trembling slightly in a way I was hoping was not visible through the bars.

A long pause. The kind of pause that had weight.

"Bold," he said. His voice was very deep, the kind of deep that resonated in the chest cavity rather than just the ears. "Collared."

He turned and spoke to one of his warriors, and I heard the word for survivor phrased as a question and then answered in the negative. The warriors moved to carry out whatever the order had been, and I decided not to watch that part.

He turned back. Those gold eyes moved over the cage with the careful assessment of someone cataloging structural information, not looking for weaknesses so much as verifying what he already knew.

"You were being taken to auction," he said. It was not a question.

"And you've come to offer a better price?" I kept my voice flat. "How generous."

Something moved in his jaw. Not anger. Something more controlled than anger, the deliberate stillness of a creature that had learned to govern itself and governed itself absolutely.

"You are not theirs," he said.

The simplicity of it was more unsettling than any threat would have been. Three words, spoken with the certainty of someone stating a fact they had already verified, and the particular quality of finality that came with decisions made before conversations began.

I understood, with a clarity that the collar could not suppress entirely, that he had not come to this caravan for me specifically. He had come for something I represented, for whatever a Catalyst was, for whatever my blood meant to people powerful enough to pay what the mercenaries had implied. The distinction between being wanted for myself and being wanted for what I contained felt important to hold onto, because it was the only leverage I had, and it was thin as paper.

"Open the cage," he said to someone behind him.

A warrior moved forward with a key, and the lock disengaged with a sound that should have felt like relief and felt instead like the next door closing.

The door swung open. I stayed where I was.

"Come willingly," Kaelor said, "or I will carry you."

There was no threat in his voice. That was what made it threatening, the complete absence of escalation, the flat certainty of a male who had already assessed the situation and arrived at its conclusion without requiring my participation in the process.

I looked at the open door. I looked at the warriors positioned around the wagon. I looked at the strange sky above the alien land and the bioluminescent growths pulsing softly in the shadows between the black rock formations, and I calculated, because that was what I did, because calculation had kept me alive through a decade of situations that should have killed me.

The math was not favorable.

I was collared. Weakened. In a realm I did not know, surrounded by warriors I could not fight, with no allies, no weapons, no resources beyond my own awareness and whatever was left of my stubbornness.

"I'm not going anywhere with you willingly," I said.

He moved.

I had understood intellectually that he was large. I had not fully understood what large meant in practical terms until he was at the cage door and then inside the cage door in a motion so fluid it barely qualified as movement, and his hands, which were massive and warm and moved with absolute precision, closed around me before I had completed the calculation of how to stop it.

I fought. Of course I fought. I drove an elbow back toward his ribs, found something that felt like stone beneath fur, and achieved nothing except bruising my own arm. I kicked, and the kick connected, and he adjusted his grip without apparent effort, shifting my weight against his chest in a way that pinned my arms and removed approximately every option I had been considering simultaneously.

The heat of him was the worst part. Not the strength, though the strength was infuriating. Not the ease of it, though the ease was humiliating in a way I was going to need significant time alone to properly process. The heat was the worst part because the collar had left me cold to the bone, cold in a way that had migrated past my skin into something deeper, and his warmth pressed against that cold with an immediacy that my body registered completely independently of my opinion on the matter.

I hated my body for noticing.

The scent of him reached me before I could prevent it: smoke, leather, iron, and something darker beneath all of that, something animal and clean and deeply, specifically him, a scent that the collar had apparently not suppressed my ability to perceive. I filed that information away with everything else I was collecting and refused to assign it any meaning beyond tactical data.

He stepped out of the cage and kept walking.

I was still struggling, still working through the limited options available to someone being carried by something significantly larger than most things I had ever encountered, and none of the options were producing results. He held me with the same quality of attention he had given the cage assessment: total, calm, and entirely unmoved by my efforts.

"Put me down," I said, because I had to say something.

He did not put me down.

The warriors parted around us as he walked, and I caught fragments of their faces, expressions I couldn't fully read but recognized in their shape: the careful blankness of soldiers watching something they had decided not to have opinions about. Whatever he had said to them, whatever the command structure here was, it held.

The Bone Road stretched ahead of us, pale and strange beneath the sky, leading deeper into the Labyrinthine Realm. The black stone formations rose on either side, and the bioluminescent growths pulsed their cold, nameless light, and somewhere in the distance a sound moved through the air that was not quite wind and not quite anything else I had a word for.

I stopped struggling. Not because I had accepted anything. Because I was saving what was left of my strength for when it would matter, and because the collar was punishing my effort with waves of nausea that made it difficult to plan anything coherent.

I would find the angle. I always found the angle.

But right now, held against the chest of a minotaur warlord who had just slaughtered an entire mercenary caravan with the efficiency of someone completing routine maintenance, being carried deeper into a world I did not know, wearing iron that silenced something in my blood I had never known existed until it was gone, the angle was not immediately visible.

I looked up at the sky, at its wrong color and its too-large light source and its faint luminescent shimmer at the edges, and I breathed through the cold and the nausea and the rage and the particular humiliation of being utterly without options.

I was not cargo.

I would need to remind them of that.

Soon.

# The Beast King

He did not put me down.

I had not expected him to, not really, but the continued reality of it was its own particular humiliation. Heat crawled up my neck and settled hot in my face, a physical betrayal of my pride that I fought to keep from reaching my expression. I kept my eyes locked on the horizon, refusing to look down, refusing to meet the heavy, assessing gazes of the armored warriors we passed. Every step he took carried me deeper into territory I did not know, surrounded by warriors I could not fight, wearing iron that turned my blood sluggish and my thoughts slow, and I was beginning to understand that struggling was costing me more than it was costing him. He had barely adjusted his grip since we left the cage. His breathing had not changed.

I hated that. I hated it with a focused, specific intensity that was at least useful, because useful anger was better than the alternative. The alternative was fear, and fear was a cold thing that would only invite the mountain wind to slip beneath my skin. I clung to that heat, wrapped it around myself like a shield against the thin altitude and the terrifying height, because I had spent too many years deciding that fear was something I processed after surviving rather than during.

The road stretched ahead, pale stone worn smooth by centuries of use, and the formations of black rock rose on either side like the architecture of something that had never intended to be beautiful. The bioluminescent growths pulsed their cold light in the shadows between the stone. The sky above remained the wrong color, too deep, too still, and somewhere in the distance those horned silhouettes moved against it, unhurried, organized, purposeful.

His forces.

I had time now, carried against his chest with my arms effectively pinned and my options effectively nonexistent, to observe them properly. What I observed made my chest tighten, a cold weight settling in my stomach that was harder to manage than the fear would have been.

They were disciplined.

Not in the loose, mercenary sense of men who followed whoever paid them and held formation only when convenient. These warriors moved in a structured formation: flanking pairs, forward scouts cycling back on rotation, and a rear guard maintaining consistent intervals. When the terrain narrowed between two massive rock faces, the column adjusted without audible command, the flanking pairs compressing inward and the spacing compensating with automatic precision. Signals passed between them in hand gestures I did not recognize but understood immediately as language. A scout simply snapped two fingers down against his thigh, a sharp, silent command that instantly dropped the three warriors behind him into a low, defensive crouch without a single head turning. It was a military shorthand developed through repetition rather than improvised on the spot.

There were rank markings. Different sigils were burned or carved into the armor at the shoulder and collar, with the more elaborate configurations belonging to the warriors who moved at the edges of the formation rather than the center. Officers. Those who held the periphery had the most authority. I filed that away.

I had been told, my entire life, in cold border taverns and mercenary camps where such things were discussed, that the beast-folk of the Labyrinthine Realm were savages. Dangerous, yes. Territorial, certainly. But not organized. Not like this. The story had always been that they were powerful and brutal and ungovernable, which was precisely why the High Fey had such a clear claim to superiority over them.

Looking at this column, I thought someone had been very deliberately telling the wrong story.

"Put me down," I said again, because silence felt like surrender and I had not surrendered. "I can walk."

"You were stumbling before I reached the cage," he said.

His voice came from above and slightly behind me, a deep, gravelly rumble that vibrated against my back and carried the steady weight of absolute authority.

"I was calculating," I said.

Something shifted in the arms holding me, not a loosening, just an adjustment, as though he found that answer worth noting. He did not put me down.

I stopped asking.

The encampment appeared as we cleared a narrowing in the pass, and it was larger than I expected, structured around a flattened stretch of mountain terrain with clear sight lines in every direction. Not a camp thrown up in haste. A temporary position chosen with precision, the kind of positioning that accounted for approach vectors and retreat lines before it accounted for comfort. At its edges, warriors maintained watch posts at intervals that left no blind angles. At its center, a command tent stood with the particular prominence of something that was meant to be visible to everyone inside the perimeter and no one outside it.

He carried me to the center and set me down.

The ground met my feet, and the muscles in my thighs immediately turned to water, cramping so hard and fast that my knees buckled. A sharp, burning spasm shot up through my calves, a direct consequence of the collar's cold weight dragging at my pulse. I locked my joints with a brutal, desperate jerk before the collapse became visible, forcing my spine straight through raw will alone, though the effort left my shins trembling against the dirt.

He watched me do it.

Those gold eyes tracked the small, involuntary shift of my weight, the barely-there catch in my breathing, and I saw the moment he assessed it because the set of his jaw shifted with a precise, deliberate finality, the way a door closes rather than slams.

He reached toward me.

"Don't touch me," I said.

"Then stand," he said.

I stood. The nausea came with it, rolling up from somewhere behind my sternum in a slow, grinding wave, and I breathed through it and kept my eyes forward and did not give any of it to my face. His hand, which had lifted toward my collar, paused. Then he did something I did not expect.

He adjusted it.

Not removing it. His fingers moved along the inside of the iron band with a focused precision that required him to be closer than I wanted him to be, his warmth reaching me in waves. The scent of smoke, leather, and something darker pressed against my awareness despite every effort to ignore it. I felt the collar shift, felt the particular grinding cold of it change pitch, and then the worst of the nausea pulled back. Not gone. Reduced. Manageable in a way it had not been since it closed around my throat.

He stepped back.

I looked at him.

"What did you do?" I asked.

"It wasn't calibrated correctly," he said. "The full setting was designed for stronger bloodlines your body was failing under it."

The information landed with a quality I did not want to examine too closely, because it meant he understood the collar's mechanism, which meant he had used them before, which meant I should feel nothing about the fact that he had just done something that made breathing easier. I should feel nothing. The fact that it had mattered was purely biological. The fact that he had noticed was probably tactical.

I hated that some small, inconvenient part of me was not entirely convinced by that reasoning.

"What are you?" I asked.

He looked at me for a long moment. The firelight from the nearest brazier caught one of his eyes and turned it the color of heated copper.

"Tired," he said.

The simplicity of it silenced me for a moment I could not afford and had not anticipated. It was not the answer of a warlord performing authority. It was the answer of something old and very honest, and I did not know what to do with honesty in a place like this.

The confrontation arrived before I could decide.

He came from the far side of the fire line, and I knew before he spoke that he was going to be a problem. Not because of his size, though he was massive in the way of something built for war rather than intimidation, broader than Kaelor and carrying the particular density of decades of combat layered into a frame that had survived things designed to end it. Not because of the way he moved, which was direct and deliberate and completely uninterested in diplomatic approach. Because of the silence that preceded him, the way the other warriors shifted slightly, not away, but into a listening posture. He commanded that kind of attention.

"You bring poison into camp," he said.

He was not speaking to me.

Kaelor turned, and the air between them had the particular quality of two gravitational forces occupying the same space and neither one intending to yield.

"I brought an asset," Kaelor said.

"You brought a human wearing a Catalyst collar into the heart of a war encampment." The other male's voice was low, military, stripped of anything decorative. "You brought something the High Fey would burn territories to reclaim. You brought something our own clans will not understand and cannot be explained to quickly enough."

The watching warriors had not moved. But they had all become very still in the way of people who were no longer pretending to be occupied with other things.

"Draevok," Kaelor said, and the name was not a warning. It was an acknowledgment, which was somehow more serious.

"She should not have reached this camp." Draevok's dark eyes moved to me, not with malice, with assessment, the flat and careful calculation of a commander evaluating a tactical problem. "She should not reach any camp. Whatever she is, whatever her blood means to the Court, having her here is more dangerous than any blade the fey have pointed at us."

I had been called a problem before. It had never been delivered with quite this quality of certainty, the tone of a male who was not angry, who was not cruel, who simply believed what he was saying with a conviction that came from somewhere deeper than opinion. It was the voice of someone who had buried consequences before and was trying to prevent burying them again.

I understood that, even while I understood it was directed at ending me.

"Your recommendation," Kaelor said.

Not a question. An invitation to state the position fully, in front of everyone, which meant Kaelor already knew what the position was and had decided to make it public rather than resolve it privately. That was a specific kind of political choice, and I filed it away alongside everything else I was collecting.

"Execute her cleanly," Draevok said. "Before the clans learn she exists. Before the High Court sends something worse than mercenaries to retrieve her. Before whatever is in her blood becomes everyone's problem."

The fire crackled. No one moved.

I kept my breathing even and my face still and looked at Kaelor, because whatever happened in the next few seconds was going to happen because of him, and I wanted to see it coming.

"No," Kaelor said.

One word. Flat and complete and delivered with the absolute absence of negotiation.

Draevok's jaw tightened. "You're letting what's in your blood do your thinking."

"I'm making a strategic decision," Kaelor said. "She was bound for the Shadow Court. That means Astrythe values her. That means she is more valuable to us alive than anything Astrythe could offer dead."

"You don't know what she is."

"Neither do you."

"Exactly," Draevok said. "That is the problem."

The silence that followed was not empty. It was full of the unsaid thing, the thing that had been referenced in the space between their words, the thing that had made two of the nearest warriors exchange a glance that meant something I couldn't read yet. Her blood. The phrase had moved through the previous exchange like a stone dropped in water, creating ripples neither of them had explained, and the fear underneath it was real. Not fabricated. Not political performance. Something they both understood and were not going to explain in front of me.

"This ends in blood," Draevok said.

"Everything does," Kaelor said.

Draevok held his gaze for three full seconds, which I suspected was a significant length of time in whatever hierarchy governed these exchanges. Then he turned and walked back toward the fire line, and the watching warriors let their attention drift away with the careful subtlety of men who had learned that appearing to witness too much was its own kind of danger.

I realized, with a clarity that settled cold through the reduced but still-present nausea, that I had just learned something important. Kaelor's authority was not absolute. It was sufficient and it was respected, but Draevok had spoken openly, in front of witnesses, in a way that meant he believed he could. That meant there were lines here, political architecture I didn't fully understand, and that Kaelor's protection of me was a position he was actively defending rather than one that required no defense at all.

It also meant that if Kaelor's position weakened, I was first against the wall.

I was still processing that when the third presence arrived.

"Well," said a voice from somewhere to my left, pitched with the casual brightness of someone who had arrived late to a very serious situation and was delighted to find it still ongoing, "she looks stabby."

I turned.

The male leaning against the supply crate was lean in the way of someone built for speed rather than force, with russet hair that looked like it had given up on any particular arrangement and amber eyes that were currently moving between me and the retreating shape of Draevok with the bright, alert attention of someone running calculations for entertainment value.

"Torren," Kaelor said, in the tone of a male who had said that name in exactly that tone many times before and had never found it resolved anything.

"I'm just observing," Torren said pleasantly. "For example, I'm observing that we've had two near-executions and one extremely tense political confrontation in the span of approximately ten minutes, which is fast even for us. I'm also observing that our guest looks like she's deciding which of us to stab first, and I want it on record that I am not a threat and should be low on any list."

"You're not on any list," I said.

"Excellent," he said. "That's exactly what I want to hear from someone with hands like that." He looked at my knuckles, the old scars and the newer raw patches from the cage bars, with the particular expression of someone who actually knew what they were looking at. "You've been in cages before."

"I've been out of them too," I said.

"Even better," he said, and something in his tone shifted just slightly, not losing the lightness but gaining something underneath it that was more careful. He glanced at Kaelor with an expression I couldn't fully read, then back to me. "For what it's worth, the food here is terrible, but it's consistent. There's something to be said for that."

I did not trust him. He was too easy, too quick, and people who arrived at the right moment with the right tonal energy had either very good instincts or very specific purposes. Possibly both. I noted him and set him aside and looked back at the fire because the collar was still doing its work, reduced or not, and I needed to think.

The cold of the mountain pass was settling into the camp now, pressing down from the peaks above with the particular weight of altitude. The fires had been built high and placed strategically, more for warmth than light, which meant someone understood the terrain and had planned for its costs. Around them, warriors moved in the ordinary rhythms of a force settling into a temporary position: armor being checked, food distributed, the low, constant murmur of men and women who were tired and professional and not wasting energy on anything nonessential.

Not savages.

The word kept returning to me, not because I had ever truly believed the stories wholesale, I had spent too many years in border territories where the stories were made by people with reasons to tell them, but because the gap between what I had known and what I was seeing was wide enough to be disorienting. This was a military culture. It had ritual, rank, protocol, and the kind of earned discipline that only came from sustained organization over time. Whatever the High Fey claimed about the beast-folk of the Iron Mountains, they had not built this.

Kaelor had built this.

I looked at him and tried to fit that fact against the shape of what he was: the horns etched with silver, the obsidian-and-gold harness, the soot-black fur, the gold eyes that were currently surveying the camp with the practiced attention of a commander taking inventory. The fractured tip of one horn meant someone had once been strong enough to challenge him and close enough to land it. The scar over his eye.

Older than me by decades, perhaps far more if the stories held any truth. Years of watching the world arrange itself against him and building something anyway.

I was not going to find that compelling. I refused to find that compelling.

I was still refusing when I heard it, two warriors speaking in low voices near the eastern supply line, their words carrying on the cold mountain air in the specific way that words carried when people believed they were out of earshot.

"If the clans learn what she is," one of them said, "this starts a war."

The other one said nothing. The silence itself was an answer.

I kept my face forward and my breathing steady and let the words settle into the place where I stored things I did not yet understand but intended to. Her blood. A Catalyst. Whatever she is. A war. Astrythe values her. Something the High Fey would burn territories to reclaim.

I had been told my whole life that I was ordinary. A smuggler's asset. Expendable, replaceable, interchangeable with any other pair of careful hands and fast feet willing to carry contraband across borders that didn't want to be crossed.

The Labyrinthine Realm was telling me a different story.

I did not yet know whether that story would kill me faster or slower than the first one had been managing. But I was going to find out what it meant, because understanding the thing that made me valuable was the only leverage I had, and leverage had saved my life more often than any blade I had ever carried.

The fire burned lower. The mountain cold pressed in. Above us, the impossible sky had deepened toward something that might have been night, and the bioluminescent growths along the rock faces pulsed their cold light in the dark, patient and strange and entirely indifferent to what was happening beneath them.

I was still alive.

For now, that had to be enough to work with.

# The Obsidian Fortress

The fortress rose from the mountain like it had been cut from it rather than built upon it, and that distinction mattered in a way I felt before I could name it.

Black stone, not the rough and broken black of volcanic rock, but something older and more deliberate, smooth where it had been shaped and brutal where it had not. The walls were thick enough to park a war wagon inside and still leave room for the soldiers walking on top of it. Towers rose at measured intervals, with the placement of someone who understood sightlines before they understood aesthetics. Torch brackets burned at consistent heights, casting overlapping pools of amber light that left no convenient shadows at the base of the outer wall. Arrow slits at three different elevations. A gate mechanism heavy enough to require multiple soldiers and a counterweight system to move.

I cataloged all of it because cataloging was what I did when I was afraid, and I was very much afraid, and the cold iron at my throat was not the only thing making it difficult to breathe.

"Good news," Torren said from somewhere behind my left shoulder, keeping pace with the column in the easy, ambling way of someone who had decided that matching military stride was optional for him personally. "You're alive."

A pause.

"That was the entire list."

I did not respond to him. I kept my eyes on the gate, on the two enormous warriors standing post at either side of it, and on the way those warriors straightened when Kaelor's silhouette came into range. Not the snap of parade discipline; rather, it was a shift of posture that moved through them like a current, lengthening their spines, lifting their chins, and redistributing their weight toward attention. It happened across the whole visible section of the wall as word traveled ahead of us.

He had not asked for it. He had not signaled for it.

They simply did it.

Order is scarier than chaos. I had known that in a theoretical way from years of moving through dangerous places. Chaos was navigable because it was unpredictable in every direction, which meant it could break for you as easily as against you. Order meant someone was in control, and someone in control had already thought three moves further than you had.

This was not a warlord's camp. This was a command structure that had been running long enough to develop its own gravity.

The gate opened without a word from Kaelor. The mechanism moved smoothly, which told me it was maintained regularly, which told me everything about how this place was run. I stored all of it away and kept walking because the guards at my back left me no other option, and because I had decided somewhere in the mountain pass that my only useful response to this situation was observation until observation became opportunity.

The interior courtyard was larger than I expected, and busy with a particular kind of organized activity. Warriors moving between buildings in purposeful lines. A training area visible through an archway to the right, scarred ground and weapon racks and the particular quality of sound that came from people practicing with real intent rather than performance. A cluster of noncombatants near a long building that smelled of food and fire and grain, a cook hall, by the architecture and the scent. Children, which I had not expected at all, moving quickly along the far wall under the watch of an older female warrior with the practiced patience of someone who had been given that particular assignment many times.

Not a military outpost. A functioning settlement wearing military armor.

My chest did something uncomfortable with that information.

Kaelor moved through the courtyard with the same unhurried certainty he moved through everything, and the space arranged itself around him without any visible effort on his part. Warriors who crossed his path offered a specific gesture, fist pressed to the opposite shoulder and held for one breath before releasing. Some version of a salute. He acknowledged it with the smallest inclinations of his head, not dismissive, not performative, just consistent. The ritual of authority that had been practiced long enough to become unremarkable.

I was taken through a side entrance and into a corridor that smelled of torch smoke and cold stone and something faintly metallic underneath both. The walls here were carved rather than rough, geometric patterns that weren't quite decorative, more like they had a function I didn't understand. The stone was black, the same black as the outer walls, and it had an almost magnetic quality to it, a subtle pull at the edge of perception that I put down to the collar and the general misery of the day.

They took me to a room that was not a cell.

That was its first and most disorienting feature. It had a door with a heavy bar on the outside, which made its purpose clear enough, but it also had a narrow window with actual glass, a cot that was not a pile of straw, and a brazier already burning with the particular low glow of something that had been lit in preparation. Someone had put a blanket on the cot. A rough wool thing, functional rather than kind, but present.

I stood in the center of it and hated how much my body wanted to sit down.

The door opened again before I had decided where to position myself, and the person who came through was not Kaelor.

She was small, or small relative to everything I had seen since arriving in this realm, with curved horns that were more suggestion than statement and quick, digitigrade legs that moved her through the doorway with a light, clipping step. Bronze curls, green eyes, and the particular satchel of a healer, worn across one shoulder and already half-open. She smelled of crushed herbs and something medicinal that burned faintly at the back of my throat.

"Oh," she said, taking in my expression with the unguarded reaction of someone who had not yet learned to manage her face in dangerous situations. "You look like you're planning something violent."

"I'm always planning something violent," I said. "Who are you?"

"Talia." She set the satchel down on the small table near the brazier without asking permission, which was either confidence or obliviousness and I hadn't decided which yet. "I'm the healer. I've been asked to look at your injuries." She glanced at the collar with the specific expression of a professional confronting something that offended her on principle. "Starting with that."

"By whom?"

"The warlord." She pulled something from the satchel, a small jar that smelled of dark resin. "He said functional. I'm choosing to interpret that generously."

I watched her move, the practiced efficiency of someone who arranged their tools the same way every time, and kept myself between her and the door out of habit. "I don't need to be looked at."

"You have iron burns at your collar line and whatever the camp travel did to your wrists, and you've been favoring your left leg since you walked in." She looked up from the jar with the direct, uncomplicated gaze of someone who had decided that being honest was less exhausting than being tactful. "I'm trying to help."

"That's what people say before knives," I said.

She blinked. Then, unexpectedly, she laughed, a short and genuine thing that had no performance in it. "I have knives. Surgical ones. But I use them for removing things that are already dead, so unless part of you qualifies, you're safe."

I said nothing.

She took my silence for the provisional permission it was and came forward, and I let her look at the collar because I wanted to know what she would say about it, and because the burning at my collar line had been a consistent background presence since the thing had closed around my throat and I was tired of pretending it wasn't there.

Her fingers were careful. Lighter than I expected. She examined the skin beneath the iron band with the focused attention of someone reading a text, and the longer she looked, the more the cheerful efficiency in her expression compressed into something quieter and more serious.

"This is a Catalyst collar," she said.

"I'd worked that out."

"The High Fey use them for transporting high-value prisoners. Magic-adjacent bloodlines, usually." She sat back slightly, not retreating, just thinking. "Extended use causes damage. Extended exposure damages the blood and the nervous system, slowly if your lucky." She looked at the collar again, then at me. "How long have you been wearing it?"

"Since the convoy."

Something moved through her expression that was not quite pity, because pity had a condescension underneath it that this didn't. "It needs to come off."

"Then remove it."

She opened her mouth and then closed it again, and the sound from the corridor outside resolved into the heavy, deliberate weight of Kaelor's footsteps a second before the door swung open.

He filled the frame. That was simply a physical fact that the doorway could not argue with. His gold eyes moved from Talia to me in a single sweep and settled.

"Report," he said to Talia, though his gaze stayed on me.

"Iron burns, soft tissue damage at the wrists, general physical stress from collar exposure." Talia's voice had shifted, professional and direct, the manner of someone reporting to a commander. "The collar needs to come off, Warlord. Prolonged use at this calibration will cause permanent damage."

The word permanent landed in the room and sat there.

I watched Kaelor's jaw set, a small, controlled movement, and waited for the calculation I could see him running.

"Not yet," he said.

The anger came up fast and clean. "Not yet," I repeated, keeping my voice level through an effort that cost me. "Because my permanent damage is a useful reminder of your authority."

"Because removing it before I understand what you are creates a risk I'm not prepared to manage." He held my gaze, and there was nothing apologetic in his expression, but there was nothing cruel in it either, which was somehow more infuriating than cruelty would have been. "The collar stays until I have answers."

"And if I don't have answers?"

"Then we will both find that very inconvenient."

I thought about driving my knee into the table and taking the jar of dark resin to his face, and rejected it on the grounds that it would accomplish nothing except demonstrating that I was frustrated, which he had presumably already inferred.

"Treat what you can around it," he said to Talia. "Anything that makes continued exposure less damaging."

Talia nodded, which was the practical response. I hated that I also understood it was the practical response.

He left without another word, and the room felt larger after he was gone, which made no sense given that he had been standing still the whole time.

"He's not cruel," Talia said quietly, working the resin jar open with practiced fingers. "That doesn't mean he's safe. But it matters."

"Not to my collar line," I said.

She applied the resin with the same careful precision she used for everything, and it was cold at first and then warm, and the burning at my throat pulled back to a manageable distance. While she worked, she talked in the way of someone who thought better out loud, and I listened the way I always listened, cataloging rather than accepting.

"People are already talking," she said. "About you. Some of the warriors think you're cursed. Some think you're a weapon the High Court lost. Some think you're an omen." She paused. "The High Fey don't mobilize the way they mobilized for that convoy for ordinary prisoners. Everyone in this fortress knows it. That creates its own kind of fear."

"Wonderful," I said.

"You really should stop trying to bite everyone," she said, which startled me enough that I almost laughed.

Almost.

She finished what she could do and packed her satchel with the same methodical care she had unpacked it, and when she left, I sat on the edge of the cot and listened to the bar slide into place on the outside of the door, and thought about what she had said, and what the collar was doing to me, and what it meant that Kaelor knew both of those things and had made the choice he had made.

He wanted answers. That was his priority, and my health was secondary to it by exactly as much as was functionally necessary. He was keeping me alive because I was valuable, not because he had made a moral decision about my welfare, and I needed to keep that architecture very clear in my thinking.

Except.

He had adjusted the collar in the camp. Before any of this. Before he had brought me here or established what I was worth. He had adjusted it when it was causing me to collapse, and he had not needed to do that.

I put that fact in the category of things I was not currently explaining and moved on.

The formal questioning happened two hours later, in a chamber that had the quality of a room used for political decisions. Not a throne room, nothing that grandiose, but a long table of black stone on a raised platform, with torches placed to illuminate the center and leave the edges in shadow. Maps on the walls. The feel of a space where strategy happened rather than ceremony.

Kaelor sat at the head of the table. Draevok stood against the far wall with the deliberate positioning of someone who had decided that sitting would imply more agreement than he was willing to perform. And to Kaelor's left sat Serathis, the female minotaur commander whose silence carried the weight of someone long accustomed to being annoyed.

She was almost as large as Kaelor, built with the solid, functional power of decades of war rather than any ornamental quality. Iron-brown fur streaked silver at the temples. One horn banded with gold. A scar that ran from jaw to collarbone, old and clean. Her left eye was clouded, and the right one tracked me with the flat, careful intelligence of someone running a threat assessment without any of the emotional noise that usually accompanied it.

She did not introduce herself. She watched me take the chair I was gestured toward and said nothing, and I understood from the quality of her silence that it was not empty.

"Your name," Kaelor said.

"You already have it."

"Your family name," he said. "Your bloodline. Where you were born."

I looked at him across the black stone table and chose my words the way I chose footholds on bad terrain. "I was born in a border village that doesn't exist anymore. I have no family worth naming and no bloodline worth the conversation." I held his gaze. "If you're looking for a genealogy, you've taken the wrong prisoner."

"The Shadow Court sent a full escort and a Catalyst collar for a woman with no bloodline worth naming," Kaelor said. The observation was not a challenge. It was delivered with the patience of someone laying facts on a table and waiting for the other person to acknowledge their weight.

"Then take it up with the Shadow Court."

"I intend to." His gold eyes held steady. "After you tell me what they know about your blood that you're choosing not to."

"Captive," I said. "Prisoner. Asset." I let the words sit. "Does changing the word make you feel noble?"

The silence that followed was complete. Draevok's jaw shifted. The female at Kaelor's left made no visible reaction at all.

"No," Kaelor said.

The simplicity of it caught me off guard. I had expected deflection, or the particular version of righteousness that powerful people used to justify their power. I had not expected the flat, undefended honesty of that single word.

"Then you understand why cooperation is not available to you," I said.

"Accuracy matters," he said. "You are not a prisoner of the Shadow Court. You are not here to be sacrificed at Astrythe's altar or used as a bargaining piece in her politics. Those are the things I am keeping you from." He leaned forward slightly, just enough that the torchlight caught the silver runes on his horns. "That does not make me the same thing."

"You're still a monster," I said.

A pause, long enough that Draevok's weight shifted against the wall.

"Yes," Kaelor said.

The word landed without apology or performance. It was the answer of something that had made its peace with what it was and found the peace more useful than the argument.

Draevok pushed away from the wall with the controlled force of a male who had been containing something and had decided to stop. "You gamble clan blood on an unknown human," he said to Kaelor, with the directness of someone who had decided that the presence of witnesses was irrelevant. "Whatever she is, whatever her blood means, every hour she sits in this fortress is an hour the High Court has to send something worse than the last convoy."

"My risks are mine to take," Kaelor said.

"When they are yours alone. These are not yours alone." Draevok's dark eyes moved to me with the same flat assessment I had received in the camp, not personal, not cruel, the calculation of a commander determining the cost of a variable. "You may be brave, human. That does not make you safe."

I did not respond to him, because he was not wrong, and arguing with things that weren't wrong was a waste of energy I didn't have.

The female at Kaelor's left spoke for the first time. Her voice was low, unhurried, and carried the weight of a woman who had earned the right to be heard and knew it.

"Sentiment is expensive," she said. "Strategy less so." Her clouded eye turned slightly toward Kaelor, then back to me. "If she is useful, use her. If she is dangerous beyond use, remove her. This conversation is neither."

I looked at her directly. "And who decides which she is?"

"I do," Kaelor said.

"We do," the female said, without heat. "That is how this command functions."

There was something between them in the exchange, not conflict, a clarification of terms that suggested it had been established through considerable prior friction and arrived at with mutual resignation. I noted that architecture, alongside everything else.

It was then, while the silence was settling after that exchange, that I noticed the wall.

I had been aware of the stone throughout the room, the same black stone as the rest of the fortress, but one section near my right side was older, the geometry of the carving different from the functional military patterns elsewhere. More complex. The kind of pattern that accumulated over time rather than being designed at once. My right hand rested on the table edge, and the table itself was the same black stone, and something along my palm, not pain exactly, more like the distant cousin of the collar's cold, stirred with a low, persistent warmth.

Not from the brazier.

From below my hand.

I looked down without meaning to, and the surface of the table was exactly what it appeared to be, ancient black stone, except that at the point of contact with my skin, something behind the surface shifted. Not visibly. Not in any way I could point to and name. But Kaelor's eyes moved from my face to my hand with the precise, unhurried attention of someone who had caught something he had been watching for.

He said nothing.

I pulled my hand back and said nothing either, and the warmth faded, and the room continued as though it had not happened.

But it had happened, and we both knew it, and the knowing of it sat between us like a third presence at the table.

The questioning continued for another hour without producing anything useful for anyone. I gave him geography and nothing else, the border territories I had worked, the names of roads that would mean nothing in this realm, the careful geography of nothing that mattered. He listened to all of it with the patience of someone who understood the difference between what was being said and what was being avoided, and when he finally signaled the end of it, it was not with frustration but with the particular settled quality of a man who had learned what he needed from a conversation even when the words themselves were useless.

They moved me after that.

Not back to the holding chamber. Down a different corridor, up a flight of stairs cut directly into the mountain stone, to a room that was unambiguously better than the first. A real window, barred but real, looking out over the inner courtyard. A larger brazier. A table and two chairs. The blanket on this cot was heavier.

Two guards outside instead of one.

I stood in the center of the room and understood the message with the same clarity I would have understood a sentence spoken directly.

I was no longer a prisoner being held because no better option existed. I was a political asset being managed because the stakes had been assessed and found significant. The improvement in my conditions was not kindness. It was investment.

The danger had not decreased. It had changed shape entirely, and the new shape was harder to navigate because it required me to constantly evaluate which part of the care being extended toward me was genuine and which part was the careful maintenance of something valuable.

I sat on the edge of the better cot in the better room behind two guards instead of one, and the collar burned at a level I had decided to call manageable, and I thought about bloodlines and fortress stone and the way Kaelor's eyes had moved to my hand with no surprise in them at all.

Not safer.

Different.

Which, in my experience, was almost always the more dangerous kind of change.

# Collateral Damage

The first thing I learned about guarded chambers was that locked doors felt exactly like cages with better furniture.

Never since crossing into this realm had I slept on a cot this soft. Real heat radiated from the brazier, and the blanket was thick wool rather than the damp, flattened thing that had been thrown at me in the convoy. None of that made the bar on the outside of the door feel like anything other than what it was, and I had spent enough years in bad situations to know that comfort offered by a captor was its own kind of pressure. Chains were honest. This was something else.

I was awake before full light reached the window, studying the room for the third time since they had left me in it, because cataloging was still the most useful thing I could do. One window, iron-barred, real glass, overlooking the inner courtyard. The glass was old, slightly warped, which distorted the torchlight below into smeared amber shapes. The door was solid, the hinges on the wrong side for forcing, and the bar I could hear through the wood was heavier than it needed to be for one person. They had thought about this room before they put me in it.

Talia arrived mid-morning, her satchel swinging from one shoulder and her expression carrying the particular alertness of someone who had already been awake for hours and had opinions about it. She smelled of crushed herbs and something sharper underneath, dragon-root, she had said before, the kind of scent that announced itself before the person did.

"You slept," she said, as though this surprised her.

"Lightly," I said.

"Still counts." She set the satchel down on the table and began unpacking with the same methodical precision she brought to everything. "I want to check the collar burns again. The salve I applied yesterday needs to be refreshed, and I want to see if the inflammation has pulled back."

I let her approach without argument, which was a different response than I had given her the first time, and she registered that without commenting on it. That restraint earned her something I wasn't ready to name yet. She worked with clean hands, careful fingers, and the kind of focused attention that had nothing performative about it. Whatever else she was, Talia was genuinely good at this.

"It's better," she said, with the slightly surprised satisfaction of someone whose treatment had worked despite the variables. "Not good. But better."

"The collar is still doing damage," I said. Not a question.

"Slower, with the salve. But yes." She sat back and looked at me directly, the way she had the day before, without the softening that most people applied to difficult truths. "Prolonged exposure at this calibration interferes with the way blood carries magic through the body. If you have any latent ability, and I think you might, the collar is essentially creating pressure without release. Eventually that causes permanent harm to the blood itself."

The word *permanent* sat in the room the way it had the first time she had used it.

"He knows this," I said.

"Yes."

"And he left it on anyway."

"He left it on because he hasn't decided what you are yet." She met my eyes without flinching. "That's not the same as not caring. Though I understand it might feel identical from where you're sitting."

"Comforting distinction," I said flatly.

She almost smiled. "If I wanted you dead, I'd be much less gentle about all of this."

"And if he wanted me dead?"

"You'd already know it." She said it simply, without drama, which was somehow more convincing than any dramatic reassurance would have been. She began repacking the satchel with the same care she used unpacking it. "The fortress is talking. I thought you should hear it from me before you heard it from the walls."

I waited.

"Some of the warriors think you're cursed. Some think you're a fey weapon that the Shadow Court lost control of. There's a faction near the western barracks that's decided you're an omen." She said it with the detached accuracy of someone reporting weather. "The High Fey don't mobilize the way they mobilized for that convoy unless whatever they're moving is worth considerable cost. Everyone here knows it. That makes you frightening before you've done anything frightening."

"I haven't done anything frightening," I said.

Her green eyes held steady. "Not yet," she agreed, and then she left, and I listened to the bar slide home behind her and thought about what it meant that the most honest person in this fortress was the healer who had been a slave.

I spent the next two hours mapping the guard rotation.

Not dramatically. Not with any theatrical urgency. I sat near the window and watched the courtyard below with the patience of someone who had learned that exits revealed themselves to people who were willing to wait for them. The guards outside my door changed at regular intervals, two hours by my counting, and the shift overlap lasted approximately forty seconds. The corridor outside ran east toward a staircase I had noted on the way up, and west toward what sounded like a supply route based on the particular rhythm of footsteps and the occasional scrape of something heavy being moved.

I waited until the shift change, used the overlap, and was through the door before the new guard had fully settled into position.

I made it to the staircase. Down one flight. Through a corridor that smelled of torch smoke and cold stone. Around a corner that opened onto a narrower passage I hadn't been shown, running parallel to what I estimated was the outer wall.

Then I turned another corner and walked directly into Kaelor.

He was not in full armor. That was the first disorienting thing. He wore a simpler war harness, the heavy shoulder pieces absent, the ceremonial obsidian work replaced by practical leather strapping that crossed his chest and left his arms bare. His fur was darker with exertion, and the silver runes on his horns caught the torchlight in the narrow passage with a cold, quiet glow. He had been in the training yard, or had just come from it. The dust of the yard still clung to his boots, and the particular controlled stillness he carried had an edge to it that suggested recent physical effort rather than the restrained authority of the war table.

He looked at me. I looked at him. Neither of us spoke for a long, measured moment.

The scars across his chest were more visible without the ceremonial harness in the way, old ones that had the clean white of complete healing and newer ones still carrying a faint ridge of raised tissue. Whatever had put them there had been significant enough to mark something that was very difficult to mark. My gaze caught on a long diagonal one that crossed from his left shoulder toward his ribs, and then I deliberately pulled my attention back to his face, because this was not the time for curiosity about Kaelor Ashhorn's history of surviving things.

"That was faster than I expected," he said.

"You anticipated this."

"You would have disappointed me otherwise."

He was not angry. That was the part that was harder to manage than anger would have been. He stood in the narrow corridor with the same unhurried certainty he brought to everything, taking up an unreasonable amount of the available space, and he looked at me with the flat, steady assessment of someone who had run the calculation and arrived at an outcome he considered predictable.

"Back," he said.

"If you're so concerned for my safety," I said, keeping my voice level, "release me."

"And deliver you to worse?"

The question landed without inflection. Not rhetorical. An actual answer in the form of a question, and the infuriating part was that I could not immediately dismantle it, because the convoy that had carried me here had not been taking me somewhere comfortable, and I knew it.

"You expect gratitude," I said.

"No." He held my gaze, and his gold eyes were steady and entirely unreadable. "I expect survival."

He turned and walked back the way I had come, and I followed because the alternative was standing in the corridor until someone less patient than him found me, and because something about the certainty with which he had said those two words had taken the argument cleanly out of my hands. Survival. Not comfort. Not safety. Not gratitude. Just the continued fact of being alive, which was the only currency he was apparently trading in.

I hated that it made a particular kind of sense.

He walked me back to the guarded chambers without touching me, without calling the guards, and without any visible frustration. The guards straightened when they saw him and had the intelligence not to comment on the fact that their prisoner was currently walking beside the warlord rather than behind the door. He stopped outside the room, and I turned to look at him before going in.

"The Shadow Court is moving," he said. It was not an explanation. It was a fact being placed between us. "Additional scouts have been spotted at three border positions in the last six days. Something is being organized, and whatever it is, it is organized around recovering what they lost." His gold eyes held mine without softening. "That is what is outside these walls. You are not being held from freedom. You are being held from something considerably worse than this room."

I studied him in the torchlight of the corridor, the controlled set of his jaw, the absolute absence of any performance in his expression, and felt the uncomfortable pressure of the possibility that he was telling the truth pressing against every assumption I had built around this situation.

"That may actually be what you believe," I said.

"Yes," he said. And then he left.

I sat with that for a long time after the bar slid home.

The second confrontation of the day came without warning.

The door opened in the late afternoon, and the figure who entered was not Talia, and was not Torren, whose footsteps I had started to recognize from the particular uneven rhythm he kept, as though he had never fully committed to walking in a straight line. This figure moved with the deliberate, controlled economy of a career soldier, taking up exactly the space she needed and none beyond it.

Serathis closed the door behind her and looked at me with her one clear eye, the other clouded and fixed at a slight angle that still managed to feel attentive. She had not removed her armor. She had not come here to be comfortable or to make me comfortable.

"I will not stay long," she said. "And I will not repeat this."

I said nothing. She had the kind of presence that made silence feel like the correct response.

"Do not mistake his restraint for weakness," she said. "He has held this alliance together through things that would have broken lesser males, and he has made decisions that cost him considerably more than you can currently calculate. His judgment is the reason these walls are standing." She paused, and the pause had weight. "If you become a liability, I will personally solve the problem. I want you to understand that clearly so there is no confusion later about what I said or what I meant."

I held her gaze. "Understood."

"Good." She moved toward the door and then stopped with her hand on the frame, not turning back fully. "He does not make personal decisions lightly. The fact that you are in this room rather than a cell is a decision he made against considerable opposition. Do with that information what you will."

She left. I sat with the quiet that followed and thought about the particular kind of warning that came wrapped in information, and what it said about Serathis that she had delivered both simultaneously.

Torren arrived approximately an hour later, and his arrival was announced by the very specific sound of someone convincing a guard to do something the guard had not initially agreed to, followed by the slightly smug footstep pattern of a person who had succeeded.

He came through the door with a cloth-wrapped bundle under one arm and the expression of a man who had accomplished something he was proud of and was waiting for someone to ask about it.

"Good news," he said. "I brought food."

A pause.

"Questionable food, admittedly." He set the bundle on the table and began unwrapping it with the casual efficiency of someone who had eaten in worse conditions than this regularly. "The cook was in a mood. There may have been an incident involving her herb stores and a certain unnamed scout who needed a distraction. I am not confirming or denying."

"You stole from the cook," I said.

"I borrowed from the cook while simultaneously borrowing her attention. It's a different category of theft." He pushed a portion toward me and dropped into the chair across the table as though he had been invited to do so. "You tried to escape today."

"Observation or accusation?"

"Admiration, actually." He tore off a piece of bread with cheerful efficiency. "You got farther than the last three people who tried it. The previous record was two corridors. You made it four, which means you either move very quietly or the guards on the east rotation are getting lazy. Possibly both." He glanced at me sideways. "He walked you back himself. That's interesting."

"Is it."

"He could have sent anyone. He came himself." Torren chewed thoughtfully. "He also hasn't put additional guards on your door, which is either confidence or a very specific message about what he thinks you'll do next." A brief pause. "Or both. With him it's usually both."

I ate, because the food was in front of me and I needed to maintain function, and because Torren's company was the particular kind of easy that didn't require anything from me except the occasional response. He talked the way some people breathed, continuously and without apparent strain, and underneath the commentary was the specific quality of attention that told me he was considerably more observant than he wanted anyone to notice.

"The Shadow Court scouts," I said. "You've seen the reports."

"I've seen everything. I have a gift for being present in rooms where important things are discussed and being somehow overlooked." He said it without modesty. "Three border positions. Six days of movement. They're not scouting randomly. They're building a picture of something." His amber eyes met mine briefly. "Whatever you are, they want you back badly enough to be obvious about looking. People like that don't do obvious unless they're either very confident or very desperate."

"Which do you think?"

"Both," he said. "Again. It's usually both."

He left with the same easy confidence he had arrived with, and I sat in the quiet that settled after him and thought about scouting patterns and retrieval forces and the particular weight of being something that two different powers wanted badly enough to move armies toward.

I needed air that wasn't the recycled warmth of the guarded chamber. The door was barred. The window was barred. But the corridor beyond the door had, in the course of my earlier escape attempt, revealed a short branching passage that ran toward what felt like the fortress's older interior, the section where the stone was different, more complex in its geometry, laid down by hands that had been working toward a purpose other than military efficiency.

The guard shift change gave me twelve seconds. I had been counting all afternoon.

I used eight of them.

The branching passage was narrower and colder than the main corridor, and the torch brackets here were spaced further apart, leaving stretches of shadow between the pools of amber light. The stone underfoot was worn smooth in a way that suggested centuries of passage rather than decades. The carvings on the walls were the older kind, the kind I had noticed in the formal chamber during the questioning, complex and layered and not quite decorative.

I pressed my fingers to the wall as I moved, steadying myself in the dim light, and felt the stone beneath my palm as I had felt the table during the questioning. Cold at first, the deep-settled cold of rock that hadn't seen direct sun in years. Then, gradually, something else.

Warmth.

Not the warmth of a heated room or a fire nearby. Something rising from inside the stone itself, specific to the point of contact with my skin, moving upward through my palm and into my wrist with the low, insistent pressure of water finding a crack. I stopped walking. My fingers spread flat against the carved surface, and the warmth intensified by a degree that made my breath catch, and then the carvings beneath my hand did something I had no vocabulary for.

They flickered.

Not light, exactly. More like the suggestion of light, the memory of something luminous moving through the grooves of the pattern, silver and faint and gone almost before I had registered it. Then a spike of pain shot from my palm through my forearm and up into my shoulder, sharp and clean as a blade, and I pulled my hand back on instinct.

The corridor was quiet. The stone was dark again.

My palm was still warm.

"I saw that."

Malakor's voice came from the shadow at the far end of the passage. He stepped forward into the nearest pool of torchlight, and I took in the details with the automatic speed of someone assessing a new threat: tall and lean, blue-gray skin marked with ritual scars burned into his forearms, silver hair tied back with severe practicality, one pointed ear partially missing. His black eyes were fixed on me with the flat, careful attention of someone who had decided to catalog rather than react.

He was not one of Kaelor's warriors. The bearing was wrong, the particular quality of it different from the disciplined military posture of the fortress soldiers. This was something older and more individual, the bearing of a man who had operated alone for long enough that hierarchy had become theoretical.

"Who are you?" I asked.

"Someone who just watched the stone respond to your hand." He said it with the same level practicality someone might use to describe weather. "Which makes you considerably more interesting than the rumors suggested."

He turned and walked back toward the main corridor without waiting for my response, and stopped at the junction, looking back at me with the flat expectation of someone who had already calculated that I would follow because the alternative was standing in a dark passage alone with a hand that was still warm from something I couldn't name.

"The warlord will want to know about this," he said.

"I imagine he will," I said.

Something shifted at the edge of his expression, not quite acknowledgment, but close enough to register. He walked. I followed, and behind us the old passage settled back into its cold silence, and the carvings were simply carvings again, and my palm had almost stopped burning by the time we reached the lit corridor.

Almost.

The warmth didn't fully fade. It sat in the center of my hand like an ember that had decided it lived there now, patient and specific and entirely mine in a way that the collar's cold burn had never been. The collar took. This had given something, though I couldn't have named what, and the distinction unsettled me more than the pain had.

Malakor said nothing else. He delivered me back to the guarded chamber with the efficiency of a man completing a task, and when Kaelor's guards found me inside the room rather than absent from it, neither of us offered an explanation for how that had been arranged. The bar slid home again. The torchlight settled into its familiar patterns against the walls.

I sat on the edge of the cot and turned my palm upward in the dim light. The skin looked exactly as it had before. No mark, no visible sign of what had happened in that passage. But the warmth remained, faint and persistent, and somewhere deep in the mountain below me the old stone held its silence, and I had the specific, unwelcome feeling of something that had been asleep for a very long time deciding that it was now awake.

It knew me.

I didn't know what that meant yet, and not knowing was its own kind of cold, sitting alongside the collar's constant pressure and the fortress's watchful quiet and the weight of everything that was apparently mobilizing beyond these walls to retrieve me.

I closed my fingers around the warmth and sat with it, and tried to decide whether it was a weapon or a warning.

I couldn't tell. That was the part that kept me awake long after the torches in the corridor had burned low.

# The Hunt Begins

I knew I was in trouble the moment Kaelor looked at the glowing stone and went completely still.

Not the controlled stillness he carried everywhere, the quiet authority of a male who had never needed to announce his presence. This was different. This was the specific absence of movement that preceded something significant, the kind of stillness that carried weight, and when his gold eyes lifted from the faintly luminous carvings to find my face, I understood that Malakor had not been the only witness in that corridor.

Word moved through a fortress the way smoke moved through a burning building. Quietly at first, through cracks and gaps, and then everywhere at once.

By morning, everyone knew.

I heard it in the way the guards outside my door spoke to each other in lower tones than they had the night before. I heard it in the particular quality of the silence that fell when Talia arrived to check my collar burns, a silence with edges, as though the air itself was holding something back. She set her satchel down and began unpacking without her usual cheerful efficiency, and the absence of her commentary told me more than the commentary would have.

"How bad?" I asked.

"Draevok called an emergency council session before dawn." She kept her eyes on her work. "I wasn't there. But I could hear the volume through two walls and a corridor."

That was informative.

"He wants me dead," I said. Not a question.

"He wants a decision made. The distinction matters to him." She pressed the salve carefully against the collar burns at my throat, and her hands were steady even if her expression wasn't entirely. "There are others who agree with him. Some want immediate execution. Some want interrogation, which in this fortress means something considerably less pleasant than questions over tea." A pause. "And then there's Kaelor."

"What does Kaelor want?"

She met my eyes briefly. "To know what you are before anyone else gets to decide."

He came for me himself, which I was beginning to understand was a pattern rather than a coincidence.

The bar lifted from outside. The door opened. He filled the frame the way he always did, not with theatrical menace but with the simple physical fact of his size, and behind him I could hear the fortress at its morning business, footsteps and armor and the distant sound of something metal being worked. He looked at me across the room with those gold eyes, and whatever he was thinking was entirely his own.

"Come," he said.

I came because the alternative was waiting to find out what Draevok's emergency council had decided, and I trusted the warlord's intentions marginally more than I trusted a room full of warriors who had apparently spent their pre-dawn hours debating my execution.

He brought me to a smaller chamber off the main corridor, a room that felt older than the rest of the fortress, its stone carved with the same layered geometric patterns I had seen in the passage the night before. A table. Two chairs. No guards inside, though I heard them position themselves outside the closed door with the quiet efficiency of soldiers who understood the order without being explicitly given it.

Kaelor sat across from me and looked at me for a long moment before he spoke.

"What are you?"

The question was direct, without preamble, without softening. I had expected it. That didn't make it easier to answer.

"If I knew," I said, "I'd be having a much better week."

Something moved briefly at the edge of his expression, gone before I could catalog it.

"The stone responded to your touch. The carvings in that passage have not activated in living memory. Malakor witnessed it. Three guards in the corridor saw the light before you pulled your hand back." He kept his voice level, but there was an intensity beneath it, controlled and deliberate. "I need you to tell me everything you know about your bloodline."

"I know that my mother died when I was four and my father died three years later and my uncle spent the following years demonstrating exactly how little family loyalty meant when personal survival was in the equation." The words came out with more edge than I intended. "I know nothing about bloodlines. I know nothing about why stone responds to my hands. I know nothing about the Labyrinth or whatever architecture runs beneath this fortress, and I have spent the better part of the last day trying to determine whether what happened in that passage was something I did or something that was done to me."

Kaelor was quiet for a moment. His eyes hadn't left my face.

"You are not lying," he said.

"Thank you for the observation."

"It complicates things."

"Enormously," I agreed, with feeling. "I find ignorance very inconvenient when it's my own."

He leaned forward slightly, his forearms resting on the table, and the silver runes on his horns caught the light from the single torch on the wall. "If you had known, you would have used it already. As leverage, as escape, as something." His voice held no accusation. "The fact that you haven't means either you are extraordinarily patient, or you genuinely don't understand what you carry."

"I've been told I'm patient," I said. "But not that patient."

He held my gaze for another beat, and then something in his bearing shifted, not softening, but recalibrating, the way a calculation adjusts when new data arrives and changes the outcome.

"Then we have a problem," he said quietly, "because the Shadow Court does not mobilize retrieval forces for ignorance. They are moving because they know what you are, and they believe it is worth the cost."

The door opened before I could respond, and Serathis entered without knocking, which told me everything about her relationship with waiting for permission. She closed the door behind her with the precise economy she brought to every movement and stood at the end of the table with her scarred jaw set and her clouded eye fixed at a slightly different angle than her clear one.

"The council is demanding your presence," she said to Kaelor. "Draevok is making arguments that are gaining traction. You need to be there before he finishes making them."

"And?" Kaelor said, because her tone suggested there was an and.

"Three more scouts have gone missing on the eastern ridge. Border movement confirmed at two additional positions." Her gaze moved to me briefly, flat and assessing. "Whatever they're organizing, it's not a retrieval. It's a retrieval force."

The distinction was not subtle. Retrieval forces didn't come to negotiate.

Kaelor stood, and the room rearranged itself around the fact of his height in the way rooms did when he moved through them. He looked at me. "Stay here. Don't make me come find you again."

"You find me every time," I said. "It's becoming embarrassing."

Serathis made a sound that might have been either disapproval or something considerably drier. Then they both left, and I sat in the old stone room and listened to the fortress around me, and thought about retrieval forces and what it meant that people who already owned considerable power wanted me back badly enough to make themselves visible.

The council chamber was loud enough that I could hear fragments of it from the corridor where a guard had placed me to wait, not unkindly, but with the firm practicality of someone following specific instructions. Draevok's voice carried the most clearly, deep and certain and genuinely angry in a way that held conviction rather than performance.

"You move her outside these walls and we bleed for it," he said, and the words arrived through stone and wood with enough clarity to catch the full shape of his certainty. "She is a fixed point. Every enemy we have is already oriented toward this location. You put her on a road and you put every warrior in that escort on a road with a target painted on their backs."

Kaelor's response was lower, controlled, and didn't carry as far. But I heard the shape of it.

"We bleed either way."

A silence. Then Serathis, precise and cold as winter water: "A fixed target is easier to destroy. We hold this position and we hand them a siege. We move and we choose the ground."

Draevok said something else that the walls absorbed entirely.

The guard beside me stared forward with the disciplined disinterest of someone who was pretending very hard not to have ears.

The decision, when it came, arrived through Kaelor's expression when he emerged from the council chamber and found me in the corridor. He looked at me with those flat gold eyes and said, without preamble: "We leave before dawn tomorrow."

"We," I said.

"You. Me. A small escort." He paused. "Torren. The healer. Malakor, if he brings what he claims to have."

The name sat in the air between us, and something in Kaelor's tone when he said it suggested that Malakor's presence was contingent on usefulness rather than welcome.

Talia found me in the corridor before I made it back to the guarded chamber, and she arrived with the particular expression of someone who had already been told the plan and had opinions about the preparation timeline.

"One day," she said. "I have one day to put together enough medical supplies for a mountain journey with no clear endpoint, in a fortress where half the herb stores are under Draevok's quartermaster's control and the other half are spoken for by the infirmary." She pulled a list from her satchel and studied it with the focused severity of someone who took supply logistics as seriously as surgery. "I'll manage. I always manage. But I want it noted that this timeline is unreasonable."

"Noted," I said.

"Also, the collar." She looked at my throat with the careful attention she always brought to it. "I've spoken to Kaelor about the calibration. He hasn't agreed to full removal. But he's considering adjustment. Enough to reduce the pressure on your blood while we travel."

I held very still. "He told you this."

"He told me to prepare for the possibility. Which from him is approximately the same as an agreement." She tucked the list back into the satchel. "I don't know what you said to him this morning, but something shifted in how he's thinking about this."

I didn't answer that, because I didn't have an answer that wasn't complicated.

Torren appeared in the courtyard while I was watching the fortress prepare itself for departure, standing near a wall with my arms crossed and my back against the stone, cataloging the patterns of movement that told me where supplies were being staged and which of the guards were assigned to the escort. He materialized beside me with the specific lack of announcement that characterized most of his arrivals.

"Wonderful," he said, surveying the organized chaos of pre-departure with the expression of a man reviewing a list of personal inconveniences. "A dangerous magical mystery road trip. Exactly what I wanted." He paused. "I had plans, you know. Perfectly reasonable plans involving staying inside these walls where it is relatively less likely that someone will attempt to kill me specifically."

"You could decline," I said.

"Kaelor didn't phrase it as an option." He tilted his head slightly. "Also, and I want it understood that I resent this, I've become somewhat invested in the continued existence of the people on this particular journey, which means I'm going to be enormously inconvenienced if any of them die." He said it with the studied casualness of someone who had decided that caring about things was a personal failing he had accepted rather than corrected.

Malakor arrived in the late afternoon.

I heard his entrance before I saw it, a change in the quality of attention in the courtyard, the specific shift that occurred when someone walked into a space, and the people already there recalibrated their awareness around the new variable. He came through the main gate with a single pack and the bearing of a man who had traveled light through hostile territory long enough that it had become his natural state. His ritual-scarred forearms were visible below rolled sleeves despite the mountain cold, and his black eyes moved across the courtyard with the flat, methodical sweep of someone building a tactical picture.

He stopped when he reached Kaelor, and they exchanged words I couldn't hear from across the courtyard. Malakor produced documents from his pack, folded and sealed with something dark. Kaelor studied them. Something in his jaw tightened.

Torren appeared at my shoulder again, quiet for once, watching the same exchange. "That one," he said very softly, "murders optimism on sight."

I had no argument with that assessment.

Malakor's gaze crossed the courtyard and found me with the specific efficiency of someone who had already noted my position the moment he walked through the gate. He held the look for a brief second, flat and categorizing, and then returned his attention to Kaelor. Whatever he had brought was enough, because Kaelor nodded once, and Malakor was apparently part of the departure.

I didn't like it. I didn't trust the measured calm of a man who carried himself like a former weapon still deciding what to aim at. But my opinion on the composition of this particular escort had not been solicited, and I had larger concerns.

The evening before departure settled over the fortress with a particular kind of quiet, the silence of preparation rather than rest, people moving through final tasks with the focused efficiency of those who knew that morning would not offer second chances to pack correctly. I stayed where I had been told to stay, which was within sight of a guard at all times, which was its own kind of message about how much the morning's conversation had actually shifted.

It was Kaelor who came to me just before the fortress bells marked the last watch hour. He came without ceremony, crossing the courtyard to where I stood near the wall, and he stopped a pace away and looked at me with those gold eyes and said nothing for a moment.

Then he reached toward my throat.

I went completely still, every instinct I had firing simultaneously, and he said, "Hold still," in a voice that was quiet and certain, and his fingers found the collar with a precision that told me he had done this before, or at least had thought very carefully about the mechanics of it.

What he did took less than a minute. I felt the pressure change, not disappear, the collar was still there and still active, but something in its function adjusted, the low constant burn that had been sitting in my blood since they put it on me pulling back by degrees until it was present but no longer insistent. The difference was like the difference between a fist and an open palm, still contact, but not force.

The relief hit me before I could stop it from showing on my face.

His eyes tracked the change in my expression with that quiet, careful attention he gave everything.

"Talia said the pressure was causing damage," he said.

"Yes," I said, and my voice came out steadier than the rest of me felt.

"I need you functional." He dropped his hand from the collar. "Not compliant. Functional."

I looked at him in the low torchlight of the courtyard, at the scarred face and the ivory horns and the absolute controlled certainty that he carried everywhere he went, and felt the particular confusion of someone whose categories had been quietly rearranged without their permission. He had adjusted the collar. He had reduced the damage it was doing. He had done it because Talia told him it was causing harm, and he had listened and come here himself to make the adjustment rather than send someone.

He was still holding me here. He was still the reason the bar had been on the outside of my door every night I had spent in this fortress. The collar was still around my throat.

None of that was simple, and I wasn't going to pretend it was.

But the relief in my blood was real, and the fact that he had created it was equally real, and I didn't have a clean category for that.

"You lie poorly when in pain," he said, and his voice held something that wasn't quite dry but was adjacent to it.

"I wasn't lying," I said.

"You were managing," he said. "It reads the same." He turned slightly, looking toward the gate and the darkness of the mountain pass beyond it. "We ride before first light. Be ready."

He was already moving away when I said, "Why does it matter to you? Whether I'm in pain."

He stopped. He didn't turn back immediately, and when he did it was with the particular deliberateness of someone who had chosen their words before speaking them.

"Because I need you to be capable of walking through what comes next," he said. "And because the Shadow Court is mobilizing an army to retrieve you." His gold eyes held mine across the distance between us. "If they want you badly enough to march an army, I need to know why."

He left, and the courtyard settled around his absence, and I stood with my hand pressed flat against my sternum where the collar's reduced pressure was still making itself known, and thought about armies and bloodlines and the warm memory of stone that had moved beneath my fingers, and tried to decide which of those things I was most afraid of.

The answer was none of them.

The answer was the specific, traitorous relief of his hands at my throat, adjusting something that hurt me, careful and deliberate and real, and the way my body had registered his proximity not with the instinctive recoil I was accustomed to but with something considerably more difficult to manage.

That was what frightened me.

The mountain wind came through the gate with the cold clarity of high altitude, carrying the smell of pine resin and stone and distance, and somewhere beyond it, moving through passes I hadn't yet seen, something was already hunting me with the confidence of those who believed the outcome was settled.

I closed my fingers around nothing, and felt the faint residual warmth in my palm from the night before, and thought: *not yet.*

The fortress prepared itself around me in the dark, iron and leather and the quiet sounds of people readying for a road that had no guarantee of safety at the other end of it, and I stood in the courtyard and breathed mountain air and decided that whatever I was, whatever the stone in my blood knew that I didn't, it was mine.

The hunt had begun. I intended to be considerably harder to catch than anyone had calculated.

## No Safe Roads

Traveling with monsters turned out to be less terrifying than traveling with people who kept trying to kill me.

I had expected the fear to be constant, the way it had been inside the fortress walls, that low-grade vigilance that never fully released its grip on my spine. Instead, somewhere between the first narrow switchback and the second ridge crossing, I realized the fear had shifted shape entirely. It was still present. It simply had better company.

The mountain pass opened ahead of us in the grey pre-dawn, cold and vast and indifferent, the kind of landscape that reminded you how small a collection of bodies on horseback really was. The wind came off the peaks with teeth in it, carrying the smell of pine resin and old stone and something wilder underneath, the scent of altitude, of places that had never been domesticated. My horse moved steadily beneath me, breath fogging in the cold air, and I sat in the saddle with my hands loose on the reins and indexed everything I could.

Kaelor rode ahead. He always rode ahead, which I had already identified as both tactical and deliberate, the position that gave him sightlines in every direction while keeping me behind him and between the flanking escort. He hadn't spoken since we left the fortress gate. The obsidian war harness across his shoulders caught the early light in dull reflections, and the silver runes on his horns had dimmed to something faint and steady, like embers that hadn't decided whether to die or ignite.

Torren materialized at my left flank with the effortless inevitability of a man who had decided that proximity to the most interesting point of danger was preferable to riding somewhere sensible.

"You've got the look of someone plotting murder," he said pleasantly.

"Helpful observation."

"I try." He tilted his head, surveying the road ahead with the expression of someone reviewing the fine print of a contract they hadn't agreed to sign. "Specifically, you've got the look of someone plotting murder while also calculating which section of this pass would offer the best cover for a fast departure. I've seen that look before. Usually on myself."

I said nothing, because denying it would have been both dishonest and unnecessary. He already knew. The interesting question was whether he would mention it to anyone else, and the answer to that question had been clarifying itself since the fortress courtyard, where I had watched him watch everyone else with the careful attention of someone whose survival had always depended on noticing what others missed.

"For what it's worth," Torren continued, "the collar reduces your options considerably. Also, Malakor has been watching you since we cleared the gate, and that one notices things with a commitment I find personally unsettling."

I glanced right. Malakor rode at a steady distance, positioned where he could see the road behind us and the ridgeline above simultaneously. His silver hair was tied back against the wind, and his black eyes were moving across the terrain in slow, methodical sweeps. He wasn't looking at me specifically in that moment. Which meant he had already finished looking at me and moved on to identifying other threats, which was somehow worse.

"Does he ever blink?" I asked.

From three horse-lengths away, without turning his head, Malakor said: "When necessary."

Torren made a small sound beside me that I chose to interpret as solidarity.

Talia rode on my right, her bronze curls escaping their pins in the mountain wind, her satchel strapped across her back with the careful security of someone who understood that her supplies were the difference between a flesh wound and a crisis. She had been quiet since we departed, her green eyes moving across the terrain with a particular alertness that had nothing to do with tactical assessment and everything to do with a woman who had learned to read environments for danger before she had learned to read them for beauty.

"The road gets narrower past the second ridge," she said, not to anyone specifically. "There are old shrine markers. I saw them on Malakor's maps last night. The Labyrinth architecture extends further up the passes than most people realize."

"Shrines to what?" I asked.

"To the roads themselves, mostly. The old builders believed the passes were living things. They left offerings to keep the stone cooperative." She paused. "I'm not entirely sure they were wrong."

I filed that away beside everything else I had filed away since entering the Labyrinthine Realm, the growing stack of information I didn't fully understand but couldn't afford to ignore. The collar sat against my throat with its reduced pressure, present but no longer grinding, and I was aware of it the way you were aware of an old injury that had stopped being acute but hadn't finished healing.

We rode for hours. The morning burned off its grey slowly, and the light that replaced it was sharp and thin at this altitude, casting long shadows from the ridgelines that swept across the road like slow clocks. The ancient Labyrinth architecture appeared gradually, at first just geometric patterns carved into roadside stones, then broader structures, crumbling archways half-consumed by centuries of mountain growth, the suggestion of walls that had once been deliberate and were now merely persistent. The roads themselves were the most striking detail: flat and precise in a way that natural stone never managed, fitted with a geometric exactness that made the surrounding wilderness feel almost improvisational by comparison.

Whoever had built this had built it to last. That they were gone anyway said something I preferred not to think about too directly.

Kaelor hadn't spoken to me since the fortress gate, but he had twice adjusted our pace without explanation, slowing the group in the specific way that meant he had heard or seen something on the ridgeline that warranted attention. Neither time had anything materialized. Which meant either the threat had reconsidered, or it was patient enough to wait for better ground.

My money was on patience.

The ravine crossing appeared mid-afternoon, and I understood immediately why Torren's expression shifted when he saw it. The road narrowed to a single-width track across a natural stone bridge spanning a drop that vanished into dark below. The bridge was old Labyrinth construction, solid enough that armies had likely crossed it in the past, but the flanking walls were crumbled to nothing, leaving the crossing fully exposed on both sides to the ridgelines above.

Kaelor raised a fist. The group stopped.

He sat still for a long moment, reading something in the air or the stone or the quality of the silence that the rest of us couldn't translate. Then he said, "Cross in pairs. Fast. Stay center."

The first escort pair moved. Then Talia and Torren, who went with the specific urgency of people who had been told to be fast and had understood why. Malakor followed with the second escort pair, his movements unhurried in the way that suggested he had already assessed the threat and made peace with the variables.

Kaelor gestured me forward.

We were three steps onto the bridge when they came off the ridgelines.

There were four of them, and they moved with the coordinated precision of people who had rehearsed the timing and chosen the location specifically because it reduced our options to nearly nothing. Shadow Court hunters, dressed in layered grey-black that had blended perfectly with the rock face above us, and they were fast in the particular way of people trained to close distance before anyone had finished identifying them as a threat.

The first one came for the nearest escort and put a blade through the gap in his armor before the alarm had finished leaving anyone's throat. The second and third split to the flanks, cutting off the retreat to solid ground on both sides. The fourth came directly for me.

I had the knife from my boot in my hand before the collision arrived. The collar flared as I moved, a sharp spike of pressure that hit my blood like a fist and stole half a second of coordination, and that half second was the difference between clean contact and a glancing block that still sent me sideways on the narrow bridge surface.

The hunter grabbed my arm. His grip was iron and practiced, and his eyes above the grey mask found mine with a recognition that was worse than threat.

"The Catalyst," he said, and his voice held no question in it.

I drove my knee into his side and got nothing useful for the effort. The collar spiked again, and my vision went briefly white at the edges, and I was still fighting the white when the hunter's grip disappeared entirely, replaced by a sound that was brief and final and very violent.

Kaelor's hand closed around my arm where the hunter had held it, steadying me on the narrow stone, and the hunter was simply no longer a problem. What remained of him was not something I examined closely.

The other three lasted less time than that.

I had seen Kaelor move in controlled circumstances. I had seen him fill doorways and cross rooms with that terrifying silent grace and understood intellectually that he was dangerous the way mountains were dangerous, something that didn't need to announce itself. What I had not seen, until the ravine crossing, was what happened when the control became purpose.

He was not chaotic. That was the detail that lodged itself somewhere beneath my sternum and refused to leave. There was no fury, no loss of precision, no explosion of violence that exceeded its target. He was efficient in the way that blades were efficient, every movement directed, every moment of force applied exactly where it achieved the necessary result and nowhere else. The third hunter made it close enough to require Kaelor's left hand, and the movement he used to address that was so economical it almost looked simple, which was the most frightening part of all.

It was over in less than a minute.

Torren, from the far end of the bridge, said: "Right. So. That was bracing."

Nobody disagreed with him.

Kaelor turned to me. The molten gold of his eyes was flat and intent, moving across me in the specific assessment of someone checking for damage rather than seeking reaction, and he held my arm another moment before releasing it.

"I didn't need saving," I said.

"You were seconds from death." He said it without emphasis, the way you stated the current altitude or the temperature. Just information.

I knew he was right. That made it considerably harder to say anything useful in response.

"One of them identified me," I said instead. "He called me the Catalyst."

Something shifted in Kaelor's jaw, a tightening that lasted one controlled breath before it smoothed out again. He said nothing immediately, and I had learned enough by then to understand that his silences were where the weight actually lived.

"Move," he said quietly, and the group moved.

We cleared the bridge and put distance between ourselves and the ravine with the focused efficiency of people who understood that a second wave was a real possibility and standing still was a gift to whoever was counting on us to do exactly that. Malakor took the rear guard without being asked, falling back with the quiet competence of a man who had covered retreats before and had opinions about how to do it correctly. The injured escort member was alive, Talia had established that with the rapid assessment of someone who had learned to triage in motion, and we kept moving until the road widened and a natural rock overhang offered cover from the ridgelines above.

Kaelor called the stop there.

The camp that night was smaller and quieter than any I had experienced in the fortress. We built no large fire, just a contained coal bed screened behind the rock face, enough for warmth and Talia's work but not enough to announce us to the dark. The mountain wind had dropped with the sun, and the silence that replaced it was the deep, particular silence of high altitude, where sounds carried strangely and the absence of them carried further.

Talia worked on the injured escort with the focused efficiency she brought to everything medical, her hands moving with confidence even in the limited light, her mouth running a quiet commentary that was as much for her patient's benefit as for her own process. "You're going to be fine. The blade didn't find anything vital, which means whoever made you is having a better night than whoever made these hunters, because their aim was poor and yours was adequate. Hold still."

Torren sat nearby, turning a piece of dry wood in his hands without purpose, and said to no one in particular: "Catalyst. Interesting word choice. Very specific. The kind of specific that suggests someone briefed them carefully before sending them to die on a ravine crossing."

"That one," Malakor said from his position at the edge of the firelight, not looking up from the blade he was cleaning, "knew exactly who she was before they moved. This was not opportunistic."

The confirmation settled over the camp like the cold did, seeping in through the gaps.

I sat with my back against the rock face and my knees drawn up and let the warmth from the coal bed work on the chill that had settled into my bones during the crossing. The collar's reduced pressure had spiked twice during the fight and was still sitting higher than its usual baseline, a slow throb that reminded me with every pulse that whatever I was, it was the kind of thing that required a leash.

Kaelor crossed the camp and crouched in front of me without announcement, which should have startled me and didn't, because I had already tracked his movement from the corner of my awareness the way I tracked anything that large in a confined space. He held out a water skin.

I took it. Drank. Handed it back.

He produced a folded cloth from the pack at his side and set it across my knee without explanation, and when I unfolded it there was dried meat and hard bread inside, the kind of provisions that kept you moving rather than making the moving pleasant. He had done it without ceremony, without the performance of generosity, just the flat practical action of someone who had identified a need and addressed it.

From his pack came a heavy wool cloak, which he dropped over my shoulders with the same absence of sentiment.

"That doesn't make us allies," I said.

"No," he said.

He stayed crouched in front of me for a moment longer, and the firelight caught the ivory of his horns and the silver runes that ran along them, and I was aware of his proximity the way I was aware of a fire, not just warmth but the potential for something considerably more significant if the distance closed.

"They called me the Catalyst," I said. "You know what that means."

"I know what it suggests."

"Then tell me."

His gold eyes held mine across the short distance between us. "There is a term in the old Labyrinth texts. A bloodline capable of activating the deep architecture. Not just touching it. Triggering it. The way a spark triggers tinder." He paused. "The Shadow Court has been searching for that bloodline for a very long time."

The fire cracked behind him. Somewhere above us on the ridge, wind moved through stone with a sound like distant breathing.

"And now they've found it," I said.

"Now they've confirmed it," he corrected. "Finding was always the easier part."

I ate the provisions he had given me because refusing them would have been both stupid and theatrical, and I had used up my available theatrical energy on the ravine crossing. The cloak was heavy and warm and smelled of leather and smoke and something darker underneath that I recognized by now as distinctly his, and I chose not to think about that with any particular attention.

Talia finished with her patient and came to sit beside me, pulling her knees to her chest and tilting her head back against the rock face with the exhausted relief of someone who had been running on focus and was only now permitting the rest of her to catch up.

"You're terrible at accepting help," she said quietly.

"I've had limited practice."

She made a soft sound that wasn't quite agreement and wasn't quite contradiction. "I know. I could tell, the first day. The way you go very still when someone does something unexpectedly kind. Like you're waiting for the cost to appear."

There was nothing comfortable to say to that, because she was right, and we both knew it.

"Get some sleep," she said. "I'll watch the collar calibration through the night."

I slept in the tent the escort had erected against the rock face, and the sleep was the flat, dreamless kind that came from pure exhaustion, the kind that felt less like rest and more like a brief suspension of consciousness. I didn't know what woke me. There was no sound that I could identify, no movement from the escort on watch, nothing that registered as threat. Just a slow, deliberate return to wakefulness, the way the body sometimes surfaced on its own schedule rather than anyone else's.

The coal bed outside had burned to near-nothing. The camp was quiet. The two escort members on watch were at their designated positions, still and reliable.

And Kaelor was standing at the camp's outer edge, alone, facing the darkness of the pass below us.

He was not positioned for watch duty. The escort had that covered, and he would have known it. He stood slightly apart from the camp's perimeter, his back to the firelight, the ivory horns a pale contrast against the black of the mountain dark, and he was utterly still in the way that had nothing to do with tactical readiness and everything to do with a male who had decided that sleep was not something he was going to permit himself tonight.

I watched him from the tent opening, the cold air moving across my face, and thought about the ravine crossing and the way he had put himself between me and the hunter with an efficiency that left no room for interpretation. I thought about the word he had used earlier, *functional*, the specific claim that protecting me was strategic rather than personal, and I thought about how clearly I had believed that claim approximately until this moment.

Nobody stood alone in the cold watching the dark for something that was strategic.

He didn't turn. He couldn't have heard me over the wind. But after a moment, without moving his gaze from the pass below, he said: "Go back to sleep."

"You're not sleeping," I said.

"I require less than you."

"That isn't what I asked."

A beat of silence. The wind moved through the pass with that low, breathing sound, carrying cold and pine and the distant smell of something I couldn't name.

"No," he said. "It isn't."

He didn't offer more than that, and I didn't press for it, because some things were better understood in silence than they were in words, and the shape of a warlord standing alone in the dark watching for threats while his camp slept was one of them. It said something that I didn't have a clean category for, the same way his hands at my collar the night before departure had said something I couldn't categorize, and I was beginning to suspect that the categories I had arrived with were simply inadequate for whatever this was.

The mountains were enormous around us. The road behind us held the memory of blood on old stone. Somewhere below, moving through passes that had been built for purposes none of us fully understood, something was still hunting us with the patience of those who believed distance was only a delay.

I pulled the wool cloak tighter around my shoulders, the one that still carried his scent, and watched the broad set of his back against the mountain dark, and felt the specific, inconvenient sensation of something settling inside my chest that I very much wished would reconsider.

It didn't.

I went back inside the tent and lay down on the bedroll and stared at the canvas ceiling and listened to the wind and the quiet sounds of the camp and the absence of any sound from the direction where he stood, and understood with the clarity that only came in the middle of the night, when you were too tired to argue with yourself, that whatever road we were on, survival was no longer the only thing making it dangerous.

That thought kept me awake considerably longer than the cold did.

# What Hunts in the Dark

I woke to the unmistakable sound of something screaming in the dark.

Not a person. Not an animal I had any name for. The sound came from somewhere beyond the camp's perimeter, low and resonant at its base and then rising into a frequency that scraped the inside of my skull like a blade dragged across wet stone. It stopped. Started again. Stopped.

Then the escort member on watch began screaming too, and that sound cut off much faster.

I was out of the tent with my boot knife in hand before the second scream finished. The mountain cold slammed into my face, and the collar flared at the sudden motion, a spike of pressure behind my eyes that stole my balance for one sickening half-second. I caught myself against the tent pole and forced my vision to clear.

The camp was chaos.

Whatever had come out of the dark was not the Shadow Court. I understood that immediately, with the specific certainty of someone who had spent enough time around human violence to recognize its shape, and this had no shape I recognized at all. The fire had been scattered, coals kicked wide across the stone ground, and in the orange fragments of their light I saw something moving at the camp's far edge that my mind refused to process cleanly. It was large. It moved wrong, too many joints articulating in directions that suggested the architecture of its body had been designed by something with different assumptions about how limbs were supposed to function. Its skin, or what covered it, absorbed the firelight rather than reflecting it, giving it the quality of a hole in the world wearing a creature's outline.

Kaelor was already moving.

He crossed the camp in four strides and drove his blade into the thing's flank, and the sound it made in response was the same resonant wrongness as the first scream, but closer now, close enough that I felt it in my back teeth. The blade didn't stop it. It turned, and for one terrible moment I saw what passed for its face, which was not a face in any way I had a clean word for, just attention wearing flesh, and that attention fixed on me.

"Move," Kaelor said, and his voice carried the specific weight that left no room for argument.

I moved.

Torren appeared from somewhere to my left, grabbing my arm and hauling me toward the tree line with the urgency of someone who had already made a tactical assessment and decided that the assessment was "elsewhere." Behind us, I heard Kaelor's blade again, and that wrong sound, and then Malakor's voice cutting sharp orders to the remaining escort.

The collar spiked hard as I ran. My legs went briefly unreliable, and Torren caught my weight without slowing, which told me he had been watching for exactly that possibility. Smart man. Infuriating man.

"What is that thing?" I managed.

"Something very old," Torren said, which was not helpful, "and very unhappy about us being here," which was also not helpful but at least felt accurate.

The trees swallowed us. Behind me, I heard the sounds of the camp fragmenting, the creature's wrong resonance moving and then changing direction, and then a sound I hadn't heard before, something between impact and collapse, and then nothing from that direction except wind.

The ground shifted under my next step. I registered the drop too late, the loose stone lip of a slope I hadn't seen in the dark, and then I was sliding, hands scraping across rock, the collar screaming at the sudden jolt of adrenaline through my blood, and I hit a ledge four feet down that knocked the air from my body in a single flat impact.

I lay there for a moment, cataloging damage. My left side had taken the worst of it. A long scrape across my ribs, deep enough to bleed steadily, and my left palm was opened on the rock. Neither was dangerous. Both hurt with the specific insistence of injuries that intended to keep reminding you of their presence.

I pushed myself upright.

The slope above me rustled, and then Kaelor came down it with the controlled descent of someone who had navigated worse terrain in worse conditions, landing on the ledge beside me without the stumble I would have expected from something his size. He took in the ledge, the dark beyond it, and me, in one sweep.

"Torren?" I asked.

"Malakor has him. Escort is moving to the secondary position." He crouched, scanning the darkness below the ledge, and his voice was flat and deliberate. "We need to move. The creature tracks by something other than sound."

"How do you know?"

"Because we stopped making sound two minutes ago and it is still moving toward this position."

I stood. The ribs protested. I ignored them.

He didn't offer his hand, but he positioned himself slightly ahead and to my left, which put him between me and the direction the creature sound was coming from, and I noticed that without wanting to notice it, the way I kept noticing things about him that I had no useful place to put.

We moved through the dark forest for what felt like a long time and was probably less than ten minutes, following a game trail that Kaelor navigated with a confidence that suggested either excellent night vision or an absolute willingness to find out what was at the end of it. The creature sounds grew more distant, then circled, then distant again. It was hunting, methodically, covering ground in expanding rings, and the wrongness of it carried even through the trees, that resonant not-quite-sound that pressed against the back of my awareness like a finger on a bruise.

The ruins appeared out of the dark as ruins in this realm tended to, suddenly and without apology. Old Labyrinth architecture, a structure that had once been deliberate and was now mostly persistence, three walls still standing and a partial ceiling of fitted stone that had held against centuries of mountain weather through sheer geometric stubbornness. An ancient shrine, or what had been one. The carved symbols on the remaining walls were geometric, precise, the same mathematical exactness as every other piece of Labyrinth construction I had encountered, though these were denser, layered one atop another in patterns that my eyes kept trying to resolve into something familiar and failing.

Kaelor ducked through the low entrance without hesitation. I followed.

Inside, the wind dropped to almost nothing. The stone held a cold that was different from the mountain cold outside, older, the preserved chill of a space that hadn't seen full sunlight in a very long time. Kaelor moved to the far wall and checked the perimeter in four efficient steps, and then he came back to me and said: "Sit."

"I'm fine."

"You are bleeding through your shirt."

I looked down. He was correct. The scrape across my ribs had soaked through the fabric on my left side in a dark spread that was larger than I had estimated in the dark.

I sat. Not because he told me to. Because my ribs were making an increasingly persuasive case for it.

He crouched beside me, and the shrine felt immediately smaller, the way enclosed spaces always did when he occupied part of them. He set his blade within reach and pulled something from the pack still strapped across his back, a cloth and a small sealed container that he opened with the efficiency of someone who carried field supplies as a matter of standard practice rather than optimism.

"I can do it myself," I said.

"Poorly," he said.

He pushed the torn fabric aside and pressed the cloth against the scrape with a pressure that was firm and deliberate, and the sting of it sharpened my breath to a point. His hands were exactly as I remembered from every other time they had been close enough to matter: rough, warm, impossibly steady. He worked without looking at my face, his full attention on the wound, and the focus of it was somehow more unsettling than being watched would have been.

The creature sounded in the distance. We both went still. It circled, the resonance pressing against the stone walls, and then moved on.

He continued.

"What is it?" I asked, keeping my voice low. "The creature. You've seen one before."

A pause. Not evasion. More like he was selecting the accurate answer from several available ones.

"Labyrinth guardian," he said. "The old texts call them anchors. They were placed here when the deep architecture was sealed. They are not supposed to still be active."

"And yet."

"And yet." He pressed the cloth more firmly, and I kept my breathing even through the effort. "The seals are weakening. Things that should be dormant are waking. This is the second one we have encountered in three months."

I absorbed that. "Second."

"The first did not find the camp."

"Lucky."

"No," he said. "Careful."

He opened the sealed container and applied something to the cloth that smelled of pine resin and something sharper underneath, and when he pressed it to the scrape the sting went briefly white-hot before settling into a duller throb. I kept my jaw locked and said nothing about it, because I had survived worse with less and complaining about it now would have been theatrical.

"You said the seals are weakening," I said. "That's connected to whatever I am."

His hands didn't pause. "It may be."

"That isn't an answer."

"It is the honest portion of one." He secured the cloth with a strip of binding and sat back on his heels, and for a moment we were closer than the wound treatment had strictly required, the dim light from the crack in the ceiling catching the silver runes along his horns and making them look like something still alive. "The bloodline tied to the Labyrinth does not merely interact with the architecture. It resonates with it. What resonates with a seal also resonates with what the seal is meant to contain."

I looked at the wall behind him. The symbols carved into it were pulsing, so faintly I might have convinced myself it was a trick of the poor light, a slow, rhythmic flicker that had not been there when we entered.

He turned and saw it too.

Neither of us spoke for a moment.

"That keeps happening," I said.

"Yes."

"In the fortress. At the ravine. Now here."

"Yes." His gaze moved back to me, and the gold of his eyes was steady and unreadable in the way that I had stopped interpreting as cold and started interpreting as something much more controlled. "It accelerated after your blood touched the stone at the ravine crossing."

I remembered the fall. My palm, opened on rock. The old Labyrinth construction of the bridge beneath me.

"You noticed that," I said.

"I notice most things."

The symbols continued their slow pulse. The creature sounded again, further now, moving away through the forest. The wind outside was the low, breathing kind, moving through stone gaps with a sound like the mountain thinking to itself.

"Do you sleep?" I asked.

The question came out more direct than I had intended it, but it had been sitting behind my teeth since the night before, since watching him stand alone in the mountain dark while the camp slept, and the shrine felt like a place where pretending not to have questions was more effort than it was worth.

Something shifted at the corner of his mouth. Not quite an expression. The suggestion of one.

"When necessary," he said, and the echo of Malakor's answer to my earlier question was close enough that I suspected it was deliberate.

"That's not an answer either."

"No." He was quiet for a moment, and the quiet had that particular weight his silences carried, the kind that meant the words were coming but on his schedule rather than mine. "Sleep requires the absence of threat. In my experience, the absence of threat is a temporary condition that punishes those who believe otherwise."

"That sounds like something that was learned badly," I said.

His jaw tightened, one controlled breath, before it released. "It was learned accurately."

I didn't push further. Some things were better understood through the shape they left in conversation than through direct excavation, and the shape this left was clear enough. War. Loss. The specific education of someone who had trusted stillness once and been corrected violently for it.

"I had a camp once," I said. It came out quieter than I had intended. "A real one. Fourteen people. We ran supply routes through the Thornwall passes for two years without losing anyone." I stopped. "Then I trusted the wrong road and the wrong contact on the same night and lost eleven of them by morning."

The shrine held the words after I said them, the stone absorbing them the way it absorbed the cold, preserving them without judgment.

"You carried them out," he said. It wasn't a question.

"The three who survived. Yes."

"And the contact."

"He didn't survive me."

A beat of silence. Then something in his expression shifted, not softening, but recalibrating, the way a scale adjusts when a different weight is placed on it.

"You have commanded," he said.

"Not like you command."

"No. But you have felt the specific weight of lives that depended on your decisions." He held my gaze, and the gold of his eyes was very steady. "That is not a small thing."

It was not a small thing. He was correct. And the fact that he recognized it without ceremony, without the performance of sympathy, without the particular condescension of someone trying to make me feel better about a thing that had no good side, meant more than I wanted it to.

"Do you always order everyone around?" I asked, because I needed to change the direction of this conversation before it carried us somewhere I wasn't prepared to go.

"Only the difficult ones," he said.

I almost smiled. I stopped it before it fully formed, but I was not certain he missed it, because his gaze tracked my mouth for exactly one moment before returning to my eyes.

The symbols on the wall behind him pulsed again, brighter this time, and the hum that came with them was no longer something I just felt in my awareness. It was in the stone beneath my hands, in the cold air, in the space behind my sternum where my heartbeat lived.

"It's responding to me," I said.

"Yes."

"And you don't know what that means. Not fully."

"I know what the old texts describe," he said carefully. "I know what the Shadow Court believes. I know what the cult has been hunting for across two centuries." He paused. "What I do not know is whether any of them are right, or whether they are all working from incomplete information toward conclusions that serve their own purposes."

"That's a generous way of saying they might all be wrong."

"It is the accurate way," he said. "Wrong and dangerous are not mutually exclusive."

The creature sounded again, very close, and we both stopped moving. The resonance pressed through the stone walls, that wrong frequency that sat at the base of every instinct I had and told them all to go quiet and stop existing. Kaelor shifted, and before I had processed what he was doing, he had moved between me and the shrine's entrance, his body between the opening and my position, one hand finding the blade he had set within reach.

We waited.

The resonance grew, pressing, filling the small space like water filling a vessel, and I felt the symbols behind me flare, a sudden bright pulse that heated the air noticeably, and then the creature sound shifted, changed pitch, and moved away. Quickly, this time. As though it had encountered something it recognized and preferred to avoid.

The warmth from the symbols faded slowly. The shrine returned to its cold self-possession.

Kaelor did not move immediately. He remained positioned at the entrance, his back to me, the broad line of his shoulders between me and the dark outside, and I was aware of how close we were in the small space, close enough that I could feel the heat he generated despite the cold, close enough that the scent of leather and iron and smoke was not just present but surrounding, and the part of my mind that was supposed to be cataloging tactical exits was doing something considerably less useful instead.

"Why save me?" The question came out before I had decided to ask it. "At the ravine. Tonight. You could have prioritized the escort. The mission. Any number of things that made more strategic sense."

He was quiet for a long moment.

"Because I was there," he said.

I waited for more. There was no more.

It should have been insufficient. It was the shortest possible answer to the question, technically complete and practically evasive, and I had spent enough years around people who used brevity to conceal the things they didn't want examined to know the difference between economy and avoidance.

But the way he said it, with that flat, absolute weight, like something that had been true for so long that qualifying it would have been dishonest, made it land differently than any longer answer would have.

He turned then, and we were closer than I had accounted for, closer than the wound treatment had required, close enough that his horns would have brushed the ceiling if he had straightened fully. The gold of his eyes caught the faint pulse from the shrine symbols, and his expression was the controlled, unreadable one I had catalogued as default, except that something behind it was different, some specific quality of attention that was not tactical and not clinical and was not, despite everything I had told myself, entirely strategic.

My breath came out carefully.

His jaw tightened, one slow breath, and he looked away first, which surprised me enough that I didn't speak for a full three seconds.

A sound from outside, boots on stone, a familiar pattern of footsteps that belonged to someone who walked like he was slightly offended by the ground beneath him.

Torren ducked through the shrine entrance with a torch he had clearly improvised from something he should not have had access to, surveyed the scene with the comprehensive assessment of a man whose primary skill was reading rooms, and said: "I leave for five minutes and everyone gets dramatically injured. Outstanding. Truly. The efficiency of this disaster is almost admirable."

Malakor appeared behind him, silent, his black eyes moving across the shrine in one sweep, settling on me, then on the symbols still faintly pulsing on the wall, then on Kaelor, and then back to the entrance with the expression of someone filing information for later use.

Talia pushed past both of them and came directly to me, dropping to her knees with her satchel already open, her bronze curls wild from the night and her green eyes sharp with the focused calm she wore when the situation required competence rather than comfort.

"Let me see," she said, and her hands were already at the binding Kaelor had applied.

"He already treated it," I said.

She examined the binding, checked the work with the critical eye of someone reviewing a procedure, and made a small sound that I chose to interpret as reluctant professional approval. "Not terrible," she said. "For a warlord."

"The creature?" Kaelor addressed Malakor.

"Gone," Malakor said. "It circled the ruins twice and retreated into the lower forest. I have not seen one move away from prey before." His eyes went to the symbols on the wall again. "Something here repelled it."

"The shrine," Kaelor said.

Malakor looked at me, not at the shrine.

He didn't say anything further, which meant he had already arrived at the same conclusion Kaelor had and was choosing not to say it aloud in a space where the walls were still humming with ancient light.

"The escort is secure?" Kaelor asked.

"Two minor injuries. Both ambulatory." Malakor's voice was its usual flat precision. "We can move at first light."

"Good." Kaelor turned toward the shrine entrance. "Rest here until dawn. I will take watch."

"You always take watch," Torren observed pleasantly. "One might wonder when the great warlord last slept through an entire night. Hypothetically."

Kaelor looked at him with the particular expression he reserved for Torren specifically, the one that communicated an entire conversation about how unwise it was to press certain subjects, without a single word.

Torren smiled the smile of someone who had survived many such expressions and had made peace with the odds.

Talia finished checking the binding on my ribs and moved to my palm, cleaning it with something that smelled of crushed herbs and cold water, her hands quick and sure. Around us, Malakor settled into a position near the entrance, and Torren arranged himself against the far wall with the practiced ease of someone accustomed to sleeping in worse places, and the shrine became, improbably, something that functioned like shelter.

Kaelor paused at the entrance. His back was to me. The silver runes along his horns had brightened again, faintly, in proximity to the symbols on the wall, and I wondered whether he knew that, whether he felt the resonance the same way I did or whether it was simply my blood reading the architecture and throwing light at whatever happened to be nearby.

I wondered too many things about him that I had no clean category for.

He stepped out into the dark without looking back.

Talia tied off the last piece of binding on my palm and sat back with the satisfied exhale of completed work. She looked at the entrance he had disappeared through, then at me, with the expression of someone choosing not to say something she had clearly already thought.

"Don't," I said quietly.

"I didn't say anything," she said.

"You were going to."

She tilted her head. Her green eyes were warm and too perceptive for comfort. "I was going to say that you should sleep," she said, entirely too innocently. "The ribs need rest to stop bleeding fully. That's all."

"That's all," I repeated.

"Completely all," she confirmed.

From across the shrine, without opening his eyes, Torren said: "For what it's worth, I have known that male for three years and I have never once seen him treat someone's wounds himself. Just something I noticed. Not saying anything about it. Simply noting it for the historical record."

I lay down on the stone floor with my back against the shrine wall and stared at the cracked ceiling and listened to the mountain dark and the distant wind and the complete absence of any wrong resonance from the forest below, and thought about a warlord standing watch in the cold again, and what it meant that I had already stopped finding it surprising.

The symbols above me pulsed once, slow and warm, like something very old acknowledging something it had been waiting a long time to recognize.

I closed my eyes.

Sleep, when it came, was not peaceful. But it was, at least, mine.

Dawn found us still in one piece, which I had decided to count as a meaningful achievement. The escort was assembled outside the shrine when I emerged into the grey mountain light, Malakor already reading the terrain ahead with his customary expression of someone reviewing a map of available disasters. Talia handed me dried fruit and a water skin without preamble. Torren was somehow already complaining about something to one of the escort members who had the look of a man who had stopped listening two sentences ago.

Kaelor stood slightly apart from all of it, watching the forest below the ruins, and his silhouette against the pale morning was the same as it had been against the mountain dark, broad and still and utterly unmoved by the fact that he had been standing in the cold for hours.

He turned when I approached, and his gold eyes moved across me in the quick, thorough assessment that I had come to recognize as his version of asking whether I was alright, rendered in the only language that seemed to come naturally to him.

"I'm fine," I said, before he could ask.

"Good," he said, and turned back to the forest.

I stood beside him for a moment, the cold morning air between us, the ruins at our backs with their still faintly glowing symbols, and the valley below, opening wide and ancient and full of whatever was coming next.

"We move," he said quietly, and we moved.

# Too Close

By morning, I hated myself for remembering exactly how warm Kaelor's hands had been.

Not the wound treatment. She had cataloged that efficiently enough, filed it under necessary and moved on. What her mind refused to release was the moment before Torren had arrived, the moment when Kaelor had turned in the shrine's dim light, and they had been closer than either of them had accounted for, and she had been aware of every single inch of the space between them with a precision that had nothing to do with combat training.

The bruise along her left ribs made itself known every time she shifted her weight on the saddle. Good. Pain was useful. Pain was a clean, uncomplicated thing that did not require her to examine her own responses with the kind of unflinching honesty she applied to everything else.

She had not slept well. She suspected she was not the only one.

The group had been moving since first light, picking up the broken Labyrinth road that wound through the lower foothills, and the silence among them was the kind that settled after a bad night rather than a comfortable one. Two of the escort members moved with the careful deliberateness of men nursing injuries they were not going to mention. Malakor rode slightly ahead, his silver hair tied back with the severe practicality that seemed to be his only concession to personal presentation, reading the terrain with a focus that had not relaxed since the ruins.

Kaelor rode at the front.

He had not looked at her since they had mounted.

This was exactly how he always behaved, controlled and distant and watchful, attending to the group's forward progress with the quiet authority that made her teeth ache. There was nothing different about him this morning. No visible evidence that anything between them had shifted or cracked or become complicated in a way she had not budgeted for.

It was deeply, unreasonably infuriating.

Talia drew her cloven-footed mount alongside mine with the gentle inevitability of a tide coming in. Her bronze curls had been braided back into something functional, and she carried her satchel across her lap rather than her back, which meant she was monitoring her patients as she rode.

"How are the ribs?" she asked.

"Fine."

"You keep shifting your weight to the right."

"I'm comfortable."

"You're avoiding pressure on the left side. That's not comfort, that's compensation." Talia's voice was pleasant in the way of someone who had learned to deliver unwelcome information in a register that made it difficult to argue with. "The binding will hold as long as you don't do anything that involves sudden lateral movement."

"I'll keep that in mind."

Talia was quiet for a moment, which meant she was either satisfied or building toward something. I had learned the difference. This was the second kind.

"You're blushing," Talia said.

"I am not."

"Your face is red."

"It's cold."

"It was colder an hour ago and your face was perfectly normal." Talia tilted her head, green eyes bright with a warmth that Elara found both comforting and extremely inconvenient. "You don't have to talk about it."

"There is nothing to talk about."

"Of course not," Talia agreed, with the serene agreement of someone who believed the exact opposite and had decided to be patient about it.

From directly behind them, Torren's voice arrived with the timing of someone who had been waiting for exactly this gap in the conversation.

"You two somehow make silence feel aggressively uncomfortable," he said pleasantly. "I've been trying to determine whether that's a skill or a symptom."

"Don't," I said.

"I'm not doing anything. I'm riding." He paused. "I'm simply noting, in a purely observational capacity, that the atmospheric tension in this group has increased significantly since last night, and I have some theories about the origin point."

"Torren."

"The creature was very dramatic," he continued, undeterred. "Very frightening. Forced proximity in ancient ruins. Wound treatment. Symbolic architecture responding to blood. I'm told it was quite the evening."

"I will push you off this road."

"Noted," he said, and finally, mercifully, went quiet.

I turned my eyes back to the road ahead, where Kaelor's silhouette moved against the gray morning sky, and hated the fact that Torren was not entirely wrong, and hated more that he knew it.

The broken Labyrinth road narrowed as the foothills steepened, leading them toward a river crossing she had clocked on Malakor's map the night before. The bridge was old Labyrinth construction, the same fitted stone as everything else in this realm, geometric and precise, but the river beneath it was running high and fast from mountain snowmelt, and its spray reached the road even before the bridge itself came into view. The stone was slick with moisture where the mist had settled and frozen in the early morning cold, and the crossing was narrow enough that they would need to go single file.

Malakor assessed it from the bank with the expression of someone doing arithmetic on available risk, then turned back to the group.

"Bridge is sound," he said. "Surface is compromised. Move carefully."

The escort crossed first, two by two, their boots finding purchase on the slick stone with the careful placement of people who had learned to treat every uncertain surface as a potential consequence. Talia went next, her goat legs giving her considerably better traction than anything built for flat ground, and she crossed quickly with the light-footed confidence of someone whose anatomy was built for exactly this kind of terrain.

Elara followed.

She was three steps onto the bridge when the collar flared.

It was not the sharp spike of the night before, not the white pain of adrenaline meeting the binding's restrictions. This was subtler, a low, sustained pressure that wrapped around the base of her skull and crept down her spine, and the effect was not pain so much as a deep, comprehensive unreliability of the signals between her brain and her legs. Her left foot slipped on the wet stone. She caught the edge of the bridge with one hand, but the impact sent a line of fire through the bruised ribs that stole her breath at exactly the moment she needed it, and for one terrible, tilting second the fast current below was not an abstract concern.

His hand found her arm before she had finished falling.

Kaelor's grip was iron and warmth and the absolute certainty of something that did not consider the possibility of dropping her, and he hauled her upright and back from the bridge's edge with a controlled force that put her firmly on her feet and kept her there, his body between her and the rushing water below.

She caught her breath.

He didn't let go.

The collar was still humming, low and insistent, and the river spray was cold against her face, and his hand was around her upper arm with a grip that was firm without being painful, and she was aware, with a sharp, specific clarity, of the exact distance between his chest and her back. Not much. Not enough for comfort, or for the kind of comfortable distance that made it possible to pretend the awareness was not there.

She turned her head, and he was already looking at her, gold eyes steady and close, and for a moment neither of them said anything, the river noise filling the space where words would have gone.

"I'm all right," she said.

"I know," he said, and still didn't let go.

One breath. Two.

Then his hand released her, slowly, and he stepped back one measured pace, and the cold air rushed into the space he vacated with the enthusiasm of something that had been waiting for the opening.

She crossed the rest of the bridge without looking back at him, and absolutely did not examine why her heart was still beating too fast for a near-fall that had lasted less than three seconds.

They stopped at midday in a hollow where the road widened beside the ruins of what had once been a waystation, the stone walls half-standing and the roof long gone, but the shelter from the wind was real, and the flat ground was enough for the group to rest and eat without losing the road entirely. I sat apart from the main cluster and worked on the water skin and the dried provisions that passed for midday meals in this part of the journey, and tried to organize her thoughts into something that resembled useful tactical analysis rather than the circular, self-indicting loop they kept defaulting to.

She was not succeeding particularly well when Malakor appeared beside her and sat without invitation, which was characteristic of him.

"The Queen is no longer searching," he said, without preamble.

I looked up. His black eyes were already on mine, level and flat with the precise neutrality of a man delivering a report he believed should change the calculus of every decision made from this point forward.

"Clarify," I said.

"The Shadow Court's previous response to your presence in the realm was intelligence-gathering. Scouts. Information networks. Patience." He paused, and the pause had the particular quality of a trained intelligence operative ensuring that the next statement landed cleanly. "That posture ended three days ago. She is hunting. The difference matters."

"How do you know?"

"Because two of the Queen's personal hunters crossed into the mountain roads forty-eight hours behind us. Not scouts. Not border patrol. Hunters. There are four types of operatives Astrythe deploys personally. This particular pair handles acquisitions the Queen has decided she cannot afford to lose."

I absorbed that. The cold of the waystation hollow felt sharper than it had a moment ago.

"You're telling me she's made this personal."

"I'm telling you the operational profile changed, and the timeline we were working against has likely compressed by at least half." His voice did not change register, which somehow made it worse. "We need to move faster."

He stood and walked away with the same unhurried practicality he brought to everything, and I stared at the half-eaten provisions in my hand and thought about a queen who commanded armies and ancient magic and apparently decided that sending her personal hunters after a single human woman was a proportionate response.

That was either deeply flattering or genuinely terrifying.

I was leaning toward the second one.

Kaelor was at the far edge of the waystation when I found him, standing at the crumbling parapet of what had once been an outer wall, his gaze on the road they had come from. An old watchtower rose behind the station, taller than the ruins around it, one corner collapsed, but the rest still stood in the stubborn way Labyrinth construction seemed to manage across centuries. He turned when I approached, and I saw from his expression that Malakor had already given him the same report.

"You knew," I said.

"I suspected. The confirmation changes our route. There is a secondary path through the Ashfall passes that will add half a day but removes us from the main roads entirely." He was already thinking in terms of logistics, already reshaping the journey's architecture around this new variable, and I recognized the quality of that focus because I had worn it myself often enough.

"Malakor said she's moved from searching to hunting. What's the difference, practically?"

"Searching is patient. Hunting has a specific objective and a willingness to accept collateral damage in pursuit of it." He turned back to the road, and the wind off the mountain moved through the ruins with a low, hollow note. "The Queen wants you alive. That means the people with me are not the primary targets, but they become acceptable losses if removing them serves the acquisition."

I was quiet with that for a moment.

"You keep saving me," I said. The words came out more measured than the ones I had planned, but the ones I had planned had been sharper, and I had decided against them somewhere between the waystation and this wall. "I haven't decided whether that's reassuring or insulting."

Something crossed his expression, a shift that wasn't amusement and wasn't offense but occupied the territory between them.

"You assume those are different things," he said.

I looked at him. He was watching the road again, the line of his jaw set against the cold, and the runes along his horns were still in the flat daylight, the silver gone matte without the dark to catch it.

"Why me?" The question came out quietly, carrying the weight of the night before and the bridge and every moment since the ravine when he had interposed himself between me and something that wanted to end me. "You have an alliance to protect. A mission. Political stakes that extend well beyond one human woman with a bloodline nobody fully understands. Strategically, I am more of a liability than an asset. So I want to understand why you keep making choices that don't align with the strategic picture."

He was silent long enough that I thought he might deflect again with brevity, the way he had in the shrine, the way that should have been insufficient and somehow never was.

When he spoke, his voice was lower than usual, and he did not look at me.

"Because I know what it is to be made into a weapon," he said.

The words hit me somewhere specific, somewhere between the sternum and the throat, with the specific impact of a truth delivered without performance or preparation.

I waited. The wind moved through the ruins. Far below the watchtower, the road wound back toward the river crossing, and somewhere behind it, two of Astrythe's personal hunters were moving toward them with the patient certainty of people who did not expect their quarry to escape.

"The clans did not unite willingly," he said, after a moment. "Some of them required convincing. Some of that convincing required me to become something that served the alliance's survival rather than my own judgment about how to conduct it." A muscle worked in his jaw. "I was effective. That is not the same as being right. And the things I was effective at are not things I can separate from what I am now, any more than you can separate yourself from the years that made you what you are."

"You think we're the same," I said.

"I think we recognize each other," he said. "That is not the same thing."

I held that carefully, the way I held anything that felt fragile and important, not examining it too closely in case the examination was what broke it.

"That's the most honest thing you've said to me since the fortress," I said.

"Don't become arrogant about it."

I almost smiled. I stopped it in time, but only just, and I suspected from the way his gaze dropped briefly to my mouth that he had clocked the effort. I looked away, out over the broken road and the valley beyond it, and tried to remember what useful, tactical detachment felt like from the inside.

I could not quite locate it.

The ruins around me were old Labyrinth construction again, the same geometric symbols carved into the watchtower's remaining walls, and I noticed with the particular, tired resignation of someone who had accepted a pattern even while resenting it that they had begun to pulse again, slow and faint, the same rhythmic flicker I had seen in the shrine. I had not touched anything. I had not bled on anything. I had simply been here, standing beside him, and the stone was responding to her presence the way it always did now, as though proximity alone was enough.

"It does it even when I'm not trying," I said quietly.

He turned and looked at the watchtower wall. The symbols there moved in their slow, warm rhythm, patient as a heartbeat.

"Yes," he said.

"Does that concern you?"

A pause. "It clarifies the stakes. That is not the same as concern."

"Malakor's already filed it away somewhere. He looks at me differently when it happens."

"Malakor looks at everything differently when it happens. That is how he has survived this long."

"And Draevok?" I watched his profile. "His messenger this morning. The one who rode ahead. That was a political update, wasn't it."

His expression did not change, but something behind it tightened.

"Draevok's position regarding your presence in the alliance has not shifted," he said. "He will continue to press the argument that you represent a variable that cannot be controlled."

"He's not entirely wrong."

"No," Kaelor said. "But being correct about the danger does not make his conclusion correct about the solution."

I looked at the pulsing symbols again. The warmth they gave off was almost pleasant, if I didn't think too hard about what it meant that ancient architecture was waking up because I was standing near it.

I was standing too close to him again.

I realized it the way you realize you have stepped into a current, not at the moment of entry but slightly after, when the pull was already there, and the question was no longer whether you felt it but what you intended to do about it. The cold air between them carried the scent of leather and iron and the specific, dark-warm smell that was simply him, and her bruised ribs were aching steadily, and I was tired in the specific way that had nothing to do with sleep and everything to do with maintaining vigilance against myself.

My hand moved.

Not far. Two inches, perhaps three, before I registered what I was doing and stopped it. My fingers had been reaching, without her permission, toward the edge of his forearm where the war harness ended, and the dark fur began, drawn by some instinct that had been building since the shrine and had apparently decided the watchtower was a reasonable place to finally act on itself.

I pulled my hand back and made a fist at my side instead.

The movement was small. It should have been invisible.

He had gone absolutely still.

Not the watchful stillness of combat readiness. Something different. Something that was the restraint equivalent of a held breath, a quality of arrested motion that told me, without a single word, that he had noticed, and that noticing had cost him something.

I kept her eyes forward and my jaw level and my voice, when I found it, measured.

"We should get back to the group," I said.

"Yes," he said, and his voice was perfectly controlled, which meant it had taken effort to make it that way.

I walked back toward the waystation hollow without looking at my own hand, and hated myself with a clean, focused efficiency that was at least something I knew how to do.

Torren was waiting near the road with the expression of a man who had observed the general direction of events from a useful distance and had formed opinions about all of it. He said nothing as I approached, which was unusual enough that I glanced at him.

His amber eyes were bright, and his mouth was doing the thing where it wasn't quite a smile but was thinking about it.

"Don't," I said.

"I'm not," he said.

I walked past him. Behind me, I heard him exhale with the quiet, compressed restraint of a man exercising the better part of his nature and finding it somewhat expensive.

Talia fell into step beside me without comment, which was the kindest thing she could have done.

Malakor was already at the head of the group, reading the route ahead, his voice flat and precise as he outlined the timeline adjustment to the escort. I caught fragments as I approached: *secondary pass, Ashfall road, move at pace, no stops after dark.*

I looked back once, despite myself.

Kaelor stood at the watchtower parapet, exactly where I had left him, his silhouette broad and still against the pale mountain sky. He was not watching me. He was watching the road behind them, the direction the hunters were coming from, standing between me and what was coming with the same quiet, absolute certainty I had been noticing since the first night in his fortress and had been telling myself, every day since, that I had not.

The symbols on the watchtower wall pulsed once behind him, slow and warm, and then went still as the distance grew between me and the old stone.

I turned back to the road ahead and kept walking.

I did not examine what my hand had almost done.

I did not think about the particular stillness he had gone when I had stopped it.

I thought about hunters on the road behind them, and a queen who had decided that patience was no longer sufficient, and the long, cold miles between here and wherever they were going.

That was enough to think about.

It had to be.

# The Breaking Point

I had survived monsters, betrayal, and magical imprisonment. Nearly touching Kaelor Ashhorn felt far more dangerous.

I pulled my hand back and made a fist at my side, and the cold air between us filled with the particular silence of something that had almost happened and hadn't, which was somehow worse than if it had. My ribs ached. My jaw was set. I walked back toward the group without looking at my own fingers, which were still humming with a fine, violent tremor that I couldn't seem to force quiet.

He said nothing.

That was the problem. I looked for the familiar hardness in his face, the sharp edge of his mouth, some dismissive flicker in his golden eyes that I could seize upon and turn into a weapon to use against him. I wanted him to lash out, to offer some cold, strategic rebuke that would let me stoke the heat in my chest. Instead he stood perfectly still, and the silence stretched between us like a wire pulled tight, and I felt the tension of it even with my back turned, even as the ruins of the watchtower fell behind me and the waystation hollow came back into view.

Torren's amber eyes tracked me across the ruined courtyard with the focused attention of someone cataloging information he would absolutely use later. I walked past him. He let me, which was its own kind of statement.

Malakor was already calling for the group to move.

We moved.

The Ashfall pass route Kaelor had chosen was choked with jagged scree and flanked by shoulder-rubbing stone walls, the stone older and less maintained, with the kind of silence that came from being genuinely isolated rather than simply unpopulated. The afternoon light was flat and gray, pressing down through a layer of cloud that hadn't broken since midday, and the cold had settled into something serious. I rode with my eyes on the terrain ahead and my thoughts doing their level best to stop circling back to the watchtower.

They were not succeeding.

We stopped at the abandoned Labyrinth watchtower as the light began its early winter collapse. It was larger than the waystation ruins, a full fortification structure from whatever era the Labyrinth's builders had considered necessary to station guards in the mountain passes. Three of its four walls still stood. The roof was gone, but the upper tower remained mostly intact, and Malakor declared it defensible with the brevity of a man who had slept in worse.

I was finding my position against the inner wall and unwrapping the provisions when the attack came.

No warning. No gradual approach. One moment, the ruined courtyard was empty. The next, two of Kaelor's escort were down. The air filled with the sharp, singing sound of bolts that were fired from something that wasn't a crossbow but moved like one. Silent. Fast. Aimed with the specific precision of people who had done this before.

Not a war party. Not a full assault.

Four of them, dropping from the upper ruins, moving in deliberate formation. Shadow Court hunters, exactly as Malakor had described. Dark armor, close to the stone, no insignia, no announcement. They did not shout demands. They did not posture. Two broke toward the group's flanks and two came directly for me, which told me everything I needed to know about their objective.

Kaelor's voice cut through the noise like cold iron.

"Move left. Now."

I didn't think. My body moved before my mind caught up, and the bolt that had been aimed at the space where I'd been standing struck the wall behind me with a sound like a stone cracking.

"I don't take orders," I said, which was a stupid thing to say while diving behind a collapsed section of inner wall, but the words came out anyway.

"Then die stubborn," he said, and the complete absence of heat in his voice was somehow more effective than any shout would have been.

He was already moving, closing distance on the nearest hunter with a speed that never stopped being wrong for something his size, and the sound that followed was short and conclusive. I pulled my blade and kept the rubble at my back, watching the angles.

Two coming for me. One flanking right, one pushing straight through. The straight approach was faster but the flanker was the real threat, using the ruined walls for cover the way someone trained for exactly this kind of close-quarters work would use them. I had maybe four seconds before the angle changed and I lost the wall advantage.

"Right side," Kaelor said, somewhere behind and to my left, still in that same controlled register, as though the firefight was a problem to be solved rather than a crisis to be survived. "Draw the straight approach. I have the flanker."

"You can't see the flanker from your position."

"I can hear them."

I processed that, and the truly infuriating thing was that I believed him, and believing him meant the tactical logic was sound, and following sound tactical logic kept me alive, and so I drew the straight approach by stepping out of cover just enough to make myself visible and immediately dropping as the shot came.

The hunter cleared the rubble three feet to my right, blade already drawn, and got exactly two steps before Kaelor arrived from an angle that should not have been possible given where I had last clocked him. The fight was not long. It was not elegant. Kaelor simply stepped inside the hunter's guard, caught the throat with one massive, clawed hand, and drove him down into the broken stone with a single, skull-cracking impact that ended the fight instantly. It was brutally efficient in the way of someone who had stopped fighting for sport several centuries ago and now only fought to end things.

The second hunter came at me directly, and I was already moving to meet them.

This one was fast. Faster than I expected, compensating for my smaller size by pressing the advantage of reach, and I spent the first few seconds purely on defensive movement, getting my measure of their style before I found my opening. They were trained for capture, not killing, which meant the strikes were aimed at disabling rather than destroying, and that told me where the hesitations would be.

I found one.

I drove my blade into the gap between armor segments at the shoulder and felt the resistance of it, and the hunter went down hard against the stone.

The courtyard went quiet.

My breath was loud in my own ears. The collar at my throat was humming with a low, sustained pressure that had been building since the first shot fired, and my hands were shaking with the specific tremor of adrenaline looking for somewhere to go, and something else was building underneath it, something that had nothing to do with the fight or the fear or the cold.

The nearest hunter was not dead. Wounded, down, attempting to drag themselves toward the cover of the far wall with the grim determination of someone who had been trained past the point where survival instinct and mission priority could be easily separated. Their eyes found mine across the ruined courtyard, and I saw recognition in them, sharp and certain, and the recognition was not of my face.

It was of something they had been briefed to expect.

The pressure in my blood crested without permission.

I did not intend it. I did not choose it. There was no ritual, no concentration, no deliberate reaching for whatever lived beneath my skin and responded to the Labyrinth's carved stone. There was only the adrenaline and the hunter's eyes and the collar's hum and something that had been coiling tighter since the shrine, since the bridge, since the watchtower wall, and it broke open all at once.

The force that came out of me was not fire and was not light. It was a shockwave, spatial and wrong, the air between me and the far wall contracting and then releasing like a held breath turned violent, and every loose piece of rubble in a twenty-foot radius moved outward from where I stood. The hunter was thrown back against the far wall with a sound that ended the fight conclusively. Two sections of collapsed masonry shifted and resettled. The geometric carvings on every Labyrinth stone surface within sight flared brilliant, burning white, and then went dark again as fast as they had come.

Silence.

My ears were ringing. My vision had gone briefly white at the edges and was returning in uneven stages. The collar was no longer humming. It was burning, a thin, precise line of fire around my throat, and my knees had decided that the ground was a reasonable destination, and I was down on the stone before I had fully registered the decision to be.

Everyone was staring at me.

Talia, from the shelter of the inner wall where she had pressed during the fight, her green eyes wide and fixed on me with an expression that was not fear but was something adjacent to it, something that sat between alarm and concern without fully settling on either. Torren stood three feet from where he had taken cover, and his face had done something I had not seen it do before, stripped of the easy humor, genuinely still, his amber eyes tracking me with a focus that had no joke waiting behind it. Malakor had gone very quiet in the specific way that meant he was filing information rather than reacting to it, and the look he gave me was already analytical, already building conclusions I did not want him to reach.

Kaelor had gone absolutely controlled.

Not surprised. Not afraid. Controlled, in the way of someone who had received information that mattered and had made the immediate decision to process it internally rather than externally, and the quality of that restraint was somehow more unsettling than shock would have been.

Torren exhaled.

"So," he said, his voice carefully level, "exploding magically. New hobby?"

"Shut up," I said, and was mildly surprised by how steady my own voice came out, given that my hands were still shaking and the collar was still burning and the courtyard felt too large and too silent and I was deeply, comprehensively terrified of myself.

Talia was at my side before I had finished the sentence, her satchel already open, her fingers light and efficient at my throat. "That looked painful," she said, which was her version of an assessment.

"I'm fine."

"You're kneeling on rubble and your collar has heat-scarred the skin beneath it." She did not make it an accusation. She made it a fact, delivered in the same tone she used for all facts, steady and clear and impossible to argue with. "Don't move quickly."

I stayed where I was and let her work, because my legs were not entirely reliable and the alternative was proving it by trying to stand.

Across the courtyard, Malakor crouched beside the fallen hunter, checked for pulse, found none, and stood. His black eyes moved to me once, flat and unreadable, and then he turned to begin securing the perimeter with two of the surviving escort, his movements unhurried and precise.

"Unknown power," he said to no one in particular, his voice carrying just far enough to reach me, "makes her more dangerous. Not less."

I had nothing to say to that, because he was not wrong, and we both knew it.

Kaelor waited until Talia had finished her assessment and moved the injured escort members to the shelter of the standing walls before he came to me. By then I was on my feet, which felt important even if my balance was still making occasional editorial comments about my recent choices. He stopped two feet away, which was close enough that I had to tilt my chin up to hold his gaze.

"Walk with me," he said.

It was not a request.

I walked with him to the upper tower's base, where a narrow stair still held, and the ruins gave us the nearest thing to privacy the situation allowed. The city of stars above was hidden behind cloud. The cold pressed down through the absent roof and the wind found every gap in the standing stones, and I crossed my arms and waited for what I already knew was coming.

"What are you hiding?" he asked.

"Nothing." The word came out too fast, and I knew it, and from the shift in his expression, he knew it too.

"That was not the power of a woman with nothing to hide."

"I don't know what that was." And the awful, infuriating, genuinely frightening part was that it was true, and the truth had no edges I could hold onto. "I didn't choose it. I didn't summon it. It simply happened, and I have no more information about it than you do, and I understand that is not a satisfying answer, but it is the only honest one I have."

His jaw was tight. His gaze on mine was relentless, gold and steady, working through what I had said and measuring it against what he had seen, and the frustration in him was not the hot kind. It was cold and precise and made of genuine concern dressed as command.

"Your blood says otherwise," he said quietly.

"My blood has been saying things I don't understand since I arrived in this realm. I have been ignoring most of them because understanding them requires information I don't have and time we haven't had." The words came faster now, cracking against each other, and I recognized the sound of my own composure finding its limit. "I did not ask for any of this. I did not choose to be whatever I apparently am. I did not volunteer my bloodline for the Labyrinth's architectural entertainment, and I did not ask to become the personal acquisition project of a queen who apparently has nothing better to do with her considerable power than hunt one human woman through the mountains."

Silence.

The wind moved through the broken tower above us.

"I know," he said.

Two words, and the steadiness in them took the edge off my anger before I had finished being angry, which was deeply unwelcome.

"I am not accusing you," he continued. "I am asking because what happened tonight confirms what I suspected, and what I suspected changes how I need to position every person in this group for the road ahead. I need to understand the scale of what we are carrying."

The frustration between us did not dissolve. It shifted, reorganized itself into something that was less about accusation and more about two people staring at the same unknown from different sides of it. I uncrossed my arms. My hands were steadier now.

"The hunters knew," I said. "Not what it was. But that it existed. The way they looked at me when they came in. They had been briefed."

"Yes."

"Which means Astrythe knows. Or knows enough."

"Enough to escalate from intelligence-gathering to personal acquisition, yes." He held my gaze, and something behind his eyes was working through implications I could only partially see. "She would not commit hunters of that caliber to a retrieval operation unless she had specific intelligence about value. Not general intelligence. Specific."

"Someone told her." The realization arrived quietly. "Someone who knew enough about my bloodline to make the case."

"That is a question we will need to answer." His voice did not change register, but something in the set of his shoulders told me the answer already had a shape in his mind, and it was not a comfortable one.

I stood with that, the cold pressing against my skin, the ruins settling around us with the occasional soft sound of old stone adjusting to the night. The collar had stopped burning and settled back into its usual low pressure, but the skin beneath it was tender in a way that would be worse tomorrow.

"I'm frightened of it," I said. I had not planned to say it. It came out anyway, in the space where all the strategic analysis had exhausted itself and the honest thing was the only thing left. "What happened tonight. I couldn't stop it. I couldn't direct it. It simply came out, and I had no more control over it than I would have over a seizure, and the thought that it could do that again, anywhere, at any time, with anyone nearby who might be in the way of it." I stopped. Steadied. "That frightens me more than the hunters did."

He was very still.

Not the combat stillness, not the cold strategic calculation. This was different, the kind of stillness that came from something landing harder than expected, from a truth delivered without armor that required a moment to receive properly.

"Isolation is not strategy." he said.

"You said something like that to me before."

"I meant it before. I mean it now." His voice was quieter than usual, and the controlled distance he maintained so precisely had narrowed, not disappeared but thinned enough that something real moved through it. "The power is yours. The fear of it is reasonable. But the isolation you are using to manage both of them is not a strategy. It is a familiar habit dressed as discipline."

My chest tightened.

"You sound certain," I said.

"I recognize it."

He moved.

Not toward my face. Not with tenderness.

One deliberate step closer, enough that the cold air between us vanished and the heat of him became a physical thing, enough that every instinct I possessed became suddenly, acutely aware of how little distance remained between us.

His hand came up, and for one treacherous second I thought he was going to touch me. Instead, his palm braced against the cold stone beside my shoulder, close enough that I felt the restrained force in the movement, close enough that my pulse immediately abandoned every reasonable pace it had previously maintained.

His gold eyes held mine.

The restraint in him was visible. Not hesitation. Not uncertainty. Restraint. The kind that cost something.

My breath caught anyway.

Then Malakor's voice cut through the tower doorway, flat and unhurried and carrying the specific weight of a man who had run the numbers and arrived at a conclusion he considered non-negotiable.

"Both of you need to hear this."

Kaelor's hand dropped. The moment closed.

I breathed.

We returned to the courtyard, where Torren and Talia had gathered near the shelter wall and Malakor stood with the posture of someone who had just finished composing a report that no one was going to enjoy receiving. His silver hair caught the faint light from the escort's small fire, and his expression was exactly as unreadable as it always was, which meant the news was bad.

"Intelligence arrived via the relay we set before the pass," he said, addressing both of us with the efficient directness of a man who had long since abandoned the practice of softening things. "The hunters tonight were advance units. Not the primary strike."

I waited. Beside me, Kaelor was completely still.

"High Queen Astrythe has entered the field personally." Malakor's black eyes were level, unblinking. "She is not directing from the court. She is not coordinating through intermediaries. She left the capital three days ago with her personal guard and an enforcer retinue. She is moving through the mountain roads herself." He paused, one brief beat. "She is coming for you."

The courtyard was absolutely silent.

Torren, to his considerable credit, said nothing at all. His face had done the stripped-bare thing again, the joke entirely absent, and he was watching me with an expression I could not quite name.

Talia's hand found my arm, light and steady.

I held Malakor's gaze and felt the cold of the mountain night settle into my bones with an intimacy that had nothing to do with temperature. The most powerful ruler in the Labyrinthine Realm had left her court. Had moved, personally, into the field. Had decided that whatever I was and whatever I carried in my blood was important enough to pursue herself, through mountains, in winter, with her personal guard at her back.

The scale of that was not a comfortable thing to stand inside.

"How far behind us?" Kaelor asked, and his voice was perfectly even.

"Two days. Perhaps less, depending on her route and how much the terrain slows the retinue." Malakor's gaze moved briefly to Kaelor. "The Ashfall pass buys us time. It does not buy us safety."

"Nothing does," Kaelor said, and began giving orders to the escort with the calm authority of a man who had already begun building the next plan before the last one had fully ended.

I stood in the ruined watchtower courtyard, Talia's hand on my arm, the collar's low pressure against my throat, and thought about a queen who had decided patience was beneath her. Thought about the shockwave that had moved through me without my permission and thrown a trained hunter into a stone wall. Thought about the Labyrinth's carvings flaring white in response to my blood and my fear and whatever it was that lived underneath both of them.

Thought about his hand, suspended in the cold air between us, waiting for a choice I had not made.

The fire was small. The ruins were old. The road ahead was worse than the road behind, and the most dangerous woman in the realm was moving through the mountains toward me with her full retinue and whatever she believed about my bloodline driving her forward.

I pulled my coat tighter and turned toward the fire.

Whatever came next, we would not be sleeping much tonight.

# No More Distance

I had spent years surviving monsters. It was wanting one that terrified me.

I lay on my bedroll long after the camp had quieted, staring at the canvas ceiling while the low fire outside threw its orange light against the walls and the cold pressed through every gap in the tent's fabric. The night had the kind of weight that follows bad news, the silence of people who were still awake and thinking hard but had nothing useful left to say. Somewhere outside, Malakor's boots moved at measured intervals along the perimeter. Two of Kaelor's remaining escort murmured something low and brief near the fire, then went quiet again.

The High Queen was in the field. Moving through winter mountains with her personal retinue, personally, because whatever I carried in my blood was worth that kind of deliberate attention from the most powerful ruler in this realm.

I pressed the heel of my hand against my sternum and breathed.

The collar had not stopped aching since the fight. Not the sharp burn from the power surge earlier, which had faded, but something lower and more persistent, a grinding pressure that had settled in beneath my collarbone and refused to release. I had been ignoring it because the alternative was acknowledging it, and acknowledging it meant admitting that Talia's expression during her assessment had been the expression of someone containing worse news than she had delivered.

The tent flap opened. Not Kaelor this time. Talia ducked inside with her satchel and a small lamp, her bronze curls loose around her face and her green eyes carrying exactly the concern I had been trying not to think about.

"I can hear you not sleeping from twenty feet away," she said, which was not technically possible but felt accurate.

"I'm thinking."

"You're catastrophizing. There's a difference." She knelt beside me and set the lamp down, already reaching for the collar with efficient fingers. "Let me look at this again."

I sat up and let her work. Her touch was light and careful, tilting my chin just far enough to see the skin beneath the metal band, and the small, controlled sound she made told me everything before she said a word.

"How bad?" I asked.

"The suppression field is degrading." She did not dress it up. I had learned early that Talia's gentleness was a quality of delivery, not a quality of honesty. "It's not designed for extended use on someone with active blood-power. It was built for containment of dormant lineages. What happened tonight, the surge, it's accelerating the deterioration. The collar is fighting your blood and losing, and the friction of that is burning the tissue underneath." She paused. "If we leave it as it is for another few days, I cannot promise the damage stays surface level."

The cold in my chest had nothing to do with the night air.

"You're telling me it needs to come off."

"I'm telling you it needs to come off soon. Yes."

I was quiet for a moment. "Does Kaelor know?"

"I told him when I finished the assessment. He sent me to tell you." She sat back on her heels, her green eyes steady on mine. "Elara. He's not going to let it hurt you further just to maintain tactical control. That's not what this is."

I did not say what I was thinking, which was that I had learned not to trust the difference between protection and possession, because the two had always looked identical right up until the moment they didn't. Instead, I said, "When?"

"Tonight. While the camp is still." She hesitated. "He wants to do it himself. The binding was keyed to his bloodline authority. Anyone else risks a backlash."

I exhaled slowly. "Of course he does."

Talia gave me the look she reserved for moments when she thought I was being deliberately difficult and chose not to say so. Then she patted my knee, gathered her satchel, and left.

I sat with the lamp and the low sound of the fire and the collar's grinding pressure and thought about how many things I had survived by keeping distance between myself and anything that felt like trust. The inventory was long and the habit was deep, and none of that changed the fact that my skin was burning and the woman who understood every herb and wound in this camp had just told me the alternative was permanent damage.

I stood up and went to find him.

He was at the far edge of the fire's reach, seated on a fallen section of timber with his war harness removed and a map weighted open across his knees. The firelight caught the runes on his ivory horns and threw the planes of his face into sharp relief, and for one unguarded moment before he registered my approach, I saw the exhaustion he never let anyone else see. It was not weakness. It was the weight of someone who had been calculating threats since before sunrise and had not stopped.

He looked up. The exhaustion disappeared behind control so practiced it was nearly invisible.

"Talia spoke with you," he said.

"She did." I stopped a few feet away and crossed my arms, which was habit more than defense. "You want to remove it tonight."

"I want to remove it before it becomes irreversible." He set the map aside and rose, and the movement reminded me, as it always did, how much space he occupied simply by existing. "The controlled conditions available to us here are not ideal. But they are better than removing it in crisis."

"And you need to be the one to do it."

"Yes."

I looked at him across the low firelight, at the measured patience in his gold gaze and the restrained intensity behind it, and said the thing I had been carrying since the moment Talia delivered her news. "If this is a trick, I want you to know I will find a way to make it deeply unpleasant for you."

Something shifted at the corner of his mouth. Not quite a smile. Something adjacent to one. "Then you may stab me afterward."

The sincerity in that was deeply unfair.

"Fine," I said.

He moved to the space between the fire and my tent, where the light was steadiest and the cold was slightly less vicious. I followed and stood still while he reached for the collar's binding point, a place at the back of the band where the seam met a small raised sigil I had noticed but not understood. His hands were careful. I felt his warmth before I felt his touch, the heat radiating from him in a way that the cold night made impossible to ignore, and then his fingers brushed the back of my neck as he found the lock point, and my entire nervous system made a series of extremely unhelpful decisions in rapid succession.

"Hold still," he said quietly.

"I am holding still."

"You are breathing differently."

"I am breathing exactly as I always breathe."

He said nothing to that, which was somehow worse.

The sigil beneath his thumb began to heat, not painfully, but with the specific quality of a binding releasing, and then the collar clicked open and came away from my throat, and the relief was so sudden and so total that my knees nearly buckled with it.

Everything hit at once.

I had not understood how much the collar had been suppressing until it was gone. Not just the power, but everything, every sense sharpened by the removal of whatever dampening field had been pressed against my blood for weeks. The night air tasted different. The fire smelled of pine resin and iron and something older underneath. I could hear the individual sounds of the camp with a clarity that felt almost violent after so much muffled silence.

And I could feel him. Not magically. Not with the Labyrinth's blood-pull, though that was there too, humming low and warm at the base of my spine. I mean I felt his presence the way you feel a fire when you have been standing in the cold long enough to forget what warmth was. His scent was leather and smoke and something dark and distinctly him, and the heat coming off his body at close range was enough to make the winter air feel irrelevant, and I stood there in the firelight with his hands still warm at the back of my neck and my pulse doing something entirely ungovernable.

He felt it too. I watched the shift move through him. His hands did not leave my neck immediately, and when they did, the withdrawal was deliberate rather than automatic.

"Elara."

My name in his voice, low and controlled and carrying something underneath the control that he was working hard to keep contained.

"Don't," I said.

"I wasn't going to say anything."

"You were about to say something responsible and strategic and I cannot hear it right now." I turned to face him, which was a tactical error because it put us at extremely close range and the firelight was doing nothing to help my composure. "I want to ask you something and I need you to answer it honestly."

His gaze was steady. "Ask."

"Why?" The word came out harder than I intended, carrying the weight of every question I had not asked since the mountain road. "Not the political answer. Not the alliance answer. Why do you keep putting yourself between me and every threat in this realm? Why does it matter to you what happens to me? What do you actually want from this?"

The silence stretched. Long enough that I thought he would retreat behind strategy and leave me holding the question unanswered.

Then he exhaled, and something cracked open behind his eyes.

"You," he said. The word was quiet, controlled, and somehow more dangerous for the restraint in it. "That is becoming the complication."

The honesty of it hit harder than anger would have.

He took one step closer. Not touching. Just close enough that the cold air between us became charged with awareness.

"This is a terrible idea," I said.

"Yes."

Neither of us moved.

His gaze dropped once, briefly, to my mouth, then returned to my eyes, and the restraint in him was so visible it became its own kind of pressure.

My pulse betrayed me.

Then the camp exploded.

Not metaphorically. The distinctive sound of a Shadow Court strike, the sharp singing whistle of silenced bolts and the percussion of something much larger impacting the outer camp wall, shattered the night so completely that my body moved before my mind had finished processing it. I was pulling my shirt back on and reaching for the blade under my blanket before the second impact landed, my hands steady with the specific, cold clarity that battle always dropped over me like a hood.

Kaelor was already upright, his war harness in his hands, his face closed down into the controlled blankness of a commander assessing incoming threat.

Outside, Malakor's voice cut through the noise, sharp and precise: "Shadow Court. Heavy unit. North and east perimeter."

Then Torren, somewhere closer: "Excellent. Impending doom always improves morale. Wonderful timing, absolutely no notes."

"Move," Kaelor said, and looked at me once, and the thing in his expression was not soft and not strategic. It was the face of someone who had something to lose now and knew it.

I moved.

The camp outside was chaos shaped into something almost organized, Malakor already directing the escort's defensive positions with the flat, rapid efficiency of a man who had run scenarios like this in his sleep. Talia was pressed against the inner supply structure with her satchel clutched to her chest and her green eyes wide but her jaw set, counting bodies, cataloging injured. Torren had two blades drawn and was positioned at the narrowest approach point with the posture of someone who complained constantly and moved when it mattered.

The attackers came from three directions simultaneously. Not a precision strike like before. This was heavier, more coordinated, built for overwhelming rather than capturing. The objective had changed.

They were not here to take me alive this time.

The realization landed with a cold, specific weight. Astrythe had escalated. Whatever intelligence she had received about the power surge in the ruined watchtower had shifted her calculation. If I could not be contained and transported intact, I could be removed.

Kaelor's hand closed around my arm, pulling me behind the supply structure as a bolt embedded itself in the post where my head had been. His grip was iron and brief, and then he was moving, intercepting the nearest attacker with that wrong, too-fast movement that still caught me off guard despite everything I knew about him.

I fought my own section of the perimeter, blade in hand, working through the attackers near Talia's position with the particular focus that comes from protecting someone who cannot protect themselves in the same way. Two down. A third circling. I drew them away from Talia's shelter, found the gap in their approach, and closed it.

The blood-pull surged without warning.

Not the full shockwave from the watchtower. Something more directed, responding to the threat with the instinctive precision of something that had been learning from my body's patterns. The attacker nearest me stumbled, thrown sideways by a force that arrived faster than any physical blow, and struck the camp's outer post hard enough to stay down.

I stood with my blade raised and my blood humming and the geometric patterns carved into the nearest Labyrinth-stone marker flaring brief and brilliant white in the darkness.

Malakor saw it. His black eyes found mine across the camp, and the expression on his face was not accusation or fear. It was the face of someone revising a threat assessment upward in real time.

"Elara." Kaelor's voice from my left, controlled and immediate. "With me. Now."

The camp was still fighting. The escort held the north perimeter with brutal efficiency. Torren had vanished into the kind of close-quarters chaos that apparently suited him, given the sounds emerging from the eastern approach. Malakor was managing the coordinated response with the flat authority of someone who had done this particular terrible thing many times before.

But Kaelor was pulling me toward the forest line, and his grip on my wrist was not captivity. It was direction, deliberate and urgent, and behind us three more Shadow Court attackers broke from the tree line specifically angled toward us.

We ran.

The forest closed over us, dark and cold and indifferent, the underbrush cracking beneath our feet as we pushed deeper into the tree line and the sounds of the camp fight faded behind us into something muffled and distant. The blood-pull was still humming, awake now in a way it had not been with the collar suppressing it, and the Labyrinth stones we passed in the darkness pulsed faint and silent as though aware of my passage.

We put distance between ourselves and the attack until Kaelor drew us up behind a massive fallen tree trunk and the forest was quiet around us except for our own breathing and the distant, diminishing sounds of combat.

I pressed my back against the bark and pulled air into my lungs and looked at him in the darkness, at the controlled tension in every line of his body and the gold of his eyes catching what little light filtered through the canopy.

"The others," I said.

"Malakor has the camp. He knows what he is doing." His voice was steady, but something underneath it was not. "We drew the pursuit. That was the point. The strike was designed to separate us."

I processed that. "They came for you too."

"They came for both of us. Together." His gaze moved through the trees, reading the dark. "The Queen has decided that the simplest solution is removing the warlord and his inconvenient human acquisition simultaneously."

The word acquisition should have stung. It landed differently now, in the aftermath of the tent and the collar and his voice saying *you* with the weight of something finally admitted.

We crouched in the dark forest with the cold pressing down and the sounds of pursuit somewhere behind us, and I was intensely, specifically aware of his warmth at my side, the brush of his arm against mine, the way the blood-connection hummed between us like a live wire that the collar's removal had finally allowed to breathe.

The attack had interrupted everything.

Nothing had been resolved.

Everything had been changed.

He turned his head and found me already looking at him, and for one unguarded moment neither of us pretended otherwise.

"We move at first light," he said. His voice was even. His eyes were not. "Keep close."

"I know," I said.

And somewhere in the dark behind us, three sets of boots moved through the underbrush toward our position, patient and precise and very certain of the direction they were following.

The hunt was not finished. It had barely begun.

And somewhere in the mountain passes to the south, a queen in a shifting gown moved through winter roads with her retinue at her back, and she was not stopping, and she was not patient, and she knew exactly what she was coming for.

I pressed my shoulder against Kaelor's arm and kept my blade ready, and the Labyrinth stones in the dark around us glowed faintly, silently, as though they had been waiting for precisely this moment to begin.

# Claimed by Fire

The explosion of the Shadow Court strike ripped through the night with a deafening roar that shattered the quiet, raining dirt and pine needles onto the tent. The worst part about being attacked in the middle of almost losing control was realizing I still wanted to finish what had started. I was moving before my mind caught up, blade already in hand, the taste of Kaelor's mouth still burning on my own and the heat of what we had almost done thrumming beneath my skin like a second pulse.

Kaelor was already moving with me, his massive frame cutting through the chaos with that terrible grace. The forest swallowed us as we ran, the sounds of the camp fight fading into something distant and muffled behind the trees. Three sets of boots followed, patient and precise, and I knew without being told that these were not ordinary soldiers. They had come specifically for us.

Branches tore at my arms. The cold bit through my thin shirt. Behind us the pursuit closed in with the relentless patience of people who knew exactly what they were hunting and had no intention of letting it escape. Kaelor's hand found my wrist in the darkness, pulling me harder, faster, deeper into the trees where the underbrush thickened and the moonlight barely reached.

The blood in my veins answered the threat before my mind could catch up. It pulsed without warning, the Labyrinth's power thrumming wild and volatile beneath my skin, and I felt the stone markers we passed humming in resonance to the vibration. They glowed faintly in the dark, ancient symbols catching fire with each step I took, and the reaction was so strong it made my knees buckle mid-stride.

Kaelor caught me before I fell. His arm locked around my waist and hauled me upright, but the movement exposed him for a single heartbeat, and that was all the attackers needed. The bolt came from the left, a dark shape cutting through the shadows, and Kaelor twisted to shield me with the whole of his body. The impact drove him sideways with a sound that was more thud than voice, and I felt the hot rush of his blood against my hands before I even registered what had happened.

"Kaelor." The word tore out of me raw and sharp.

He kept moving. The wound was bad, I could feel that much, but he did not slow and he did not let me go. We crashed through the last line of trees and into a clearing where the moonlight finally found us, and the ruined outpost rose from the darkness like something half-forgotten. Stone walls, broken and weathered, with a heavy door hanging crooked on rusted hinges. It was shelter. It was the only thing we had.

We reached it just ahead of the pursuit. Kaelor drove his shoulder into the door and it gave with a scream of metal, and then we were inside, the darkness closing around us like a second skin. He slammed the door behind us and dropped the bar across it, and the sound of the attackers hitting the other side made the whole structure shudder.

The interior was small. A single chamber with a low ceiling and walls carved with symbols I recognized from the watchtower, the same geometric patterns that had flared when my power awakened. There were no windows. Only one way in, one way out, and the door would not hold for long against determined force.

Kaelor sagged against the wall and I smelled the blood, thick and metallic, and the fear that had been building in my chest since the attack finally found a shape. I reached for him without thinking, my hands finding the wound in his side where the bolt had driven deep between his ribs. The fur there was soaked through, and when I pressed my fingers against the injury he made a sound that was more growl than voice.

"You're bleeding."

"I noticed." His voice was tight, controlled, but I could hear the strain beneath it. "The bolt missed anything vital. It will hold until we can reach the others."

"That's not the point." My hands were shaking. I could feel the tremor in my own fingers as I tried to assess the damage, and the intimacy of the moment hit me all at once. We were alone. The door was barred. The camp was somewhere behind us fighting for its life, and Kaelor was bleeding because he had put himself between me and the attack without hesitation.

"You're shaking," he said quietly.

"You're bleeding."

The silence that followed was thick with everything we had not said in the tent before the attack tore us apart. I could still feel the ghost of his mouth on mine, the weight of his hands, the way the blood connection between us had burned so bright it had nearly consumed every rational thought. Now he was hurt. Now we were trapped. Now the hunger that had been building between us for weeks had nowhere left to hide.

"Let me help," I said.

"Elara."

"Don't argue with me right now." I tore a strip from the bottom of my shirt and pressed it against the wound, applying pressure the way Talia had taught me. The blood soaked through almost immediately, warm and slick against my fingers, and Kaelor did not stop me. He watched me work with those molten gold eyes, and the intensity in his gaze made my skin feel too tight.

The ruined outpost was colder than the forest had been. The stone beneath my knees bit through the thin fabric of my pants, and I could hear the attackers outside circling, testing the door, speaking in voices too low for me to catch. They knew we were trapped. They were waiting for us to weaken or for reinforcements to arrive.

"You should have let me take that bolt," I said without looking up. "It would have hurt less."

"That is not how this works."

"How what works?" The words came out sharper than I intended. "You deciding that my life matters more than yours? You throwing yourself in front of every threat like I'm some fragile thing that needs saving?"

"You are not fragile." His voice was low, steady, and it carried the kind of weight that made me stop what I was doing and meet his eyes. "You are the opposite of fragile. But that does not mean I will stand by while they try to kill you."

"Why?" The question hung between us like a blade. "You keep saying it's because of what I am, because of the bloodline, because of the Labyrinth. But that's not all of it. I can feel that it's not all of it. So tell me the truth for once instead of wrapping it in strategy."

Kaelor was quiet for a long moment. The wound beneath my hands had stopped bleeding quite so freely, but the damage was still there, still raw, and I could feel the way his breathing had changed with the pain. When he finally spoke, his voice was rougher than I had ever heard it.

"I lost people before you." The admission came slowly, carefully, like something he was not accustomed to giving away. "Whole clans. Warriors who trusted me to lead them through fire and did not come back out the other side. I made choices that cost lives, and I told myself those choices were necessary, that the cost was worth the outcome. But the truth is simpler than that. I was willing to sacrifice anyone who was not mine."

"And now?"

His jaw tightened.

"Now losing you would be strategically catastrophic," he said.

"That's not what I asked."

A long silence. Then, quieter:

"No."

That landed harder than any speech could have.

"I don't know what this is," I said quietly. The words came out before I could stop them. "I don't know what you are to me or what I am to you. All I know is that when you touch me, I stop thinking about survival. I start thinking about what it would feel like to stop running."

"Neither do I." His thumb traced once along my jaw, then stopped, as though even that much contact cost him restraint.

"Want is not the problem," he quietly said.

The air between us felt too thin. The sounds outside had faded to something distant, the attackers still circling but not yet committed to breaking down the door. We had time. Not much, but enough for the tension that had been building since the night Kaelor first appeared in my tent to finally break.

I did not tell him to stop. Instead, I rose up on my knees and closed the distance between us, and when my mouth found his, the kiss was nothing like the first one. That had been desperate, interrupted, a collision of need and fear and the certainty that we were about to die. This was slower. Deeper. The kind of kiss that came from weeks of wanting and fighting and denying, and it tasted like surrender and defiance all at once.

Kaelor's hands found my waist and pulled me closer, and the size of him made me feel small in a way that should have been terrifying but wasn't. He was careful even now, even with the wound in his side and the blood on both of us and the knowledge that death was waiting just outside the door. His mouth moved against mine with a hunger that matched my own, and when I opened for him the sound he made was low and rough and entirely involuntary.

Kaelor's hands moved beneath my shirt, calloused palms sliding over the scars on my ribs, and the touch was so careful it made my chest ache. He mapped every mark like he was learning a language, like he wanted to understand the shape of every hurt I had survived, and when his fingers found the edge of my breast I felt the tremor that went through him.

"Elara." My name in his voice was a question and a warning and a plea all at once.

"I know." I pulled back just far enough to look at him, to see the gold of his eyes gone dark with want and the way his horns caught the faint light filtering through the cracks in the ceiling. "I know what this means."

"You should care."

"I spent years caring about survival. About staying one step ahead of everyone who wanted to use me or kill me or sell me. I'm tired of it." My hands found the fastenings of his war harness and worked them loose with fingers that were steadier than they had any right to be. "I'm tired of pretending this isn't happening. That I don't want you."

I pushed him back against the wall and straddled his thighs, and the position put us at eye level for once. His hands settled on my hips with a possessiveness that should have felt like a cage but didn't. It felt like being chosen. Like being wanted for reasons that had nothing to do with bloodlines or politics or the war that had brought us together.

I kissed him again, harder this time, and the last of his restraint snapped. His hands tightened on my hips and pulled me down against him, and the hard length of him pressed against the thin fabric of my pants made my breath catch. He was huge in every way that mattered, and the knowledge of what was about to happen sent a thrill of fear and want through me so strong it made my vision blur.

Kaelor's mouth moved to my throat, and the scrape of his teeth against the sensitive skin there made me arch into him. His hands worked my shirt up and over my head, and the cold air hit my bare skin for only a moment before his warmth replaced it. He was careful with the scars, tracing them with his tongue like he was learning the map of every battle I had survived, and when his mouth closed over one nipple the sound that escaped me was embarrassingly loud in the small space.

"Quiet," he murmured against my skin. "They are still outside."

"Then you should stop doing that."

"I am not going to stop." His voice carried the kind of certainty that made my stomach flip. "I have wanted this for too long to stop now."

His hands moved lower, finding the fastenings of my pants and working them loose with a patience that contradicted the hunger in his eyes. When his fingers slipped beneath the fabric and found the heat between my thighs, I had to bite my lip to keep from making another sound. He explored with the same careful attention he had given my scars, learning what made me gasp, what made me tremble, what made my hips rock against his hand with a desperation I could no longer hide.

"Kaelor." His name came out broken, and I felt him smile against my throat.

"I have you." Two of his fingers slid inside me with a slow, deliberate pressure that made my whole body clench around him. "I have you. Let go."

I came on his hand with a shudder that went through me like a shockwave, and the release was so intense it left me gasping against his shoulder. He held me through it, his fingers still moving, drawing out every last tremor until I was limp and shaking and completely undone.

When I could think again, I reached between us and found the hard length of him straining against the fabric of his pants. He was even larger than I had imagined, and the knowledge that I was about to take all of him sent a fresh wave of heat through me. I worked his pants down with hands that were not entirely steady, and when he sprang free, I had to pause for a moment just to look at him.

"Elara." There was a warning in his voice, a note of concern that cut through the haze of want. "If this is too much—"

"It's not." I wrapped my hand around him and felt the way his breath caught. "I want this. I want you. Stop trying to protect me from something I chose."

He made a sound that was almost a laugh, rough and broken, and then his hands were on my hips again, lifting me, positioning me. His head pressed against my entrance, and I felt the stretch, the burn, the overwhelming fullness of it as he pushed inside me with a slow, careful thrust that gave me time to adjust to every inch.

It hurt. It felt incredible. It was too much and not enough all at once, and when he was finally seated fully inside me I had to rest my forehead against his chest and breathe through the intensity of it. Kaelor held still, his hands stroking my back, his breath ragged against my hair.

"Tell me when," he said quietly.

"Now." I rocked my hips experimentally and felt the way he shuddered beneath me. "Now. Please."

He moved then, lifting me and lowering me with a strength that made me feel weightless. Each thrust went deeper than the last, and the angle was perfect, hitting something inside me that made stars explode behind my eyes. I clung to his shoulders and let him take what he needed, and the sounds he made were low and rough and entirely mine.

The blood connection between us burned brighter with every movement. I could feel it like a live wire, like something ancient and hungry waking up beneath my skin, and the ruined outpost responded to the surge. The symbols on the walls began to glow, faint at first, then brighter, until the whole chamber was lit with a pale silver light that had nothing to do with the moon outside.

"Elara." Kaelor's voice was tight, strained. "Your power—"

"I know." I could feel it building, the same wild surge that had nearly destroyed the watchtower, but this time it was different. This time it was tied to something more than fear. This time it was tied to him, to us, to the connection that had been growing between us since the moment our paths collided at the auction block.

I came again with his name on my lips, and the release triggered something in the stone beneath us. The floor shuddered. The symbols flared white-hot. And then the whole chamber seemed to come alive, ancient mechanisms waking from centuries of sleep, responding to the power in my blood like it had been waiting for exactly this moment.

Kaelor followed me over the edge with a groan that vibrated through his entire chest, and the force of his release made my vision go white. For a moment, there was nothing but heat and light and the overwhelming sensation of being connected to something far larger than either of us. The Labyrinth's power sang through my veins, through his, and the ruined outpost drank it in like parched earth drinking rain.

When the light finally faded, we were both breathing hard, and the symbols on the walls had gone dark again. But something had changed. I could feel it in the stone beneath us, in the air, in the blood connection that now hummed with a new kind of awareness. The ancient mechanism had not just awakened. It had recognized me. Claimed me. And I had a terrible feeling that whatever it had set in motion was only the beginning.

Kaelor's arms tightened around me, and I could feel the question in the gesture, the uncertainty of what came next. I pressed my face against his throat and breathed in the scent of him, leather and smoke and something darker that I could not stop associating with him, and I knew that nothing would ever be the same.

"This complicates things," I said against his skin.

"Massively." His voice was rough, but there was something almost gentle beneath the roughness. "The others will know. Malakor will disapprove. Draevok will try to use it against me. And the Queen will redouble her efforts to separate us."

"I don't care about any of that right now." I pulled back just far enough to look at him, to see the gold of his eyes gone soft in a way I had never seen before. "I care about the fact that you are still bleeding and we are still trapped and something just woke up beneath us that I don't understand."

"One problem at a time." He shifted carefully, and I felt the loss of him as he slipped free. The emptiness was immediate and strangely painful, and I had to fight the urge to pull him back. "First we survive the night. Then we deal with what this means."

The door shuddered again, the attackers outside growing impatient. We dressed in silence, the intimacy of what we had shared settling between us like a new kind of armor. When Kaelor looked at me, there was something different in his gaze. Not possession. Not strategy. Something closer to wonder, and it made my chest feel too tight.

"Elara." He said my name like a promise and a warning all at once. He held my gaze for one hard second, then turned back toward the door.

"I know." And I did. The certainty of it sat in my chest like a stone, heavy and real and impossible to ignore. "That's what terrifies me."

The floor beneath us gave another shudder, and I felt the ancient mechanism responding to the blood still singing in my veins. Whatever we had awakened was not finished. It was only beginning, and I had a feeling that when it finally revealed itself, the world we knew would never be the same.

Kaelor moved to the door and tested the bar, and I could see the tension in every line of his body as he prepared for whatever waited on the other side. The wound in his side had stopped bleeding, but I could see the strain in the way he held himself, the careful control that came from years of fighting through pain.

"Stay behind me," he said quietly. "If they break through, I will hold them as long as I can. You run."

"I'm not running without you."

"Elara."

"Don't ask me to do something I can't." I moved to stand beside him, blade in hand, and the look he gave me was equal parts frustration and something that might have been pride. "We do this together or not at all."

The door shuddered again, and this time the wood began to crack. Kaelor positioned himself in front of me, his massive frame blocking the worst of the threat, and I could feel the power in his blood responding to the danger just as mine had responded to our intimacy. The blood-connection between us still hummed, volatile and unfamiliar, beyond the bloodline, beyond anything either of us had planned for.

The door gave way with a final crack, and the first attacker came through in a rush of dark armor and drawn steel. Kaelor met him with a roar that shook the stone walls, and I followed with my blade already swinging, the taste of him still on my tongue and the knowledge that whatever came next, we would face it together.

The ancient symbols on the walls began to glow again, responding to the violence, responding to my blood, responding to something I could not yet name. And as the fight erupted around us, I had one last coherent thought before the chaos claimed everything.

This was only the beginning.

# Aftershocks

Waking ancient magic during sex had not been on my list of catastrophic life choices.

It was, however, rapidly climbing to the top of it.

The chamber shuddered again beneath us, and I grabbed the nearest wall with both hands as the stone buckled. The symbols carved into the ancient surfaces were no longer dormant suggestions of forgotten script. They blazed, white-hot and hungry, cycling through patterns that pulsed with the rhythm of something breathing underground. The ceiling groaned. A section of carved stone near the far wall split along a seam that had probably been sealed for centuries, releasing a gust of air that smelled of iron and old magic and something else entirely, something mineral and cold, like the inside of a place that had never once seen sunlight.

"Move," Kaelor said.

He did not say it loudly. He did not have to.

I was already pulling my shirt back over my head, fingers fumbling with the laces of my pants, acutely aware of every place his hands had been and how spectacularly unhelpful that awareness was right now. The floor shuddered in three sharp intervals like a pulse. The glow from the carvings threw strange shadows across the low ceiling and made Kaelor's horns look like they were carved from living flame.

He had his war harness half-fastened. The wound in his side was still visible, the makeshift bandaging I had pressed there dark and damp, and I had approximately two seconds to feel guilty about that before the floor buckled hard enough to send me stumbling sideways into the wall.

Kaelor caught me. Of course he did.

His arm closed around my shoulders, steady and immediate, and the warmth of that contact after everything we had done made my chest do something complicated that I refused to examine.

"The passage," he said. "There is a secondary corridor behind the eastern wall. I saw it when we entered."

"You were injured when we entered."

"I was also paying attention."

Arrogant. Bleeding. Entirely correct.

I pushed off from the wall and followed his lead as the stone ceiling split with a deafening crack, showering us in limestone dust and stinging grit. Another section of ceiling cracked and dropped a palm-sized chunk of stone that shattered on the floor where I had been standing three seconds earlier. The carvings pulsed faster, their light shifting from white to silver to something faintly violet at the edges, and I felt my blood respond to the change like a tuning fork struck too close to my ear. The sensation moved through my veins in a slow, deep vibration that was nothing like pain, which made it somehow worse.

"Elara." Kaelor was at the eastern wall, pressing his hands flat against the stone, and I watched the runes near his palms flicker in recognition. Not of him. Of me, standing close enough that my proximity apparently counted as presence. A section of wall grated inward with the reluctant sound of machinery untouched for lifetimes.

I did not ask how that worked. The passage beyond was dark and narrow and smelled of damp earth, and I went into it without hesitation because the alternative was being buried under collapsing ancient stone.

Kaelor came behind me, and the wall groaned shut at his back.

We moved in near-total darkness. His hand found my shoulder and stayed there, less a grip than a point of contact, a way to keep track of each other without demanding anything. I was grateful for it. I was also acutely, infuriatingly aware of it in a way that had nothing to do with survival instinct and everything to do with the fact that an hour ago that same hand had been on my skin for entirely different reasons.

The passage was not short.

Neither of us spoke for the first several minutes, and the silence was its own specific kind of torture. Not the comfortable quiet that sometimes settled between us during long watches or tense patrols. This was the silence of two people who had done something irreversible and had not yet agreed on what it meant.

He was not going to bring it up first. That much I already knew.

I was not going to bring it up at all, ideally never, possibly forever.

The passage sloped upward and eventually narrowed enough that Kaelor had to angle his horns sideways to avoid scraping the ceiling. I would have found that undignified under any other circumstances. Right now it was simply another detail in the ongoing disaster of the evening.

The passage ended at a stone door that opened onto the forest. Cold night air hit my face like a correction, sharp and clean after the charged atmosphere of the ruins. I stepped out into the dark and breathed it in, and the vibration in my blood slowly, reluctantly quieted.

Behind me, Kaelor emerged from the passage and straightened to his full height. Moonlight caught the silver runes on his horns and the dark stain at his side, and I made myself look away from both.

"The others will be moving toward the secondary rally point," he said. "Northeast. Forty minutes on foot."

"Right."

"Elara."

"We're not discussing it."

A pause that lasted precisely long enough to be deliberate.

"That," he said, "seems unlikely."

I started walking northeast.

He fell into step beside me without another word, and the fact that he let it go, for now, was either respect or strategy. Knowing him, probably both.

The ruins had shown me something before the walls started trying to kill us. I kept turning it over as we walked, the memory of those final carvings before everything went violently wrong. Not the geometric patterns I had seen before. Something older, layered beneath the more recent script like a palimpsest, visible only when the light surged to its brightest. Figures. Human-shaped, or nearly. And beside each figure, a specific symbol I did not have a name for but recognized on instinct with a certainty that sat cold and uncomfortable in my stomach.

The same symbol was in my blood. I had felt it when the ruins responded to me. When the mechanism recognized me.

And there had been more than one figure in the carvings.

I filed that thought away behind a door in my mind and nailed it shut. One catastrophe at a time.

We reached the rally point with enough time to spare that Torren had apparently decided the worst had happened and was in the process of delivering what sounded like a particularly pessimistic eulogy to the rest of the group when we stepped out of the tree line.

"And that," he was saying, "is why following a bloodline-cursed human woman into hostile ruins in the middle of the night without a secondary escape plan remains one of our least defensible decisions. A decision I did, for the record, object to.

"Torren," I said.

He turned. The relief that crossed his face was immediate and genuine before he buried it under something approaching casual indifference.

"Oh, excellent," he said. "Another catastrophically irresponsible decision-maker, alive and ambulatory. Wonderful. My peace is ruined."

"Good to see you too."

Kaelor stepped out of the tree line behind me, and I watched the moment the group took us both in. The proximity. The state of my clothes. The fact that Kaelor was injured and I was the one who had, evidently, done the bandaging, based on the strip of my shirt still pressed against his side.

Talia's eyes moved between us once, quick and quiet, and she pressed her lips together in an expression that managed to be simultaneously supportive and deeply knowing. She crossed to Kaelor immediately, healer's instincts overriding any other response, and he submitted to her examination with the particular stillness of someone who had learned it was easier not to resist Talla when she was in professional mode.

Malakor stood apart from the group, as was his habit. His black eyes moved from me to Kaelor and back again, and whatever conclusion he reached settled into his expression like stone cooling into its final shape. He said nothing. He did not need to. The disapproval did not require words.

Torren, predictably, was not going to let it rest.

"I don't need details," he said, falling into step beside me as I moved toward the fire someone had managed to keep burning low and well-screened. "I absolutely already know enough. The ruins had an opinion about it, apparently, which is a new experience for all of us, and you both came back with the combined energy of people who have either survived something terrible or done something catastrophically inadvisable, and given the state of Kaelor's bandaging, I'm guessing both, and I'm going to stop talking now because you're giving me the look."

"I'm not giving you any look."

"You're giving me the look. It's the one that means I'm correct about something and you resent it. I recognize it because I see it frequently."

"Torren."

"Stopping now," he said pleasantly, and handed me a waterskin. "Drink that. You look like someone who ran through ancient ruins on an adrenaline crash and needs hydration significantly more than dignity."

I drank it. He was right about the adrenaline crash. My hands had started shaking somewhere around the second mile of walking, and the tremor had not fully stopped.

Talia finished with Kaelor and came to me next, her hands quick and methodical as she checked for injuries I had not mentioned, which was most of them. She found the bruises on my ribs from where I had hit the wall during the chamber's collapse, pressed gently, and made a sound that was not quite disapproval.

"Complicated timing," she said quietly, low enough that only I could hear it.

"That's one word for it."

"Are you all right?"

The question was so simply and directly delivered that it caught me off guard. Not all right from the ruins. Not all right from the attack. Just all right. As a person. Right now.

"I don't know yet," I said, which was more honest than I had intended.

Talia nodded like that was a perfectly reasonable answer and wrapped a bandage around my ribs without making me ask for it.

Malakor waited until she had moved away before he crossed to where I was sitting. He crouched to my eye level, which was a gesture he rarely made and which meant he was about to say something he considered serious enough to deliver without the implicit power differential of looming.

"Emotional compromise," he said, "is rarely strategic."

"Thank you, Malakor."

"I'm not looking for gratitude."

"I know."

"What happened in there?"

"The ruins activated. We escaped. That's what happened."

His expression did not change. "And the other thing."

"Malakor."

"I'm not asking for reasons of personal interest," he said. "I'm asking because he is going to become more protective in ways that are visible, and visible protective behavior from a warlord toward a human woman is going to create political pressure that we are not currently equipped to manage. I need to know how serious this is so I can begin managing the fallout."

He was not wrong. That was the infuriating part. He was being entirely, clinically, unhelpfully correct.

"Manage the fallout," I said. "That's what you're concerned about."

"Yes."

"Not about the fact that whatever is in my blood just woke up an ancient mechanism that hasn't moved in centuries and reacted to me specifically."

A pause. "That," he said, "concerns me more than the other thing. But I considered it less likely you would discuss it."

He rose, gave me one final unreadable look, and returned to his post at the perimeter.

Across the fire, Kaelor was watching me.

Not obviously. He was speaking to one of the scouts in the low, controlled voice he used for strategic briefings, his attention apparently entirely elsewhere. But he was watching, and I could feel it the way you could feel weather changing, a shift in pressure, a gathering before the storm declared itself.

He had been like this since we left the ruins. Controlled. Composed. Entirely present in every tactical sense and entirely, deliberately absent in every other one. Whatever he had been in that chamber, whatever had moved behind his eyes when he looked at me afterward, it had been packed away behind the warlord's face with a precision that should not have bothered me as much as it did.

I had told him we were not discussing it.

I had not expected him to agree quite so efficiently.

Talia reappeared with dried meat and hard bread, pressed it into my hands, and sat beside me in companionable quiet for a few minutes while the camp settled. She did not push. She was good at that, knowing when words helped and when they only created more noise in an already crowded head.

Then she said, carefully, still looking at the fire: "The ruins reacted to you specifically."

"Yes."

"Not just to your power. To your blood."

"Yes."

"The carvings," she said. "Did you see them? Before the walls started moving?"

I looked at her. "You know what they said."

"Not exactly. But I've seen similar script before, in the medical archives the High Fey used to catalog their experiments. There was a word that appeared in reference to certain bloodlines." She hesitated, and the hesitation was uncharacteristic enough that I felt my stomach tighten. "They called them Catalysts."

The word landed with the weight of something I had already half-known.

"It was in the carvings," I said slowly. "In the ruins. That specific word, or close to it."

"It's old script," Talia said. "Pre-High Court. It refers to a bloodline specifically created to interact with the Labyrinth's architecture. Not born with power in the ordinary sense. Created. Engineered." She paused again. "The High Fey records I saw described them as keys. Living keys, designed to open or seal specific structures within the Labyrinth itself."

The fire crackled. Somewhere in the dark, an owl moved through the trees.

"Created," I said. "Not born."

"That's what the records suggested. Though the records were incomplete, and some were clearly destroyed deliberately."

I thought about my mother, whom I had never known well enough to mourn properly. I thought about the border village that had burned when I was seven. I thought about every narrow escape and every hand that had reached for me with intent and about my uncle, who had known something, who had always known something he had never seen fit to share.

"If I was engineered," I said, keeping my voice very level, "then someone made the decision to create my bloodline for a specific purpose. And someone else has been hunting me to use that purpose."

"Yes," Talia said quietly. "That's what I'm afraid of."

The camp was settling into its night rotation. Kaelor had finished with the scout and was now standing at the perimeter with Malakor, their conversation too low to catch. I watched the line of his shoulders, the way he stood, the particular quality of stillness that he carried like a second skin.

I pushed to my feet and crossed to him.

Malakor, to his credit, recognized the look on my face and removed himself without being asked. Kaelor turned to face me, and his expression gave away nothing, which was precisely the problem.

"We need to talk," I said.

"About the ruins."

"About all of it."

He studied me for a moment. Then he moved away from the camp's edge, toward the shadow of a large pine where the firelight did not reach, and I followed.

"The carvings," I said, keeping my voice low. "Talia explained what Catalyst means. What the High Fey records said about bloodlines like mine."

Something moved through his expression. Not surprise. He had known, or suspected, and the fact that he had not told me lit a small, hot flame behind my sternum.

"You knew," I said.

"I suspected. I did not have confirmation."

"That's a distinction that matters a great deal less to me than you might think right now."

"Elara."

"Don't." The word came out sharp. "Don't say my name like that, like it's supposed to calm me down. You had information about what I am, what my blood does, why people have been hunting me, and you made a strategic decision to withhold it."

"I made a decision to avoid alarming you with incomplete intelligence before I had something useful to give you."

"That is not your decision to make."

His jaw tightened. The muscle there moved once, and then he was very still again. "No," he said, after a moment. "It was not."

The admission caught me off guard enough that the anger lost some of its edge. Not all of it. But enough.

"What do you know," I said, "and what do you suspect?"

"I know that your bloodline reacts to Labyrinth structures in ways no ordinary human bloodline should. I know that the High Court has been specifically hunting your family line for at least two generations. I know that the cult's interest in you is not incidental. They have been tracking a specific bloodline." He paused. "And I know that the mechanism that activated tonight responded to you in a way I have not seen any other blood-tied individual trigger. The ruins recognized you in a manner that suggested you were expected."

"Expected," I repeated. "By whom."

"By whatever created the mechanism in the first place."

The silence stretched between us, heavy with everything we were not saying. I could feel the warmth radiating off him despite the night cold, could still feel, somewhere beneath the anger and the fear and the exhaustion, the ghost of his hands on my skin and what it had felt like to be fully present in my own body for the first time in years.

I hated that I could feel both things simultaneously.

"It happened," I said.

His attention sharpened. "Yes."

"That doesn't change anything."

The silence that followed lasted long enough that I started to think he was going to let it stand, which would have been the right strategic decision and would have made me unreasonably furious.

"That," he said, "is where we disagree."

I looked at him. He looked back, and there was nothing controlled in his eyes right now, nothing packed away or managed. Just the direct, steady weight of what he actually meant, laid out without the warlord's armor to soften it.

"Kaelor," I said, and my voice came out quieter than I intended.

"I am not going to pretend it did not happen," he said. "But I will not let it rule my judgment either."

"That's not the point. The point is that we are in the middle of a war, with a cult hunting my blood and a High Queen who wants me as a weapon and an ancient mechanism that just woke up because we were reckless, and adding this to the list of things that could get us both killed seems like exactly the kind of decision we should be making with more caution that either of us showed tonight."

"I agree," he said. "It is also done."

"That is not helpful."

"No," he said. "It is honest."

I wanted to be angry about that. I almost managed it.

Then Torren's voice cut across the camp with the particular urgency he used when something had gone wrong that was not his fault but that he was going to be blamed for anyway.

"We have a problem," he called, carefully quiet but distinctly tense. "A scout just came in from the eastern trail. You are both going to want to see this."

Kaelor turned immediately. I was a half-step behind him, and the thing I had been about to say dissolved into the cold air and was gone.

The scout was young, one of the fox-kin runners who worked the outer perimeter, and she was holding a piece of stone in both hands with the careful distance of someone handling something she did not want to touch. The stone was roughly palm-sized, broken from a larger surface, and the carvings on it were visible even from several feet away.

The same script as the ruins. The same geometric patterns. But in the center of the carvings, burned dark and deep as though something had seared through the stone from the inside out, was the Catalyst symbol.

Beside it, a second symbol I had not seen in the ruins tonight.

Talia was the one who identified it. She had gone very still, and the color had drained from her face in a way that made my stomach drop before she even spoke.

"This is a sealing mark," she said. "The second symbol. It means the Catalyst it was tied to has been closed off." She swallowed. "Burned out. The mechanism they were connected to consumed them."

The camp went very quiet.

"Where did you find this?" Kaelor asked the scout.

"Eastern ruins," she said. "Half a mile. There are more like it. And there are remains." She paused. "Human remains. Old, but not old enough."

The implications settled over me like cold water. A Catalyst. Someone like me, with the same blood, the same ancient engineering in their veins, connected to the Labyrinth's architecture. And whatever had happened to them, whatever the mechanism had done, it had consumed them completely.

The stone in the scout's hands had their seal burned into it.

Their end, recorded in ancient script, half a mile from where my blood had just woken the same machinery.

Kaelor's hand came to rest on my shoulder, the contact brief and grounding and entirely deliberate. He did not speak. He did not need to.

I stared at the stone and understood, with a clarity that felt like the floor dropping out from under my feet, exactly what I might be looking at.

Not a unique bloodline. Not a singular accident of birth or design.

A series. A pattern. Catalysts created, used, and burned through by the very architecture they had been made to open. And somewhere, in whatever records the High Fey had destroyed and the cult had hoarded and the ancient ruins were slowly releasing piece by piece, there was a count.

How many had come before me.

How many had not survived it.

"She's not the only Catalyst," Torren said, very quietly, looking at the stone. "She never was."

Nobody argued with him.

The fire burned low, and the forest held its breath around us, and the seal burned into the stone kept staring back at me from the scout's careful hands like a warning written in a language I was only beginning to learn.

# Bad Decisions

If Kaelor was going to pretend nothing had changed, I was prepared to become deeply inconvenient.

He had been at it since before dawn. Strategic. Focused. Entirely in command of himself and everyone around him, issuing orders with the calm efficiency of a man who had simply decided that the previous night had been locked behind whatever iron control he used on himself. He spoke to the scouts. He reviewed the route. He consulted with Malakor in low, measured tones that carried authority without effort and told me absolutely nothing about what was happening inside his chest.

I watched him from across the camp and felt the particular, grinding frustration of knowing I had expected something and received its exact opposite.

The stone with the Catalyst seal was now wrapped in cloth, packed into Talia's satchel for safekeeping. Nobody had said much after Torren's quiet observation last night. There was not much to say. The evidence spoke for itself in a language that did not require translation: someone like me had come before. Someone like me had been consumed. And the ruins held their bones half a mile east of where I had slept.

We broke camp at first light and moved.

The forest trail was dense and green, morning mist threading through the undergrowth in slow, dissolving ribbons. The air smelled of wet bark and pine resin and the faint metallic edge that had been following me since the ruins, which I was beginning to suspect was less the forest and more whatever was happening inside my own blood.

My power had been misbehaving since we left the ruins. Small things. A flicker of light along my palms when my concentration slipped. A pulse of warmth through my veins when something startled me, heat moving outward in a wave that made Talia, walking beside me, glance sideways without comment. Once, when a branch snapped too close, and my body went instinctively taut with alarm, the air around me contracted sharply enough that Torren, three feet behind, stumbled mid-step.

"That," he said, recovering his footing with admirable dignity, "was new."

"Ignore it."

"Absolutely. Ignoring it now. Pretending it did not happen." He paused. "The tension here could physically injure someone, for what it's worth."

"Torren."

"Stopping."

He did not stop. He simply moved slightly further behind me, which I appreciated more than I was going to admit.

Kaelor walked ahead with Malakor, and I watched the line of his shoulders against the morning light and tried, with limited success, to be a reasonable person about all of it. He had not ignored me. He had checked on me twice during the early morning hours in ways that were so carefully positioned as tactical concern that I almost believed he meant them that way. Almost. He had adjusted the group's pace when my ribs ached from the bruising I had taken in the ruins. He had placed himself between me and the direction the scouts reported potential pursuit without making a production of it.

Protective. Absolutely. Infuriatingly, consistently, and deliberately protective in every way that did not require him to acknowledge a single thing that had happened between us.

Talia matched her stride to mine. She had been doing that since we set out, quiet and steady, and I was grateful for it in a way that made me feel slightly unsteady, which was its own specific problem.

"You two are exhausting," she said, conversationally, as though she were commenting on the weather.

"We're not anything."

"That is a very committed position for someone who hasn't stopped watching him since we left camp."

I made myself look at the trail ahead instead. "My power is unstable. He's the warlord. Watching him is tactically appropriate."

Talia made the small sound she made when she was being politely unconvinced, and we walked in comfortable silence for another quarter mile before she said, "The instability is going to get worse before it gets better. Whatever the ruins activated, it's still active. Your body hasn't finished responding to it."

"What does that mean, practically?"

"It means strong emotions are going to trigger surges. Fear, anger." She paused. "Anything heightened."

That was spectacularly unhelpful given current circumstances. I kept that observation to myself.

The first skirmish came at midmorning.

Two of the outer scouts came back through the trees at a run, and Kaelor had his hand up, halting the group before they had fully emerged from the undergrowth. The scouts reported what we had all suspected: pursuit. A fey unit, light cavalry, and trackers, moving fast along a parallel route to the northeast. They had found our camp from the previous night. They were not guessing anymore. They knew the direction.

The skirmish was brief and ugly. Four of the cavalry pushed through the tree line before the scouts could redirect them, and the fight happened in close quarters among the roots and low branches, messy and fast. Kaelor moved through it with a controlled violence that was almost mechanical, efficient, like someone who no longer needed to think about the mechanics. Malakor fought with precise, economical strikes, taking down his target in two movements and moving to the next without breaking stride.

I put a knife through a soldier's shoulder joint where the armor separated, dropped him, and felt the pulse of heat move up my arm the instant his blood touched the blade. Not intentional. Not controlled. The air around my hand shimmered faintly before I clamped down on it, jaw tight, and forced the sensation back.

Torren, who had theoretically been watching the rear, materialized at my left elbow with a short sword and the expression of someone who had made several poor decisions in quick succession and had committed to seeing them through.

"Good news," he said, driving his blade home with more accuracy than his general demeanor suggested he was capable of, "I found the other two."

"Bad news?"

"They found me first. Obviously." He stepped back, breathing harder than he wanted to show. "We should move."

We moved.

The halt came an hour later, a natural shelter formed by three massive pines growing close enough that their lower branches created a dense screen. Kaelor called the stop for water, and a brief assessment of their injuries, and the group spread out in the practiced quiet of people who had done this many times before.

I found a tree to put my back against and watched my hands. The faint shimmer was gone, but the warmth was not. It sat in my veins like banked coals, waiting for something to fan it.

"Emotional triggers," Talia had said. The skirmish had been an excellent demonstration. I did not particularly want to consider what the evening's argument would do to my sense of power and stability, because I had already decided the argument was happening.

Kaelor was standing at the edge of the shelter speaking to one of the scouts, and I waited until the scout moved off before I crossed to him. He saw me coming. He always saw me coming. He simply adjusted his weight and turned to face me with the particular stillness he wore when he had already assessed a situation and chosen his response in advance.

"You don't get to touch me like that," I said, keeping my voice low enough that it did not carry, "and then become a wall."

Something moved in his expression, controlled and deliberate. "I am trying to think strategically."

"Try harder."

He studied me, molten eyes steady and unreadable, and the quiet stretched between us until it became its own kind of pressure.

"What would you have me do," he said. It was not quite a question.

"Acknowledge that something happened. Not dissect it. Not solve it. Simply stop pretending I don't exist in any capacity that isn't tactical."

"I have not pretended that."

"You adjusted my pace this morning without saying a word to me."

"Your ribs are injured."

"That is not the point."

"I am aware of what the point is," he said, and his voice dropped further, something rougher moving beneath the control. "I am also aware that we are in the middle of a pursuit, that your power is unstable, that we have evidence of a dead Catalyst half a mile from where we slept, and that my judgment needs to be functional right now."

"Your judgment," I said, "is not my concern. What you do with it is your business. But you do not get to make decisions about my emotional reality for me by simply refusing to engage with it."

His jaw tightened. The muscle there shifted once.

"You told me we were not discussing it," he said.

"I changed my mind."

"You are infuriating."

"I am furious with you," I said. "There is a difference."

Something cracked open in his expression. Not much. Just enough that I saw the actual heat of it before he brought it back under control, and then his hand was at the back of my jaw, not gentle and not rough, just certain, tilting my face up, and his mouth came down on mine with all the restrained frustration of someone who had been holding a door shut against a flood for hours and had finally stopped pretending the door was winning.

I kissed him back with every ounce of the anger that had been building since dawn, and it was nothing like the ruins. Nothing like surrender or desperation or the strange, reverent quality of something finally giving way. This was teeth and heat and the specific fury of two people who wanted something they could not stop wanting and resented each other for it. His hand fisted in my hair, pulling my head back just enough to change the angle, and I grabbed the front of his war harness and held on because my knees had become spectacularly unreliable.

The warmth in my veins surged. Not dangerously. Just present, flooding upward like a tide responding to the moon, and I felt it move outward through my skin in a wave that was not quite power and not quite anything else, just the raw, unprocessed energy of everything I had been clamping down since last night.

He felt it. His breath changed against my mouth, something between a sound and a word that he did not finish, and then he pulled back just enough to look at me, both hands framing my face, his chest moving harder than his controlled exterior had suggested.

"Noted," he said, rough and low, and I would have laughed if my throat had been working properly.

Thirty seconds was all the forest allowed us.

"Contact, northeast." Malakor's voice, clipped and utterly devoid of inflection, came from approximately twelve feet away.

Kaelor pulled back. His hands released me in a single, deliberate motion, and he turned toward Malakor with a composure that I genuinely could not account for given the previous thirty seconds of evidence.

Malakor stood at the edge of the tree screen, back to us, looking northeast with the rigid posture of a man who had assessed the situation and filed it in a mental file he would absolutely reference later, at the worst possible moment. His voice, when he spoke again, was addressed to the trees.

"Scouts report a second unit has joined the pursuit. They will reach this position within the hour if we do not move." A pause. "Emotional instability is exploitable. I suggest we address the more pressing issue."

The look on Kaelor's face when Malakor finished speaking suggested that the next tactical briefing was going to be a chilly affair.

I straightened my shirt, checked my knife, and decided that what had just happened was going to haunt me for the foreseeable future, whether I permitted it or not, and there was nothing to be done about it.

We moved again.

The afternoon ground on. The pursuit pressure remained consistent, scouts reporting in at intervals with updates that all conveyed the same basic message: the fey units were not falling back and were methodical. Whoever commanded them understood patience as a tactic.

My power surged twice more without invitation. Once, when a branch broke too close to Talia, the fear hit before my reason did. Once, when

Kaelor moved ahead of me around a blind corner, some animal part of my brain registered his absence as a threat before I could correct it. Both times, the warmth moved outward in a pulse that I caught, barely, before it became visible.

By the time we reached the secondary shelter, a rocky overhang at the base of a ridge that Malakor had apparently known about and shared only when necessary, the afternoon light had gone orange, and my head was aching from the sustained effort of keeping everything inside the lines.

Torren dropped down beside me against the rock face with the boneless exhaustion of someone who had been moving hard all day and had opinions about it.

"I'm going to say something," he said, "and I want you to understand that I say it from a position of genuine personal concern and absolutely no desire to be involved."

"Then don't say it."

"Malakor saw you," he said. "Just so you have complete information about the political situation. He saw you, and he made a face that I can only describe as deeply disappointed in several directions simultaneously, and he is going to do something bureaucratic and unpleasant about it at the first available opportunity."

"I know."

"Right." He stretched his legs out. "Good. I also want it noted that I personally found it validating because I have been watching the two of you, and I remain committed to not being involved."

"Torren."

"Going quiet now," he said pleasantly, and closed his eyes.

Talia had been moving through the group with her kit since we stopped, checking injuries with quick, certain hands. She reached me eventually, crouched down, and pressed two fingers against the bruising at my ribs without preamble.

"The surges are getting more frequent," she said.

"I know."

"Are you managing them?"

"Mostly."

She sat back on her heels and studied me with the expression she wore when she was deciding how much truth was useful. "The Catalyst connection to the Labyrinth architecture doesn't go dormant once it's been activated. Whatever the ruins woke up, it's looking for something to do. If you don't give it a controlled outlet, it's going to find an uncontrolled one."

"How do I give it a controlled outlet when I don't understand what it is yet?"

"You probably can't," she admitted. "Not fully. But awareness helps. Don't suppress it completely. Let it move through you without directing it. Like holding water in your hands without squeezing."

I thought about the feel of it moving through my veins, the warm tide of it, and tried to imagine not fighting it every time it surfaced. That sounded like the opening line of a disaster.

"I'll try," I said.

Night came down fast under the ridge. The scouts reported that the pursuit had halted a quarter mile east, where they were setting up their own camp, which meant they were waiting for morning rather than pressing through the dark. Small mercy.

The group settled into a muted, watchful quiet. Kaelor spoke briefly to each of the senior fighters in turn, working the perimeter with the methodical thoroughness that was so fundamental to how he operated that it had stopped registering as deliberate and simply felt like weather.

He came to me last.

He did not crouch down. He sat, which was unusual enough that it registered. His back against the rock beside me, close enough that his arm pressed against my shoulder, and he said nothing for a stretch of time that might have been five minutes or fifteen. The warmth of his proximity was something I had stopped being able to pretend was neutral.

"Malakor," I said finally.

"I'm aware of Malakor."

"He's going to make it a problem."

"He already has." Kaelor's voice carried no particular heat. "He raised it formally with me before we stopped. Concerns about judgment and stability and exploitable vulnerabilities."

"And?"

"And I told him that his concerns were noted and that his assessment of my judgment was not a decision he was authorized to make."

I turned that over. "That's going to create friction."

"Yes." He paused. "I find I am willing to sustain it."

The fire burned low between the rest of the group and us, and I felt something in my chest do the complicated, unwelcome thing it had been doing with increasing frequency since the ruins, since before the ruins, since the first time he had appeared in my tent and I had reached for a dagger, and he had caught my wrist like it was nothing.

"Kaelor." I kept my eyes on the fire. "The Catalyst in the ruins. The one the mechanism burned through." I had to stop and start again. "How many do you think there were?"

He was quiet. Not avoidance. Consideration.

"I don't know," he said. "The records we have recovered suggest multiple. The cult's interest in bloodline tracking implies they have been monitoring the pattern for generations."

"Generations," I said. "Meaning this has happened before. Multiple times. And nobody stopped it."

"Nobody who survived it was in a position to stop it."

That sat between us like something with weight.

"I am not going to let that happen to you." His voice did not shift, did not rise, did not convey conviction. It simply stated a fact. "Whatever I have to do."

"You can't promise that."

"No," he said. "I can make it very difficult for anything else to occur."

I almost said something sharp. The reflex was still there, the reach for distance when something got too close to mattering. But I was tired, and my ribs ached, and the warmth in my veins had settled into something almost bearable, and I let myself lean slightly into the solid heat of his shoulder instead of pulling away.

He did not comment on it. He simply adjusted his weight almost imperceptibly to hold mine more securely.

Torren, from across the fire, cracked one eye open, assessed the situation, and closed it again with the practiced neutrality of a man who had learned when not to speak. Progress, for him.

It was Talia who found it.

She had been combing through the scout reports while the rest of us rested, cross-referencing the eastern ruin fragments with the carved stone they had brought back. She came to me quietly, crouching down, and her face in the firelight was carefully composed in the way it got when she was managing something difficult.

"There's more," she said. "From the ruins. The scouts did a secondary sweep before dark, and they brought back additional fragments." She set two pieces of stone on the ground between us. "I've been reading them."

Kaelor straightened beside me. Malakor materialized from the shadows at the perimeter with the uncanny timing he always seemed to manage, and Torren sat up and stopped pretending to sleep.

"The second symbol," Talia said, pointing to the fragment on the left, "the sealing mark I identified last night. There are six of them in the fragments. Six separate sealing marks, each with a slightly different configuration. Not the same Catalyst. Different ones." She looked at me directly. "Six individual bloodlines that the mechanism recorded as consumed."

The number settled over me like cold stone.

"And the second fragment?" Malakor asked before I could find a response.

Talia hesitated. In anyone else, it would have been a small pause. From Talia, who hesitated at nothing medical and almost nothing else, it was significant.

"The second fragment has a seventh mark," she said. "But it's different. The sealing burn isn't complete. The process was interrupted." She pressed her lips together. "Which means the seventh Catalyst was not consumed. The mechanism tried to close the connection, and something stopped it."

Silence moved through the group like water finding low ground.

"Stopped it how?" Torren said.

"I don't know. The fragment doesn't say." She picked up the stone and turned it in her hands. "But the seventh mark is open. Which means whoever that Catalyst was, they were not destroyed. They were just..."

She searched for the word. "Disconnected. Cut off from the mechanism mid-process."

"Corrupted," Malakor said flatly. "The word you're looking for is corrupted. A partial severance from Labyrinth architecture would not leave the bloodline intact. It would leave it damaged."

Talia did not disagree with him. That told me everything.

My power moved in my veins, restless and warm, and I held Talia's instruction in my mind and did not squeeze. Let it move. Let it be there without directing it.

"Someone like me," I said slowly, "connected to the same architecture, partially severed mid-process, left alive and damaged. Where would they be?"

Nobody answered immediately.

Then the fox-kin scout who had brought us the stone last night stepped forward from the edge of the camp. She had been quiet since, but her expression now carried something that looked like a mix of reluctance and decision.

"The eastern ruins," she said. "When we did the secondary sweep. We found more than fragments."

She looked at Kaelor, then at me.

"There is a chamber," she said. "Deeper in. We did not go inside. But there is something in it that is still alive."

The words hit me the way a blade hit bone, not just the surface pain but the deeper, resonant shock of it moving through everything beneath.

Still alive.

A Catalyst, partially consumed, improperly severed, still existing somewhere in the wreckage of a ruin half a mile away. Still alive in whatever state the mechanism had left them after trying to burn through their bloodline and being interrupted.

Kaelor rose. He turned to the scout, and his voice was measured and precise. "Show me the approach."

"We're not going back there tonight," Malakor said.

"No," Kaelor agreed. "At first light. With the full forward unit." He looked at me, and the look was not a question. It was an acknowledgment. He already knew I was going.

Malakor turned away without argument, which was its own specific kind of alarm. He was saving it for later. He was very good at saving things for later.

I sat with the fragments in front of me and the fire burning low, and I counted six sealed marks and one open one, and I thought about the ruins recognizing me. About the mechanism responding to my proximity. About whatever had been engineered into my blood by people who had lived and died before I was born, who had made decisions about what I would be and what I would be used for without ever considering that I might have opinions about it.

Six consumed. One corrupted. And me, still walking around with the same architecture running through my veins, newly awakened and increasingly unstable.

The warmth moved through me again, and this time I let it, the way Talia had described, open hands, not clenched. It moved like breath, like tide, like something that had a natural rhythm if I stopped fighting it long enough to feel it.

It was still terrifying. But it was mine.

That was the thing I kept coming back to. Whatever they had engineered, whatever purpose they had designed the bloodline to serve, the power itself was mine. And if I was going to die the way the six sealed marks suggested was possible, I was going to do it with full knowledge of what I carried rather than half-understood fear of it.

Kaelor settled back beside me in the dark. His shoulder pressed against mine again, warm and solid and present in the particular way he had of being present, which was total and quiet and without demand.

"You're thinking very loudly," he said.

"Six," I said.

He did not pretend to misunderstand. "Yes."

"And one who might still be there."

"Yes."

"And me."

His hand found mine in the dark, not gentle and not possessive, just present, fingers closing around mine with a steadiness that moved through me more effectively than anything he could have said.

"And you," he said quietly. "Who we are going to understand before anyone else decides your fate."

I did not tell him I believed him. I was not sure I did, not entirely, not yet. But I held his hand in the dark and let the fire burn low, and I stopped fighting the warmth in my veins, and I let myself be afraid without running from it.

Tomorrow we would go back to the eastern ruins. Tomorrow we would find whatever remained of the seventh Catalyst and learn what the mechanism had left behind.

Tonight, the forest held its breath around us, and somewhere half a mile east in a chamber that had been sealed for longer than anyone remembered, something was still alive that should not have survived what had been done to it.

I thought about that, and about six sealed marks, and about my blood moving through the Labyrinth's architecture like a key turning in a lock, and I understood, with a clarity that sat cold and certain in my chest, exactly what I might be walking toward in the morning.

Not a warning. Not a record. A mirror.

A mirror that breathed, and survived, and was going to show me what I could become if the wrong hands reached me first.

# What They Made

I have expected many terrible things in my life. Finding out that I might have been manufactured was not one of them.

The chamber was deeper than the scouts had described. We descended through a passage cut into bedrock so old the stone had gone smooth from moisture and time, torchlight sliding off the walls in ways that made the shadows move wrong. The air smelled of stale iron and the sweet, organic decay of a wound closed too long without cleaning. My power moved in my veins before my eyes had adjusted to the dark below.

Talia walked close to my left shoulder. She had her satchel open, one hand resting on the strap, and her jaw was set with the tight, deliberate stillness she wore when she was scared and choosing not to show it.

Malakor descended first, torch in hand, scanning every recess before he allowed the rest of us to follow. He had not said much since we entered the ruins. What he had said was economical and cold and exactly as useful as intended.

Torren was the last one down the stairs. I heard him behind me, a careful footfall and then a sharp exhale. "I officially hate this place," he said. "I want that noted. For the record. Historically."

Nobody answered him. Even Torren seemed to understand that this was not a moment that required a response.

The chamber opened ahead of us like a held breath finally released. Kaelor moved to my right, his presence a solid, deliberate wall, and I had stopped pretending his proximity was tactical three chambers ago. The rune light on his horns was dim here, suppressed, as though even his power understood that this place did not welcome it.

What we found stopped us all.

The room was wide, low-ceilinged, carved from the same dark stone as the passage. But someone had worked it. Someone had spent considerable time and deliberate intent making it functional for a purpose I was only beginning to understand and already did not want to understand.

Restraint systems ran along the far wall. Not crude chains. Engineered systems, articulated brackets, and anchoring points set at specific heights, spaced for a human body, with mechanisms built to hold without killing. The stone beneath them was stained dark in patterns that had nothing to do with water damage.

Ritual markings covered every surface. Not decorative. Functional, the same architectural language I had seen in the upper ruins, but denser here, layered, as though this room had been used repeatedly and the markings had been refreshed each time.

"I don't think these were patients," Talia said quietly. Her voice was completely steady. The stillness of it was worse than if she had sounded afraid.

Malakor moved along the right wall, examining a series of apparatus mounted to the stone. His torch held level, he studied each component with the focus of an examiner rather than a reactor. "Blood extraction points," he said. "Modified containment sigils. This was not a place of study. It was a place of process."

I moved toward the restraint wall before I had consciously decided to. My boots found the floor one step at a time, and the warmth in my veins began to rise the closer I got, not aggressively, not the surge I had learned to brace for, but a slow, reaching quality, like something recognizing something else.

The markings around the brackets were the same sealing architecture Talia had identified on the stone fragment. I could read enough of it now, after three days of Talia's patient translation work, to understand the intent. Not containment. Direction. The restraints had been designed to keep a body in place while the Labyrinth's architecture was deliberately activated through the bloodline and then channeled outward. Harvested.

The word arrived in my mind with a cold precision that made my stomach turn.

"They were being used," I said. "Not studied. Used. Someone built this to extract the connection from the bloodline while the person was still alive, and channel it somewhere else."

Talia had moved to the central basin. She crouched over it, torch close to the dried residue, and her expression as she looked up confirmed what I already knew before she spoke. "The markings around the drainage points are Catalyst-specific. They're not designed to contain power generally. They're keyed to this bloodline specifically." She paused. "Someone knew exactly what they were building this for."

Kaelor's hand settled at the back of my shoulder, not restraining, just present. The warmth of his palm through my shirt was grounding in a way that both annoyed and steadied me.

"Do not look at me like I'm broken," I said, keeping my voice low.

"I am looking at you like you are hunted," he said. "There is a difference."

I turned away from the wall before I could think too long about the height of the restraint brackets, which matched mine closely enough that the observation needed no elaboration.

Malakor had found the records. They were not paper; nothing so fragile could have survived this long. Carved tablets, a dozen of them, stacked in a recessed alcove behind the apparatus, each incised with the same dense script as the walls. He lifted one and passed it to Talia without comment.

She read in silence for a moment that stretched too long. Then: "Six subjects. Documented over what appears to be multiple decades. Each one identified by bloodline designation rather than name." She turned the tablet slightly. "The terminology used is agricultural. Yield. Extraction rate. Viable duration."

The silence after that was thick enough to press against.

"Agricultural," Torren said flatly, and for once, there was no performance in his voice. Just the word, stripped bare.

"They bred this bloodline deliberately." I said. The word felt like biting down on metal. "Someone bred this bloodline deliberately, built this facility to process what the bloodline produced, and documented it the way you document a harvest." I stopped. Something cold settled into my chest and did not move. "And if they were breeding it deliberately, then my parents, my family, none of it was accidental. Someone made decisions about what I would be before I existed."

Kaelor said nothing. He did not reach for me. He simply turned to face me fully, and the weight of his attention was a different kind of steadiness than his hand had been, something that asked nothing and simply refused to look away.

"What if that becomes me?" I asked. It came out quieter than I intended.

"Not if we understand it first."

"You don't know that."

"No," he said. "I know that we leave this place with full information, and that full information makes prevention possible. I know that you are standing here aware of what this is, which none of the six before you were given the chance to be." His voice did not soften. It simply stayed certain. "That is not nothing."

It was not enough. But it was honest, and I had learned to value his honesty more than his comfort, because his comfort was rare enough that I still did not fully trust it.

Talia had moved deeper into the chamber, past the basin line, and her torch threw long shadows against the far wall. "There's another passage," she said. "Behind the apparatus. Sealed, but not permanently."

Malakor was beside her before the sentence finished. He examined the sealing mechanism, ran his fingers along the frame, and stepped back. "Recent use. The seal has been disturbed within the last few years." He looked at Kaelor. "The seventh."

The warmth in my veins surged, a single hard pulse that moved outward through my hands before I caught it. Not power. Recognition. The same reaching quality I had felt near the restraint wall, but stronger now, directional, pulling toward the sealed passage like a tide finding its source.

I knew what was on the other side before we opened it.

The passage beyond was short, ending in a holding cell barely large enough to stand in. The restraint system here was simpler, cruder, a secondary containment space rather than a processing chamber. The markings on the walls were incomplete, some of the sigils trailing off mid-inscription, as though whoever had been working them had been interrupted or had simply stopped caring about precision.

What occupied the space in the far corner was the thing that had been alive when the scout reported it.

She had been a woman once. The structural evidence was still there, the height, the shape of her hands, the remnants of clothing that had once been functional. She was seated against the wall with her knees drawn up, and she was breathing, which was the most disturbing part, because breathing implied survival, and survival implied awareness, and awareness of what this room had done to her was too enormous to look at directly.

The Labyrinth architecture had burned through her incompletely. The partial severance Talia had theorized was visible, literally visible, the veins at her throat and wrists tracing patterns of blackened silver beneath the skin, the same color as the drainage channels in the outer chamber, as though the process had begun and then been interrupted mid-extraction, leaving the power half-severed and the body half-consumed. Her eyes, when they opened, were wrong in a way that was difficult to name precisely, not blind, not empty, but occupying a place between awareness and somewhere else entirely.

Talia made a sound behind me, quiet and involuntary, and pressed her fingers to her mouth.

Torren had gone very still.

I took one step into the cell and stopped. My power pulled toward her the way iron pulls toward a lodestone, a physical sensation of recognition that moved through my chest and would not stop. She was the same architecture. Damaged, corrupted, partially unmade, but the same.

Her head turned toward me.

The movement was slow and deliberate, tracking me with the patience of something that had been waiting in one place so long that time had lost its texture. When her gaze found mine, whatever was left of her attention focused with a sharpness that was at odds with every other terrible thing about her.

She opened her mouth.

The voice that came out was dry and faint, carrying the quality of something speaking from a very long way away through a very small opening. But the words were clear. Every word was clear.

"The Queen always comes for hers."

The air pressure in the cell changed. My power did not surge. It contracted sharply, pulling back toward my center as though it had recognized something and retreated from it. The warmth in my veins dropped cold for one terrible second before my control reasserted itself, and when I breathed again, the air tasted of iron and old stone and the specific, body-deep fear that comes from understanding something completely.

Then Malakor's voice cut through the silence like a blade through rope. "Contact. Upper level. Multiple entry points."

And the facility became a death trap.

The noise arrived a half-second after his warning, boots on stone overhead, the particular cadence of a coordinated entry rather than a patrol stumbling into something unexpected. They had known we were here. They had been waiting for us to go deep enough that retreat required passing through them.

Kaelor moved before the sound fully registered. "East tunnel," he said, his voice dropping to the register that carried without echoing. "Talia, with me. Torren, rear guard."

"Rear guard is a beautiful way to say sacrifice," Torren said, already moving.

"Move."

I did not look back at the cell. I could not afford to, and looking would not have changed anything. She was beyond what we could carry, beyond what could be undone in the time we had, and the knowledge of that sat in my chest like a stone as I ran.

The east tunnel was narrower than the passage we had descended, carved low enough that Kaelor had to angle his horns to clear the ceiling, and it wound in a direction that felt like it was taking us further from the surface before it began to rise. Malakor ran point, torch in hand, moving with the efficiency of someone who had memorized the route before we entered, which I suspected was exactly the case. He had been too calm about the exit for it to be improvised.

The sounds behind us clarified as the fey unit reached the main chamber. I heard the moment they found the holding cell, a sharp exchange of voices in the high, precise cadences of court Fey, and then orders moving through their ranks with the snap of a coordinated response.

They were fast. Faster than the previous units we had avoided.

The first of them found the east tunnel entrance as we reached the first ascending turn. I heard them behind us, too close, and felt the pulse of my power respond to the threat before I had consciously processed it. Not a surge. A wave, moving outward and backward through the tunnel air, a shockwave that had no color and no flame but carried enough force that the two soldiers in the lead stumbled, the rhythm of their pursuit breaking for three crucial seconds.

Not intentional. Absolutely not controlled. But functional.

"That was you," Torren said from directly behind me, not a question, the words coming out between controlled breaths as he ran.

"Keep moving," Kaelor said, and his hand found my arm as the tunnel curved, steering me through the turn without breaking stride, the contact lasting exactly as long as it needed to and releasing cleanly.

We were working together without discussing it. I noticed that somewhere between the second and third turn of the ascending passage, the way you notice something that has been true for longer than you realized. He moved, and I adjusted. I slowed, and his pace accounted for it. The coordination had a quality that felt earned rather than assigned, and the part of me that had spent a lifetime trusting nothing and no one registered it with a specific, uncomfortable warmth.

The second wave of power left me on the final ascent, where the tunnel narrowed to a single-file approach and the fey unit compressed into a bottleneck behind us. This one I felt coming before it happened, a rising pressure in my chest that I recognized as the same sensation that had preceded every uncontrolled surge, and this time, instead of clamping down, I did what Talia had told me. Open hands. Let it move through without directing it. I exhaled and let the pressure release outward, and the wave that hit the tunnel behind us carried enough concentrated force to make the stone groan and the torchlight in the passage gutter out entirely.

The sounds of pursuit stopped.

Not permanently. But enough.

Malakor looked back at me as we broke into the open air of the forest exterior, dawn light gray and thin through the canopy. His expression carried nothing readable, which was its own specific communication.

"Panic later," he said. "Move now."

We moved. The extraction point was a quarter mile north, a dense stand of old growth where the scouts had positioned horses and a secondary pack. The run through the forest was quiet and hard, the kind of movement that uses everything available and leaves nothing to spare. My lungs burned. My ribs ached with the bruising that had not fully healed. The warmth in my veins had settled into something distant and exhausted, like a fire burned down to coals after putting out too much heat too fast.

We reached the extraction point without contact. The scouts were there, the horses were ready, and the group mounted with the wordless efficiency of people who had done this too many times to need instruction.

I did not speak until we were a mile clear of the ruins and the forest had thickened enough around us that sound would not carry. Then I pulled my horse to a walk and let the others move ahead, needing thirty seconds of space that had nothing to do with distance and everything to do with the fact that if I did not stop moving for a moment, I was going to come apart in a way that would be witnessed.

Kaelor's horse matched my pace without his having to signal it. He simply stayed beside me, unhurried, and waited.

The words came eventually, rougher than I intended. "If someone bred that bloodline deliberately. If my family, my mother, was selected for this. Then nothing about my life happened because of chance or choice. I was engineered. Like a weapon someone built and then misplaced."

He did not offer a correction. He did not reframe it into something easier. He simply stayed at my pace and let the words exist.

"And that woman in the cell," I continued. "That is what happens when the process goes wrong. That is the outcome for someone like me if the wrong people reach me first." My voice held steady, which required more effort than anything I had done in the tunnel. "I have spent my entire life believing I was surviving on my own terms. My own choices. My own refusals." I stopped. "What if none of it was mine?"

"The power is yours," he said. "What you do with it is yours. What you have survived to reach this moment is yours." He was quiet for a beat, and when he continued, his voice had dropped to the register I had learned meant he was not speaking tactically. "Everything they designed, they designed without accounting for the fact that you would become yourself rather than their instrument. That is not engineering. That is failure on their part."

I did not say anything for a long stretch of the trail.

Then: "She knew. The woman in the cell. She knew who sent her there. 'The Queen always comes for hers.' That was not random speech. That was memory."

Kaelor's jaw tightened. The shift in his expression was small and cold, carrying the quality of something locked into place. "Yes," he said. "It was."

"Which means Astrythe knows what I am. Not generally. Specifically. She has known for longer than we have."

"Yes."

"And the facility. The documentation. The six before me." I pushed through it. "You think she sanctioned it."

"I think," he said carefully, "that we have considerably more information than we had this morning, and that acting on it requires a clear head." His gaze found mine, steady and direct. "Which means you are allowed to fall apart for a moment before we discuss strategy."

The unexpected gentleness in that landed somewhere undefended. I had not been braced for it. I was always braced for his authority, his practicality, his controlled protectiveness. The simple permission to be a person who had just seen something terrible, offered without condition, was harder to receive than any of it.

My throat tightened. I did not cry, and I was not going to cry, but the tightening was there, and it was real, and I let it be real instead of grinding it down immediately.

"I don't want to be treated like I'm fragile," I said.

"You are not fragile," he said. "You are shaken. Those are different things, and you know it."

By midday, the group had reached the secondary shelter, a ruined waystation built into the slope of a rocky hillside, its walls intact enough to break wind and conceal firelight. The scouts cleared it in minutes and reported the immediate area clean. We had outpaced the fey unit by enough margin that the pressure, for the moment, had eased.

Talia went immediately to work, moving through the group with her kit, assessing the minor wounds from the tunnel run with quick, certain hands. She reached me eventually, pressing her fingers along my ribs with a professional briskness that I had learned was how she managed her own distress, by treating everyone else's.

"How are the surges?" she asked.

"The two in the tunnel were unintentional," I said. "The second one I partially managed."

"Partially is progress." She kept her eyes on her work. "The woman in the cell. I need you to understand something medically." She paused, choosing her words. "What happened to her required sustained intervention over a long period of time. It was not an accident or a single catastrophic failure. Someone kept her in that process for years. What you saw was the result of deliberate, prolonged harm." She looked up. "You have not been in that process. What happened to her cannot happen to you through proximity or bloodline activation alone. I want that to be clear."

It helped more than I expected. Not completely. But more.

Torren appeared at my other side, dropping down against the waystation wall with a flask that he offered without ceremony. "I have several observations about this morning," he said, "and I have decided to withhold most of them out of respect for the general emotional atmosphere." He paused. "The one I will share is that you stopped a tunnel full of armed soldiers with your bare hands and an exceptionally unpleasant morning, and I think that deserves at least a moment of acknowledgment before we return to being terrified."

I took the flask. Whatever was in it burned going down and tasted of pine resin and bad decisions. "Thank you, Torren."

"You're welcome. I am choosing not to mention the part where I screamed a little in the tunnel." He took the flask back. "That stays between us."

The afternoon settled into a quiet that felt fragile rather than peaceful, the kind that comes after something large has passed and left the air too still. Malakor kept watch rotations running with methodical efficiency. Kaelor spoke to each of the scouts in turn, working through the intelligence from the facility with a thoroughness I recognized as the way he processed things that unsettled him: by making them tactical.

I sat with my back against the waystation wall, watching the light move through the broken roof beams, and let myself feel the full weight of what the morning had contained without running from it.

Manufactured. Designed. Bred toward a purpose by people who had never considered that the bloodline they were cultivating might develop opinions.

The anger arrived later than I expected, clean and cold and very specific. Not the hot, reactive fury I had carried since the ruins first activated my power. Something older and quieter, the kind that comes from understanding the full shape of what was done to you rather than just the surface of it.

When Kaelor came to me, the light outside had gone orange and long. He settled beside me without announcement, close enough that his shoulder pressed against mine, and I felt the familiar warmth of his presence move through me before I had consciously registered his approach.

Neither of us spoke for a moment that stretched and held.

Then I turned toward him, and the movement was deliberate and mine, entirely mine, the choice made from the clear, exhausted, still-standing place I had reached after a day of terrible knowledge. I pressed my face into the curve of his neck and shoulder, and his arm came around me with a steadiness that did not ask anything or claim anything, simply held.

He was warm. He smelled of leather and iron and something darker that had stopped frightening me, and his chest rose and fell with a slow, even rhythm that my body borrowed without permission.

"I don't know how to be something that was made," I said against his shoulder. "I only know how to be what I chose."

His hand moved slowly up my back, a steady, deliberate pressure. "Then continue choosing," he said. "Everything from this moment forward. That is the only answer that matters."

I lifted my head and looked at him, at the scarred lines of his face and the molten gold of his eyes catching the last of the afternoon light, and something in me that had been braced for impact since the tunnel finally, slowly, stopped bracing.

I kissed him. Not with anger, not with the frustrated, reckless heat of the previous day, but with something quieter and more deliberate, the kind of contact that says I am choosing this, specifically, now, with full awareness. His response was careful and certain, his hand framing my jaw with a gentleness that was somehow more undoing than force would have been.

We stayed like that until Malakor's voice came from the far side of the waystation, clipped and carrying the specific flatness that meant something had changed.

"Kaelor." A pause. "Intelligence from the forward scouts. You need to hear this now."

Kaelor drew back slowly. His hands released me in a measured motion, and when he rose, the shift in his bearing was immediate and total, warlord replacing everything else with the completeness of a door closing. He looked at me once before he turned, and what was in his expression held everything that the moment had been, acknowledged and carried rather than dismissed.

Then he walked toward Malakor, and I followed, because I was not going to be managed away from intelligence that was almost certainly about both of us.

Malakor stood with a sealed message in his hands, broken open, his black eyes carrying the particular quality of controlled gravity that meant the news was genuinely bad. He did not look at me when Kaelor approached. He looked only at Kaelor, which told me exactly who the message concerned.

"Draevok has moved," Malakor said. "Formally. He has called a council session in your absence and framed it as a question of command stability. Three of the secondary clan leaders have aligned with him." He set the message down. "He is arguing that your judgment has been compromised and that the alliance requires a period of collective leadership until the situation is resolved." A pause, and now his gaze did move to me, briefly and without inflection. "He has named the specific compromise."

The silence that followed had weight and edges.

Kaelor's expression did not change. Not the jaw, not the eyes, not the set of his shoulders. He simply absorbed the information with the stillness of someone who had been expecting a door to open and was not surprised to find it had.

"And his proposed resolution?" Kaelor said.

Malakor's voice was flat and final. "He has not stated it explicitly. He does not need to."

The warmth in my veins had gone very still. I did not look at Kaelor. I looked at the broken seal on the message, at the waystation wall behind Malakor, at the last of the light dying outside the open roof, and I understood with complete and terrible clarity exactly what Draevok's unnamed resolution required.

And I understood, equally clearly, what answering it would cost the male standing three feet away from me.

Kaelor turned and looked at me directly, without the usual strategic distance. The expression that crossed his face was brief and tightly controlled, but I saw enough to understand the shape of the problem. Draevok intended to force a choice.

The forest was very quiet. Somewhere in the ruins a mile south, a failed Catalyst sat in a holding cell and breathed, and the Queen who had made her was already moving.

# Hold On to Me

By midday we reached the secondary shelter. A ruined waystation sat built into a rocky hillside, its walls intact enough to break wind and hide firelight. The scouts cleared it quickly and reported the area clean. We had outpaced the fey unit by enough margin that the immediate pressure eased. Talia moved through the group with her kit, assessing minor wounds from the tunnel run. She reached me eventually, pressing her fingers along my ribs with professional briskness.

"How are the surges?" she asked.

"The two in the tunnel were unintentional. The second one I partially managed."

"Partially is progress." She kept her eyes on her work. "The woman in the cell. I need you to understand something medically. What happened to her required sustained intervention over a long period of time. It was not an accident or a single catastrophic failure. Someone kept her in that process for years. What you saw was the result of deliberate, prolonged harm. You have not been in that process. What happened to her cannot happen to you through proximity or bloodline activation alone. I want that clear."

It helped more than I expected. Not completely. But more.

Torren appeared at my other side, dropping down against the waystation wall with a flask that he offered without ceremony.

"I have several observations about this morning," he said, "and I have decided to withhold most of them out of respect for the general emotional atmosphere. The one I will share is that you stopped a tunnel full of armed soldiers with your bare hands and an exceptionally unpleasant morning, and I think that deserves at least a moment of acknowledgment before we return to being terrified."

I took the flask. Whatever was inside burned going down and tasted of pine resin and bad decisions.

"Thank you, Torren."

"You are welcome. I am choosing not to mention the part where I screamed a little in the tunnel. That stays between us."

The afternoon settled into quiet that felt fragile rather than peaceful. Malakor kept watch rotations running with methodical efficiency. Kaelor spoke to each of the scouts in turn, working through the intelligence from the facility with the thoroughness I recognized as the way he processed things that unsettled him. By making them tactical.

I sat with my spine against the waystation wall and watched the light move through the broken roof beams. Manufactured. Designed. Bred toward a purpose by people who had never considered that the bloodline they were cultivating might develop opinions. The anger arrived later than I expected, clean and cold and very specific. Not the hot, reactive fury I had carried since the ruins first activated my power. Something older and quieter. The kind that comes from understanding the full shape of what was done to you rather than just the surface of it.

When Kaelor came to me the light outside had gone orange and long. He settled beside me without announcement, close enough that his shoulder pressed against mine. I felt the familiar warmth of his presence move through me before I had consciously registered his approach. Neither of us spoke for a moment that stretched and held.

Then I turned toward him. The movement was deliberate and mine. Entirely mine. The choice made from the clear, exhausted, still-standing place I had reached after a day of terrible knowledge. I pressed my face into the curve of his neck and shoulder. His arm came around me with a steadiness that did not ask anything or claim anything. It simply held. He was warm. He smelled of leather and iron and something darker that had stopped frightening me. His chest rose and fell with a slow, even rhythm that my body borrowed without permission.

"I do not know how to be something that was made," I said against his shoulder. "I only know how to be what I chose."

His hand moved slowly up my back, a steady, deliberate pressure.

"Then continue choosing," he said. "Everything from this moment forward. That is the only answer that matters."

I lifted my head and looked at him. At the scarred lines of his face and the molten gold of his eyes catching the last of the afternoon light. Something in me that had been braced for impact since the tunnel finally, slowly, stopped bracing. I kissed him. Not with anger. Not with the frustrated, reckless heat of the previous day. But with something quieter and more deliberate. The kind of contact that says I am choosing this. Specifically. Now. With full awareness.

His response was careful and certain. His hand framed my jaw with a gentleness that was somehow more undoing than force would have been. We stayed like that until Malakor's voice came from the far side of the waystation. Clipped. Carrying the specific flatness that meant something had changed.

"Kaelor. Intelligence from the forward scouts. You need to hear this now."

Kaelor drew back slowly. His hands released me in a measured motion. When he rose the shift in his bearing was immediate and total. Warlord replacing everything else with the completeness of a door closing. He looked at me once before he turned. What was in his expression held everything that the moment had been. Acknowledged and carried rather than dismissed. Then he walked toward Malakor. I followed. I was not going to be managed away from intelligence that was almost certainly about both of us.

Malakor stood with a sealed message in his hands. Broken open. His black eyes carried the particular quality of controlled gravity that meant the news was genuinely bad. He did not look at me when Kaelor approached. He looked only at Kaelor. Which told me exactly who the message concerned.

"Draevok has moved," Malakor said. "Formally. He has called a council session in your absence and framed it as a question of command stability. Three of the secondary clan leaders have aligned with him. He is arguing that your judgment has been compromised and that the alliance requires a period of collective leadership until the situation is resolved."

He set the message down.

"He has named the specific compromise."

The silence that followed had weight and edges. Kaelor's expression did not change. Not the jaw. Not the eyes. Not the set of his shoulders. He simply absorbed the information with the stillness of someone who had been expecting a door to open and was not surprised to find it had.

"And his proposed resolution?" Kaelor said.

Malakor's voice was flat and final.

"He has not stated it explicitly. He does not need to."

The warmth in my veins had gone very still. I did not look at Kaelor. I looked at the broken seal on the message. At the waystation wall behind Malakor. At the last of the light dying outside the open roof. I understood with complete and terrible clarity exactly what Draevok's unnamed resolution required. I understood equally clearly what answering it would cost the male standing three feet away from me.

Kaelor turned and looked at me directly. Without the usual strategic distance. The expression that crossed his face was brief and tightly controlled. But I saw enough to understand the shape of the problem. Draevok intended to force a choice.

The forest was very quiet. Somewhere in the ruins a mile south, a failed Catalyst sat in a holding cell and breathed. The Queen who had made her was already moving.

We did not stay at the waystation long. Kaelor gave orders with the same controlled efficiency he had shown since Malakor delivered the message. We would push toward allied territory before nightfall. The scouts had located a temporary refuge deeper in the forest. A place where we could regroup without immediate risk of interception. I mounted my horse without waiting for assistance. Kaelor did not offer it. The shift between us registered as something small and painful. A distance that had not existed an hour earlier.

The group moved with renewed urgency. Talia rode near me, her usual brightness tempered by everything we had seen. Torren kept his commentary light but watchful. Malakor rode point with the same grim focus he always brought to difficult terrain. Kaelor stayed ahead of the column. Not beside me. Not behind. The choice to maintain separation felt deliberate. I told myself it was tactical. I told myself it did not matter. Neither statement held much truth.

The temporary refuge turned out to be an abandoned hunter's shelter built against a rocky outcropping. Stone walls. A low roof. Enough space for the group to rest without exposure. The scouts had already cleared it. Kaelor posted sentries while the rest of us dismounted and began the work of making camp. Talia started a small fire. Torren sorted through supplies with practiced efficiency. Malakor reviewed the route ahead with two of the scouts.

I found a place against the outer wall and sat with my knees drawn up. The forest around us had gone dark. Night air carried the scent of pine and damp earth. The quiet felt different here. Not peaceful. Simply absent of immediate threat. That absence created its own kind of pressure.

Kaelor approached after the sentries were set. He moved with the same silent grace that always made his size seem impossible. He settled beside me without asking permission. The distance he had maintained on the trail had vanished. Or perhaps it had simply shifted into something more complicated.

"You should eat," he said.

"I am not hungry."

"That does not change the requirement."

I looked at him. The firelight caught the edge of his profile. The scar over his eye. The curve of his horn. He met my gaze without flinching.

"You are pulling away," I said. "I can feel it."

"I am adjusting priorities. That is not the same thing."

"It feels the same."

He was quiet for several breaths. When he spoke again his voice carried a note I had not heard before.

"Draevok has named you as the reason my judgment cannot be trusted. Three clan leaders have already aligned with him. If I remain visibly attached to you while the challenge builds, I give him exactly what he needs to fracture the alliance further."

"So you distance yourself. To protect the alliance."

"To protect you. From becoming the target they can reach without touching me."

The honesty of that landed harder than any evasion would have. I swallowed against the tightness in my throat.

"I did not ask for protection that costs you your people."

"You did not ask for any of this. Neither did I."

Talia approached with two bowls of something that smelled like stew. She handed one to each of us without commentary. The gesture felt deliberate. A quiet acknowledgment that we needed the space to finish whatever conversation had started. She returned to the fire without looking back.

We ate in silence. The stew was hot and simple. Root vegetables. Dried meat. Enough to keep strength in the body. When the bowls were empty Kaelor set them aside. His hand found mine in the darkness between us. The contact was careful. Measured. As though he had decided the cost of distance outweighed the cost of being seen.

"I meant what I said," he said. "This is not strategy anymore. I do not know what this has become. But I know that I will not watch you become another name in someone else's record."

The words settled into the space between my ribs. I turned my hand beneath his. Our fingers interlaced. The simple contact carried more weight than any declaration could have managed.

"What if that thing is what I become?" I asked. "What if the process they started in the ruins is already inside me, waiting to finish what it began?"

"Then the world will learn to fear us both."

The answer was not comforting. It was not meant to be. It was simply true. And truth had become the only currency I trusted between us.

The night deepened. The fire burned lower. Torren and Malakor took the first watch rotation. Talia found a place near the shelter wall and curled into her bedroll with the efficiency of someone who had learned to rest whenever rest was available. Kaelor remained beside me. The sentries stayed at the perimeter. The forest held its breath around us.

I did not know who moved first. Perhaps it did not matter. One moment we sat with our hands joined in the darkness. The next I was on my feet and he was following. We moved away from the shelter. Not far. Just far enough that the firelight would not reach us. Just far enough that the others would not hear what passed between us.

The ruined hunter's shelter had a small lean-to attached to the eastern wall. It offered partial cover from wind and sight. We stepped beneath it. The space was tight. His presence filled it completely. I pressed my back against the rough stone and looked up at him. The darkness made his eyes almost black. The runes on his horns caught what little light remained and held it like captured stars.

"Why are you doing this?" I asked.

He was quiet for a long moment. When he answered, the words came slowly. As though each one required careful consideration before release.

"Because pretending otherwise has stopped being effective."

The honesty of that broke something open inside me. I reached for him. My hands found the broad plane of his chest. The fur was soft beneath my palms. The muscle beneath it was unyielding. He bent his head. His horns angled carefully to avoid the low roof. His mouth found mine with a hunger that had nothing to do with conquest and everything to do with need.

The kiss deepened. His hands moved to my waist. Lifted me. Pressed me more firmly against the stone. I wrapped my legs around his torso. The position brought us closer. The heat of him bled through my clothing. The strength of him surrounded me without trapping me. I could have pulled away at any moment. I did not want to.

When he entered me, the stretch was overwhelming. The size of him. The heat of him. The way he filled every empty space inside me. I gasped against his shoulder. His hand found mine. Our fingers interlaced. He held still just long enough for me to adjust, then he began to thrust. Slow at first, then deeper, with a restraint that lasted all of seconds before need overtook discipline entirely.

I lost track of time. Of place. Of everything except the feeling of him moving inside me. The weight of him above me. The way his breath caught when I tightened around him. The way his hand tightened around mine when release approached. It came in waves. First for me. Then for him. His body went rigid. A sound tore from his throat that I had never heard before. Something raw. Something honest. Something that belonged only to this moment and this choice.

We stayed joined afterward. Breathing. Trembling. The night air cooled the sweat on our skin. His weight remained a comfort rather than a burden. I traced the line of his spine with one hand. Felt the small tremors that still moved through him. He pressed his face into the curve of my neck. His breath warmed the skin there.

"I meant what I said," he murmured against my skin. "This is not strategy anymore."

"I know."

"I do not know what this has become."

"I know that too."

We dressed in silence, the kind that was no longer awkward and had become something heavier, more aware.

When we returned to the shelter, the others remained at their posts, and if anyone noticed our absence, they had the courtesy not to comment.

Kaelor resumed command with the same seamless efficiency he always wore, which should have annoyed me more than it did. Instead, exhaustion finally caught me.

I slept badly.

Dawn arrived cold and gray, with mist hanging low between the trees and the camp already beginning to stir around the remains of the fire.

Malakor stood near the coals with the expression of a man carrying unwelcome intelligence.

The moment I saw the sealed dispatch in his hand, I knew the morning had plans for us.

He approached Kaelor directly.

"Draevok has mobilized," Malakor said. "He is moving openly now. He has called a formal challenge to your authority. The council will convene within the week. He is bringing evidence. Witnesses. Arguments framed as concern for the alliance rather than personal ambition."

Kaelor took the message and read it without expression.

"He names Elara specifically?" Kaelor asked.

"Yes."

"He names her as the reason your judgment has been compromised. He argues that your attachment to a human Catalyst puts the coalition at risk. That her presence invites the Queen's attention. That her power is unstable and cannot be controlled."

"And the proposed resolution?"

Malakor's expression did not shift.

"He has not stated it explicitly. But the implication is clear. Either you step back from command. Or she is removed as a liability."

Kaelor turned away from the fire. He moved toward the edge of the shelter where the sentries watched the forest. I followed. The morning air felt cooler away from the fire. He stopped at the perimeter. His silhouette against the trees was massive. Unmistakable. The horns that nearly brushed the canopy above him marked him as something other than human. Something the clans had chosen to follow through fire and blood.

"You should rest," he said without turning.

"I should know what happens next."

What happens next is strategy. The specifics are still being determined."

"You could let me go," I said. The words came out before I could stop them. "Send me away. Remove the liability. Keep your people together."

He turned then. The motion was slow. Deliberate. His eyes found mine in the darkness.

"Is that what you want?"

The question hung between us like a blade balanced on its point.

"No," I said. "But I do not want to be the reason your people die either."

"Then we find another path. One that does not require your absence or my surrender."

"And if there is no other path?"

"Then we force one into existence."

The certainty in his voice should have been comforting. Instead it settled into the space beneath my ribs like a promise I was not sure either of us could keep. The forest around us remained quiet. The sentries maintained their watch. The fire crackled behind us with the soft sound of wood settling into ash.

Kaelor reached for my hand. The contact was brief. Deliberate. A reminder of what we had chosen in the lean-to. A reminder of what now stood in the way of keeping it.

"Rest," he said. "Tomorrow brings enough trouble without adding exhaustion to the list."

I nodded. The gesture felt small. Insufficient. But it was all I had to offer. I returned to the shelter. Found my bedroll. Lay down with my back to the fire and my eyes open to the darkness above. Sleep came eventually. It did not bring peace. It brought only the knowledge that morning would arrive with its own demands. And that the choice Kaelor faced was one no warlord should ever have to make.

# The Cost of Wanting

Peace had lasted exactly long enough to become dangerous.

I should have known better. I had spent enough years reading silences to understand that the comfortable ones were always the most treacherous. The kind that settled into your bones like a warm hearth-fire, loosening your muscles until your grip on your weapon slackened, making you believe that you had earned a moment to breathe. That was when the world remembered you owed it something.

The morning after the waystation, Kaelor gave orders with the controlled efficiency I had come to recognize as the face he wore when strategy had fully replaced everything else. His voice had lost its gravelly warmth, clipped and flat as a blade striking wood, and the rigid line of his broad shoulders held a stiffness that made him look more like an iron monument than a living male. No warmth. No residual closeness from the lean-to. Just the warlord, assembled so completely that the male who had pressed his face into the curve of my neck and admitted he did not know what this had become might as well have been a different creature entirely.

I told myself it was necessary. I even believed it, mostly.

The group moved fast through the forest, following a route Malakor had mapped the previous night. Toward allied territory. Toward the war council staging camp where Serathis would be waiting with her assessment of the political damage and whatever cold strategic clarity she had prepared for the occasion. The trees thinned as we pushed east, the dense pine giving way to scrub oak and rocky ground that made the horses work harder. The pace left no room for private conversation. Which was, I suspected, intentional.

Torren pulled his horse alongside mine sometime around midmorning, wearing the expression of a man deeply unhappy about the situation but unwilling to waste perfectly good suffering on silence.

"I miss simpler problems," he announced, to no one in particular. "Like assassination attempts. Those at least had a clear resolution. Someone tries to kill you, you either die or you don't. Clean. Comprehensible. None of this." He gestured vaguely at the general atmosphere of controlled tension moving through the column. "Political drama is so much worse because everyone survives and has feelings about it afterward."

"Not everyone survives political drama," I said.

"You had to go and ruin my comfort with facts." He glanced ahead toward where Kaelor rode at the front of the column, spine straight, bearing utterly closed. "He's doing the thing," Torren said, dropping his voice to something less carrying. "The thing where he becomes entirely made of iron and strategy. I've seen it before sieges. Never after something that looked more like the opposite of a siege."

"Drop it, Torren."

"Dropped. Gone. Forgotten entirely." A pause. "I'm just noting that you're doing the matching version. The one where you carry everything alone and dare the world to comment on it."

I had no good answer for that, so I did not offer one.

Talia rode on my other side for a stretch, her bronze curls pulled back against the wind, her satchel bouncing against her hip. She did not say anything for a while, which was unusual enough that I glanced at her. Her green eyes were moving over the group with the quiet assessment she generally reserved for patients she was worried about.

"Malakor thinks we'll reach the staging camp before nightfall," she said eventually.

"Good."

"Serathis will be there."

"I know."

She adjusted the strap of her satchel and kept her voice carefully neutral. "Serathis is very practical."

"That's a diplomatic way to prepare me for something."

"I'm a healer. Diplomacy is most of the job." She hesitated. "Just don't let her make you feel like a problem. You're not a problem. You're a person in a complicated situation. Those are different things, even when they look the same from a command tent."

The kindness in that settled somewhere uncomfortable in my chest. I had not realized how much I needed someone to say it plainly until she did.

"Thank you, Talia."

She nodded and urged her horse slightly ahead, and that was that.

Malakor rode up beside me near midday, with the particular flat economy of motion that meant he had something to say and had already decided how to say it. He did not bother with preamble.

"Political enemies are often deadlier than armies," he said. "Armies require resources. Political enemies require only doubt. Draevok has been cultivating doubt in the secondary clans for weeks. Possibly longer. This is not a sudden reaction to current events. This was prepared."

"He planned this before the waystation."

"The waystation gave him a sharper argument. The planning preceded it." His black eyes remained on the trail ahead. "I am telling you this because understanding the shape of a threat is more useful than reacting to its surface. Draevok is not irrational. He is a strategist who has reached a conclusion you should take seriously."

"That I should leave."

"That your presence creates a vulnerability he believes will be exploited. He is not wrong about the exploitation risk. He may be wrong about the solution." He paused. "I have been wrong about solutions before. It is worth noting that Draevok has not."

He returned to the front of the column before I could formulate a response, which I suspected was entirely deliberate. Malakor delivered truths the way some people delivered knives: cleanly, precisely, and then gave you space to bleed privately.

The staging camp appeared through the trees as the light began its late-afternoon descent, turning the sky the color of old bronze. It was larger than I expected. A proper command installation, ringed with sentries and marked with the clan sigils I had come to recognize on Kaelor's war harness. The sounds of it reached us before the sight did: armor shifting, boots on packed earth, the distant beat of a hammer against metal, voices carrying in the flat way voices do when the wind is right and men are not trying to be quiet.

Serathis was waiting at the camp's entrance.

She stood exactly as I had imagined she would, arms crossed over her battle-marked chest, silver-streaked fur and that clouded eye catching the evening light. The gold band on her horn caught it too, like a small wound of brightness against the iron reality of her presence. She watched Kaelor dismount with the expression of a commander assessing whether her general had returned from the field intact. Then her gaze moved to me, and the assessment did not soften.

Kaelor went to her directly. They exchanged low words I could not hear. Her jaw tightened once. Then her eyes cut back to me with a clarity that required no interpretation whatsoever.

She knew. She had probably known before we arrived.

Torren appeared at my shoulder as I dismounted. "She is very alarming," he murmured, "and I respect her enormously, and I am going to stand somewhere else now." He drifted sideways with the practiced ease of a man who had survived many rooms by being peripheral.

Serathis crossed to me without waiting for an invitation. She stopped at a distance that was respectful but not warm, and she studied me the way you study a structural problem before deciding whether to reinforce or dismantle.

"Attachment makes leaders predictable," she said. Not cruelty. Statement of fact, delivered with the same tone she might use to describe weather conditions or supply shortages. "Predictable leaders lose wars. That is not opinion. That is recorded history."

"I am aware," I said.

"Then you understand that this," she said, and she did not specify what *this* was, but her meaning was complete, "will be used against him. Not because his enemies are right. Because they are opportunists, and you have given them an opening."

"I did not choose to give them anything."

Her clouded eye gave her gaze an unbalanced quality, as though one part of her was always watching something the rest of us could not see. "What you choose is what you do once you realize what you've become."

She walked away before I could answer. Which was, I was beginning to understand, how Serathis ended every conversation she considered sufficiently concluded.

The war council convened inside the command tent as the sun fully dropped. The structure was large enough for the assembled commanders, maps spread across the central table, lanterns burning amber against the canvas walls. I stood slightly apart, by Kaelor's right side, where I had positioned myself with enough deliberate intent that moving me would have required someone to make it an explicit act.

No one moved me.

Malakor delivered the strategic assessment with his usual stripped-down precision. The alliance's current position. The timeline before the council session Draevok had called. The three secondary clan leaders who had already aligned with the challenge. The intelligence gaps that needed filling before any response could be calibrated.

Serathis added tactical specifics. Supply lines. Troop positioning. The two forward camps that would be most vulnerable if political uncertainty fractured the command structure at the wrong moment.

Then the message arrived.

It came through one of the camp's senior scouts, sealed with a mark I did not recognize. Kaelor broke the seal without visible reaction and read the contents. When he set it down, the silence in the tent carried an edge.

"Draevok's formal accusations," he said. His voice was measured, each word placed with the same deliberate weight he used when the information was worse than he intended to show. "Submitted directly to the secondary clan representatives. Entered into the council record before our arrival."

Serathis made a sound low in her chest. "He moved faster than projected."

"He always does." Kaelor's eyes moved over the assembled faces. "The accusations are as expected. That my judgment regarding the Catalyst has been compromised. That her presence invites targeted attention from both the High Queen and the shadow cult. That the risk to the alliance is unacceptable and the situation requires correction." A pause. "He has been specific about what correction means."

Every eye in the tent found me.

I had known it was coming. I had felt the shape of it since the waystation, since Malakor had set down that broken seal and let the implication speak for itself. Knowing did not make the moment easier. It made it more precise, like a blade pressed to skin without the mercy of quick motion.

"He wants her removed," Malakor said, flat and informational. "That is the formal position."

"He wants her dead," Torren said, from the back of the tent, where he had apparently decided that periphery was no longer a sufficient distance from the conversation. His voice had lost its usual lightness entirely. "Let's say what it is."

Kaelor's bearing did not shift. But something moved through the set of his jaw, brief and tightly controlled. "The answer is no. On every version of the question."

"Kaelor." Serathis spoke quietly. Not arguing. Warning. "Your answer in this room is not the problem. Your answer in the council session will be. And if the secondary clans see what I am seeing in this tent tonight, they will have the evidence Draevok needs before he makes a single argument."

The temperature in the room seemed to drop several degrees.

"What are you seeing?" Kaelor asked.

Serathis held his gaze without flinching. "This will be used against you," she said. "You know it. I know it. Everyone in this tent knows it. What matters is whether you can walk into that council session and give them nothing to confirm."

The tent held that tension for a long beat. Then Kaelor gave a single, controlled nod and returned his attention to the maps. The council continued. But the moment had already done its work, and every person in that tent had felt it land.

I waited until the others had filtered out before I spoke to him directly.

The tent had emptied down to the two of us and the dying lamp. The maps were still spread across the table. His hands rested on the surface, studying routes and positions with the focus of a man who found strategy easier than the conversation he knew was coming.

"If I am the problem," I said, "I can leave."

He turned from the table. The motion was slow, deliberate, and the expression that crossed his face carried something I had not seen there before, something rawer than the controlled authority he wore like armor.

"No," he said.

One word. Absolute. The kind of refusal that did not leave room for negotiation.

I held his gaze. "That was not a request for permission."

"I am aware."

"Then you understand that I can make this choice without your agreement. I am not your prisoner, Kaelor. We established that. If leaving removes the leverage Draevok is using against you, then leaving is a reasonable tactical option and you know it."

Something shifted in his posture. Not softening, nothing so forgiving as that. It was the kind of shift that happens when a structure under pressure finds its limit. His hands left the table. He moved around it, closing the distance between us with a measured deliberateness that sent my pulse spiking before my mind caught up with the reason.

He stopped close enough that I had to angle my chin upward to keep his face in sight. The lantern threw long shadows across his features. The scar over his eye. The fractured tip of one ivory horn. The runes that caught light and held it in ways that had nothing to do with fire.

"You are not a tactical option," he said. His voice had dropped to something low and controlled that made the air between us feel too dense. "You are not a variable to be removed for cleaner mathematics. And I will not stand in that council session and argue for your absence as though it is a strategy I have considered."

"Then what are you going to do?" My voice came out steadier than I felt. "Because Serathis is right. They can see it. Whatever this is, they can see it, and Draevok is going to stand in front of those clan leaders and make it mean exactly what he wants it to mean."

"Let him." The certainty in those two words was not comfort. It was something more unsettling than comfort. Something that sounded like a decision already made at a level that strategy could not reach. "I did not build this alliance by making choices that were easy. I built it by making choices that were correct. You are not the liability he needs you to be. And I will not hand him that argument by treating you as though you are."

The space between us had become very small. I was aware of his warmth, the solidity of him, the way his presence seemed to rearrange the atmosphere of whatever room he occupied. My body registered all of it with an inconvenient, unwelcome thoroughness.

"You are being possessive," I said. "You know that."

"Yes."

"It is going to cost you."

"Leadership has always carried costs."

The honesty of it landed somewhere between my ribs and stayed there. I wanted to argue. I wanted to find the clean, tactical angle that made leaving the correct answer, the one that protected him and his people and the fragile, blood-soaked thing he had spent decades building. But the argument would not form cleanly, because some part of me that I had not fully managed to silence did not want to find it.

I stepped back before I did something unwise. His expression registered the movement and held itself very still.

"We will find another path," he said, echoing words from the night before. "I told you that."

"And if the path requires something neither of us wants to give?"

"Then we decide together what we are willing to pay." His eyes held mine with an intensity that felt like pressure against the skin. "Not Draevok. Not the secondary clans. We decide our response. not them."

I left the tent before he could say anything else, because another thirty seconds in that enclosed space with that particular quality of unresolved tension between us was going to produce consequences I was not prepared for tonight.

The camp outside was busy with the particular organized movement of a military installation settling into night routine. Sentries rotating. Fires being banked. The distant sound of someone sharpening a blade with the methodical patience of a soldier who had learned to keep his hands busy when sleep was unavailable.

I sat outside against the command tent's outer wall and let the cold air work on the heat still sitting in my face. The sky above was clear, thick with stars, the kind of sky that looked beautiful and felt enormous and made a person feel very small against the weight of everything moving around them.

Torren appeared from the direction of the supply tent with two cups of something hot, sat down beside me without ceremony, and handed one over.

"Don't," I said.

"I wasn't going to say anything."

"You were building to it."

"I was building to offering you a hot drink and sitting here quietly, which I consider a significant exercise in personal growth." He wrapped both hands around his own cup and stared at the stars. "He's not going to make this easy," Torren said. "Which, for the record, is either admirable or catastrophically inconvenient. Possibly both."

I drank the hot liquid, which turned out to be some kind of spiced grain tea that tasted considerably better than it smelled. The camp moved around us, orderly and purposeful, the kind of structured activity that reminded you exactly what was at stake if the structure failed.

I was still sitting there when the sound reached me.

Not the expected sounds of the camp. Something else beneath them, a disruption at the eastern perimeter, voices pitching upward, the flat thud of something heavy hitting ground. Torren was on his feet before I was, his hand already at his belt.

Then the shout went up from the sentry line, sharp and carrying.

Movement at the camp entrance. A figure, massive and unmistakable, flanked by warriors bearing the markings of a different clan. The firelight caught dark chestnut fur streaked with black, a face that was a map of old violence, and two scarred horns, one fitted with crude iron reinforcement.

Draevok Bloodhorn walked into the camp as though he had always planned to arrive exactly at this moment, and the way the sentries parted told me everything I needed to know about how much authority he still commanded.

His eyes moved across the camp with the unhurried assessment of a general taking inventory of a position. Then they found me, sitting against the command tent wall, and they stopped. Not with surprise. With the specific, settled recognition of a man who had been expecting to find exactly what he found.

He had arrived in person.

And from the look on his face, he had not come to negotiate.

# Blood and Authority

Draevok Bloodhorn looked exactly like the kind of man who would tear kingdoms apart and sleep soundly afterward.

He stood in the firelight with the unhurried certainty of someone who had never needed to announce himself, because the space around him adjusted without being asked. The sentries had parted. The warriors nearest the entrance had gone still. Even the ambient noise of the camp seemed to lower itself by a degree, the way sound does when something more significant than routine has entered the room.

I stayed where I was, my back pressed against the canvas wall, my cup of spiced tea cooling in my hands. Moving would have looked like retreat. Retreating would have looked like guilt.

So I watched him complete his assessment of the camp, and I waited for his eyes to find me again, and when they did, I made sure my face gave him nothing useful.

Torren had gone very still beside me. "Right," he murmured, barely above a breath. "I miss enemies who announce themselves properly."

"Go inside," I said.

"Absolutely not." A pause. "But I am going to stand slightly behind you."

Kaelor emerged from the command tent before Draevok crossed the halfway point of the camp. The two of them stopped at a distance that was not quite confrontational but left no ambiguity about the nature of the meeting. No embrace. No warrior greeting. Just two massive, dangerous males taking the measure of something that had been building for a long time.

I watched Kaelor's bearing from where I stood. Controlled. Upright. Every line of him radiating the kind of authority that had nothing to prove because it had already been proven too many times to count. But there was something in the set of his jaw that had not been there earlier tonight, a tightness that Serathis had been right to identify as a liability.

The council convened within the hour.

---

The command tent felt smaller with Draevok in it.

He was broader than Kaelor, built with the solid, battering weight of a siege engine rather than the controlled lethality of a duelist. The iron reinforcement on his damaged horn caught the lamplight each time he moved, and the trophies on his armor told stories in a language made entirely of violence. He had not come to intimidate. He was simply the kind of presence that made the room reorganize itself around him without his consent.

Serathis stood on the opposite side of the map table. Malakor occupied the far corner with the quiet neutrality of a man who had already calculated every possible outcome and was simply waiting to see which one materialized. Torren had positioned himself near the tent entrance with the practiced invisibility of someone who understood that the safest place in a room full of dangerous people was the one closest to the exit.

I stood at Kaelor's right, because that was where I had been and moving would have been its own kind of statement.

Draevok looked at me once, directly, with those dark eyes that missed nothing. Then he addressed Kaelor as though I had ceased to exist, which was somehow worse.

"The secondary clans have reviewed the formal accusations," he said. His voice was lower than I expected, rough-edged and flat, each word given exactly the weight it needed and nothing more. "Three have already committed their formal concern. Two more are considering. You walk into the council session tomorrow carrying this situation, and you walk in with half your alliance already asking whether your judgment can be trusted."

"My judgment," Kaelor said, "has held this alliance together through circumstances that would have destroyed lesser coalitions. That record does not disappear because you have chosen to question one decision."

"One decision." Draevok's eyes moved to me again, briefly, with the impersonal assessment of a man categorizing a strategic variable. "The Catalyst's bloodline draws every enemy we have directly to us. The High Queen wants her controlled. The shadow cult wants her consumed. And you have placed her at the center of your command structure, where every intelligence operative from both courts can observe exactly how much she matters to you." He returned his gaze to Kaelor. "That is not one decision. That is a cascading liability with a human face."

"She is not yours to judge," Kaelor said.

Draevok's expression did not change. It was not the response of a man who had been surprised. It was the response of a man who had been expecting exactly that answer and found it confirmed everything he feared.

"That answer," he said, "proves my point."

The tent was very quiet after that.

Serathis placed both hands flat on the map table. "Truth and strategy are not always allies," she said, addressing the room rather than either of them specifically. "The question is not whether the risk exists. It clearly does. The question is whether removing the risk resolves the vulnerability or creates a different one." She looked at Draevok with the direct, unadorned regard of someone who respected him and disagreed with him simultaneously. "If Kaelor removes her under political pressure, every warlord in this alliance learns that pressure produces compliance. That is not a precedent any of us can afford."

"And if he keeps her," Draevok said, "every warlord in this alliance learns that sentiment outranks strategy. That is worse."

Malakor spoke from his corner. "The secondary clans are responding to perceived instability rather than confirmed tactical failure. Managing perception is more efficient than executing the source of the concern." He paused. "At this stage."

"Helpful," Torren said, very quietly, to no one.

Kaelor cut across the room's tension with a measured deliberateness that I recognized as the particular control he used when the alternative was something considerably less measured. "The council session will proceed tomorrow. The alliance will hear my position. I will not alter the substance of that position because of tonight's conversation." He looked at Draevok with an absolute, settled certainty. "You built this alliance beside me. You know what it cost. Do not mistake my refusal to sacrifice a person for a political argument as weakness. You know better."

Something moved through Draevok's expression, brief and tightly contained. Not anger. Something that looked almost like grief, which was far more unsettling.

"I know what it cost," he said. "That is exactly why I am standing here."

He left before the lamp burned another quarter-inch lower, and the tent breathed out when he was gone.

---

I found him at the training grounds.

Not by searching. By following the sound, the rhythmic, controlled violence of steel meeting the wooden practice frame at the camp's eastern edge, where the firelight barely reached and the shadows were deep enough to feel private. I had gone looking for air and found him instead.

Kaelor moved through the forms with a savage, focused precision that was nothing like the economical violence I had seen him use in actual combat. This was something else. Each strike drove into the wood with a force that should have splintered it, and might have, if the frame had not been reinforced with iron banding that spoke to exactly how many times it had been used for this purpose. His war harness was gone. He wore only the close-fitted garments beneath it, and the lamplight from a single torch caught the old scars across his chest and shoulders, the ones I had let myself be curious about more times than I would willingly admit.

He knew I was there. He always knew. But he finished the sequence before he stopped, one massive hand resting against the frame, his breathing controlled despite the visible effort.

I should have gone back to my tent.

Instead I walked closer, until I was standing a few feet behind him, and I said the thing that had been sitting in my chest since Draevok's eyes had found me across the camp entrance.

"What if he's right?"

Kaelor turned. His molten gold eyes found mine with an immediacy that made the space between us feel charged, and his expression sharpened in a way that was not quite anger but lived in the same territory.

"He is not," he said.

I held his gaze. "That was not convincing."

His jaw tightened. He stepped away from the practice frame and the distance between us narrowed without either of us making a deliberate decision about it, the way things tended to happen around him, gravity asserting itself without asking permission.

"He is a strategist who has assigned your existence a cost and decided the cost is unacceptable," Kaelor said. "He is not wrong that there are costs. He is wrong that the calculation ends there."

"He said you would lose everything because of me." The words came out steadier than they felt. "He came to me privately, after the council. Before you ask."

Something went very still in Kaelor's posture. The particular kind of stillness that preceded significant decisions.

"When."

"An hour ago. While you were reviewing the maps." I crossed my arms, not for warmth. "He was not cruel about it. That was the worst part. He looked at me like I was a structural flaw he genuinely regretted finding. He said he did not hate me." I paused. "He said he hated what my existence would cost."

Kaelor was quiet for several seconds. When he spoke, his voice had dropped to something that resonated in the chest rather than the ears. "What did you say to him?"

"Nothing." I met his eyes. "Because I could not find the argument that proved him wrong, and I was not willing to lie to his face when he was telling me the truth as he understood it."

"Elara."

"He may be partially right, Kaelor." The guilt had been building since the council tent, since Serathis had looked at me and named what I had become without using any of the words that would have made it easier to dismiss. "I did not come here to fracture your alliance. I did not ask for whatever is in my blood that makes every dangerous faction in this world want to use it. But wanting something is not the same as causing it, and the fact that I did not choose this does not change what it is costing you."

"Stop," he said.

"I am being rational."

"You are taking Draevok's argument and applying it to yourself with more thoroughness than he managed." He covered the remaining distance between us in two steps, and the sheer physical reality of him this close, the heat radiating off his skin, the controlled tension in every line of his body, made rational thought considerably less reliable. "You are not the liability. The war that was already coming is the liability. The High Queen who has wanted this alliance destroyed since before you arrived is the liability. Your blood is a complication we are managing. Removing you would not remove any of those things. It would simply remove the one concession I refuse to offer."

My pulse was doing something inconvenient. "That is possessive."

"Yes."

"I told you last time that it was going to cost you."

"You did." His eyes stayed on mine, steady and burning and utterly unrepentant. "I have not changed my position."

The anger and the guilt and the exhaustion and the attraction were all occupying the same space inside my chest, and none of them were willing to yield to the others. I wanted to step back. I wanted to step forward. I wanted to say something sharp that would restore the distance between us to a manageable measurement.

I said, "You cannot protect me from the political consequences of my own existence, Kaelor. No matter how much you want to. Draevok is going to stand in front of those clan leaders tomorrow and he is going to be compelling and persuasive and he is not going to be entirely wrong, and I do not know how you hold that together."

"By walking into that room and making the case that has always been true." His voice had gone very quiet. "That you are not the cause of this war. That the clans were already fracturing before you arrived. That your blood is the only reason we have any intelligence on the shadow cult's movements at all. That losing you would not stabilize the alliance. It would simply remove the only leverage we hold that neither the High Queen nor Veltheris can replicate." He paused. "And if that is not sufficient for Draevok's faction, then the fault is not yours."

Something in my chest cracked along a line I had been carefully bracing.

"You actually believe that," I said.

"I do not say things I do not believe."

I knew that was true. It was one of the more unsettling facts about him, that his words carried actual weight because he had never learned to use them as decoration.

The torch behind him guttered in a passing breeze, and the shadows moved across his face, and I was standing close enough to feel the warmth coming off his skin, and the night was very quiet around us, and I made a decision I would probably examine more carefully in the morning.

I closed the remaining space between us and pressed my forehead against his chest.

It was not graceful. It was not tactical. It was simply the only honest thing I had left, and I was too exhausted to dress it up as anything else.

His hands came up slowly, with the deliberateness he used for everything he considered worth doing carefully, and settled around me with a weight that felt nothing like captivity and everything like a decision made at a level beneath calculation. His chin lowered until it rested against the crown of my head.

Neither of us spoke.

The camp moved around us in its ordinary rhythms, and the torch burned, and somewhere on the perimeter a sentry made his rotation, and I breathed in the scent of leather and iron and smoke and the specific, particular warmth that was only ever him.

"I am not leaving," I said, into the fabric against my face.

Kaelor gave a single controlled nod. "Understood."

I stepped back before either of us did something that would complicate tomorrow further. His hands released me without resistance, which was either discipline or its own kind of answer, and I could not decide which interpretation made the ache in my chest more difficult to manage.

"Try to sleep," he said.

"You first," I said. "You were taking your frustration out on reinforced timber. That seems like a poor substitute for actual rest."

Something shifted at the corner of his mouth. Not quite a smile. But the thing that lived adjacent to one, the expression that appeared rarely enough that each occurrence felt like finding something rare in difficult ground.

I walked back toward my tent before I stayed long enough to ruin it.

---

Sleep came eventually, which was more than I had expected.

What woke me was not a dream.

It was the sound of something moving outside my tent that was not the pattern of a sentry rotation. The wrong rhythm. The wrong weight distribution against the packed earth. The quality of footfall that belonged to someone trying not to be heard rather than someone who had every right to be present.

I was sitting up with my dagger in my hand before I had fully assembled a conscious thought about it.

The tent entrance moved.

I threw myself sideways an instant before the blade came through, and it missed my neck by a distance I would have nightmares about for the rest of however long I continued to have nights. The figure came through the entrance low and fast, moving with the practiced efficiency of someone who had done this before.

I did not give them a second chance.

The fight was short and ugly and conducted in near silence because neither of us wanted to announce what was happening. My elbow connected with something that crunched satisfyingly. His knee found my ribs in a way that stole my breath for three crucial seconds. I used the seconds anyway, because I had learned a long time ago that waiting for breath to return was a luxury that got people killed.

When I drove my knee into his midsection and he went down, I sat on him and pressed my dagger to his throat and screamed for the guard.

The camp came apart around us in the space of a minute.

Torches. Boots. Shouted orders. The heavy tread of minotaur warriors moving at combat speed, which produced a sound like controlled thunder on packed earth. My tent was surrounded before the attacker had finished deciding whether struggling was worthwhile.

Kaelor arrived in the kind of silence that was louder than noise.

He took in the scene, my knee on the figure's chest, my dagger at his throat, the shallow cut on my forearm where the first strike had grazed me, and something moved through his expression that I had never seen there before. Not anger. Something colder and more complete than anger, something that occupied the same space anger would have used and left no room for anything else.

"Get up," he said to me, his voice carrying a quiet that raised the hair on my arms. "Let them take him."

I stood. The attacker was hauled upright by two of Kaelor's warriors, and he did not fight it, which told me he had already assessed those odds and found them terminal.

Serathis appeared at the tent entrance, taking in the scene with the rapid inventory of a general who has been interrupted mid-sleep and is already constructing tactical responses. Her one good eye moved from the attacker to the blood on my forearm to Kaelor's face, and I watched her arrive at a conclusion that made her jaw tighten.

"Camp-standard gear," she said. "No external markings." She looked at the attacker with a directness that was more frightening than shouting. "He is one of ours."

The weight of that settled over the assembled warriors like weather.

Not an external threat. Not an enemy who had breached the perimeter. Someone who had eaten at the same fires, rotated the same watch schedules, worn the same sigils.

Torren appeared at the back of the gathered crowd, took one look at the situation, and pressed his fist briefly against his mouth. Even he did not have anything to say.

Malakor materialized from the direction of the command tent. He studied the attacker for a long moment, then turned to Kaelor with the flat, informational precision that never softened for context. "He did not come for you," he said. "The tent was hers. The approach vector confirms it."

Kaelor's eyes moved to me.

The coldness in them did not recede. If anything, it deepened, and beneath it, barely visible beneath the controlled surface, was something that looked like the specific terror of a person who had almost been too late and was choosing not to examine what that meant while witnesses were present.

"Take him to the interrogation post," Serathis said, and her authority was absolute enough that no one looked to Kaelor for confirmation. "Secure the perimeter. Double the rotation. No one moves between sections without direct authorization until I say otherwise." She looked at the assembled warriors with the expression of a commander who would accept no ambiguity about the gravity of the moment. "This stays inside this camp. No word to the secondary clan representatives until we have information. If Draevok's faction hears about this before we have facts, the political fallout becomes unmanageable."

People moved. The crowd dispersed with the disciplined urgency of soldiers who understood urgency without requiring it explained twice.

Kaelor crossed to me.

He took my injured forearm in both hands with a gentleness that was entirely at odds with the controlled lethality still radiating off him, and he examined the cut with a focus that felt less like medical assessment and more like a man making himself look at evidence he was not ready to accept.

"It is shallow," I said.

"I can see that."

"Kaelor."

"Do not tell me you are fine." His voice was very quiet. "Not tonight."

I looked at him, at the set of his features in the torchlight, at the way every muscle in his body was still wound at the same tension as a weapon ready to discharge, and I made the decision not to argue with him about it. Not right now. Not when the adrenaline was still burning through my system and my hands were not entirely steady and there was blood on my forearm that could have been considerably more if my instincts had been a fraction slower.

"All right," I said.

Something in his posture shifted fractionally, the way a structure settles when one critical pressure point is released.

Serathis appeared at my shoulder. "Talia is being summoned. She will see to the wound." She held Kaelor's gaze for a brief, direct moment. "The interrogation will begin within the hour. We need whatever he knows before the council session." A pause. "The attempt was not aimed at you. That will matter politically, and not in ways that help us. Be prepared for what Draevok's faction will say about it."

"That it validates the risk," I said.

Serathis looked at me. "Yes."

I appreciated that she did not soften it. The truth delivered plainly was always less damaging than the truth discovered through the wreckage of misplaced reassurance.

"Then we get ahead of it," I said. "Before the session. Whatever the interrogation yields, we control the framing of what it means, and we present it first."

Serathis was quiet for a moment. Then she said, to no one in particular, "She is irritatingly useful."

It was not warmth. But from Serathis, it was something.

Talia arrived at a run, her satchel bouncing against her hip and her bronze curls in spectacular disarray from being woken at speed. She took one look at my arm, made a sound of professional displeasure, and steered me toward the tent entrance with the authority of someone whose domain this now was.

I went.

Behind me, I heard Kaelor speak to Malakor in a voice that was still carrying that particular cold quiet, and the words were tactical, precise, and entirely controlled. He was not going to fall apart. He never fell apart.

But I had seen his face when he looked at the cut on my arm, and I knew what it had cost him to keep the surface that still.

Inside the tent, while Talia cleaned the wound with something that smelled aggressively medicinal and muttered about entry angles and reaction times, I sat and breathed and let myself feel the shape of what had just happened. Someone inside the camp had tried to kill me. Not Draevok, probably. Serathis had said it herself, too convenient, too obvious, more likely someone in his orbit who had acted without sanction. But the attempt had been real, and the blade had been real, and the distance between my neck and the edge of that steel had been real, and the camp that had felt like imperfect safety now felt like something else entirely.

"There," Talia said, tying off the bandage with a neat, firm knot. "It will close properly by morning. You were lucky." She looked at me with those wide green eyes that saw considerably more than most people expected. "Are you all right? And I mean actually, not the version you tell people."

"No," I said. "But I will be."

She nodded, and she did not press it, and that was exactly the right response.

Outside, the camp had settled back into movement, but the quality of it had changed. The watch rotations were tighter. The voices were lower. The kind of disciplined quiet that follows the discovery that the danger was never outside the walls.

It was inside.

And somewhere in the interrogation post, the man who had come through my tent entrance was about to tell Serathis exactly who had sent him, and whether his answer pointed toward a disgruntled faction sympathizer or something with longer, more dangerous reach.

I sat in the lamplight and waited, and the night settled around me with all the weight of a world that had just reminded me, efficiently and without sentiment, that survival was never something you could finish earning.

# Enemies Within

The first thing I understood was that someone inside Kaelor's camp had decided I needed to die.

The second thing I understood, standing in the interrogation area with bandages on my forearm and blood still drying under my fingernails, was that the man they had caught was not going to tell us much. Not because he was brave. Because he did not know much. A paid blade. A name passed through two intermediaries and a coin purse that had already changed hands too many times to trace cleanly. He confirmed what Malakor had already suspected: the attempt was not faction-sanctioned. Someone in Draevok's orbit, maybe, or someone connected to a connection connected to the Shadow Court, or both, wearing the same face. The ambiguity was the point. The ambiguity was the weapon.

Serathis had the interrogation wrapped within forty minutes. She was not gentle about it, but she was efficient, and by the time she emerged from the holding post with her jaw set and her clouded eye hard, the camp already knew something had shifted in the night and could not be unshifted.

"Paid agent," she said, to Kaelor and me and Malakor, who stood together near the dying fire at the camp's center. "No direct clan affiliation confirmed. Two names given, neither verifiable at speed. Possible Shadow Court routing, but no certainty. He was a tool. Someone handed him a target and a direction and let him run." She looked at me without softening it. "The target was specific. He was shown your face. Not described. Shown."

Whoever sent him had access to visual intelligence on me. That meant eyes inside the camp, or close enough to it that the distinction barely mattered.

The fire popped. No one said anything immediately.

Torren materialized from the shadows at the perimeter's edge, his flask in one hand and his expression stripped of its usual performance. "I am officially requesting less betrayal," he said. "I realize that is not a strategic suggestion. I am making it anyway."

"Draevok needs to be informed before the council session," Serathis said. "If he hears it from the secondary clan representatives first, the political framing belongs to whoever told him, and that is not a conversation we can afford to lose."

"He will say it validates his position," I said.

"He will say it regardless," Kaelor replied. His voice had not risen above a quiet that had nothing to do with calm. He had not looked away from me since Malakor confirmed the target. Not in the hovering, suffocating way. In the way of a man cataloging damage he was still deciding how to answer for. "Let him make that argument. The argument does not change the facts. The attempt failed. The attacker is contained. The intelligence gap is the priority."

Serathis nodded once. "Fear makes factions stupid. We control the framing or the factions fill it with whatever story suits them best."

She left to handle Draevok before the sun cracked the horizon. Malakor went with her, silent and purposeful as a blade returned to its sheath. Torren lingered for exactly three seconds before reading the specific quality of Kaelor's silence correctly and finding somewhere else to be.

That left the two of us beside the dying fire, and the camp moving around us in its tight, watchful new rhythms, and the night pressing close with everything it had already shown us.

"Stop looking at me like I nearly died," I said.

"You nearly did."

The flatness of it landed harder than anger would have. Anger I could have deflected. That was just fact, delivered without ornamentation, and it sat in my chest like a stone dropped into still water.

"I am aware," I said. "I was there."

He crossed the space between us, and his hand came up to my jaw, tilting my face toward the firelight with a deliberateness that made my pulse do something inconvenient. He examined the bruising along my cheekbone where I had hit the ground avoiding the first strike, and his thumb brushed the edge of it with a careful, controlled touch that was doing nothing to restore my equilibrium.

"I am not something you lock away," I said, because I needed to say it before the tenderness of his touch convinced me to let the point go entirely.

His eyes lifted to mine. Something moved behind them, contained but present.

"Today," he said, "I considered it."

The honesty of that hit harder than any deflection. He was not apologizing for the impulse. He was not pretending it did not exist. He was simply telling me the truth of what the night had cost him in the places where his control lived, and the fact that he was still standing here, hands steady, voice measured, rather than acting on it, told me more than any reassurance could have.

I pulled back, not sharply, just enough to reclaim the boundary.

"Then we understand each other," I said. "You considered it. You are not going to do it. And I am going to pretend I did not see the exact look on your face when Malakor said the tent was mine."

His jaw tightened. "Elara."

"I know." I said it quietly, because I did. I knew what it had cost him to keep the surface still while the inside of him was doing whatever it had been doing since the moment he walked into my tent and saw blood on my arm. "I know."

The fire burned lower. The camp held its breath around us.

And then he said, with the same measured quiet he used for everything that mattered: "Come with me."

His command quarters were spare. A cot built for function rather than comfort, a weapons rack along one wall, maps weighted flat on a folding table, a single lamp burning low. The tent smelled of leather and old steel and something that lived beneath both, something specific to him that I had stopped pretending I did not notice.

He secured the entrance behind us.

I stood in the center of the space and watched him cross to the weapons rack and set his hand against it, his back to me, breathing with the deliberate control of a man deciding something.

"This is a terrible idea," I said.

"Yes."

The single word dropped into the room and occupied all of it.

My pulse was loud in my own ears. The adrenaline from earlier had not fully cleared my system. The bruise on my cheekbone ached. My forearm, under Talia's bandaging, stung with each heartbeat. I was standing in a warlord's tent after surviving an assassination attempt with my hands still not entirely steady, and the specific fear-sharpened awareness running through my body had nowhere left to go except toward him, because he was the only solid thing in a night that had shown me, efficiently and without sentiment, that the ground I stood on could shift at any moment.

He turned.

The lamplight caught the old scars across his chest. His horns cast wide shadows against the canvas. His molten gold eyes found mine and stayed there, and there was nothing restrained in them now, nothing managed or measured. There was only the same adrenaline running through him that was running through me, wearing a different shape, carrying a different weight.

"If you want to leave," he said, "leave now."

I crossed the space between us instead.

The first touch was not gentle, and I did not want it to be. His hands found my waist and pulled me against him with a directness that matched the exact pitch of everything burning through my system, and I felt the sheer physical reality of him against me, the heat and the mass and the barely-contained force, and some part of me that had been coiled tight since the blade came through my tent entrance finally, finally unclenched.

I got my hands against his chest and felt the scar tissue beneath my palms, rough and complex, the map of everything he had survived, and he made a low sound when I pressed my fingers flat against it and tilted my face up to his.

He kissed me like he was still angry about the blade, like the anger had nowhere else to go and I was the only place that made sense for it. His hand came up into my hair, and the grip was firm enough to make my breath catch, and I answered it by digging my fingers into his shoulders and pulling him down rather than standing on my toes to meet him, because I was not interested in the version of this that was delicate.

Neither was he.

He walked me back until my knees hit the cot's edge, and I sat, and he dropped to one knee in front of me with a deliberateness that made the breath leave my lungs entirely. His hands found the fastenings of my jacket and worked them with a focused efficiency that told me he had been thinking about this far more carefully than his controlled exterior suggested, and when he pushed the jacket off my shoulders and got his hands on the shirt beneath, I stopped thinking about the interrogation post and the assassin and the political fallout and what Draevok's faction would say in the morning.

I stopped thinking about most things.

His mouth found the bruise along my cheekbone and pressed there, careful enough to make my chest ache, and then moved lower, tracing the line of my jaw, the curve of my throat, the place at my collarbone where tension had been living for the past several hours. I got my hands into the close-cropped fur at the back of his neck and held on, and he made another sound against my skin, something lower and more unguarded than anything I had heard from him before.

When he pressed me down against the cot and covered me with the heat of him, I arched up into it rather than away from it, and his forehead dropped to mine, and we stayed there for one suspended moment, breathing the same air, both of us still carrying the particular rawness of a night that had gone close enough to catastrophe to leave marks.

"I have you," he said. Low. Direct. Not a reassurance. A statement of fact that he was making as much for himself as for me.

"I know," I said, and meant it in ways I was not ready to examine clearly yet.

He moved, and I stopped being able to think in complete sentences.

He was not gentle. Not entirely. But he was present in a way that made the roughness feel like its own kind of attention, every shift calibrated to what my body did in response, and the adrenaline and the fear and the anger and the relief all collapsed into each other until I could not have separated them if I had tried. I did not try. I let them run together, let the heat of him and the weight of him and the specific, deliberate focus of him burn through the tangled mess of the night until there was nothing left but this, the sweat and the bruises and the breathlessness and his name in my mouth when I finally, finally let go.

He followed me there, his control breaking apart with a low, rough sound that I felt more than heard, his hands gripping me hard enough to leave marks I would notice tomorrow and did not object to tonight.

Afterward, we did not speak immediately. My pulse was still loud. His breathing was controlled in the way of a man reassembling himself from the inside out. The lamp burned its steady, indifferent flame. Outside, the camp held its tightened watch rotation, and the night went on being the night it had always been, regardless of what had just happened inside this tent.

The emotional consequences arrived immediately.

I lay staring at the canvas overhead and felt the complicated weight of it settle over me with the same efficiency as everything else this night had delivered. The fear was still there, rearranged but present. The awareness of how close the blade had come. The awareness of how much that had mattered to him, and how much his mattering about it mattered to me, and how neither of those things was simple or safe or easily contained.

"I am not all right," I said, to the canvas. "In case you were going to ask."

Kaelor's breathing shifted. He turned his head toward me, and I felt his gaze on the side of my face without looking at him.

"I know," he said.

"Good." I kept my eyes on the ceiling. "I needed you to know that this did not fix anything."

"It was not intended to."

"Then what was it intended to do?"

A pause. Then, with the measured weight he gave to things he had considered carefully before saying: "Because after tonight, pretending otherwise seemed inefficient."

I did not have an answer for that. So I said nothing, and the lamp burned, and I breathed, and the complicated tangle in my chest did not resolve but it did, fractionally, loosen.

I was still staring at the ceiling when the tent entrance opened.

Malakor did not apologize for the intrusion. He never did. He stood in the entrance with his storm-gray complexion flat and unreadable, and he looked at neither of us with any particular judgment, because Malakor had no emotional investment in our personal decisions and was constitutionally incapable of pretending otherwise.

"Get dressed," he said. "Both of you."

Kaelor was already sitting up. "What."

"They are moving faster than they should be able to." Malakor's black eyes moved to Kaelor with the weight of someone delivering a fact he had already decided how to use. "My contact at the eastern relay confirmed it an hour ago. The Shadow Court advance units have already passed the second waypoint. They anticipated the route." He paused. "This camp is compromised. Not maybe. Confirmed. We have hours, not days."

The cold of it went through me like a blade finding a gap in armor.

"How," Kaelor said.

"The same way they knew her face," Malakor replied. "Someone talked. Or someone listened. The distinction matters less right now than the fact that staying here finishes what the assassin started."

I was already moving, pulling my shirt over my head, reaching for my jacket. The bruise on my cheekbone throbbed. My arm stung under the bandaging. I filed both observations away and kept moving.

Kaelor rose from the cot with the same controlled urgency and crossed to the weapons rack. His war harness went on with practiced efficiency, each buckle fastened with a focus that had nothing personal in it anymore. The warlord had returned to the surface, and whatever we had been to each other in the past hour was folded away into the space where he kept the things that could not be permitted to cost him precision.

I understood it. I was doing the same thing.

"Serathis," Kaelor said.

"Already woken," Malakor said. "She is preparing the reduced party now."

"Torren."

"Awake, complaining, and currently locating the supply packs. He was the first one I told." A brief pause. "He did not take it well, but he is moving efficiently despite that."

"Talia."

"Packing her medical supplies. She was told to take only what she can carry at speed."

Kaelor looked at Malakor with a directness that asked the question he had not said aloud, the one about Draevok and the secondary clan commanders and the political machinery that could not simply be abandoned in the night.

Malakor answered it anyway. "Draevok will remain with the larger force. Serathis has already spoken to him. He was not pleased." A pause that held something that might have been dry acknowledgment. "He said, and I am delivering this accurately, that if you get her killed on the road, he will find the manner of it personally insulting."

I stopped in the middle of fastening my jacket.

"That is the closest thing to a protective sentiment I have ever heard from him," I said.

"Do not let it comfort you excessively," Malakor said. "He still believes you are a structural liability. He simply prefers his liabilities to remain alive long enough to be properly evaluated." He turned back to Kaelor. "We move within the hour. Anything that slows us gets left behind."

He left. The tent entrance fell closed behind him.

Kaelor crossed to me and stood there for a moment, his war harness fully fastened, his expression composed into the particular controlled authority that would carry us through whatever the road ahead was going to demand. He looked at the bandage on my forearm, then at my face, and something passed through his eyes that was brief and unguarded before it went back under the surface where he kept it.

He touched my jaw once, carefully, with the backs of two fingers.

Then he picked up his sword belt and walked out to give orders.

I stood alone in the tent for exactly three seconds, breathing the air that still smelled of him, letting myself feel the full weight of the night one final time before I locked it down and followed him out into the cold pre-dawn dark.

The camp broke in forty-five minutes. I had seen military camps broken before, during the border campaigns when I was still young enough to think speed under pressure was impressive rather than desperate, but this was different. Smaller. Quieter. The particular efficiency of people who understood that the thing behind them was real.

Serathis moved through it like weather, giving orders that were obeyed before the words finished forming. Torren appeared at my elbow with a pack slung over his shoulder and his expression stripped to its functional core, the version of him that existed beneath the performance and only showed when the stakes were high enough to make the performance a waste of energy.

"I want it noted," he said, falling into step beside me, "that I have not slept, I was in close proximity to an assassination attempt, and I am now being asked to walk out of a camp in the dark with enemies on three sides and a party small enough that I am statistically significant as a casualty risk." He paused. "I am not requesting sympathy. I am establishing a record."

"Noted," I said.

"Excellent." He handed me a strip of dried meat from somewhere inside his layered jacket. "Eat. You look like someone who survived an assassination attempt and then made a sequence of deeply questionable personal decisions."

I took the dried meat and did not respond to the second half of that.

Talia found me near the supply line, her satchel packed tight and her bronze curls pinned back with the severity of someone who had accepted that practicality was the order of the night. Her wide green eyes moved over my face with the rapid assessment she used when she was determining whether something needed immediate treatment or could wait until circumstances permitted.

"The arm is holding," she said. "Don't stress the bandaging. If it bleeds through, tell me immediately and do not wait until it becomes a problem."

"I will," I said.

She looked at me for a beat longer than the medical assessment required. "The rest of it. Are you managing?"

"I will," I said again, meaning something different.

She nodded, and she did not push it, and I was grateful for that in the particular way I was always grateful when people understood that some things needed time rather than words.

We moved out as the first gray suggestion of dawn began to dilute the dark at the horizon's edge. Eight of us, plus a small elite guard of six warriors Kaelor had hand-selected, moving quietly along a road that became less road and more intention the further we traveled from the encampment. The main force remained behind with Draevok, and the political fallout from the night would have to be managed at a distance, by people with more patience for it than I currently possessed.

The cold was sharp and clean. My breath fogged. My boots found the frozen ground with each step, and the rhythm of walking did what it always did, settled the scattered pieces of my mind back into something resembling order.

I was alive. The camp was behind us. Whatever came next, I was moving through it with my own legs, and that had to count for something.

Malakor moved at the column's front with Kaelor, their voices low and continuous, the tactical conversation of two people working through variables at speed. Serathis held the rear. Torren drifted in the middle with the practiced invisibility of a man who had survived many years by being the person no one tracked until they needed something.

I walked near Talia, which was where I needed to be, and I watched the road, and I thought about nothing that was not immediately relevant, because the alternative was examining the night's accumulated weight and I was not ready to do that yet.

The sun came up eventually. Cold and pale and offering more light than warmth, but present, which was enough.

We kept moving.

# The Road That Bleeds

By dawn, I had learned that surviving an assassination attempt did not make people trust you more.

It made them watch you differently. Quietly. With the specific, measuring calculation of people trying to determine whether the thing that had nearly gotten you killed was going to get them killed next. The elite guard Kaelor had selected moved with that awareness behind their eyes, professional enough not to show it openly, experienced enough that I noticed it anyway.

The road we traveled was not a road in any conventional sense. It was a suggestion of one, worn into the mountain stone over centuries by boots and hooves that no longer existed, cutting through terrain that the main passes avoided for reasons no one in our group had bothered to explain until Malakor fell back to walk beside me and said, without preamble, "Beast-clan routes. Old ones. They run along Labyrinth veins."

I looked at the ground under my feet with a different attention than I had been giving it.

"Which means what, exactly?"

"Means most travelers avoid them." He kept his eyes forward, his voice carrying the flat precision he used for everything that mattered. "The stone can be unpredictable near vein-lines. Fey soldiers especially. Their magic interacts badly with old Labyrinth resonance."

"And mine?"

A pause that was not uncertainty, only deliberateness. "That is the question, isn't it."

He moved back to the front of the column without further elaboration, which I had come to recognize as Malakor's version of saying he did not yet have a satisfactory answer.

The cold was honest, at least. Sharp and clean and entirely indifferent to whatever complications we had accumulated overnight. My breath fogged with each exhale, and the mountain wind cut through the layered wool of my jacket in a way that kept me present and focused rather than drifting into the tangled territory I was actively avoiding. The bruise along my cheekbone had settled into a dull, persistent throb. My arm, under Talia's careful bandaging, stung when I flexed my fingers, which I did periodically just to confirm everything still worked.

Kaelor walked twelve paces ahead of me.

I was counting. Not intentionally. My attention kept returning to him the way it returned to an unhealed cut, against my better judgment and without my permission.

We had not spoken since breaking camp. There was nothing wrong with that, precisely. There was nothing to say that the road wasn't already saying more efficiently. But the silence between us now carried a different texture than it had two days ago, weighted with things that had been said without words and could not be unsaid, and I was finding it considerably harder to ignore than the wind.

Torren appeared at my shoulder with the specific timing of someone who had been watching me stare at Kaelor's back for thirty seconds too long.

"I vote," he said conversationally, "that we adopt a formal policy against roads that bleed. Just as a general travel standard. Something the group agrees on before we find ourselves on another ancient cursed path that smells faintly of old catastrophe."

"The road doesn't bleed."

"Not yet." He adjusted the pack on his shoulder. "I notice you've been looking at it the way you look at things that are about to become complicated."

I had not realized I was doing that.

The truth was that I had been sensing the road for the past two hours without having a word for it. Something beneath the stone, rhythmic and faint, like a heartbeat heard through several walls. The symbols carved into the occasional waymarker stones along the path caught my attention in a way they should not have, pulling my focus even when I was looking at something else entirely. I had said nothing about it, because there was nothing useful to say yet, and because admitting that the ground was speaking to me in some language I was only beginning to half-understand felt like exactly the kind of information that would cause everyone around me to stop and stare.

I kept moving instead.

The waystation appeared three hours into the march, set back from the path into a shallow rock alcove. Stone walls, a collapsed roof on one end, the remnants of a fire circle long gone cold. Kaelor signaled the halt before any of us had said anything, which meant he had already known it was there.

What none of us had known was what was inside.

Serathis went in first, which was habit and hierarchy and the particular kind of command instinct that put the most experienced body between the unknown and everyone else. She emerged three seconds later with her jaw set and her clouded eye hard.

"Old site," she said. "Years. Not recent."

We went in anyway.

The bones were small.

That was the first thing I registered, and my throat went instantly dry, the air catching in my chest with a sharp, physical hitch that bypassed every defensive layer I had built over years of border campaigns and narrow escapes. Not soldiers. Families. The evidence was still there in the arrangement of what remained, preserved by the cold and the stone: cook pots, a child's leather boot, the rusted fragments of tools that had nothing to do with war. Whatever had happened here, it had not happened to combatants.

Talia made a sound beside me that she quickly swallowed. Her knuckles were white around the strap of her satchel.

Kaelor stood in the center of the space and said nothing. The muscle along his jaw worked once, controlled and deliberate, but his eyes moved across the remnants with a dark, hollow sharpness that was different from his usual unreadable composure. This was not a man suppressing emotion. This was a man who recognized something.

"High Fey," Malakor said, crouching near the far wall. His fingers traced the edge of a burn pattern scored into the stone, the precise geometric signature of fey-made fire rather than any natural source. "The pattern is consistent with military-grade destruction. Not punitive. Systematic."

"How old?" I asked.

"Fifteen years. Possibly twenty." He straightened. "During the consolidation campaigns."

I looked at Kaelor again.

He felt it. He turned, and his molten gold eyes found mine across the cold space, and neither of us said anything about the fact that this was why he had fought, why he had bled, why he had built an alliance through sheer brutal strategic will in a world that had given his people exactly this as the alternative. The political abstraction of his war had just become a child's boot in a ruined waystation on an abandoned road, and I could not unknow it.

Serathis moved to stand beside him. "We knew about this site," she said quietly. "We have known about forty-seven sites like it." Her voice carried no performance. Just fact, delivered to me directly, because she had decided I needed to hear it clearly. "This is what we are fighting to prevent from continuing."

I nodded once. It was all I had.

We moved on. We did not linger, because lingering would not give anything back, and the road ahead still needed covering.

It was another hour before the road responded to me.

I felt it before I saw it. The pulse beneath the stone intensified without warning, climbing from faint background awareness into something that resonated in my sternum and ran up through the soles of my feet. The waymarker stones on both sides of the path lit at the edges of my vision, faintly, briefly, inscriptions burning blue-white for a half-second before returning to ordinary rock.

I stopped walking.

Kaelor stopped two paces later, turning without being signaled, because he had been watching me. Of course he had.

"Elara."

"Something is here." I pressed my left hand flat to the nearest stone wall, and the pulse came back immediately, stronger, directional. "Below us. Or behind the stone. There's a—" I searched for a word that would not sound entirely unhinged. "A passage. Closed."

Malakor was beside me before I finished speaking.

Torren, to his credit, stayed where he was and simply muttered, "I would like to register that I have a bad feeling about this, formally and for the record."

The stone did not wait for any of us to decide. The moment I pressed my palm flat against the wall, something happened beneath my skin, a drawing sensation, brief and almost painless, like a door recognizing a key it had been waiting centuries to feel. A hairline crack split the face of the rock, running in a vertical line from the ground to a height just above my head, and then the stone simply moved, folding inward with a grinding weight that sent dust cascading and made the two nearest guards step back with weapons drawn.

Beyond it: darkness, and ancient air, and something that smelled of stone and old fire and the particular mineral cold of a place sealed against time.

"Nobody asked for that," Torren said. "Noted."

We went inside.

The passage widened after the first ten paces, opening into a chamber that should not have existed beneath the mountain road, large enough to hold all fourteen of us with space remaining. The walls were covered floor to ceiling in murals, not painted, carved, the stone itself worked into images so detailed and so old that the technique predated any artistic style I could name.

Talia held a torch up, and the light moved across the images in slow revelation.

Figures stood before a vast, spiraling structure that could only have been the Labyrinth rendered in ancient iconography, its paths branching in impossible geometries. The figures nearest the structure were human-shaped but marked distinctly, lines of light running from their hands into the stone, their postures neither worshipful nor afraid but purposeful. Functional. They were not praying to it. They were working with it.

"Catalysts," Malakor said, and the word landed with the weight of something he had suspected and was now seeing confirmed.

Above the Catalysts, in the upper register of the mural, other figures watched. Tall, elongated, crowned, their features carved with a precision that made them unmistakable despite their age. High Fey. Not interacting with the Labyrinth. Observing. Recording. Taking.

And at the center of the composition, massive, dominating the entire right wall of the chamber, a horned figure stood before the Labyrinth's heart, one hand pressed to its surface, runes running up both arms in patterns that bore a disturbing resemblance to the markings on Kaelor's own horns.

Beside the horned figure, smaller but no less clearly rendered, a woman with dark hair and lines of light running from her palms into the stone.

The silence in the chamber was the kind that happened when too many people understood too much at once and needed a moment before anyone spoke.

"That," Torren said carefully, pointing at the dark-haired figure, "looks remarkably like someone I know."

"It does not," I said.

"It genuinely does."

"It is an ancient carving of a generic—"

"Elara." Kaelor's voice, quiet, carrying the particular weight he used when he was telling me to stop deflecting.

I stopped.

The figure in the mural had sharp cheekbones and lines of light running from her hands into the Labyrinth's stone. The horned figure beside her was massive, ivory-marked, and the runes on his horns were rendered in a detail that no casual artist would have invented.

"It is a coincidence," I said. "Archetypes repeat in ancient imagery. This is not—this does not mean anything specific."

"Prophecy is rarely kind to those named in it," Malakor said, still studying the upper register, his tone carrying none of Torren's performative alarm and all of his actual concern, which was considerably more unsettling.

Kaelor moved to stand beside the central composition. He examined the horned figure with his arms crossed and his expression controlled, but something underneath that control was pulling taut, and I could feel it from six feet away.

"Can you read any of the inscription?" Serathis asked Malakor, nodding toward the carved text that ran along the base of the murals in a dense, archaic script.

Malakor crouched, bringing his torch lower. He was quiet for nearly two minutes, which was a long time for him. His lips moved slightly over certain word-forms, the unconscious habit of someone translating internally before committing to spoken interpretation.

Talia moved beside me during the wait. She kept her voice below the range of the others. "Being afraid of what you are does not make you dangerous," she said, and there was no preamble to it, no softening. Just Talia, saying the thing that needed to be said with the directness she used when she had decided someone needed to hear it. "Refusing to learn does."

I wanted to argue. I had a very coherent argument prepared, actually, about the difference between learning and being conscripted into a narrative someone else had written before I was born.

I did not make it, because Malakor spoke.

"Much of it is damaged or uses dead dialect forms." He rose, his expression unreadable in the way that meant he was still deciding how to present what he had found. "But the lower inscription is legible." He looked at Kaelor first, then at me, with the black eyes that never telegraphed anything before he decided to give it. "When blood joins horn, the sleeping maze remembers."

The chamber went very still.

"No," I said.

Everyone looked at me.

"No," I said again, because the first one had clearly not been sufficient. "That is not what this is. That is not what any of this is."

Kaelor turned from the mural. His expression was controlled, but something behind it had gone sharp and cold, and I recognized it as the same rejection I was feeling, wearing his particular shape.

"We are not a prophecy," he said.

"Agreed," I said.

We were in perfect alignment, and somehow that made it worse, because the perfect alignment felt like evidence rather than reassurance, and the carved figures on the wall behind him were not helping.

"I need to ask you something," I said, because I had not been asking it since before dawn, and the chamber had removed my last reason to keep waiting. "And I need you to answer it honestly."

Kaelor waited. He was very good at waiting.

"Do you want me," I said, keeping my voice level, "or do you need what I am?"

The silence stretched. Torren, to his considerable credit, was suddenly very interested in a section of mural on the far wall. Serathis remained precisely where she was, because Serathis did not pretend not to hear things.

"Both," Kaelor said after a beat. "I would distrust any answer that claimed otherwise."

The honesty of it landed exactly as hard as I had known it would.

"That answer is supposed to reassure me," I said.

"It is not supposed to be anything. You asked for the truth." He crossed the space between us, not rushing it, and stopped close enough that I had to tilt my chin to hold his gaze. "I do not know how to separate you from what is waking inside you. I have tried. The answer is the same regardless." His voice dropped, carrying a restrained intensity that made the back of my neck tighten. "But if you are asking whether I would still be standing here if the Labyrinth burned tomorrow, the answer to that is also yes."

I wanted to believe that. I also knew that wanting to believe something was not the same as having evidence for it, and that I had built a significant portion of my survival record on keeping those two categories separate.

"A ruler may love," Serathis said, without moving from her position, her voice carrying the flat practicality of someone stating a structural reality rather than offering an opinion. "He may not become ruled by it."

"Thank you, Serathis," Kaelor said.

"That was for her," Serathis replied. "Not you."

I looked at the general. She met my gaze with the steady, unsentimental attention of someone who had decided I was worth speaking to directly, which from Serathis functioned as something close to a gesture of respect.

I understood what she was telling me. That his wanting me was real. And that his needing what I was was also real. And that neither of those things absolved either of us from thinking clearly about what that combination cost.

"I hear you," I said quietly, to both of them.

Torren turned back from the wall. "Excellent. Existential complications acknowledged. Now, and I raise this with genuine urgency, the floor has been vibrating for the past four minutes and I would very much like someone to address that."

He was right. I felt it the moment my attention shifted back to the physical chamber, the pulse beneath the stone had changed from its steady resonance to something more irregular, more urgent, like a held breath approaching its limit.

"The chamber is waking," Malakor said, and he was already moving toward the entrance. "We need to leave. Now."

The stone moved faster than any of us had expected. The far wall shifted inward by six inches with a sound like grinding bone, and a crack split the floor in a jagged line toward the center of the room. Dust fell from the ceiling in thin curtains.

"Move," Kaelor said, and it was the warlord's voice, carrying the weight of absolute command, and everyone moved.

The passage back toward the exterior was no longer the passage we had entered through. The stone had rearranged itself in the way of a living thing settling into a new position, and the corridor that should have led straight to the outside bent sharply to the left after twenty paces and then opened into a second, smaller chamber I had not seen on entry.

I heard the others' voices ahead, Talia calling back that she could see the original passage, Torren producing a stream of commentary that served no tactical function whatsoever. The vibration under my feet intensified, and then the floor dropped two inches on one side and I stumbled, and the section of wall to my right sealed itself with a grinding finality that cut the sound of the others off entirely.

Kaelor caught my arm before I hit the stone.

We stood in a narrow stretch of corridor, alone, the passage ahead sealed and the chamber behind us still shifting, the air thick with ancient dust and the mineral cold of a place that had been deciding something for a very long time.

His hand was still on my arm. I was still close enough to feel the heat of him despite the cold, close enough that the scent of leather and iron and the darker, specific thing that was only him wrapped through the dust and the centuries and reminded me, inefficiently and without permission, of the previous night.

"There will be another exit," he said, scanning the walls with the focused attention of someone who had navigated confined spaces under worse conditions than this. "The passage opened to my blood once before. It will open again."

"This is the Labyrinth doing it," I said. "Not coincidence."

"I know."

"It separated us deliberately."

"I know that too." His eyes came back to me. "Are you going to let it decide something for you?"

The question hung in the narrow space between us, and I understood it precisely. The prophecy, the mural, the ancient inscription, the chamber arranging us into this specific proximity with the deliberateness of something very old and very purposeful. I could feel the pull of it, the way the stone itself seemed to lean toward him, the way my own blood was quieter here, closer to him, than it had been anywhere else on the road.

"No," I said.

He studied my face for a beat. Then he said, quietly, "Prophecy can name a door. It cannot decide whether we walk through it."

Something in my chest shifted at that, not resolving, not simplifying, but settling into a new arrangement, one where the prophecy and the wanting and the uncertainty could coexist without any of them erasing the others. He was not telling me the inscription was wrong. He was telling me it did not own us.

The wall to our left gave way with a low groan, a seam of cold light splitting the stone, and the passage beyond was narrow but navigable and smelled of open air.

We moved through it quickly, not speaking, the sound of the others growing louder as the corridor wound upward through the mountain's bones. Torren's voice was audible before anyone else's, which was reliable as a directional tool.

The passage ended at a rough stone arch, and beyond it the mountain opened into a high overlook, pale sky above us, the road below visible in both directions, the cold wind immediate and real and entirely welcome after the ancient air of the chamber.

The group was already assembled. Talia's relief was visible in the loosening of her shoulders. Malakor had already turned to assess the terrain below with the systematic efficiency of a man who had decided the immediate problem was the one that required attention.

Serathis spoke before anyone else.

"Look at the valley."

I looked.

Below, on the road that curved through the mountain's base, banners moved in the wind. Silver and black, the colors catching the pale morning light with an elegance that had nothing to do with warmth and everything to do with power. The formations beneath them were precise, unhurried, and very deliberately placed across the only viable exit route through the pass.

High Fey banners.

Astrythe's forces had arrived first.

Torren stood beside me and looked down at the valley with the expression of a man whose formal travel policy suggestion had just been retroactively validated.

"The road," he said, "is bleeding."

# The Horned Prophecy

I had been called many things in my life, but destiny felt the most insulting.

I stood at the edge of the overlook with the cold mountain wind pulling at my hair and the valley spread below us, and I tried to make sense of what I was seeing. The banners were unmistakable even at this distance, silver and black, elegant and deliberate, arranged in formations that did not look like a patrol and did not look like coincidence. They looked like an answer to a question we had not known we were asking aloud.

Torren stood to my left. He was quiet, which was the most unsettling thing about the situation, because Torren was almost never quiet.

"How many?" Serathis asked. She had already moved to the highest point of the overlook, scanning the valley with the practiced, unhurried assessment of a commander who had made decisions on worse terrain with worse numbers.

"Two hundred, minimum," Malakor said. He stood at her shoulder, his voice carrying no particular alarm, just measurement. "The formations on the eastern slope suggest a second unit held in reserve. They are not trying to hide."

"No," Kaelor said, from directly behind me. "They are not."

I turned. His molten gold eyes were already on the valley, jaw set, arms crossed over the breadth of his chest with the controlled stillness of a man deciding several things simultaneously and not planning to share any of them until the decision was made.

"They knew we would emerge here," I said.

"Yes."

"Which means they tracked us. Or tracked the passage opening." I paused. "Or someone told them where to wait."

No one answered immediately, and the silence carried enough weight to make the back of my teeth ache. I did not look at anyone in particular, because accusation without evidence was a luxury we could not afford on a mountain overlook with two hundred soldiers in the valley below. But I noted the way Serathis's expression did not change, and the way Malakor's eyes moved briefly across our small group before returning to the terrain.

"We address that question later," Kaelor said. "Right now we address the valley."

"Agreed," Serathis said.

Torren found his voice again. "I am going to say, for the record, that I strongly favor addressing it from a location that is not directly above two hundred High Fey soldiers." He squinted downward. "Do they have archers on the eastern ridge?"

"Yes," Malakor said.

"Wonderful. Absolutely wonderful."

The answer from below came before we had finished deciding anything. A single rider separated from the main formation and moved to the center of the road, stopping where the sight lines from the overlook were clearest. Even at this distance, the rider's white armor was visible, ceremonial and cold as the mountain air.

The voice that carried up to us was amplified by magic, clear and deliberate, every word placed with surgical precision.

"Lord Ashhorn. You are offered terms. Surrender the human woman alive and unharmed. Your escort leaves this mountain without further engagement. You have until the sun moves one hand's width."

The words landed like stones dropped into still water.

I felt every person on the overlook process them in the specific, private way people calculate the cost of a single life against a group. Serathis didn't look at me, but her hand drifted down, her fingers resting lightly on the pommel of her sword, her thumb tracing the worn leather grip in a slow, deliberate rhythm. I had made that calculation about myself before. I was familiar with the shape of it, the way it felt when you could see people doing the math and waiting to see what the answer would be.

"No," Kaelor said.

He said it immediately, without deliberation, and it was not addressed to anyone on the overlook. It was loud enough to carry, and it did.

Serathis exhaled once through her nose. "Then we fight our way through." She turned to Malakor. "The eastern ridge archers. How long before they can range this position?"

"Ten minutes. Less if they move now."

"They will move now." She began issuing quiet orders to the elite guard, her voice dropping into the flat efficiency of command, organizing angles and positions and movement priorities with the calm of someone who had done this so many times that crisis had become simply another kind of work.

I stood where I was, my mind racing to find a thread of logic in the timing. The arrival of the High Fey could not be coincidence. Not after what we had just witnessed in the chamber beneath the mountain—the carved basin reacting to my proximity, the walls shifting us into deliberate arrangements, and the Labyrinth actively separating Kaelor and me from the others during our escape.

It was also awake enough, I suspected, to be useful now, if I could figure out how to ask it.

Talia appeared beside me. She had her satchel pulled tight across her chest and her green eyes were very bright, the kind of brightness that happened when she was frightened and had decided to be useful instead. "Tell me what you need," she said quietly.

"I don't know yet." I pressed my palm flat against the nearest section of mountain stone, not the overlook wall but the solid face of the cliff behind us, and felt for the pulse I had been tracking since the waymarker stones on the road. It was there. Stronger now, resonating up through the rock with an urgency that felt almost intentional, almost responsive.

"Old magic lies as often as people do," Talia said softly, watching my hand against the stone. "But it also remembers things people forgot."

"I'm counting on that."

The first arrow from the eastern ridge hit the overlook wall six feet to my right, and then everything happened at once.

Serathis's guard moved into formation without a sound, shields up, closing ranks around the group's core with practiced speed. Malakor was already moving toward the cliff's eastern face, drawing his blade in a single smooth motion. Torren had somehow produced a crossbow from somewhere inside his layered leathers and was tracking the ridge line with an expression that had shed every trace of his usual irreverence.

Kaelor was beside me before the second arrow landed.

"Tell me you have something," he said.

"I might." I pressed harder against the stone and felt the pulse climb into my palm, into my wrist, moving up through my arm with a heat that was not fever but was not entirely comfortable either. "I need a minute."

"We have considerably less than that."

"Then stop talking."

He stopped.

I closed my eyes and focused on the resonance under my hand, following it the way I had followed the road's pulse on the approach, tracing it down through the mountain's bones toward something older and larger and deeply patient. The chamber had responded to proximity. The passage had opened to contact. This was the same mechanism, just larger, and as I pushed deeper, the memory of the chamber's vision slammed back into me through the stone—the physical sensation of other Catalysts screaming in chains, a crowned woman watching with star-filled eyes, and a horned figure kneeling in old blood. The Labyrinth was awake, its attention locked entirely onto me, the carved basin in my mind's eye leaning toward my blood without needing to draw it.

The vision came back in fragments. Catalysts screaming. Chains. A crowned woman watching with those star-filled eyes. A horned figure kneeling in something dark and wet. The Labyrinth opening like a wound in the world's side.

I pushed past the images and reached for the structure beneath them, the architecture, the way the passages had moved and breathed and responded, and I asked it, not in words but in intent, not *open* but *here, now, through*.

The cliffside answered.

The stone groaned, a low, interior sound that vibrated through the soles of my boots and up through my knees, and a section of the cliff face split along a seam I had not seen, folding outward and back to reveal a passage wide enough for two people abreast, angled sharply downward into the mountain's interior. Cold air poured out of it, smelling of deep stone and old dark and something faintly mineral and alive.

The effort of it hit me immediately.

It was not pain, precisely. It was depletion, sudden and total, like the moment a held breath becomes impossible to sustain. My knees gave out, and the stone under my palm went from resonating to silent so fast it felt like a door slamming.

Kaelor caught me before I hit the overlook wall. His arm came around my ribs from behind, solid and immediate, and he took my weight without stumbling, holding me upright while the world tilted and resettled.

"Move," Serathis called to the guard, already directing the group toward the passage. "Now. Fast."

I tried to say I was fine. What came out was more like a breath that had forgotten to become words.

"I have you," Kaelor said, and he was already moving, carrying me forward with the kind of unhurried certainty that made the statement feel like a structural fact rather than a reassurance.

I did not argue. My legs were working, mostly, but the coordination required to insist on doing this myself felt like a luxury I could revisit once the arrows stopped.

The passage swallowed us.

Behind us, I heard the sound of the formation below reacting, shouted orders, the clatter of armor shifting into pursuit, and then the mountain's stone closed across the entrance with a sound like a held breath finally released. The passage had not done that at my direction. The Labyrinth had decided, and I was too depleted to find that anything other than marginally reassuring.

The descent was steep and fast. Torren produced a torch from somewhere with the specific efficiency of a man who expected to need fire at short notice and planned accordingly. Malakor took the lead without discussion, reading the passage's angles and gradients with the attention of a scout who defaulted to terrain assessment under pressure.

Halfway down, a sound came from somewhere behind us in the mountain, not the passage we had come through but from the walls themselves, a low resonant note like a horn heard through deep water. It lasted for three seconds and then stopped.

No one spoke about it. We kept moving.

My strength had knitted back together enough to walk under my own weight by the time the passage leveled out and widened into a natural cavern that opened, eventually, onto the lower ravine floor. Kaelor kept pace beside me, close enough that his arm brushed mine at every step, not holding me up anymore but not moving away either.

The ravine outside was shadowed and cold and blessedly absent of silver-and-black banners.

Behind us, I heard something else. A single sound, sharp and final, from somewhere in the mountain's upper passages. Malakor's pace did not change. But his jaw tightened, and I saw his hand move to the blade at his hip and then release it again, a gesture I recognized as the physical form of something being consciously set aside.

"Malakor," I said quietly.

"Keep moving." His voice was flat, not harsh, just sealed shut.

I kept moving.

The ruined signal tower appeared at the ravine's far end as the pale light shifted toward afternoon. Three walls standing, one collapsed inward, the remnants of a beacon platform at the top still wearing its iron bracket for a fire long since gone. It was defensible enough, sheltered enough, and far enough from the road's main line that Serathis approved it without debate.

We assembled inside what remained of its walls. The guard took positions at the collapsed side. Talia moved immediately toward the two soldiers who had taken shallow cuts on the overlook, working with the quick, methodical focus she brought to anything that needed fixing. Torren sat on a fallen stone and appeared to be conducting a private inventory of everything in his pockets, which seemed to be his version of stress management.

I sat against the standing wall and let my head rest against the stone, feeling the hollow ache in my chest where the Labyrinth's pull had dragged itself through my veins. The depletion was already fading, but slowly, like color returning to a room after a lamp has been moved. Whatever the Labyrinth had drawn from me to open that passage, it had taken it efficiently and without asking, and the fact that I had initiated the request did not make that feel any less invasive.

Kaelor crouched in front of me. He studied my face without touching me, his molten eyes moving across my features with the focused attention of someone taking inventory rather than offering sentiment.

"Tell me what it felt like," he said.

"Honestly?" I considered the question. "Like the floor fell out from under a house I was standing in. The structure held. The floor did not."

Something moved through his expression, too quick to name.

"It will not do that again," he said. It was not a question.

"Not without rest." I paused. "I don't know how much rest. I've never done that before."

"Then you will not do it again today."

"That is not a decision you make."

"No," he agreed, and the agreement carried its own weight, because he meant it. "But I am asking."

The asking was harder to deal with than a command would have been. Commands I knew how to refuse. This I had to actually decide about.

"I'm not planning to," I said.

He rose. Malakor had been standing near the collapsed wall, separated from the group by a few feet and his own particular silence, the kind that had a specific shape to it tonight. I had learned to read the difference between his ordinary economy of expression and the deliberate blankness he used when something had landed hard and he was not going to discuss it.

"The person in the passage," I said, keeping my voice below the range of the others. "You knew them."

He did not look at me. His black eyes stayed on the ravine beyond the broken wall.

"A captain I served under," he said, after a moment. "Before." The word carried the full weight of what it was standing in for: the campaigns, the massacres, the decades of following orders that he had eventually decided he could not keep following. "He recognized me. He was not going to allow us to leave."

"I'm sorry," I said.

His jaw shifted once. "Don't be. He was not a good man. I simply knew him when he was." He turned away from the ravine. "There is something else."

He crossed to where Kaelor stood with Serathis, and I pushed myself up from the wall and followed, because whatever it was had the texture of information that needed to be heard immediately.

"The commander who gave the terms," Malakor said. "Before we entered the passage, I heard a second message. Passed through their signal system, not meant for us. I caught it because I know their protocols." His voice remained precise and level, carrying the flat weight of something he had been holding since the overlook. "The standing orders from the High Queen are not what was announced publicly."

Serathis's eyes narrowed. "Explain."

"The public offer was surrender Elara, the escort leaves. The actual orders are different." He looked at Kaelor directly. "Astrythe wants the woman alive. She also wants you alive, Lord Ashhorn. Both of you. Together."

The silence that settled over the ruined tower was a different quality from the one that had followed the prophecy inscription in the chamber. That one had been startled. This one had a terrible weight to it, sealed by the sudden, sharp transition of Kaelor's gaze meeting mine—a look that showed no hesitation, only the grim, instant recognition of a trap we had both walked into with our eyes wide open.

"She is not hunting a Catalyst," I said slowly.

Torren, who had apparently been listening from his position on the fallen stone, looked up from his pocket inventory. "She is hunting the union," he said, and there was no irony in his voice at all, which was how I knew he understood exactly what it meant. "Blood and horn together. The prophecy. She wants the complete equation."

"If she controls both elements of the inscription," Malakor said, "she controls whatever the Labyrinth does when they unite. She does not want to stop the waking. She wants to direct it."

Serathis made a sound low in her chest, not quite a word, just the sound of a tactical mind recalculating everything it thought it understood. "Astrythe inherited more than a throne," she said. "She inherited knowledge of how the Labyrinth works. And she has been waiting for the pieces to appear."

"Malakor said it in the chamber," Kaelor said. His voice was very controlled, very quiet, in the register he used when something had genuinely surprised him and he was not planning to let the surprise show beyond that single moment of stillness. "If the murals predate the Shadow Court, she built her empire on what she stole from the Labyrinth's history."

"She did not just steal knowledge," I said, and the vision came back to me with sudden, cold clarity: the crowned figure watching from shadow, the Catalysts in chains, the precise detachment of someone observing a mechanism rather than witnessing human suffering. "She has done this before. Or tried to. The vision I saw in the chamber, the chains, the other Catalysts. That was not ancient history for its own sake. She was showing me what had already been attempted."

"The failed ritual," Talia said from across the tower floor. She had been listening too, her hands still working but her attention fixed on us. "The mural showed a ritual that fractured the worlds. If Astrythe knows what went wrong the first time, she knows how to correct it. And if she has both of you under her control when the Labyrinth fully wakes—"

"She shapes what comes through," I finished.

Kaelor turned to me. His expression was unreadable in the way I had learned to read anyway, the controlled surface and the thing beneath it that was considerably less controlled, and what I saw underneath was not fear and was not anger but something colder and more purposeful than either.

"Then she does not get both of us," he said. It was not addressed to the group. It was addressed to me, specifically, quietly, carrying the full weight of what he meant by it, which was not a strategic assessment but a declaration.

I held his gaze for a long moment, feeling the weight of that prophecy settle not in my mind, but like a cold, physical pressure behind my ribs—a sudden tightening in my lungs that tried to crowd out my own breath and replace it with the ancient narrative of inscriptions, murals, and destiny wearing the shape of two people who had not chosen any of this.

I refused to let it.

"No," I agreed. "She doesn't."

Torren stood, brushed stone dust from his leathers, and surveyed the ruined tower with the resigned expression of a man accepting that his formal travel policies were going to continue being ignored. "Right," he said. "So. We have a prophecy we refuse, a Queen who wants to weaponize it, two hundred soldiers behind us, and a Labyrinth that is apparently developing opinions." He tucked something back into his pocket. "I am going to suggest, strongly, that we find a route out of these mountains before nightfall, because I have a very reliable instinct for when a situation is about to become dramatically worse, and it is working overtime."

"For once," Serathis said, "I agree with the thief."

Torren blinked. "I want that written down. Someone should write that down."

Malakor was already studying the ravine's far end, mapping the terrain with the steady, forward-facing attention of a man who had set something difficult aside and replaced it with the next necessary task. He would carry whatever the mountain passage had cost him, and he would not discuss it, and he would continue to be useful, and I understood that, because I had been doing versions of the same thing for years.

I pushed away from the wall and stood fully upright, testing the steadiness of my legs and finding them adequate. The depletion had not fully resolved, but it had receded enough that I could move without assistance, and that would have to be sufficient.

Kaelor fell into step beside me as Serathis began organizing the group's movement toward the ravine's far passage. His shoulder nearly brushed mine, close without being touching, present without being possessive, and I was aware of it with the same involuntary precision I had been aware of him all day, which was inconvenient and showed no sign of becoming less so.

"The prophecy named us," I said quietly, not looking at him. "Astrythe believes it. The Labyrinth is acting on it." I paused. "And you still think it cannot own us."

"I think," he said, equally quiet, "that it can describe what exists without having created it. The inscription did not build what is between us, Elara. It found words for something already there." He paused, and the pause had weight. "What Astrythe does with those words is her choice. What we do is ours."

The wind moved through the ravine below us, cold and indifferent, carrying the distant sound of the mountains settling into late afternoon.

I did not have an answer to that, not one I was ready to say aloud. So I kept walking, and he kept pace beside me, and somewhere behind us the Labyrinth continued its slow, patient waking, full of ancient memory and stolen knowledge and the particular certainty of something that had been waiting a very long time for the right door to open.

We were not going to make it easy for anyone to decide what happened next.

That, at least, I was certain of.

# Banners in the Dark

The High Fey were waiting beneath the mountain like they had been written there by fate itself.

That was the thought I carried down from the overlook, through the ravine, and into the cold shelter of the ruined signal tower. It sat behind my ribs alongside the depletion and the residual chill of deep stone, and the memory of Kaelor's arm around me, steady and immediate, while the world had tilted sideways under my feet.

We had survived the ambush. That was the fact I kept returning to when the rest of it threatened to become too much weight to carry.

We had survived, and now we knew something we had not known before: Astrythe did not simply want me. She wanted both of us, together, the complete equation the prophecy described, because a Catalyst without a horned warlord was only half a key, and Astrythe had clearly decided she wanted to own the entire lock.

The signal tower's remaining walls offered enough shelter from the wind that the cold became merely uncomfortable rather than dangerous. Talia had finished with the wounded soldiers and was now sitting near what remained of the eastern wall, her satchel open beside her, mixing something that smelled sharp and medicinal. Torren had found a higher vantage point inside the collapsed section and was watching the ravine with a focus that, on anyone else, I might have called vigilance. On Torren, it looked like a man looking for his exit.

Serathis stood near the tower's broken threshold, back to the rest of us, scanning the terrain below with the methodical patience of a commander who did not permit herself the luxury of visible unease. She had been in that position since we arrived, and I suspected she would remain in it until we moved again.

Malakor had not spoken since we entered the tower.

He stood apart from the group, near the fallen section of the northern wall, and his expression had settled into the particular blankness I had learned to recognize as the surface he wore when something had cut deep enough that even his considerable discipline was working hard to keep it contained. The skin around his temples was pulled tight, a muscle ticking in the hard line of his jaw as he stared into the dark, his throat moving with a slow, heavy swallow that he tried to hide by tilting his chin down. His hand had moved to his blade twice in the last hour and released it both times without drawing, a habit I recognized as grief wearing the shape of a soldier's reflex.

I crossed to him. Not because I had something useful to say, but because he had stood beside me through an ambush, through a passage opening that had nearly flattened me, and through a battle that had cost him something he was not going to name, and the least I could do was stand beside him in the aftermath.

"The commander," I said, keeping my voice low enough that it did not carry. "The one who recognized you."

Malakor's jaw shifted once. His black eyes stayed on the ravine.

"Caerevyn," he said. "He served under me for eleven years. He was twenty-three when I first assigned him."

He did not say anything else, and he did not need to. Eleven years was a long time to serve beside someone. Long enough to know the sound of their footsteps and the way they held their blade and what they looked like when they were frightened.

"He called you traitor," I said.

"Eventually," Malakor said. "That was my answer too." His voice was precise and sealed, carrying no invitation for further questions. "He was not wrong about what I was. He was simply wrong about whether I should have been."

I let the silence hold for a moment before I said, "I'm sorry he didn't defect with you."

Something moved behind his eyes, quick and gone. "He never questioned the orders. He was loyal to the structure, not the people inside it. That distinction matters." He paused. "It was always going to end this way. I knew that when I left."

There was nothing I could offer that would improve on that, so I didn't try. I simply stood beside him until he exhaled slowly and turned away from the ravine, and then I let him go without requiring anything else from the moment.

Kaelor was watching me when I turned back toward the group. He was leaning against the intact section of the western wall, arms crossed over the breadth of his chest, molten eyes tracking me across the tower floor with that focused, unhurried attention that I had stopped pretending I did not notice.

"You should rest," he said, when I reached him.

"I've rested enough."

"Your legs gave out an hour ago."

"They recovered." I sat down against the wall beside him, not because I needed the support but because my body had developed the inconvenient habit of orienting itself toward him without consulting me first. "The depletion is mostly gone. It fades faster than I expected."

He studied my face the way he did when he was deciding whether my self-assessment was reliable or convenient. "How much faster?"

"Faster than whatever you're imagining." I paused. "It draws from something. I don't know what, exactly. But whatever it is replenishes. I can feel it."

"That is not reassuring."

"You keep saying that like reassurance is what I'm offering."

His expression shifted slightly, a fractional movement around the mouth that was not quite a smile but was in the same neighborhood. "You could have died today," he said.

"You could have died today. Serathis could have died today. Malakor just watched someone he knew for eleven years die today." I held his gaze. "I used what I had. It worked."

"It nearly collapsed you."

"You keep saying that like it's rare," I said.

Something tightened in his jaw before he released a slow breath. His shoulder pressed against mine where we sat together against the wall, warm and solid and deliberate in a way that did not demand anything, which was somehow harder to deal with than demand would have been. Demand I knew how to answer. This quiet, steady presence required something more complicated from me.

"You trusted me," I said, after a moment. Quietly. Not an accusation, just the plain shape of what had happened.

"Yes," he said.

"It cost you something."

"Trust always costs something." His voice was level, unhurried, carrying the weight of someone who had reached that conclusion through experience rather than philosophy. "I would rather pay the cost than choose to doubt you."

I did not have an answer for that. My chest did something complicated and I looked away from him, out through the gap in the tower wall toward the ravine below, where the afternoon light was beginning to thin toward evening.

Talia appeared at my shoulder, holding out a small clay cup of something that steamed faintly and smelled like pine needles and burnt herbs. "Drink this," she said. "Whatever you just did to that mountain, it pulled from your blood, and your blood needs replacing, which this technically helps with, and also it tastes terrible, which means it is definitely working."

I took the cup. It did taste terrible. I drank it anyway.

"Whatever you just did," Talia added, sitting down on the other side of me with her satchel tucked against her knees, "do less of it next time."

"I'll pass that along to the mountain."

"Please do." She glanced across me toward Kaelor, and the glance carried the specific, sidelong quality of someone filing away information they had already decided to have opinions about later. She did not comment. She simply organized her herbs with the brisk efficiency of a woman who knew when to be quiet and had made a conscious decision to exercise that knowledge.

Serathis turned from the threshold. "We cannot stay here past dark," she said, addressing the group. "The High Fey will widen the search perimeter once they lose our trail in the ravine. By nightfall, they will have riders on both ravine exits." She crossed to where we had spread the rough map on a section of fallen stone. "We need a route through the lower passes before the light goes."

Malakor moved to the map without being asked. He traced the terrain with one finger, his black eyes moving across the routes with the quiet, forward-facing attention of a man who had set his grief aside and replaced it with the next task. "The southern pass is too exposed. They will have it covered. The lower ravine continues northeast, and there is a secondary track here," he indicated a line on the map, "that descends to the foothills outside their standard patrol range. It will add hours, but it keeps us off the primary roads."

"Hours we can afford," Serathis said. "A patrol we cannot."

"Agreed." He straightened. "There is one other thing." He looked at Kaelor. "The commander's standing orders. What I heard before the passage closed. I have been thinking about what it means beyond the immediate tactical consequence."

"Tell me," Kaelor said.

"Astrythe's forces were positioned precisely at our exit point. Not along the road. Not covering multiple possibilities. Exactly here." Malakor's voice was measured. "That is not tracking a blood signature or predicting a route. That is specific intelligence about where we would emerge, and when. Someone with knowledge of the Labyrinth passages gave her that information. Someone who knew what Elara's power would do."

The silence that followed had a different texture from ordinary quiet. It was the silence of people who trusted each other performing the uncomfortable act of wondering if they should.

"We are a small group," Serathis said, her voice flat. "We address the possibility when we are not standing in the open with pursuit behind us. Not before."

"I am not accusing anyone," Malakor said. "I am naming the reality so it cannot be ignored."

"It is named," Kaelor said. "And Serathis is right. We move first."

Torren, from his perch on the fallen stone, raised one hand without looking away from the ravine. "In full support of moving. Enthusiastically. Immediately."

We moved.

The descent through the lower ravine took two hours, following the secondary track Malakor had identified, single file through terrain that was narrow enough to make conversation impractical and steep enough to demand full attention. The light faded as we walked, the pale afternoon giving way to the blue-gray of early evening, and the cold that came with it was sharp and clean and smelled of stone and distant snow.

I walked behind Malakor and ahead of Kaelor, and I was aware of Kaelor's presence behind me with the same involuntary precision I had been aware of him since the overlook, the specific weight of his footsteps on the loose rock, the occasional brush of his shoulder against mine when the path narrowed, the steadying hand he put against the small of my back once when I misjudged a step and nearly went sideways on a slick section of trail.

He didn't say anything about it. Neither did I.

We emerged from the ravine an hour after dark, onto a broad, flat section of foothills that stretched south toward the distant tree line. The mountain rose behind us, dark against a sky full of hard, cold stars. There were no banners visible. No silver armor catching the moonlight. No sound except wind and the distant movement of something in the scrub that was almost certainly a night animal and not a High Fey scout.

Torren checked both exits anyway.

"Clear," he said, returning with the quiet economy of a man who knew how to move without announcing himself. "For now."

"There is a farmhouse a mile south," Malakor said. "Empty. I scouted this area two seasons ago. The family relocated when the border roads became unsafe. It will serve for tonight."

It did serve. Low-ceilinged and cold, smelling of old hay and damp timber, with two rooms and a hearth that still drew well enough to allow a small fire. Serathis organized the guard rotation with the same flat efficiency she brought to everything, and Talia found a corner to set up her supplies and bullied two of the soldiers into drinking something that made them grimace. Torren disappeared briefly and returned with what appeared to be a length of dried meat from somewhere, which he distributed without explanation or acknowledgment of anyone's curiosity about its origin.

I sat by the fire and let the warmth work on the remaining stiffness in my hands.

Kaelor settled across the hearth from me, exhaustion softening some of the rigid control in his posture. The fire filled the silence between us with something quieter than tension, but no less charged.

"Astrythe wants the union," I said, finally. "Not just me. Not just you. Both of us together, because the prophecy requires both, and she wants to control what happens when the Labyrinth wakes fully."

"Yes."

"Which means every step we take toward each other is a step toward giving her what she needs."

His molten eyes held mine across the fire. "Or a step toward denying her the ability to control it," he said.

"That is a very convenient reframe."

"It is also accurate." He leaned forward slightly, forearms resting on his knees, voice dropping into the register he used when he was saying something he had thought through rather than reaching for it. "Astrythe's power over the Labyrinth depends on controlling both elements. If those elements act of their own will, she loses the advantage. She needs us passive. Captured. Compliant." A pause. "She does not need us choosing."

I looked at the fire for a moment. The logic was sound. That was the infuriating part. "You are telling me that the most defiant thing we can do is exactly what we are already doing."

"I am telling you that Astrythe's plan requires us to be afraid of what we are to each other. She is counting on that fear to make us manageable."

His voice was very steady. "I am not manageable, Elara. And neither are you."

The fire crackled between us, sending a brief scatter of sparks upward toward the low ceiling.

There was something underneath the argument, something that had been building since the overlook, since the passage, since his arm around me in the dark while the mountain groaned and the world tilted, and it was not going to be talked past or strategized away. I had tried that. My body had already made an argument; my caution was losing.

I rose from my seat and crossed to his side of the fire, and he tracked the movement with his eyes without changing his position, waiting, giving me the full choice of what happened next. That was the thing about him that I had never been able to dismiss, not even when I wanted to. He never reached. He waited, and he let me decide, and that specific restraint was more disarming than anything else about him.

I stopped in front of him. "This is reckless," I said.

"Yes."

"It makes us a target."

"We are already a target." His voice was very quiet. "The question is whether we are a target that bends, or one that chooses."

I reached out and put my hand against the side of his jaw, feeling the warmth of his skin and the faint edge of old scar tissue beneath my fingers, and felt him go very still in the way a large and dangerous thing goes still when something reaches for it gently and it is deciding whether to allow that.

He allowed it.

"This is not prophecy," I said. "I need you to understand that. This is not the Labyrinth or the inscription or destiny deciding anything."

"I know." His hand came up and covered mine, large and rough and warm, pressing it gently against his face. "I have known for longer than you have, and I did not need ancient stone to tell me."

I kissed him, and he kissed me back, and there was nothing tentative about it on either side. It was a deliberate act, fully chosen, carrying the weight of everything that had been held back since the mountain passage and the overlook and every charged, careful moment before that. His hands found my waist and drew me down to him, and I went without argument, settling against the solid warmth of his chest while his arms closed around me with a steadiness that felt nothing like captivity and everything like someone who had decided to hold something precious without crushing it.

What followed was not gentle in the way of careful things, but it was deliberate in the way of chosen ones. It was urgent and close and entirely chosen, and for a little while, the war outside the farmhouse ceased to exist.

Afterward, I lay against him in the low firelight, his arm heavy and warm across my ribs, his breathing slow and steady beneath my ear.

"We cannot keep running blind," I said, after a while.

"No." His chest rose and fell. "We need answers before she moves again."

"The murals in the chamber, the vision, the failed ritual. Someone who is older than all of this would know what actually happened. Not Astrythe's version. Not the cult's version. The real history of what the Labyrinth is and what it does to people like me."

"There is one possibility," he said.

"Tell me."

"An oracle. Ancient. She does not belong to any court. She has refused allegiance to the High Fey, to the clans, to every faction that has tried to claim her knowledge." He paused, and the pause carried weight. "She has been called Mother Isyra. She was old when the first beast-clan wars were fought."

I sat up slowly. The name landed like a physical blow, a sudden, cold weight in the pit of my stomach that made my breath catch in my throat. “You know where she is?”

"I know where she was," he said. "Three years ago. She moves, but she leaves traces, and Malakor has contacts who track old knowledge. It is possible."

"Then that is where we go."

He studied me for a moment, and then he nodded, and the decision settled between us with the quiet finality of something that had already been decided and only needed naming.

I dressed and returned to the main room while the guard shift changed outside. Malakor was awake, sitting near the window with his blade across his knees in the posture of a man who had decided sleep was not worth the attempt. He looked up when I entered, and something in his expression registered the decision I was carrying before I said a word.

"We need to find Mother Isyra," I said.

He was quiet for a moment, not surprised, just considering. "She has been sought before," he said. "By rulers, scholars, factions with resources far greater than ours."

"I know."

"She does not answer to power. She does not answer to need. She answers to whatever calculus she alone understands, and she has turned away empires." He looked at me steadily. "I am not saying it cannot be done. I am saying it is not a simple thing."

"Nothing about any of this is simple."

"No." He turned the blade once in his hands, a slow, habitual motion. "If Isyra still lives, there is a reason even the Queen leaves her alone." His voice was flat and certain, carrying the weight of a man who had served the High Fey long enough to know which names made their courts go quiet. "Whatever she knows, Astrythe has decided it is safer to leave her undisturbed than to attempt to extract it."

The fire in the hearth had burned down to coals. Outside, the wind moved through the foothills with a low, continuous sound that reminded me of the mountain's breathing, the deep interior resonance I had felt under my palm before the cliff had opened. The Labyrinth was still there, somewhere beneath everything, patient and old and full of knowledge that people had been killing each other over for centuries.

I was done being the thing they killed each other to possess.

It was time to be the one asking the questions.

"Then we find her," I said.

Malakor held my gaze for a moment. Then he set the blade aside and reached for the map, and his expression settled into the forward-facing focus of a man who had decided the next task was the only one that mattered.

Behind me, Kaelor filled the doorway, his presence as solid and certain as the mountain we had just survived, and I did not need to look to know he was there.

I already knew.

# The Queen's Terms

The first message from High Queen Astrythe arrived wearing a woman's face and a god's patience. It came through the thin air of the abandoned watchpost where we had taken shelter, a shimmer of silver light that bent the shadows into something colder than night. I felt it before I saw it, a pressure against the skin that made the hairs on my arms stand up and the blood in my veins turn sluggish with recognition.

Kaelor had already gone still beside me, his massive frame blocking the worst of the wind that slipped through the broken stones. The others had gone quiet too. Torren's hand had drifted to one of his hidden knives without conscious thought, while Serathis simply straightened her posture as though facing down an enemy required the same discipline as any battlefield. Malakor's expression had gone blank in that particular way that meant he was already calculating exits and casualties both.

The light gathered itself into shape. Astrythe appeared as a projection, her figure suspended in the air between the broken walls, too elegant to belong to any ruin. She wore black silk that moved like liquid shadow, and her hair fell in a cascade of white-gold that caught no light from our meager fire. Her eyes were the worst part. They held entire constellations behind the darkness, and they looked at me the way a collector might examine a rare specimen.

"Little blood-key," she said, her voice carrying the smoothness of someone who had never needed to raise it to be obeyed. "You have been carried from hand to hand by lesser creatures long enough."

I felt the words land like a slap. My fingers found the hilt of my dagger before I had decided to reach for it, and the metal was cold against my palm. "Come closer and call me that again."

Her mouth curved, not quite a smile. "Still so quick to bare your teeth. That spirit will serve you well when you learn to point it at the correct targets."

Kaelor shifted slightly, and the movement drew her attention. His horns caught the firelight, casting long shadows across the stone floor, but he kept his voice measured when he spoke. "You dress rebellion in armor and call it a kingdom."

"And you dress fear in silk and call it civilization," she replied, the words flowing like she had rehearsed them. "How predictable that a beast would mistake conquest for destiny."

The insult rolled off him, but I saw the way his jaw tightened, the slight narrowing of his molten eyes. He was holding himself in check with visible effort, and that restraint made something hot and defiant curl in my chest. She wanted us afraid. She wanted us divided. I refused to give her either.

"I will not repeat my terms," Astrythe continued, turning her attention back to me. "Elara Thorne will come to the Shadow Court of her own will. Kaelor Ashhorn will kneel and accept binding. In exchange, his people will be granted a temporary reprieve from the cleansing that has already begun in the eastern valleys."

The lie was beautiful. It was the kind of offer that sounded reasonable until you examined the edges, where the threats waited like knives wrapped in velvet. I tasted copper in my mouth and realized I had bitten the inside of my cheek.

"My people are not bargaining chips," Kaelor said, each word falling with deliberate weight.

"They are already lost," Astrythe replied, as though she were commenting on the weather rather than the fate of an entire alliance. "The question is whether you will watch them die slowly or quickly. The choice remains yours, though I suspect your attachment to this human has already clouded your judgment."

She knew about the prophecy. That truth settled into my bones like a second weight, heavier than the exhaustion from the passage. She knew what we were to each other, or at least what we could become, and she meant to use it. The knowledge made my skin crawl.

"You speak of prophecy as though it were a chain," I said, surprised by the steadiness in my own voice. "But chains can be broken."

Astrythe's expression shifted, and for the first time something like genuine interest flickered behind those star-filled eyes. "Your mother thought the same thing. She hid you well, buried your bloodline beneath layers of ordinary human misery, hoping the courts would forget what you carried. She was wrong about many things, but her final act was almost clever."

The words hit me like a physical blow. My mother had known. She had known what I was, had hidden me deliberately, and had died without ever telling me why. The grief I had carried for years twisted into something sharper, something that tasted like rage mixed with betrayal.

Kaelor's hand found my wrist, his grip warm and grounding. The touch was public. It was a declaration. I felt Astrythe notice it, felt her catalog the intimacy with the same cold precision she had used to dissect my mother's choices.

"How touching," she murmured. "The beast comforts his key. I wonder if he understands that every moment he spends drawing closer to you only makes the Labyrinth hungrier."

"You want this," I said, the realization cutting through the fog of anger. "You want whatever exists between us. You think you can control it."

"I think I can contain it," she corrected, her voice remaining perfectly calm. "The difference matters more than you realize. Come to me willingly, and I will teach you how to survive what your blood will unleash. Refuse, and you will learn the lesson through suffering instead."

The projection flickered once, a ripple in the silver light that suggested the magic required to maintain it was beginning to strain. Astrythe's form wavered, but her voice remained clear.

"You have until the next moonrise to decide. After that, the eastern valleys will burn, and your warlord will have nothing left to protect."

The light collapsed inward, folding into nothing, and the watchpost felt colder in its absence. No one spoke for several long moments. The fire popped, sending a brief shower of sparks toward the broken ceiling, and I watched them die against the stone.

"I miss when our enemies just stabbed people," Torren said finally, his voice carrying the dry edge that meant he was covering fear with sarcasm. "At least then you knew where the blade was coming from."

"Astrythe does not bargain," Malakor said, his tone flat. "She arranges obedience. That was not an offer. It was a demonstration of reach."

I pulled my wrist free from Kaelor's grip, though the loss of his warmth made something inside me protest. The anger was building now, a slow burn that had nothing to do with the High Queen's words and everything to do with the truth she had wielded like a weapon. My mother had hidden me. My mother had known. And now Astrythe knew more about my own history than I did.

"She wants us afraid of each other," I said, the words coming out sharper than I intended. "She wants us to believe that what we feel is just the prophecy pulling strings."

"She is not wrong about the danger," Kaelor replied, his voice carefully neutral. "The bond between us strengthens the Labyrinth's response. That is a fact we cannot ignore."

"So we ignore each other instead?" The question came out bitter. "We pretend we feel nothing so the Queen can claim us both anyway?"

His eyes met mine across the small space between us, and I saw the same fury I felt reflected there, banked and controlled but burning nonetheless. "I will not let her define what we are to each other."

"Then stop letting her control what we do about it."

The words hung between us, and I felt the shift in the air, the moment when the argument became something else. The others had moved away, giving us the illusion of privacy even though we all knew how thin these walls were. Serathis had taken up a position near the entrance, her back turned with deliberate courtesy. Malakor had found a corner where he could watch both the approach and our conversation without appearing to do either. Torren had disappeared entirely, probably to scout or to give us space, or both.

Kaelor took one step toward me, and the movement was enough to make the air feel charged. "You are angry."

"I am furious." The admission came easier than it should have. "She spoke about my mother like she was a failed experiment. She spoke about you like you were a mistake she could correct. And she expects us to thank her for the opportunity to surrender."

"She expects us to break."

"I will not give her that."

The tension between us had been building for days, weeks, since the first moment he had pulled me out of the courts and refused to treat me like property. It had been building through every careful distance we had maintained, every moment of restraint that had left us both raw and wanting. The Queen's words had only sharpened it, turned it into something that demanded an outlet.

I moved first, but not with urgency, not this time.

The anger was still there, but cleaner now, stripped down into something colder and far more deliberate. I stepped into his space, put my hand against his chest, felt the steady power beneath fur, scar, and muscle, and held his gaze until he understood exactly what I was choosing.

“This is still reckless,” I said.

“Yes.”

“Good.”

Something changed in his expression then, subtle but unmistakable, some final restraint giving way.

The kiss that followed was slower than the fury between us warranted, and somehow that made it infinitely more dangerous. Every measured touch felt intentional. Every second of restraint sharpened the anticipation instead of easing it.

His hand slid along my jaw, then down the line of my throat with enough pressure to make my breath hitch, and the control in the movement made heat coil lower in my body far faster than urgency ever could.

“You are angry,” he murmured against my skin.

“Yes.”

“Good.”

The word sent a shiver through me.

When his hands moved beneath my clothing, they did not pull me flush against him. Instead, he stepped behind me, his massive chest a solid wall of heat pressing against my spine. He didn't force me down; he waited, his breath hot against the nape of my neck, his large hands resting on my hips with a heavy, grounding pressure that left the choice entirely mine. I leaned back into him, yielding to the solid weight of his body, my hands reaching behind to grip his muscular thighs. By the time I bent forward slightly over the cold stone ledge, using it to anchor myself, this no longer felt like rage.

It felt like a decision.

A dangerous one.

And decisions are harder to regret than impulses.

When he entered me from behind, it was not with violence or haste, but with a deliberate, agonizingly slow certainty that stole the breath from my lungs all the same. The sheer reality of him behind me, the deliberate control in every movement, stole the breath from my lungs. The intensity of what we were choosing in that moment made my hands grip the rough edges of the stone slab ahead of me, my knuckles turning white as I pushed back against him, demanding more of his weight.

The pace he set afterward was merciless in its precision rather than its force, his hands anchoring my hips, guiding each deep, heavy thrust. Every movement was measured enough to drag every reaction out of me, his thick shaft sliding against my highly sensitive walls until restraint became its own kind of torment. He leaned over me, his massive chest pressing down against my back, his horns framing my face as he growled low in his throat, the sound vibrating straight through my bones.

I pressed my cheek against the cold stone to muffle the shameless, high-pitched sounds he was pulling from me with every relentless stroke.

"Elara," he said, rough and low, and hearing my name in that voice nearly undid me.

When release finally came, triggered by the friction of his heavy body driving deep inside me, it felt less like surrender and more like impact, sharp enough to leave me trembling against the stone while he shuddered violently, spilling himself inside me. The world slowly reassembled itself around the broken stone and dying fire as he held me tightly against him, his breathing ragged against my neck.

When he finally let me go, my legs were unreliable, and his hands stayed at my waist, gently turning me around to face him until he was certain I could stand.

Neither of us spoke immediately.

We didn't need to.

Kaelor studied my face for a moment, and I saw the calculation there, the weighing of risks against the need for truth. Finally, he nodded, and the decision settled between us with the weight of something inevitable.

We rejoined the others, and if any of them noticed the change in the air between us, they were wise enough not to comment. Serathis continued her watch at the entrance with the same rigid discipline she brought to everything. Malakor had moved to the map we had spread across a fallen stone, his fingers tracing routes with the focused attention of a man already planning our next move.

"We need to find Mother Isyra," I said, addressing the group without preamble.

Malakor looked up, his black eyes meeting mine with that unflinching directness that made most people uncomfortable. He was quiet for a moment, considering rather than surprised. "She has been sought before. By rulers and scholars with resources far greater than ours. She does not answer to power or to need. She answers to her own understanding of what the worlds require."

"I am not asking for permission," I said. "I am stating a direction."

"I am not denying the need," he replied, his tone remaining neutral. "I am warning you that she is not a solution. She is a threshold. Crossing it means accepting whatever truth she offers, whether we are prepared to hear it or not."

Torren appeared from the shadows near the broken northern wall, his russet hair catching the firelight as he moved into the circle of warmth. "I miss when our enemies just stabbed people," he repeated, the words carrying the same dry humor as before. "At least then you knew the blade was coming. This feels like walking into a trap we designed ourselves."

"It is not a trap," Malakor said, though his voice carried no conviction. "It is a gamble. Isyra does not deal in comfort. She deals in consequence."

Serathis turned from her position at the entrance, her clouded eye catching the light as she faced us. "If we seek her, we do so with open eyes. She will not protect us from what she reveals. She will simply show us the shape of the blade that has always been aimed at our throats."

The words should have been discouraging. Instead, they felt like the first honest assessment I had heard since Astrythe's projection had vanished. We were not seeking salvation. We were seeking truth, and the difference mattered.

"We move at first light," Kaelor said, the command settling over the group with the weight of authority. "The route to Isyra's last known location will take us through the old passes. It will not be easy. The terrain is sacred to the clans, and the dead are buried there in numbers that make even our strongest warriors uneasy."

"I have walked among the horn-stones before," Serathis said, her voice carrying the flat certainty of experience. "The dead do not trouble the living who come with purpose. It is the living who trouble each other."

Malakor rolled the map carefully, his movements precise. "The Queen will not wait for our decision. She will continue her campaign regardless. Seeking Isyra buys us knowledge at the cost of time."

"Time we were going to lose anyway," I said. "At least this way we choose what we lose it to."

The watchpost settled into the rhythms of a temporary camp, with guards posted and watches arranged. I found a corner where the stones still held some warmth from the fire, and Kaelor settled nearby, his presence a solid weight in the darkness. The others had given us space again, a courtesy that felt both welcome and exposing.

"Your mother hid you," he said quietly, the words not quite a question.

"She did." The admission tasted like ash. "And now I have to decide whether that makes her a coward or a strategist."

"It makes her someone who loved you enough to try."

The kindness in the statement made my throat tight. I had spent years believing my mother had simply been another victim of the border wars, another casualty of a conflict that cared nothing for the people caught between armies. The truth that she had acted with intention, that she had chosen to hide me rather than fight openly, changed the shape of my grief into something more complicated.

"Astrythe will use that truth against me," I said. "She will twist it until I doubt every memory I have of her."

"Only if you let her."

I looked at him, at the massive form that should have terrified me and instead had become the one constant in a world that kept shifting beneath my feet. "You are remarkably calm for someone who just heard a queen threaten to burn his people."

"I am not calm." The admission came with a slight edge to his voice. "I am focused. There is a difference."

"And what does that focus tell you?"

"That we cannot win by playing her game. She controls the board, the pieces, and the rules. The only way to survive is to change what game we are playing."

The logic was sound. It was also terrifying. Changing the game meant stepping into unknown territory, following paths that even the clans considered dangerous. It meant trusting an oracle who might give us answers we did not want to hear.

"Then we find Isyra," I said. "And we learn what the Queen has been hiding from us."

Kaelor reached out, his hand covering mine in the darkness. The touch was simple, almost chaste compared to what we had just shared against the wall. It was also a promise, a declaration that whatever came next, we would face it together rather than apart.

The night deepened around us, the cold settling into the stones with the thoroughness of winter's approach. I closed my eyes and tried to quiet the racing of my thoughts, but the Queen's words kept circling back. My mother had hidden me. My mother had known what I carried. And now that knowledge was being used as a weapon against us both.

Sleep came in fragments, interrupted by the sound of guards changing shifts and the distant howl of wind through the passes. Each time I woke, Kaelor was there, a solid presence that kept the worst of the fear at bay. When dawn finally crept through the broken walls, I felt no more rested than I had the night before, but the decision had settled into something solid.

We would seek Mother Isyra.

We would learn the truth.

And whatever the Queen had planned for us, we would meet it on our own terms.

The first light of morning found us already moving, the watchpost abandoned behind us as we descended into the passes that would take us toward answers. The weight of the Queen's threat hung over us all, but beneath it ran a current of something else. Defiance. Purpose. The knowledge that we had chosen this path rather than having it forced upon us.

Kaelor's hand brushed mine as we walked, a brief contact that carried more weight than any words could hold. I did not pull away. The Queen wanted us to be afraid of what we were becoming. She wanted us to believe that every step toward each other was a step toward our own destruction.

She was wrong.

She wanted fear. Submission. Distance. She was getting none of them.

# The Woman Beneath the Mountain

The path to Mother Isyra's sanctuary began with bones.

I stepped carefully around the intentional markers—not scattered remnants or the careless dead of battle, but horn-stones driven deep into the frozen earth at intervals. Each one was carved with heavy clan sigils, and I had to duck my head slightly to avoid brushing against the bleached skull of a prey animal crowning the closest marker. Beside it, a braided rope threaded with small carved beads swayed in the freezing wind, brushing against my shoulder as I passed. I paused, my boot heel catching on a fragment of an old weapon half-buried in the frost, its metal long since turned to rust-colored lace under the elements.

I pulled my cloak tighter against the mountain cold and watched the warriors ahead of me. Kaelor's men, hardened veterans who had walked through fire and siege and the particular brutality of the clans' long wars, were moving differently here. Slower. More deliberate. Their voices had dropped to nothing, and even Torren, who had maintained a steady stream of quiet commentary since we left the abandoned watchpost at dawn, had gone silent when we crossed into the burial grounds proper.

The cold up here had teeth. Every breath came out as vapor, and the stone beneath our boots was laced with frost that cracked and shifted with each step. The peaks above us were lost in cloud, and the sky between them was the pale, washed-out gray of old iron.

"How far?" I asked Serathis, keeping my voice low without quite knowing why. The silence demanded it.

She did not glance back at me. Her war armor caught the flat morning light, etched clan sigils dulled by weather and use. "Far enough that you will understand what you are asking before we arrive."

That was not an answer. I had learned it was also Serathis's version of one.

Kaelor walked ahead of us both, and I studied him without meaning to. He moved through the burial grounds differently than he moved through a war camp or a fortress. The command was still there, that absolute, unthinking authority that made his warriors instinctively clear space. But underneath it was something else, something heavier that settled across his shoulders like a second cloak. He paused twice at horn-stones, not speaking, not touching them, simply stopping long enough to acknowledge them before continuing. No one else did this. Only him.

I moved up beside Serathis. "What is he doing?"

She kept her gaze forward. "Paying respect." A pause. "These are not strangers to him. Many of the dead here fought under the old alliance. Some died in campaigns he led."

The weight of that settled into me slowly. I had understood, in an abstract way, that Kaelor had built his coalition through war, that every scar on his body and every fractured negotiation in his history had cost something real. But watching him stand silent before a carved horn-stone in the mountain cold made the abstraction collapse into something immediate and human. These were his dead. His people's dead. And the homeland he was fighting to protect was not a political concept for him. It was a debt.

Torren appeared at my left shoulder, his breath fogging in the air. "I dislike places where the rocks feel judgmental," he murmured, his voice stripped of its usual sharpness. He was watching the burial grounds with an expression that suggested he was not entirely joking.

"They are not judging you," Serathis said flatly. "They have no interest in you at all."

"Somehow that is worse."

Malakor said nothing. He had said almost nothing since we set out, moving along the flank of the group with the measured, economical pace of a man who had learned long ago that silence was its own form of armor. His storm-gray face was unreadable, his silver hair pulled back with severe practicality. He was watching the ridgeline above us, not the burial markers below. Some old instinct keeping him focused on threats rather than history.

The horn-stones grew denser as we climbed, the path narrowing between them until we moved in single file. I noticed the carvings more closely now. Not only sigils. Faces. Simplified, stylized, but unmistakably intentional, the features of the dead preserved in stone by whoever had buried them. Some stones were old enough that the carvings had blurred with weather. Others were newer, the lines still sharp. One bore the shape of a female minotaur, her horn-crest detailed with a precision that spoke of grief too specific to be ritual.

Serathis noticed me looking at it. "This is not a place for lies," she said quietly. "Even silent ones. Whatever you carry into Isyra's sanctuary, she will find it."

"I carry a great deal."

"Then you will have a great deal to answer for." She said it without cruelty. "She does not offer comfort. She offers truth. Truth usually costs something."

I had been told this already. It felt different up here, surrounded by the careful record of generations of dead, with the mountain cold pressing down and Kaelor's silent grief visible in every pause along the path. Isyra's truth would not arrive in a warm room with soft light. It would arrive here, in the same space where everything real and permanent eventually ended up, carved in stone and left for the wind.

The sanctuary appeared without announcement.

I had expected something grand, some carved entrance or towering structure that announced its own importance. Instead, the path simply curved around a shoulder of rock, and there it was: a low building pressed against the mountainside as though it had grown there rather than been built, its walls made from the same stone as the peak above it, its roof slanted and covered in moss and frost. A single column of smoke rose from somewhere inside, thin and pale against the gray sky. The door was old wood, iron-banded, and slightly open.

Nothing about it suggested power. Everything about it felt like it.

Kaelor stopped at the threshold. The warriors with us halted further back, and I noticed that none of them made any move to approach. Even Serathis stayed a few paces behind, her posture rigid with something that was not quite reluctance but was not comfortable ease either.

"She already knows we are here," Kaelor said. His voice was level, but the usual certainty in it had been replaced by something more careful.

The door swung open before any of us moved toward it.

Mother Isyra was smaller than I had expected. She sat on a low wooden chair beside a fire built in a wide stone hearth, her feet tucked beneath her robes, her white-braided hair falling over both shoulders in uneven lengths threaded with bone charms and carved stones that clicked softly when she turned her head. Her skin was the deep weathered brown of old bark, marked with ritual ink that had blurred with age into something closer to shadow than pattern. Her eyes were clouded, white as winter sky, sightless in any physical sense.

She was looking directly at me.

The sensation was deeply unpleasant.

"You smell of iron, fear, and a king who has forgotten how not to want," she said. Her voice was unhurried, dry, and carried the precise enunciation of someone who had long since stopped bothering to soften what she said. "Come inside. All of you. The mountain cold is wasted on manners."

The interior was small and dense with presence: scrolls stacked on low shelves beside dried herbs, clay vessels sealed with wax, stones arranged in patterns on the floor that may have been decorative or may have been something else entirely. The smoke from the fire smelled of incense and something older beneath it, something mineral and cold, like deep water over ancient rock.

Kaelor had to duck through the doorway. His horns came within a breath of the ceiling beams, and the room shrank considerably with him in it. Isyra tilted her head at the sound of his entrance.

"Kaelor Ashhorn," she said. "You have grown heavier since the last time you stood in my doorway."

"It has been twenty years," he replied.

"I know how long it has been." She gestured toward the floor near the fire. "Sit. You tower, and it irritates me."

He sat. Without argument, without ceremony, with the ease of someone who understood that some authority was simply older than his own. I found a low bench near the wall. Serathis and Malakor positioned themselves near the door, and Torren tucked himself into a corner with the practiced invisibility of a man who had survived many dangerous rooms by making himself furniture.

Isyra's clouded gaze moved through the space, landing on each of us in turn with an attention that had nothing to do with sight. When it reached me again, it stayed.

"You have come because the Queen has shown you her teeth," she said.

"Among other reasons," I said.

"Must everyone insist on speaking of me like I am an object?" The words came out before I had fully decided to say them.

The corner of Isyra's mouth curved, dry and sharp. "Then stop standing between worlds." She folded her hands in her lap, the bone charms in her hair clicking once as she settled. "What you are has a name. It has had many names, depending on the age and the people doing the naming. Catalyst is the most recent. It is also the least accurate."

The fire crackled. Nobody else spoke.

"You are not a key," Isyra continued, her voice carrying the same unhurried certainty it had held since we entered. "You are a junction. Your blood does not only open the Labyrinth's doors. It can choose which ones stay sealed. The difference is considerable, and those who hunt you have understood only half of what you are. The useful half, from their perspective."

I processed that slowly. Astrythe, who had spoken about my blood with the precision of someone cataloging tools, who had described me as a possession mislaid rather than a person making choices. Veltheris, whose name I had only heard in the careful, lowered tones people reserved for catastrophes. Both of them wanted me for my blood. Both of them understood what I could open.

Neither of them, apparently, had fully understood what I could close.

"Astrythe tried to control the Labyrinth once," Isyra said. "This was before your mother's time. Before the current age of her empire. She believed that if she could hold the junction stable, she could use it to reshape the borders between the realms, to expand fey territory into spaces previously inaccessible." A pause. "She failed. The Labyrinth does not respond to command. It responds to blood. And her blood was not the right kind."

"And Veltheris," Kaelor said. He had not moved since sitting, his massive frame utterly still.

Isyra turned her sightless gaze toward him. "Speak plainly," she said.

"You first," he replied.

A beat of silence. Then something shifted in her expression, the dry edge of someone genuinely surprised. She inclined her head slightly, an acknowledgment between equals that felt significant coming from her.

"Veltheris wants to complete what Astrythe could not," she said. "But his intention is not control. He wants dissolution. He believes the separation between worlds is a structural flaw, that existence itself would be truer without the boundaries that currently hold it in shape." She said it calmly, the way one might describe a flood or a fire, a natural disaster rather than a choice. "He has spent centuries positioning himself to use the junction when the right blood became available. He did not create you. But he watched your bloodline for a very long time."

The incense smoke moved slowly toward the ceiling. I could feel the mountain cold pressing against the walls from outside, held back by nothing more than old stone and a small fire.

"They are enemies," I said. "Astrythe and Veltheris."

"Profoundly," Isyra agreed. "They want entirely different outcomes. And yet both roads require you." She let that sit for a moment. "You are the only point on which their interests converge. Which means you are the most dangerous position on the board. Not because of what you are. Because of what you can choose to do."

"Prophecy," Kaelor said. A single word, carrying the weight of a question.

Isyra made a short sound, not quite a dismissal, not quite a laugh. "Prophecy is a coward's name for consequence. People speak of blood and horn as though the stars themselves arranged it. They did not. Power reflects the will of those who hold it. What you are is not your fate. It is your capacity. What you do with it remains entirely your own."

Something loosened in my chest at that, a knot I had not entirely noticed carrying since Astrythe had spoken about my mother, since the revelation that I had been hidden deliberately, that my blood had been known and feared before I was old enough to understand what fear was.

Isyra's head tilted slightly, as though she had heard the loosening.

"There is one more thing," she said, and the quality of her voice changed, becoming quieter, more deliberate. Her clouded eyes settled on Kaelor. "The bond between you and this woman. It is not caused by the Labyrinth. But the Labyrinth responds to it. Every time you deepen what exists between you, the junction becomes more sensitive. More active. Those who know how to read the signs will be able to feel it."

The fire popped. Kaelor said nothing. I did not look at him.

"That does not mean you should stop," Isyra added, with the flat practicality of someone describing weather rather than desire. "It means you should understand the cost. Power is never free, and connection is power whether you intend it to be or not."

The silence that settled after that was complicated. I was acutely aware of Serathis near the door, of the careful stillness in her posture that suggested she had filed this information away with the same precision she applied to military intelligence. I was acutely aware of Kaelor's breathing, measured and steady, giving nothing away.

And I was acutely aware of how much I did not want to discuss any of this in front of witnesses.

Isyra rose from her chair with the slow deliberateness of great age and crossed to the fire, crouching before it and feeding a small piece of wood to the flames. The bone charms in her hair clicked with the movement.

"Come here," she said, without turning her head. The instruction was clearly directed at me.

I crossed the room and crouched beside her. The fire was warm against my face, the incense stronger this close to the hearth.

"Give me your hand," she said.

I hesitated for less than a second before I held it out. Her fingers closed around my wrist, and her grip was dry and surprisingly strong, the bones of her hand visible beneath the skin like something architectural. She turned my palm upward and pressed her thumb against the pulse point there.

The room did not disappear. There was no dramatic shift, no sudden darkness or blinding light. Instead, the fire simply became the center of everything, and around its edges, images began to form in the smoke, not quite visible, not quite imagined, somewhere in the uncertain space between the two.

A woman I recognized in the shape of her hands and the line of her jaw, though I had never seen her clearly in any memory I trusted. My mother. She was running, her dark hair unbound, her arms wrapped around something she was carrying. A child. The child's face was turned away, but the recognition that settled into my bones was absolute and devastating.

The scene shifted. A room I did not know, firelit, full of documents and low voices. Valerius, younger, his hair darker, his hands steadier than I had ever seen them. He was speaking to someone across a table, his posture the careful, eager lean of a man offering something he hoped would be accepted. Across from him, the suggestion of a fey courtier, pale and still, watching him with the patient attention of someone who already knew what was being offered was worth taking.

My mother's name. Her bloodline. Her location.

The room shifted again. Astrythe's agents moving through streets I did not recognize, arriving too late at a house already emptied, the fire still warm in the hearth but the inhabitants gone. My mother had run before they arrived. She had known they were coming because someone had warned her, some final mercy from a source the vision did not make clear.

And then, at the edge of the smoke-image, barely present, a figure that stood apart from all the others. Tall and unnaturally thin, wrapped in layered robes, his face turned toward the scene with academic interest rather than urgency. Watching my mother's flight as though it were a calculation he had already accounted for. Veltheris. Not acting. Not intervening. Simply observing, and noting, and filing away what he learned for a future he was patient enough to wait for.

Isyra released my wrist.

The smoke was only smoke again.

I became aware that I was breathing too fast, the cold mountain air too sharp in my lungs, the firelight too bright against eyes that were suddenly stinging. The vision had lasted only seconds by any real measure of time. It felt like I had been inside it for an hour.

"Your uncle did not sell you first," Isyra said, her voice steady and without apology. "He sold your mother."

The words did not land the way a blow lands. They landed the way a foundation shifts, slowly, the damage spreading outward from a center that had seemed solid until the moment it was not. Everything I had understood about my own history rearranged itself around a new fact, and none of the pieces fit in quite the same places they had before.

My mother had not simply been a victim of the border wars. She had been specifically hunted, specifically betrayed by family, specifically targeted by people who had known what she carried and wanted it. She had run. She had hidden me. And she had done all of it knowing the cost, because someone had told her what Valerius had done and she had run anyway, and hidden me anyway, and chosen to disappear rather than let what I was become a weapon in someone else's hands.

She had not abandoned me.

She had protected me with the only thing she had left.

I pressed my free hand against the hearthstone and focused on the texture of it under my palm, rough and cold and very real. The grief I had carried for years, the one shaped like abandonment and loss and a child left behind, was changing into something that had no clean name. It was still grief. But it was also something closer to awe.

Behind me, I heard Kaelor move. Not toward me, not yet, but the shift in the room's air was unmistakable, his attention sharpening and fixing on the line of my shoulders with an intensity I could feel without seeing.

Isyra straightened and returned to her chair as though she had done nothing more consequential than tend a fire. She settled her hands in her lap, the bone charms going still.

"The betrayal is older than you knew," she said. "That does not make it larger. It makes it clearer." She paused. "Your mother understood what she was. She chose to give you the chance to discover what you are on your own terms. Whether you honor that choice is now your own business."

Malakor spoke from near the door, his voice as flat and precise as always. "The Queen's timeline. The cult's movements. Are they connected?"

Isyra's head turned toward him with the unhurried attention she gave everything. "Veltheris is moving. The Labyrinth's heart has been quiet for generations, but the seals are old and the pressure against them has been building since Astrythe's failed attempt generations ago. He has been patient. He is becoming less so." She folded her hands. "Astrythe knows he is moving. She wants to bind what she cannot control before he can reach it. Both of them need the junction. Both of them are running out of time to acquire it peacefully." The dry edge returned to her voice. "For varying definitions of peacefully."

"And Draevok," Serathis said from the door, her voice carrying the clipped directness of someone who had been thinking through military implications since the moment we arrived. "The rebellion within the clans. If it fractures the alliance before we can act—"

"Then both your enemies will have the opening they need," Isyra finished. "Divided, you are manageable. United, you are a problem they cannot solve cleanly." She did not offer comfort around this. She simply stated it. "You should return to your people before the fracture becomes irreparable."

Kaelor rose. The movement was controlled, decisive, and I recognized the shift in him, the warlord reassembling himself around whatever weight he had carried quietly through the burial grounds. He looked at Isyra with an expression I had no good word for, something that acknowledged a debt without diminishing it.

Isyra looked back at him with her sightless eyes.

"There is a price," she said.

The room went still.

"The knowledge I have given you tonight is not free. It never was." She turned her clouded gaze to me, and the sensation of being seen by someone who could not see remained as deeply uncomfortable as it had been from the moment I walked through the door. "The junction must be opened willingly, by the blood that carries it. Not the Labyrinth's full power. A sealed memory within the blood itself. You open it, and you gain the ability to sense sealed Labyrinth gates, to feel their locations the way you feel the pressure of weather before rain." Her voice remained level. "But the Labyrinth will also be able to sense you more clearly than it already does. Power is never contained to one direction."

Torren made a quiet sound from his corner. Not words. Just the sound of someone deeply unhappy with the way an evening was developing.

I looked at Isyra. At her ancient, weathered face, her ritual-marked hands, her bone-threaded braids. I thought about my mother running through streets in the dark with a child in her arms, making choices that cost everything so that child might one day stand somewhere and choose for herself.

"All right," I said.

Kaelor's gaze moved to me, sharp and immediate, but he did not speak. He trusted me to make this choice. That trust sat in the air between us, quiet and solid as the horn-stones outside.

Isyra held out her hand again. I placed mine in it.

This time, she pressed something cold and precise against the center of my palm, a carved stone seal, its surface etched with symbols I did not recognize. The cold spread upward through my hand, along my arm, moving through my blood the way winter moves through water, slow and absolute. There was a moment of resistance, something deep and private that had been sealed for longer than I had been alive, and then it opened.

It did not hurt.

That surprised me more than if it had.

What came instead was awareness, vast and directional, like developing a new sense organ overnight. I could feel the mountain beneath us, not as stone and cold but as structure, as sealed places, heavy with old purpose, doors that had not been opened in generations pressing against my new awareness like landmarks I had never been able to see before. There were three of them within range. Three sealed Labyrinth gates, their locations as clear to me now as the firelight on the walls.

Isyra withdrew her hand.

The sensation remained, quieter now, settled into the background of my awareness like a sound you stop noticing only when it stops. I realized, with a chill that had nothing to do with the mountain air, that it was not only working in one direction. Something beneath the peaks, vast and patient and impossible to assign any human quality to, had just turned its attention toward me the way a sleeper turns toward sound in the night.

Not awake. Not moving. But aware.

I stood up slowly and kept my face as steady as I could manage.

"We should move quickly," I said.

Kaelor was already moving.

# The Price of Blood

By the time we left Isyra's sanctuary, betrayal had become something far less clean than a knife. I had not known it could be an inheritance.

The word turned in my mind as I stood outside Isyra's sanctuary, the mountain cold pressing against every exposed inch of skin, the smoke from the old woman's fire still faint in my nostrils. My hand still held the ghost of that carved stone seal against my palm, and beneath the peaks, three sealed gates pulsed with a slow, patient awareness that had not existed in my perception an hour ago.

Something vast had noticed me. It had not moved. It did not need to.

Kaelor was already past the threshold and standing in the snow, and the warriors who had waited at a respectful distance were stirring, reading his posture the way soldiers read weather. Serathis was at his shoulder within moments, her voice low and clipped, already working through the logistics of the return journey. Malakor had positioned himself on the high side of the path, studying the ridgeline with his usual expectation of ambush.

Torren fell into step beside me as I moved away from the door.

"I preferred mysteries," he said, his voice stripped of its usual brightness, "before they began dismantling everyone in the vicinity."

"Go stand near someone else," I said.

"There is no one else who looks like they need company as desperately as they claim not to." He glanced at me sideways. His crooked grin was absent, and without it his face looked older, sharper. "Are you all right?"

The question was genuine enough that I could not immediately dismiss it.

"No," I said. "But I will be."

He accepted that without pressing further, which was the most useful thing he had done all evening.

The path back through the burial grounds was the same stone and frost as before, the horn-stones standing in their patient rows, the carved faces blurred or sharp depending on how recently grief had arrived at this mountain. I moved through them differently now. Every step felt weighted with a specific, private knowledge that had no clean way to settle.

My mother had run through darkness with me in her arms, knowing exactly what Valerius had done and doing it anyway, choosing the cold and the flight and whatever end came after, because the alternative was letting me become what Astrythe and Veltheris both wanted me to be. A junction, controlled by someone else's hands.

She had not abandoned me.

That should have been a relief. It was, underneath everything else. But grief does not simply transform because its shape changes. It reorganizes, and the reorganization hurts in different places than the original wound.

Kaelor came up beside me without announcement, his footfall nearly silent despite his size. He said nothing. He simply matched his pace to mine and walked, his presence as solid and certain as the mountain itself.

I stared at the path ahead.

"She didn't leave me," I said.

His voice was quiet and even. "No."

"She saved me."

"Yes."

Two words. No elaboration, no gentle expansion toward comfort, no suggestion that what I was feeling should be reframed into something tidier. He simply confirmed what I had said and let it stand, and somehow that was more bearable than any amount of carefully chosen sympathy would have been.

I pressed my teeth together until the tightness in my throat eased.

"Valerius knew," I said. "He knew what she was. He knew what I would be. He sold her to people who would have turned her into a tool, and when that wasn't enough, he eventually found a way to sell me too."

Kaelor's jaw shifted, the muscle there tightening once before releasing.

"Yes," he said again, the single word carrying a weight I recognized as controlled fury, the kind he kept in check not because it was small but because releasing it would not serve any immediate purpose.

"I want him to pay for it," I said. The words came out flat and certain, without the heat of immediate rage. Something colder than rage. "Not because of what he did to me. For what he did to her."

Kaelor did not answer right away. When he did, his voice was measured and deliberate. "He will."

It was not a promise designed to soothe me. It sounded like a fact being stated in advance of its occurrence, and I believed it the way I believed in the cold and the stone beneath my feet.

We walked in silence after that. The burial grounds thinned and then fell behind us, and the path began its long descent toward the lower passes. The sky had moved from iron gray to the deep, bruised purple of a mountain evening, and the first stars were beginning to press through in the east.

Behind us, I heard Isyra's door close.

I had not heard her move toward it. I had not heard it creak. It simply closed, and the sanctuary was sealed again, and we were back on the mountain with everything she had given us and every price we had paid for it.

The grief was still there. It would be there for a long time, I suspected. But underneath it, something else had taken root, quiet and stubborn. Not comfort exactly. Something closer to clarity. My mother had understood what she was and had chosen what to do with it. She had not been defeated by the knowledge that her blood made her a target. She had used the time that knowledge bought her to make sure I had a chance to choose something different.

I intended to.

Serathis dropped back from her position near the front of the group and fell into step on my other side. She did not look at me directly, her gaze still moving across the terrain with professional habit.

"Isyra's warning about Draevok," she said, her voice low enough that only I and Kaelor would hear. "We need to assess the situation before we arrive. If he has moved during our absence, we cannot walk back into the encampment without intelligence."

"Torren," Kaelor said, without raising his voice.

Torren appeared from somewhere near the middle of the group with the aggrieved expression of a man who had been hoping to avoid being assigned anything. "I am already composing my objections," he said.

"Ride ahead," Kaelor said. "Full assessment. Do not engage. Return to us before the last pass."

"Naturally." He looked at Kaelor with the particular weariness of a man who had made his peace with his own usefulness. "You know, most commanders express gratitude occasionally. For morale."

"Your morale is fine," Kaelor said. "Go."

Torren went, peeling away from the group with a speed that suggested he was, despite all theatrical protest, genuinely capable and motivated when the situation required it.

Malakor appeared at Kaelor's shoulder, his expression unchanged from its baseline of grim assessment. "Veltheris is moving now," he said. "If Isyra's read is accurate, we have days, not weeks. The cult's infiltration capacity is significant. We should assume any breach in our perimeter has already been exploited."

"Noted," Kaelor said.

The three gates I could feel beneath the mountain pulsed faintly at the edges of my new awareness, distinct from each other, each with its own particular texture, old and sealed and heavy with purpose. I had no words yet for the quality of that sensation. It was like learning to hear a sound that had always existed but that my ears had not previously been built to register.

Something beneath the mountains turned with it, that vast and patient attention, not threatening yet, not awake, but undeniably aware. Present in the way a deep current is present beneath still water.

I kept my face steady and focused on the path.

We made camp briefly at the last pass before the descent into Kaelor's territory, waiting for Torren's return. The fire was small and practical, and no one spoke much. Malakor cleaned his blades with the systematic focus of a man who needed his hands occupied. Serathis reviewed the route back with one of the senior warriors, her voice a low, continuous murmur of tactical assessment. The remaining warriors ate in silence and maintained their positions at the camp's perimeter with the quiet discipline of people who understood the stakes of inattention.

I sat near the fire with my knees drawn up and let myself feel the weight of the evening.

Kaelor settled beside me without ceremony, close enough that the warmth of him cut through the mountain cold. Not touching. But present in every way that mattered.

"You do not have to hold all of it right now," he said, his voice pitched low enough for only me.

I exhaled slowly. "I know."

"But you are going to anyway."

"Old habit."

He was quiet a moment. The fire snapped between us.

"She was brave," he said. "Your mother. What she chose cost everything."

The grief rose sharply, unexpected after I had thought I had it contained, and I let it come because fighting it would have been exhausting and pointless and there was no audience here worth performing control for. My eyes stung. I did not cry, not fully, but the pressure of it was real and I did not pretend otherwise.

Kaelor did not move to fix it. He did not offer words designed to redirect the feeling into something more manageable. He simply sat beside me in the dark and the cold, his shoulder near mine, his breathing steady, and let the grief be what it was until it found its own level.

That was, I thought, the most honest kind of comfort I had ever been given.

After a while, the tightness in my chest eased. Not gone. Just rearranged into something I could carry.

"Isyra told you something before we left," I said. "When she spoke to you alone. About not being able to protect me from becoming what I am."

His gaze moved to the fire. "She said I cannot protect you from becoming what you are. I told her I could protect you while you choose it."

I absorbed that. The distinction mattered, and he knew it mattered, and the fact that he had made it without prompting settled into my chest alongside the grief and the new awareness of sealed gates and the memory of my mother running through dark streets with me in her arms.

"She wasn't wrong," I said.

"No," he agreed. "Neither was I."

I turned my head to look at him directly. His profile was lit by the fire, the strong lines of his face, the fractured tip of his ivory horn, the scar that crossed near his eye. The molten gold of his gaze was fixed on the flames with an expression I was learning to read as something close to fierce, careful wanting, the kind that had learned to hold itself at a disciplined distance because the alternative was too large to manage.

I understood that particular architecture of feeling better than I wanted to admit.

"Thank you," I said. "For pulling me back from the vision before it took me under."

He looked at me then, and the quality of his attention shifted in that way it sometimes did, becoming more direct, less guarded. "You were shaking," he said. "The magic was pulling too hard."

"I know. I felt it." I had felt the vision beginning to consume rather than show, the smoke and memory reaching past observation into something that wanted to absorb me entirely. His hand had closed around my arm at precisely the right moment, warm and impossibly grounding, and the vision had released its hold with a reluctance I could still feel at the edges of my awareness. "You have good timing."

"With you," he said, "I am always paying attention."

The honesty of it landed with more force than he had probably intended. Or perhaps he had intended exactly that much, and I was simply not yet accustomed to being the subject of that kind of direct, unselfconscious attention from someone who meant it without condition or agenda.

I looked back at the fire before my face betrayed anything I was not ready to name.

Torren returned before the hour was out, his horse blowing hard from a pushed pace, his expression carrying the specific tightness of a man delivering news he had hoped to be wrong about.

"Draevok has been busy," he said, dropping from the saddle and speaking to Kaelor directly. "He has not moved against the command structure outright. But he has consolidated. His warriors are positioned throughout the encampment in a pattern that is not casual. He has been receiving visitors from at least three other clan war-bands. Word has spread about the oracle visit, the prophecy talk, the human woman, the power involved." He glanced at me briefly, without apology. "The mood is not warm."

"How many of the garrison have shifted toward his faction?" Serathis asked.

"Enough to matter. Not enough to be decisive. Yet." Torren paused. "He will push when we return. He has been waiting for it."

Kaelor stood, his full height drawing the eye of every warrior in the camp without any particular effort. "Then we will not make him wait," he said.

The descent was fast and cold, and we reached the encampment well after dark. The fires were lit throughout the sprawling settlement of tents and temporary structures that had grown up around the fortress's outer walls, and the shapes of warriors moved between them with a tension that was immediately legible. Too many grouped conversations breaking off as we passed. Too many eyes tracking Kaelor's movement with assessment rather than simple attention. Too many deliberate gaps in the usual easy noise of an encampment at rest.

Draevok was waiting near the central fire. He had not staged anything theatrical. He had simply positioned himself where he could not be avoided, his massive frame silhouetted against the flames, his war armor undecorated and practical, his expression carrying the flat certainty of a man who had decided what needed to be said and was prepared to say it regardless of the consequences.

Beside him stood two clan commanders I recognized from earlier councils, their presence making Draevok's position explicit without requiring any declaration.

Kaelor stopped. His warriors fanned out behind him with the unconscious precision of people who had learned to read the terrain of political confrontation the same way they read a battlefield.

"Ashhorn," Draevok said. His voice was low and carried without effort, the voice of a man accustomed to being heard across distances. "You went to the oracle without council consultation."

"I did," Kaelor said.

The simple confirmation visibly steadied Draevok, as though he had expected deflection and found the honesty disarming. He adjusted quickly. "The warriors are asking questions I cannot answer. About the human woman. About the prophecy. About what was said at the oracle's sanctuary and what it costs us." His gaze moved to me, brief and direct. "They deserve answers."

"They will have them," Kaelor said.

"Now," Draevok said. Not a question.

The fire crackled between them. Around us, the encampment had gone quiet in that specific way that told me every warrior within hearing distance was listening while pretending not to.

I stepped forward.

The decision did not feel strategic in the moment. It felt necessary, the way stopping a wound feels necessary when you can see it bleeding and the bandage is right there in your hand.

"The oracle confirmed that my blood is tied to the Labyrinth," I said. My voice came out clear and level, which surprised me somewhat. "She confirmed that both the High Queen and Veltheris's cult want me for it. Not for the same purpose. They want different outcomes, and they are enemies, and I am the only point where their interests overlap."

The encampment was very quiet.

"I am not going to tell you I am not dangerous," I continued. "I am. I don't fully understand what I can do, and that makes me more dangerous, not less, because it means I cannot predict how my power will behave under pressure. I know what I cost this alliance simply by being here. I am not ignorant of it." I held Draevok's gaze. "But removing me does not make the threat disappear. Astrythe and Veltheris do not stop wanting what my blood can do simply because I am no longer standing in your camp. They will keep moving regardless. At least here, you know where I am."

Draevok studied me with the unreadable focus of a commander assessing a position report. His expression did not soften. But something shifted in it, a very slight recalibration, the look of a man encountering a variable he had not fully accounted for.

"Brave words," he said. "You have said them before in different forms."

"Yes," I agreed. "And every time I say them, the situation has gotten more complicated. Because I'm telling you the truth, and the truth keeps getting worse." I paused. "That is not a coincidence. That is what the truth does when the people involved are genuinely dangerous."

One of the clan commanders beside Draevok exchanged a look with the other. I caught it.

Draevok's jaw tightened, and he turned back to Kaelor. "Your judgment has been questioned by your own people. That is not something I manufacture. It exists."

"I know," Kaelor said, his voice carrying the same controlled weight it always held, authority without aggression, certainty without dismissal. "I have never asked you to follow without question. I have asked you to trust that the questions are worth sitting with before they become fractures. The oracle's information changes the situation. The cult is moving now. Not as a future threat. As a present one."

Draevok opened his mouth to respond.

And then I felt it.

The sensation arrived with the abruptness of a sound in a silent room, a sudden, specific pressure beneath the ground where the encampment stood, focused and directional in a way that was entirely unlike the three distant gates I had felt on the mountain. This was close. This was beneath us.

Not sealed. Not fully.

Something had opened it, or partially opened it, recently enough that the disturbance was still warm in my awareness like a coal that has just been uncovered from ash.

"There is a gate beneath this encampment," I said.

The conversation stopped completely.

Draevok's gaze snapped to me.

"Not one of the old sealed ones," I said, already moving toward the sensation, trusting the direction instinctively the way you trust the direction of wind on skin. "This one has been breached. Recently. Someone came through it."

Kaelor was beside me in three strides, his hand not touching me but close, his attention on the ground ahead rather than on me. "Can you feel where?"

"Yes." The awareness was clear and insistent, tugging like a current. "Southeast. Near the supply storage."

Serathis was already issuing orders, her voice cutting through the encampment's frozen silence with the clipped efficiency of someone who had been waiting for exactly this kind of concrete crisis to replace the political one. Warriors moved. The encampment reorganized itself around the emergency with the speed of people who drilled for this.

Draevok followed without being asked. I noticed that.

The breach was not visible to the eye. It was a patch of frozen ground behind the largest supply tent, indistinguishable from the surrounding earth. But beneath it, I could feel the seam, the place where the gate had been cracked open from below and then partially resealed with something less permanent than the original binding. A temporary patch, hastily applied.

"Here," I said, stopping over it.

Malakor crouched and pressed his palm flat against the ground. His expression did not change, but his eyes moved in a way that suggested he was reading something in the earth. "Disturbed within the last several hours," he said. "And there." He pointed toward the supply tent's rear wall. "Boot marks. Pressed deep. Someone stood here for a while."

The search took less time than I expected. The infiltrator was found in the lower storage, tucked behind barrels with the practiced stillness of someone trained to wait indefinitely. He was fey, narrow-faced and pale, wearing the layered dark clothing of a courier rather than a soldier. He carried no weapons that were immediately visible, which made him more alarming rather than less.

He did not resist when Kaelor's warriors pulled him into the firelight. He looked at me across the space between us with an expression I recognized after a moment as something academic, the look of a person cataloging a result rather than experiencing a crisis.

The interrogation was efficient and not gentle, conducted by Malakor with the systematic precision of someone who had spent decades extracting information under pressure. The infiltrator offered it with less resistance than expected, which itself was information. He was not protecting a secret. He was delivering a message.

Veltheris was moving. His cult had been in position throughout Kaelor's territory for three days, moving through breach points that had been identified and partially opened over the preceding weeks. This infiltrator was not a spy. He was a scout confirming that the network was in place.

The message he carried, written in a hand that smelled faintly of incense and old stone, was three lines long.

Malakor read it aloud without inflection. "The bloodline has opened. The heart will answer. Come willingly, or do not come at all."

The fire crackled in the silence that followed.

Draevok stood at the outer edge of the gathered commanders, his arms crossed, his expression no longer readable in the way it had been minutes ago. He was watching me, and this time the assessment in his face was different from what it had carried during our confrontation by the fire. Not warmer. But recalibrated. The way a general looks at a piece of intelligence that has just rearranged his understanding of the battlefield.

"You felt it," he said. Not a question.

"Yes," I said.

He was quiet a moment. Then, with the painful economy of a man who chose his concessions carefully: "That is useful."

It was not an apology. It was not a welcome. It was Draevok acknowledging a fact because the facts had shifted, and he was, beneath all the ideology and the genuine political danger he represented, a commander who valued truth over comfort.

I accepted it for what it was.

Kaelor looked at the assembled commanders, his gaze moving through them with the deliberate attention of someone who was counting loyalties rather than faces. "The cult is already inside our territory," he said. "The political question we were debating tonight has become a survival question. Every resource we spend on internal fracture is a resource we are handing to Veltheris." A pause, brief and weighted. "We have one night to make a choice about what we are."

No one spoke immediately.

Then Serathis, her voice carrying the flat authority of someone who had made her decision before the question was fully formed: "We secure the perimeter. Full gate assessment at dawn." Her gaze cut to me with the directness I had learned to expect from her, blunt and entirely without apology. "If she can sense the breach points, we use that. Every tactical advantage on the table."

The other commanders followed, not unanimously and not without visible reluctance from some, but they followed.

Draevok uncrossed his arms. He did not pledge anything aloud. He simply turned and began issuing orders to his own warriors, directing them toward the perimeter with the efficiency of a man who had decided that the argument could wait for a time when the encampment was not actively compromised.

Torren appeared at my shoulder, his voice barely above a murmur. "For what it's worth, that was either extremely brave or extremely reckless. I genuinely cannot tell which." He paused. "Also, excellent timing on the gate thing. Deeply inconvenient, but excellent."

"Go help with something," I said.

"Already planned," he said, and melted into the activity around us with the practiced ease of someone who had survived many years by being useful precisely when it mattered.

The encampment was in motion now, the paralysis of political confrontation replaced by the focused urgency of a threat everyone could agree on. I stood at the center of it and let the new awareness in my blood guide me, feeling the sealed gate beneath my feet and the three distant ones on the mountain and the vast, patient attention of the Labyrinth itself, resting somewhere far below all of it, awake enough now to notice the shape of me.

My mother had chosen sacrifice so I could stand here and choose something different.

I intended to make it count.

Kaelor stopped beside me in the controlled chaos of the reorganizing camp. He did not speak immediately, but his presence settled against my awareness the way it always did, solid and certain and warm in ways I was running out of good reasons to resist acknowledging.

"The cult is here," I said.

"Yes."

"And Veltheris knows the bloodline has opened." The message had been addressed to me. Not to Kaelor. Not to the alliance. To me, specifically, using the language of the Labyrinth itself. "He felt it when Isyra broke the seal in my blood."

Kaelor's jaw moved. "Then he knows exactly where you are."

"He probably always did," I said. The thought arrived with a chill that settled deep and stayed there, the recognition that Veltheris's patience had never been passive. He had been watching the bloodline for generations. He had watched my mother run. He had watched me exist without knowing what I was, and he had waited, and now the thing he had been waiting for had announced itself as clearly as a signal fire on a dark night.

Far beneath the encampment, something ancient turned its awareness toward mine.

It did not move.

It simply waited, the way it had always waited, vast and patient and aware.

And I understood, with the clarity that comes from choices that cannot be undone, that the waiting was over.

# Fracture Lines

The war council ran until the fire burned to coals.

Nobody slept. Not really. The encampment had locked down hours ago, perimeter doubled, every gate sealed with physical bolts and fresh sentries rotating at intervals short enough to prevent the drowsiness that made men careless. The infiltrator was in a holding cell somewhere beneath the fortress's outer wall, which left us with his message and the cold, specific knowledge that Veltheris had been patient enough to position his people inside our borders for three days before announcing himself.

Three days. While we rode to Isyra's sanctuary and back. While Draevok consolidated his influence. While I learned what my blood could do and what that would cost. The cult had been beneath the camp the entire time, moving through a breach none of us had known to look for, and the thought of it sat in my chest like swallowed iron.

Serathis had commandeered the war command pavilion with her usual lack of ceremony, spreading maps across the central table with both hands and speaking in the clipped, continuous shorthand of someone who processed crisis through action rather than reaction. I stood at the far side of the table and watched her, watched Kaelor to her right, watched Malakor trace routes across the parchment with one finger while his expression betrayed nothing at all.

Torren sat at the table's edge with his boots up and his arms crossed, his usual restlessness suppressed into something quieter. He had not made a joke in nearly an hour, which told me more about how seriously he was taking the situation than anything he might have said aloud.

"The breach beneath the supply stores is the one we know about," Serathis said. She pressed two fingers against the map. "If Veltheris built an infiltration network, he did not build it through a single point. He is not that careless. There are more."

"How many?" Kaelor asked.

Malakor's gaze moved to me before he answered. The motion was deliberate and entirely without apology. "That depends on how far her sensing range extends."

Every pair of eyes at the table settled on me with varying degrees of expectation and calculation. I had grown accustomed to being looked at as a problem over the past weeks. Being looked at as a potential solution was different in texture, not entirely comfortable, but at least pointed in a more useful direction.

"I don't know the limits yet," I said honestly. "The breach beneath the camp was clear because it's recent and close. The gates on the mountain felt different, older, more settled. If there are other compromised points nearby, I should be able to feel them." I paused. "I'd need to move through the camp systematically. Not just stand in one place."

"Then we do that at first light," Serathis said, as though the matter were resolved.

"Before that," Malakor said, his voice flat and measured, "we address the other problem." He did not look up from the map. "The infiltrator did not find our breach point through luck. The Labyrinth gates are not visible to standard fey scouts without significant magical preparation. Someone inside this camp either led them to it or made it possible to identify."

The silence that followed had a physical weight to it, pressing down on the pavilion until the only sound was the dry hiss of the embers. No one moved. Serathis kept her fingers locked on the edge of the table, her knuckles white, while Malakor's gaze remained frozen on the map as if waiting for the ink to shift. Even Torren's chest rose and fell in a shallow, quiet rhythm, his posture stiffening as the air in the room grew too thin to draw easily.

Torren dropped his boots from the table and sat forward. "He's right," he said, his voice stripped of performance. "I've been going over the timing. Three days of positioning, moving through a point that's behind our supply stores. That's not improvised. Someone gave them a map."

Kaelor's jaw set. "You have a name?"

"Not yet." Torren's expression was unusually careful. "But I have a pattern. The warriors who rotated through supply duty over the last week, cross-referenced with anyone who has had contact with Draevok's extended faction. It's not a short list. But it's not a long one either."

Serathis looked up from the map with the specific stillness of someone containing a response that would not serve the moment. "Draevok himself?"

"No," Torren said. "I don't think he knows. Which somehow makes it worse." He pushed a folded piece of parchment across the table toward Kaelor. "Someone close to his faction made this decision without his knowledge. If that becomes public before we handle it carefully, it either exonerates him in a way that makes him politically stronger, or it fractures his own people's trust in him." A pause. "I cannot tell you which outcome is more dangerous."

Kaelor unfolded the parchment, read it once, and set it flat against the table. His expression did not shift. But something in the set of his shoulders changed, a tension that settled rather than released, the kind that came from absorbing information that required a specific, deliberate response rather than an immediate one.

"Keep the name contained," he said. "No accusation until we have evidence that holds. I will not give anyone grounds to claim we manufacture enemies for political convenience." His gaze moved to Torren. "Find the evidence."

"Already planned," Torren said, and the ghost of his usual tone was back, thin and dry but real. He stood and disappeared through the pavilion entrance without further ceremony.

Malakor watched him go. "If the cult has an informant in Draevok's faction, they are not simply scouting. They are engineering the internal fracture deliberately. Veltheris wants the alliance to break before any military confrontation becomes necessary."

"Divide the structure from within," Serathis said. "Let us exhaust ourselves on politics while he positions."

"Yes." Malakor's voice carried no particular emotion. It was simply fact delivered without decoration. "The cult is not here to fight us. Not yet. They are here to make us fight each other."

I had already understood this, somewhere beneath the urgency of the past hours, but hearing Malakor state it plainly made the air in my throat turn to frost. A cold, heavy weight settled behind my ribs, stilling my breath until the map on the table seemed to sharpen, its lines turning into a cage. Veltheris had spent generations perfecting patience as a weapon. Three days of positioning. Weeks of preparing the breach points. Longer than that engineering the conditions inside the alliance that would make any breach exploitable. He had not simply arrived. He had been building the architecture of our collapse long before we knew to look for it.

The thought made my stomach tighten in a way that had nothing to do with fear and everything to do with fury.

Kaelor looked at me across the table. His voice was quiet enough that it did not carry beyond the two of us. "Get some rest. You will need clarity for the morning sweep."

"I'm not tired," I said.

"I did not ask if you were tired."

It was not a command. His voice never quite landed as command when it was directed at me, even when the words were structured that way. It was closer to the kind of statement that trusts the other person to hear the care underneath the directness without requiring it to be spelled out.

I looked at him steadily. "A few hours," I said. "Wake me before dawn."

He held my gaze a moment, then nodded once.

I left the pavilion and walked through the locked-down camp under a sky that had gone fully dark, the stars sharp and close the way they only got at altitude when the air was clean and cold. Sentries moved at every boundary, their armor catching the torchlight in brief, metallic flashes. The encampment had the particular atmosphere of contained readiness, not panic, because panic was a luxury that disciplined soldiers could not afford, but the kind of taut, focused alertness that comes from knowing the danger is specific and near and not yet fully mapped.

My assigned quarters were a small room off the fortress's inner corridor, stone walls and a narrow cot and a lamp that burned low. I sat on the cot without undressing, my back against the wall, and closed my eyes.

The awareness came immediately, the way it had been arriving since Isyra broke the seal in my blood. The three distant gates on the mountain, patient and deeply settled, like stones that had been underwater for centuries. The breach beneath the supply stores, still faintly disturbed, its edges rougher than a proper gate's clean architecture. And something else, two other points, both farther than the first breach, one to the north of the encampment's boundary and one somewhere below the fortress's lower storage levels, fainter than the compromised gate but distinct enough to register.

I sat very still, throwing my senses outward and letting my awareness thread through the cold stone to touch each point separately.

The new awareness was not comfortable. It was not painful exactly, but it was constant, the way a sound you cannot unhear becomes part of the background of every room you enter. The Labyrinth existed beneath everything in this territory, threaded through the stone like roots through soil, and now that I could sense its architecture, I could not stop sensing it. I was not sure I would ever stop.

I was not sure I wanted to, which was the more unsettling realization.

I pressed my palms flat against the cold stone floor and concentrated on the two fainter points, trying to determine whether either of them had been recently disturbed. The northern one felt clean, sealed with the same heavy permanence as the mountain gates. The one beneath the fortress was harder to read. Older than the supply breach, but not as undisturbed as it should have been. Not recently opened. But touched, recently and carefully, by something that understood gate architecture well enough to probe without triggering it.

The cult had been mapping us. Not just entering through the one breach. Cataloging every gate in reach, testing the seals, identifying weaknesses. The supply breach was the one they had used. The fortress point was the one they had been preparing.

I was on my feet and moving before I had fully decided to stand.

Kaelor was still in the war pavilion when I pushed back through the entrance. Serathis looked up from the map. Malakor had not moved.

"There's a second point," I said. "Beneath the fortress itself. Lower storage. It hasn't been breached, but it's been tested. Recently. They know exactly where it is."

Serathis straightened. "How certain?"

"Certain enough to tell you before sleeping."

She and Kaelor exchanged a look that communicated several things at once without requiring words. Then Serathis turned and began issuing instructions to the warriors stationed outside, her voice carrying the flat authority that made people move without needing to be asked twice.

Malakor looked at me with his unreadable black eyes. "How many total?"

"Two compromised within camp territory. One used, one targeted. Three sealed gates on the mountain that feel untouched." I paused. "I want to sweep the full perimeter at first light. There could be others I can't feel from this distance."

He gave a single, slow nod. "Then we sweep."

I went back to my room. I did not sleep, but I rested, which was the closest thing available, and I kept my awareness on the two disturbed points throughout the remaining hours of darkness, monitoring them the way you monitor a wound you cannot afford to have worsen overnight.

Dawn arrived gray and bitterly cold. The sweep began an hour after first light, and Draevok was waiting at the pavilion entrance when we assembled.

He had not been invited. He had come anyway, which was entirely consistent with everything I had come to understand about him. His massive frame was already armored, his expression set in the particular flat readiness of a commander who has made his decision about where he intends to be and does not plan to negotiate the point.

"I will walk with you," he said to Kaelor, not a request and not quite a challenge. Something more careful than either. "My warriors are part of this camp. If there are breach points in our perimeter, I have the right to know their locations."

Kaelor considered him for a moment, his gaze steady and measuring. "You walk at the rear of the formation," he said finally. "You observe. You do not interfere with the sensing process."

I held his gaze. There was nothing in his face that resembled warmth, but there was a kind of blunt honesty that I could work with, a man who said what he meant and meant what he said and did not require me to perform gratitude or deference in exchange for his basic acknowledgment that I was present. That was, in its own stark way, a form of respect.

"Then let me remove some of the uncertainty," I said. "Give me an hour at the supply breach. If I can seal it, you'll know what I can do. If I can't, you'll know that too, and we plan accordingly."

Draevok was quiet for a long moment. Then he stepped back, a deliberate movement, creating space without quite conceding anything. It was not agreement. It was permission to proceed, which was, from him, close enough.

The work at the supply breach took closer to two hours than one. I knelt on the frozen ground behind the supply tent and pressed both palms flat against the earth and tried to find the seam the cult had opened, feeling for it through the new awareness in my blood the way you feel for a splinter you can't quite see but can precisely locate by pressure. The breach was there, unmistakable once I focused, a ragged gap in the gate's architecture where someone had forced an opening with a method that prioritized speed over precision.

Closing it was harder than finding it. Isyra had not taught me this, only shown me that the ability existed. I was learning the mechanics by feel, which was an uncomfortable way to learn anything, and twice the effort slipped and I had to start again, my jaw aching from how hard I was clenching it against the frustration.

Kaelor crouched beside me at some point during the second attempt, not touching, not speaking, only present. His proximity steadied something in my concentration that I could not have explained rationally and did not try to. I focused on the breach and pushed, and on the third attempt, I felt the gate's architecture respond, the way a wound's edges will draw together when properly supported, and the gap closed with a sensation like pressure releasing from a room that had been sealed too long.

I sat back on my heels and breathed.

"Done?" Kaelor asked.

"Done." My hands were shaking slightly, which I found irritating. "It's not permanent. The gate was never designed to hold against deliberate reopening from someone who knows what they're doing. But it will take them time to breach it again, and I'll feel it when they try."

"That is enough," he said.

I stood, and the world tilted briefly before settling. Kaelor's hand came up near my elbow without quite making contact, a reflex checked at the last moment, and I noticed both the gesture and its restraint.

"You did not need to speak last night," he said, his voice low enough that only I would catch it. He meant the confrontation with Draevok, my decision to step forward and address the assembled commanders directly.

"Apparently I did," I said.

The corner of his mouth shifted, not quite a smile, but something adjacent to one. It was rare enough that I cataloged it without meaning to.

We found Torren waiting near the pavilion entrance when we returned, and his expression had settled into the specific, carefully neutral arrangement that meant he had found what he was looking for and was not particularly pleased about it.

"The informant," he said to Kaelor, without preamble. "I have a name and enough evidence to make it hold. He is not one of Draevok's inner commanders. He is a supply officer, three levels removed from direct contact with Draevok's leadership. He has been passing access routes to cult contacts for approximately two weeks." Torren paused. "He does not appear to understand what the cult actually is. He was paid, and he was told it was a rival faction scouting operation. He believed it."

Serathis's expression did not change, but her posture shifted, the kind of adjustment that meant she was containing something she would address more fully once the immediate situation was resolved. "Draevok does not know."

"No," Torren confirmed. "Which means when we bring this forward, we do it carefully. Draevok learns his own people were used against him without his knowledge. How he receives that information depends entirely on how it is delivered." He looked at Kaelor. "I would suggest delivering it to him directly. Before it reaches anyone else."

Kaelor was already moving toward the far side of the pavilion, where Draevok had settled after the morning sweep with two of his own commanders. The large minotaur looked up as Kaelor approached, his expression carrying the patient readiness of a man who had learned to prepare for news he did not want.

I did not follow. I stayed near the table with Serathis and watched Kaelor speak to Draevok in a voice too low to carry across the room, watched Draevok's expression move through several things in rapid succession before settling into something that was not quite anger and not quite grief. More like the controlled recognition of a man who has just been shown precisely how his own good faith was exploited.

Draevok looked at the floor. His hands, I noticed, were very still, the deliberate stillness of someone who has decided not to move because movement would express something they are not ready to express publicly.

Serathis spoke quietly beside me. "If we collapse before the enemy arrives, we save them the effort."

"Yes," I said.

She looked at me sideways, a brief, assessing glance. "The gate work this morning was useful." She did not elaborate or soften it. From Serathis, that was as close to an endorsement as the situation was likely to produce, and I received it in the spirit it was offered.

Malakor appeared at my other side with the soundless efficiency that still occasionally startled me. "The cult is not scouting," he said, which was nearly word for word what he had said in the small hours of the previous night, but his tone was different now, carrying the weight of confirmed intelligence rather than strategic assessment. "They have been inside our territory for three days. They have mapped four gate points. They have an informant. They have a prepared breach and a secondary target." He paused. "If the cult is inside our borders, they are not positioning for a future operation. They are already executing one."

I thought about the message the infiltrator had carried. The three lines written in a hand that smelled of incense and old stone. *The bloodline has opened. The heart will answer. Come willingly, or do not come at all.*

Not a threat. An invitation. Or rather, a statement of inevitability dressed as an invitation, which was, I was beginning to understand, exactly how Veltheris communicated. He did not threaten because he did not believe threats were necessary. He stated what he considered to be the predetermined shape of events and waited for reality to conform to his expectations.

The fury that had settled in my chest the previous night was still there, banked low and steady, the kind that did not burn itself out quickly. I had been a destination on someone else's map for my entire life. My uncle had drawn the first routes. The High Court had added their lines. Veltheris had been laying his own cartography over all of it for longer than I had been alive, patient and precise and utterly certain that I would end up exactly where he had designed for me to arrive.

I intended to be a significant inconvenience to that certainty.

"Torren," I said.

He materialized from somewhere to my left. "Present and trying to appear useful."

"I preferred interpersonal dysfunction when it involved less prophecy," I said, echoing something close to what he had said the previous night, and watched his eyebrows lift with genuine surprise before his mouth curved into something real.

"That is almost exactly what I was thinking," he said. "Deeply concerning."

Kaelor returned from his exchange with Draevok, his expression carrying the controlled steadiness of a man who has delivered necessary information and is now calculating what comes next. Draevok had not followed him back. He was still on the far side of the pavilion, speaking quietly with his own commanders, his posture altered in some way I could not fully read from this distance.

"He is angry," Kaelor said, arriving at the table. "Not at us. At the situation. At being used without his knowledge." A measured pause. "He will not fracture the alliance over this. It would validate the cult's intent." Another pause. "He is also intelligent enough to know that."

Serathis nodded once, the sharp economy of someone filing information and moving forward. "Then we address the fortress gate point next and reassess the northern marker before nightfall. Full council this evening with all faction commanders. No more separate briefings."

"Agreed," Kaelor said.

I stood at the table with the map spread between us and let the awareness in my blood run steadily through the camp's architecture, feeling the sealed supply breach, the probed fortress point, the flagged northern marker. Three places where Veltheris had reached into Kaelor's territory like fingers testing the give of a door. Three places where he had decided, with the patient certainty of someone who had never been truly stopped, that entry was possible.

He had been watching the bloodline for generations. He had watched my mother run and chosen to wait. He had watched me exist without knowing what I was and chosen to keep waiting. And now the seal in my blood had broken open and announced itself across whatever distance the Labyrinth's awareness spanned, and his patience had shifted into action.

Somewhere beneath the mountains, the Labyrinth turned with its vast, slow attention, aware of me the way a river is aware of a stone dropped into it, not hostile, not welcoming, simply registering the disruption and adjusting its current around it.

I pressed my palm flat against the map and felt the stone beneath the table beneath the ground beneath the camp, and I thought about my mother running through dark streets with me in her arms, and I thought about Veltheris waiting for generations with the calm certainty that the bloodline would eventually come to him.

He was wrong about the inevitability. He was going to be wrong about a great many things.

But first, I needed to understand the full shape of what he had already built inside our walls, and I needed to dismantle it before he decided the time for patience was over.

Malakor set a sealed report on the table near my hand, his voice level and precise. "The morning's intelligence has confirmed one thing beyond the gate locations." His black eyes moved around the assembled commanders with the calm of someone delivering news they have already accepted. "The cult entered Kaelor's territory not to scout and withdraw. They entered to stay." A pause, brief and weighted. "Veltheris is already here."

The camp outside the pavilion moved and breathed and maintained its disciplined vigilance, and the fire at the pavilion's center burned with steady orange heat, and nobody spoke for a moment that lasted exactly long enough to make the truth of it land fully.

Then Serathis reached forward and pressed two fingers against the map, marking the fortress's lower storage, and said, "Then we find him first."

# The Cult Beneath

The ground beneath Kaelor's camp was breathing.

Not as imagination. Not as fear inventing movement where none existed. I felt it through the soles of my boots, through the stone floor of the pavilion, through the awareness in my blood that had not gone quiet since Isyra cracked it open. A slow, rhythmic pressure, like something vast and patient drawing air into lungs that should not have existed beneath solid rock.

Veltheris was already here.

Malakor's words from the night before had not settled so much as calcified in my chest, and now the camp was moving on them, every gate sealed and every perimeter doubled. Kaelor's voice carried through the pavilion entrance as he issued orders in the clipped, deliberate cadence that meant he had already processed the worst possibilities and was now working backward from them.

I stood near the center table with my palms pressed flat against the map and let my senses thread downward through the layers of stone and cold earth, following the architecture of the Labyrinth the way I used to trace the jagged ridge of my uncle's old saber scar when I was small enough to believe his stories. The sealed supply breach held. My work from that morning was still intact, its edges drawn tight with the particular pressure of something reluctantly closed. But below that, deeper, the fortress gate point I had flagged in the small hours of the previous night was moving.

Not opening. Not yet. But something was testing it from the other side with the patient, methodical pressure of someone who already knew the lock's design.

"They're at the fortress point," I said.

Serathis looked up from the route she had been marking on the map. "How active?"

"Testing. Not forcing." I kept my focus on the sensation, trying to read its texture the way Isyra had described, pressure rather than panic. "Someone who knows what they're looking for."

Kaelor came through the pavilion entrance before she could answer. He read the room in a single sweep, his gaze settling on me with the steady weight of someone who has learned to read urgency by the way a person stands rather than by what they say.

"We go down," he said.

My fingers curled tighter into the map's linen backing, the rough fibers anchoring me as he scanned the assembled faces: Serathis already rolling the map into its cylinder, Malakor straightening from the table's corner, Torren pulling his layered leathers tighter in the manner of someone preparing for something he would rather be anywhere else for.

"Small team," Kaelor continued. "Fast, quiet, no unnecessary exposure. We find the ritual preparation before they finish it."

Malakor checked the blade at his hip without comment. Serathis had already moved toward the pavilion exit.

Torren looked at the ceiling. "I would like to formally apologize to every above-ground problem I ever complained about."

Nobody laughed, but the tension in the room shifted by a precise, necessary degree.

Draevok was waiting at the pavilion entrance when we stepped outside into the cold morning air. He had his armor on, his horns catching the pale light, his posture set with the deliberate solidity of a commander who has made his decision and is not interested in arguments about it.

"I will come," he said, to Kaelor directly.

Kaelor stopped walking. The two of them occupied the same few feet of space with the careful, loaded quality of two immovable objects that had learned, over long years, how to coexist without collision.

"No," Kaelor said.

Draevok's jaw tightened. "You deny me because you think me traitor."

"I deny you because I cannot afford uncertainty below ground." Kaelor's voice carried no heat. It never did when he was being most serious, and that absence of heat was somehow worse than anger. "Above ground, if your judgment fails me, I can manage the cost. Below, in confined tunnels, against blood-magic, with the Labyrinth active beneath our feet, I cannot afford uncertainty from any direction. That includes people I trust."

Draevok was still for a moment that stretched long enough to hear the wind move through the camp's pennants overhead.

"When I return," Kaelor said, "you will be here. That is not punishment. It is deployment."

Something shifted in Draevok's expression, not softening, but adjusting, the recalibration of a military mind receiving orders it disagrees with from a commander it still, despite everything, respects. He stepped back. A single, deliberate motion.

We descended into the sealed service tunnels through an access point beneath the fortress's lower storage, a narrow hatch set into stone that had not been opened in years before Torren found it on his maps that morning. The air below was immediately different. Cold in a way that had nothing to do with altitude, dense with damp stone and something metallic that sat at the back of the throat like copper wire. My torch threw orange light across walls that closed in on both sides, barely wide enough for Kaelor to move through without turning his shoulders.

His horns scraped the ceiling twice in the first corridor. He did not acknowledge it. Neither did I, though I noticed, and filed the image away in the part of my mind that cataloged things I had no business paying attention to during active infiltration operations.

Malakor moved at the rear of our small group with the quiet, economical step of someone trained to occupy hostile environments without announcing himself. Serathis was directly behind Kaelor, her hand resting on the war blade at her side. Torren was beside me, his usual restless energy compressed into something more focused, his sharp eyes moving across every surface we passed.

The cult markings appeared on the walls about forty feet in.

Not painted. Burned. The stone itself had been scorched in patterns that spiraled inward toward centers I did not want to stare at too long, because the longer I looked, the more the shapes seemed to move at the periphery of my vision. I looked away and kept walking.

"How old are these?" I asked, keeping my voice low enough to carry only to the people immediately around me.

"Days," Malakor said from behind us. His voice carried no particular inflection. "Not weeks. They were placed after the initial breach."

Three days. They had been down here for three days, moving through tunnels beneath a camp full of soldiers, drawing their markings on the walls, preparing something, and none of us had known to look.

The fury came back, low and steady, and I used it to keep my breathing even.

The whispers started around the same time as the second set of markings.

Not voices, not exactly. More like the sensation of sound just below the threshold of language, threading through the rock from somewhere ahead and below. The Labyrinth's awareness was closer here, the way a river current strengthens as you move toward the source, and what I felt through it was not only the cult's presence. Something older ran beneath that, patient and vast and not entirely unaware of me, the way I had learned to sense the Labyrinth's attention since Isyra broke the seal in my blood.

I focused on separating the two. Cult above, older thing below. The cult's presence had a texture like scar tissue, rough and deliberate, while the deeper awareness was something else entirely. Smoother. More certain. Not hostile.

Not welcoming either.

Simply present, the way deep water is present beneath thin ice.

"You hear it," Kaelor said. Not a question. He had slowed slightly, matching his pace to mine, his shoulder close enough that the heat of him registered even through the tunnel's cold.

"The Labyrinth runs deep here. Deeper than the breach points above." I kept my gaze forward. "The cult chose this location deliberately. They wanted to be as close to the heart architecture as possible."

"For the ritual," Serathis said ahead of us.

"Yes."

The chamber opened without warning at the end of a passage that had been narrowing for the past twenty feet, and for a moment none of us moved.

It was larger than it had any right to be, carved from the natural rock with the assistance of something that was not natural at all. The walls bore the same spiral markings but more elaborate here, denser, layered over each other in concentric rings that drew the eye toward the chamber's center with a pull I felt in my sternum rather than my vision. A stone platform occupied the center, low and circular, etched with channels that had been used recently. The dried residue in them was dark enough to be blood and exactly the right color for it.

At the platform's four cardinal points, objects had been placed with careful precision. A shard of iron. A coil of hair bound with black cord. A sealed vial of something that moved slightly when nothing in the room was moving. And a small piece of parchment, folded once, with writing I could read from where I stood because my name was on it.

Not the name I used now. My full name, the one from before the border raids, the one only my mother had used.

Something cold moved through my chest that had nothing to do with the tunnel air.

"Torren," Kaelor said quietly.

Torren was already moving along the chamber's perimeter, his eyes tracking the floor and walls with the practiced attention of someone looking for things that should not be where they are. He crouched near the northern wall, examining something I could not see from my position, and his expression did the thing it did when he found what he was looking for and wished he had not.

"There," he said, and pointed. Tucked behind a natural protrusion of rock was a leather satchel, the kind used in supply rotations, bearing the stamped insignia of Kaelor's camp quartermaster. "Someone carried provisions down here. Recently and more than once." He looked up, his voice stripped of everything except the information. "They had access to supply rotation schedules. Someone gave it to them."

"The supply officer," Malakor said behind me.

"Or whoever he reported to." Torren did not move the satchel. He was cataloging it. "Either way, someone inside this camp knew this chamber existed and kept it quiet."

Kaelor's silence was the kind that precedes decisions rather than follows them.

The ambush came from the passage we had entered through.

Not from ahead, not from the chamber's shadows where instinct would have suggested, but from behind, from the corridor we had already walked, which meant they had let us pass and sealed themselves at our back. Four of them, moving fast, wearing robes the color of old ash with their faces wrapped in binding cloth. No conventional weapons. Their hands were already moving in the gestures I had seen described in the intelligence reports, fingers trailing dark light the way a torch trails smoke.

Blood-magic.

Malakor moved before anyone else, placing himself between the passage entrance and the rest of us with the reflexive precision of a former military captain who had not entirely abandoned his training when he abandoned his allegiance. He took the first strike on a ward I had not known he carried, a flat disc of etched bone that cracked under the impact and absorbed enough of the blow to keep the rest of it from being immediately lethal.

Serathis was already drawing her blade. Kaelor moved toward me with one arm extended, not grabbing, not restraining, simply positioning himself at my flank while his other hand reached for the weapon at his hip.

The Labyrinth surged beneath my feet.

That was the only way I could describe it. The awareness in my blood, which had been a steady background hum since we descended, suddenly amplified into something that pressed against the inside of my skull and demanded attention. The ritual platform behind me was active. Not completed, but active, its channels carrying a residual charge that the blood-magic in the air was feeding, and the combined pressure of it pulled at something in my chest with a direction I recognized from the mountain gates.

It was pulling me toward the platform's center.

Not physically. I was not moving. But the pull was there, insistent and specific, and it carried the cold certainty that if I did not consciously resist it, my feet would follow without my permission.

Kaelor's hand came to my arm. Not a grip. Contact, steady and warm, and I held onto the sensation of it the way you hold onto a fixed point when the ground is moving beneath you.

"You cannot keep standing between me and everything that wants me," I said, and my voice came out steadier than I had expected.

"Watch me," he said.

Behind us, Malakor took another strike and kept his feet, which was remarkable and also deeply concerning regarding how much punishment one person could absorb before the mathematics stopped working in their favor. Serathis had engaged the nearest cultist with the focused efficiency of someone who had been fighting longer than the person opposite her had been alive. Torren, to his considerable credit, had produced a blade from somewhere in his layered leathers and was making himself useful in the passage entrance, blocking a fifth attacker I had not initially seen.

The pull intensified.

I stopped fighting it through resistance. That had not been working. Resistance was panic wearing the costume of control, and panic was what the ritual was designed to exploit. I had understood this somewhere in the back of my awareness since Isyra described the Labyrinth's architecture, the way its gates responded to force by drawing harder, and gates responded to will by yielding.

I stopped pulling back and started reaching instead.

The difference was immediate and nauseating. Reaching meant opening the awareness fully, letting the Labyrinth's pressure flood through rather than bounce against the wall I had been holding, and for three seconds that felt considerably longer, I was not entirely certain where the chamber ended and the stone began. The ritual platform's channels lit with a pale, cold light that had nothing to do with the torches. The markings on the walls moved, genuinely moved, their spirals tightening inward as the residual charge tried to complete the circuit.

I found the breach point at the chamber's floor. Not a gate, not like the ones above, but a crack in the Labyrinth's architecture where the cult's ritual had begun to force an opening. Raw and specific, the way a splinter is specific, and I could feel the shape of what they were trying to build through it. A mark. Not physical. Something that would remain in my blood like a signature, directing the Labyrinth's heart awareness toward Veltheris's reach rather than my own.

They had not needed to touch me. They had only needed me in the chamber long enough for the ritual to complete around me.

I closed it.

Not elegantly. Not with the careful, controlled pressure I had used on the supply breach that morning. I drove my awareness into the crack the way you drive a wedge into splitting wood and pushed, and the Labyrinth's architecture responded with the shuddering, pressurized release of something that had been held in unnatural tension. The chamber's light died. The markings stilled. The pull in my chest collapsed into a hollow ache that would probably hurt considerably more once the adrenaline finished metabolizing.

The cultists stopped moving.

Not all of them. Two were already down, courtesy of Serathis and Malakor. The remaining three hesitated in the passage entrance, their hand gestures halted mid-form, their blood-magic severed from its anchor point.

In that hesitation, the fight ended quickly and badly for anyone wearing ash-colored robes.

I sat down on the chamber floor because my legs had decided the courtesy of holding me upright was no longer strictly necessary. The stone was cold through my clothing, and the awareness in my blood was running at a low, exhausted frequency, like a torch burning on the last of its fuel.

Kaelor crouched in front of me. His molten gold eyes moved across my face with the focused attention of a field assessment, checking for damage rather than offering comfort, which was exactly the right approach and I appreciated it more than I would have been able to articulate at that particular moment.

"You sealed it," he said.

"Most of it." My voice felt distant from my body. "The breach is closed. The ritual can't be completed now, not from this point. They would need to start again somewhere else."

"Then we have time."

"Some." I pressed my palms against the floor, feeling for the Labyrinth's current. It had settled back into its deeper rhythm, vast and slow and no longer pressing against me with the urgency of the last several minutes. "The exposure worked both directions. I felt where the breach was reaching. But the reach goes both ways."

Kaelor's gaze sharpened. He had understood before I finished the sentence.

The dying cultist at the chamber's edge moved.

Not from life. The movement was wrong, the specific wrongness of a body animated by something other than its own volition, joints bending at angles that the living do not achieve without considerable pain. Malakor stepped back from it, his expression the closest to unsettled I had ever seen it reach. Serathis raised her blade, but Kaelor lifted one hand and she held.

The cultist's mouth opened.

The voice that came from it was not the cultist's voice. It was measured, quiet, and carried the particular quality of someone who had never once doubted that the person they were speaking to would listen. Not because they commanded it. Because they considered themselves genuinely interesting.

"You are learning to close doors," Veltheris said, through a dead man's throat, with the gentle, approving tone of a teacher whose student has finally grasped a lesson they had been patient enough to wait for. "Good. Soon you will learn what begs to come through them."

Nobody in the chamber moved.

The cold in the room was absolute. My breath misted in front of my face. The torches had stopped flickering, standing upright and perfectly still in air that should have moved them.

"I have watched your bloodline for a very long time," the voice continued, with the same measured patience. "Your mother was stubborn. You are stubborn differently. She ran. You stay and fight." A pause, brief and surgical. "She thought that would protect you. That distance would be enough. That if she ran far enough, the Labyrinth would forget the shape of her blood." Another pause. "It does not forget. I do not forget."

My jaw was locked. I could feel Kaelor beside me, the heat of him, the absolute controlled stillness, and I could feel Torren at my peripheral vision standing very carefully without speaking, which was one of the most jarring things I had witnessed since descending into these tunnels.

"She had a name for you," Veltheris said, and my blood went cold. "Not the name she gave you publicly. The one she used when you were frightened. The one she used in the dark." The cultist's borrowed mouth shaped something that was not quite a smile. "She called you *vareth*. Her little flame."

The air in the chamber weighed approximately twice what it had thirty seconds ago.

I had not heard that word in eleven years. I had not heard it since a burning street and a woman's voice telling me to run, to keep running, to not look back. I had not heard it since the last time I had felt entirely safe and entirely destroyed in the same moment.

Nobody knew that name. Nobody alive had ever heard my mother use it. I had not spoken it aloud to another person in over a decade.

Veltheris let the silence hold for exactly as long as it needed to.

"Your mother said many beautiful things when she believed they might save you.," he said.

The chamber was very quiet.

The cultist's body settled back against the stone with the loose, final weight of something that no longer had any use for the shape it had been given. The borrowed voice was gone. The cold began, slowly, to lift.

Kaelor's hand closed around mine where it rested against the chamber floor. Not pulling me up, not repositioning me, not doing anything except making contact with the steady, deliberate certainty of someone who had decided that this was where his hand was going to be and nothing in the room was going to change that.

The warmth of it moved up my arm and into my chest and settled somewhere near the hollow ache the sealed breach had left behind, and I sat with it, and breathed, and did not speak.

I was not going to break in front of the chamber's stone walls and the cooling bodies of cult dead and the smell of blood-metal and old ash. I was not going to give that voice, even absent now, even gone back to wherever it had come from, the satisfaction of a response it could catalog and use.

But my fingers tightened around Kaelor's, and he let them.

Malakor's voice came from somewhere to my left, quiet and precise, stripped of everything decorative. "The cult does not worship death."

I looked at him.

"That's supposed to comfort me?" My voice came out steadier than I had any right to expect.

His black eyes held mine without apology. "No. It is supposed to frighten you accurately."

I absorbed that. Accurate fear was more useful than comfortable ignorance. I knew this. I had built my entire survival on this principle.

Knowing it did not make the chamber smell less like copper and old stone. It did not make the dead cultist on the floor look less like a discarded vessel that something else had finished using. It did not make the word *vareth* stop ringing against the inside of my skull like a bell struck too hard.

But it was accurate, and accuracy was what I had instead of safety, and I had been working with that trade-off long enough to manage it.

I stood, and Kaelor rose with me, and I did not let go of his hand until I was fully upright and certain my legs had remembered their function.

Then I let go, and I turned toward the passage that led back to the surface, and I put one foot in front of the other.

"We need to move," I said. "He knows I sealed it. He will send something else before we reach the top."

Kaelor fell into step at my flank without comment. Serathis took the lead. Malakor and Torren covered the rear, and nobody wasted breath on anything that could wait until we were above ground and breathing air that did not smell like the specific intersection of old ritual and recent death.

Torren managed, somewhere in the last forty feet of tunnel, to arrive at something that was almost his normal register. "I want it on record," he said quietly, to no one in particular, "that I was significantly more useful down here than my general reputation would suggest."

Nobody argued with him, which was, by Torren's own stated standards, the highest form of validation available.

The hatch opened onto cold afternoon air and gray sky and the controlled, locked-down movement of a camp that had been waiting for us to come back up. Talia was at the perimeter of the access point with her satchel and her wide green eyes and the specific expression she wore when she was cataloging injuries before anyone had finished speaking. She counted us with a quick, practiced sweep and some of the tension in her shoulders released by a fraction.

Draevok was exactly where Kaelor had left him, which I had not entirely expected. He read our faces as we emerged, and whatever he found in the assembled expressions of Kaelor's strike team settled something in his posture that was adjacent to relief and nothing like it at all.

The breach was sealed. The ritual was disrupted. The team was alive.

And somewhere beneath the mountains, in the dark architecture of the Labyrinth's oldest corridors, Veltheris had already turned his patient, certain attention toward the next door.

The one I had not yet learned to close.

# When Horns Break

Veltheris had not struck me with a blade, but I bled from it all the same.

The word *vareth* had not left my skull since the tunnel. It sat behind my eyes with the particular weight of something exhumed, brought into cold air after years of deliberate burial, and I could not put it back. We had climbed out of that chamber into gray afternoon light and locked-down camp movement, and Talia had cataloged our injuries with her quick, practiced hands, and Draevok had read our faces without speaking, and all of it had happened around me while I stood in the shape of someone functioning normally.

My hands were so cold they felt hollow, the skin across my knuckles tight and bloodless as I stared at the cup without seeing it.

But there was no time for that, which was perhaps the only mercy the situation offered.

The news broke within the hour. Torren's evidence from the chamber, the supply satchel with the quartermaster's stamp, the careful record of access rotations, the proximity of the cult's preparations to one specific faction's supply chain, all of it pointed toward the same conclusion with the cold, inevitable logic of a trap that had already sprung. One of Draevok's lieutenants. A warrior named Casseth, trusted, decorated, who had served in Draevok's direct command through three campaigns and had apparently been serving something else for considerably longer.

The camp cracked open like a fault line under pressure.

I heard it from across the war council pavilion, where I had positioned myself near the eastern wall with a cup of something hot that I had not yet drunk, listening to the argument build in layers the way the Labyrinth's deeper gates grind together before they lock, distinct pressures colliding until the air itself becomes dangerous. Draevok's faction commanders were loud. Kaelor's inner council was controlled, which was worse. The warriors in the outer ring of the pavilion were quiet, and quiet soldiers deciding what to believe were more dangerous than any amount of shouting.

"One man," Draevok said. His voice carried without effort, the deep resonance of someone accustomed to being heard across battlefields. "You hold one man's corruption against an entire faction."

"I hold your faction's corruption against your faction," Serathis said, from her position at the table's far end. "There is a difference."

"Casseth acted alone."

"Casseth provided the cult with supply rotation schedules, access point timing, and three days of undetected operation beneath our feet." Malakor spoke from the wall to Draevok's left, his tone stripped of everything except the information. "Alone or not, the access required knowledge that only your chain of command possessed."

Draevok turned toward him with the slow, deliberate movement of something large that has decided a smaller obstacle requires direct attention. "You have no standing to speak on corruption, traitor."

Malakor's expression did not shift. "No. But I have standing to speak on intelligence failures. That is rather the point."

The pavilion had gone very still. Outside, through the canvas walls, I could hear the camp moving with the compressed, tense energy of soldiers who knew something had gone wrong and were waiting to find out exactly how wrong. Veltheris had not needed to breach our defenses with force. He had needed only this, the moment when Kaelor's alliance began checking whether the man beside them was worth trusting.

My breath caught, a sharp, cold stitch in my chest that went suddenly still as the truth of it settled.

Kaelor stood at the head of the council table. He had not raised his voice once since the meeting began, which meant every word he spoke carried the full weight of a man who had already decided what he was going to do and was simply allowing the room to arrive at the same conclusion on its own schedule. His molten gold gaze moved across the assembled commanders with the steady attention of someone reading a map, cataloging positions and distances and where the ground was weakest.

"Casseth will face judgment," he said. "Public. Before the full war council. No private execution, no quiet burial of the evidence." He looked at Draevok. "You asked for that. You will have it."

Draevok's jaw worked. "That is not the argument I am making."

"Then make the argument you are making."

The silence stretched between them, taut as a bowstring at full draw.

"You think this proves me wrong?" Draevok said, finally, and beneath the bluntness of it there was something rawer, something that had not been there before the tunnels. A crack in the certainty he wore like armor.

Kaelor held his gaze without flinching. "No. I think it proves we are both late."

Something moved across Draevok's face, not concession, not agreement, but the subtle recalibration of a man receiving information that his existing framework does not entirely accommodate. He did not speak again immediately, and in that silence, I could feel the war council's attention shifting, pulling toward the center of the room where the argument had been loudest, and then pulling further, toward me, because I was standing at the eastern wall and I had not spoken, and in rooms full of people deciding what to fear, quiet observers become focal points whether they want to or not.

Casseth was brought in under guard twenty minutes later.

He was a broad warrior, dark-furred, with the kind of build that suggested decades of physical conditioning. He held himself with the residual dignity of someone who had decided, sometime between the guards arriving and this moment, that he would not give anyone the satisfaction of watching him fold. His eyes moved across the assembled faces and settled on Draevok with an expression I could not read precisely but felt somewhere in my sternum, the specific anguish of someone who has betrayed a person they genuinely respected and is now standing in front of that person with no useful explanation available.

Draevok looked at him for a long moment without speaking. When he did speak, it was quieter than anything I had heard from him.

"Why."

Not a question. The shape of a question without its function, because the answer was already present in the room and everyone could feel it.

Casseth's composure held for approximately four seconds. Then something in his posture shifted, the particular collapse that comes not from physical defeat but from the exhaustion of maintaining a position that has become untenable. Casseth swallowed once, jaw locked hard enough to show the muscle jumping beneath the skin. "He promised survival," he said. "Not victory. Survival. For the clans. He said the human woman was the price and if we paid it, the rest of us would be allowed to exist."

The pavilion went absolutely silent.

Several warriors near the outer ring had stilled in a way that told me the information was landing somewhere complicated, because survival was not an abstraction to people who had spent their lives being hunted, and Veltheris had known exactly which argument would find purchase in the cracks of an alliance held together by shared threat rather than shared trust.

He did not need to defeat Kaelor's army. He only needed to make the army wonder if it was fighting for the right thing.

My boots pushed off the canvas wall, a sudden, sharp impulse in my legs carrying me forward before my mind had fully cleared the fog of the past hour to decide on the movement.

The room's attention followed me, and I felt it, the weight of collective focus settling across my shoulders like something physical. Kaelor tracked my movement from the head of the table, and I saw the precise moment he understood what I was about to do, because his expression shifted in that way it had, not softening exactly, but adjusting, making space for something he had not anticipated.

He did not stop me.

"Casseth," I said, and my voice was steadier than the situation warranted, which was something I had learned to be grateful for when it happened. "Pull up your left sleeve."

The warrior went very still.

"Veltheris marks the people he works through," I said, to the room rather than to any individual in it. "Not with ink. Not with a blade. With something older. I felt it in the chamber below. I think I know what it looks like in the Labyrinth's architecture." I held Casseth's gaze. "Pull up your sleeve, or I will do it for you, and one of those options will be unpleasant."

Draevok made a sound that was not quite a word and was not quite agreement, but which fell somewhere in the space between them.

Casseth pulled up his sleeve.

The mark was there. Not visible to the naked eye, nothing so simple as a tattoo or a burn, but when I let my awareness extend the way Isyra had taught me, the way I had used it in the tunnels to feel the breach points through solid stone, I could see it the way you see a shadow rather than the thing casting it. A signature. Deliberate and specific. The same architecture as the ritual chamber's markings, compressed into the space beneath living skin.

I reached toward it without touching him, and the Labyrinth's awareness responded to my intent, pulling the mark's structure into visibility the way lamplight pulls shapes from darkness.

It appeared on the surface of Casseth's skin like frost forming on glass, intricate and unmistakable, spreading from his wrist to his elbow in the geometric spiral pattern that every person in this pavilion had seen burned into the tunnel walls two hours ago.

The room's silence had a different quality now.

It was the cold, hollow stillness of people realizing they had no name for what they were watching.

I withdrew my awareness, and the mark faded back beneath the skin, but it had been seen. Every person in the pavilion had seen it. The evidence was no longer a supply satchel and a chain of circumstantial logic. It was written on a man's body, and I had pulled it into the light, and there was no interpretation of that fact which did not come with significant implications about what I was.

Draevok was staring at Casseth with an expression I had not seen him wear before. Not rage. Something older and more specific than rage, the grief of a commander who has discovered that a soldier he trusted carried a war inside himself without ever saying so.

"He is compromised," I said to the room. "Not corrupted by choice alone. The mark is a tether. It keeps Veltheris's reach inside anyone it's placed on, feeding information, shaping decisions, making surrender feel like pragmatism." I looked at the assembled commanders. "He promised survival. That is precisely what Veltheris does. He finds the thing you cannot afford to lose and he holds it in front of you until you forget to ask what the payment actually costs."

Nobody spoke immediately.

Kaelor's voice came from the head of the table, measured and absolute. "Casseth will be confined and examined by our healers. The mark requires removal before any judgment can be fair." He looked at the gathered commanders with the steadiness of someone who has decided the room's fear will not be allowed to become the room's governing force. "The cult's strategy was to fracture us. To make us afraid of each other until we did their work for them." A pause. "We are not going to do that."

Draevok turned toward him slowly. His gaze moved from Kaelor to me, and I met it without flinching, because flinching in front of Draevok was a concession I had no intention of making regardless of how my hands felt beneath the surface.

"You used that power in front of my warriors," he said. His voice was flat, not accusatory, but flat in the way of a man cataloging something significant.

"Yes," I said.

"They are afraid of you now."

"I know."

His gaze held mine for a moment that had enough weight to be felt across the room. "Good," he said, finally. "Fear of the wrong things has killed more armies than enemy blades."

It was not absolution. It was not even acceptance. But it was a line drawn somewhere new, and I understood it for what it was.

Kaelor moved around the table to my side. He did not touch me. He simply positioned himself at my flank with the unhurried, deliberate certainty of someone making their position physically legible to every person in the room. Before the full war council, in front of Draevok's faction commanders and his own inner circle and the warriors standing at the pavilion's outer ring, he stood beside me, and the statement of it needed no words.

Serathis looked at the ceiling briefly. "If you fools are finished bleeding pride, we have actual enemies below us."

The attack came at dusk.

Not from one direction. That was the first thing that told me this was not an opportunistic strike. The cult had been preparing multiple breach points simultaneously, using the primary chamber's disruption as cover for the secondary work, and when the seals gave way, they gave way all at once, from three separate locations along the camp's perimeter, close enough to create overlapping chaos and far enough apart that no single response could cover all of them.

The alarm horns sounded in rapid succession, each one carrying the specific cadence that meant *multiple points* rather than single engagement, and the camp transformed in the space of thirty seconds from a locked-down political crisis into something considerably more immediate.

I was moving before the third horn finished.

The nearest breach had opened at the camp's eastern storage yard, and I could feel it through the Labyrinth's awareness before I could see it with my eyes, a tear in the architecture that carried the specific wrongness of something forced open from the wrong side. Cultists poured through it in the gray dusk light, robed figures carrying blood-magic already active between their fingers, spreading through the supply rows with the organized movement of people who had studied the camp's layout from below.

Torren appeared at my left shoulder, breathing hard from running. "Good news," he said, slightly winded. "I found the breach on the south side."

"And?"

"He found me first." He produced a blade from his layered leathers with the practiced motion of someone who had never entirely stopped being a thief. "I have never missed ordinary assassins more. Simple people. One knife, one direction."

The eastern breach was the largest. I went for it, because the others could be managed by Kaelor's warriors with conventional weapons, but the Labyrinth architecture required something the warriors did not have. Behind me I could hear the camp erupting into organized combat, Serathis's voice cutting through the noise with the sharp efficiency of a battlefield commander directing traffic through disaster, Malakor's quieter instructions threading through the shouting with the precision of someone who has managed worse.

The breach point was a wound in the ground itself, a crack in the stone from which cold light seeped upward like light through a broken seal. Cultists were still emerging from it in a stream. I planted myself ten feet from its edge and reached into the Labyrinth's awareness the way I had in the chamber below, not fighting the pressure, not bracing against it, but threading my intent through it with the control I had not possessed three hours ago and was still only partially certain I possessed now.

The crack resisted. There was something on the other side, not Veltheris himself, but his architecture, the deliberate structural damage he had designed into the Labyrinth's foundation at these points, and closing it required more than will. It required addressing the damage rather than simply overriding it.

Something slammed into me from the left.

Not a blade. The impact carried the specific wrongness of blood-magic, a strike that bypassed physical contact and hit the awareness I had extended instead, like a blow aimed at the part of me that was currently threaded through stone. The pain was disorienting in a way that ordinary pain was not, because it came from a direction the body does not have defenses for.

I went down on one knee, my focus fracturing.

The cultist was already raising their hands for a second strike, fingers trailing the dark light that meant the next one would not be disorienting. It would be conclusive. I could feel it building in the air between us with the specific, inevitable quality of something that has already been decided by someone other than me.

Then Draevok stepped between us.

He moved with the mass and speed of a siege engine that had decided to become a duelist, his war blade already drawn, intercepting the cultist's strike with a counter that scattered the blood-magic sideways into the storage yard's stone walls. The cultist went for him instead, which was a significant miscalculation, and the fight lasted approximately four seconds before Draevok ended it with the economical brutality of a commander who had been killing things for forty years and had long since stopped wasting motion on it.

He turned back to me without ceremony. A cut had opened across his left shoulder at some point in the engagement, dark against his chestnut fur, and he was favoring his right side with the subtle shift of someone who has taken impact damage and is managing it rather than acknowledging it.

"Do not mistake this for fondness," he said.

I was already rising, pulling my focus back together. "Wouldn't dream of it."

He grunted, which I took as acknowledgment, and turned to engage the next cultist pushing through the breach.

I went back to the work.

The second attempt at the breach point was different. I had learned something from the first failure, or rather, the first failure had taught me something I had not been willing to accept in the abstract. Closing a forced breach was not the same as closing a seal. A seal had been placed deliberately, with intent and architecture, and closing it was a matter of returning that intent to its original position. A forced breach was damage. And damage required not closure but repair, working with the Labyrinth's own structural awareness rather than imposing my will over the top of it.

I stopped trying to close it and started listening to it instead.

The Labyrinth's awareness met me with the same vast patience it always carried, ancient and specific and entirely uninterested in the urgency I was bringing to the interaction. It knew the breach was there. It had known since the moment it was made. What it needed was not force but direction, someone whose blood was woven into its architecture acting as the instruction rather than the hand.

The breach sealed from the inside out, the crack in the stone drawing closed with the slow, grinding certainty of tectonic movement compressed into seconds, and the cold light from below went dark.

The cultists still above ground were cut off from reinforcement.

The battle's tenor changed immediately. Kaelor's warriors recognized the shift, the moment when the enemy stops receiving and starts being contained, and the camp's chaos began resolving itself into something with edges and outcomes. Serathis was already directing the systematic engagement of isolated cultists with the methodical focus of someone closing a net. Malakor had taken the southern breach, working alongside Torren, and from the distant sounds of that engagement it appeared to be going adequately, measured by the fact that Torren's voice was still audible and still sarcastic.

The western breach was Kaelor.

I found him at the camp's far perimeter, standing at the edge of a third breach point with three cultists already down around him and his war harness marked with dark residue from blood-magic strikes that his size and speed had apparently not entirely allowed him to avoid. The breach itself was smaller than the eastern one, more controlled, more deliberately placed, and he had held the perimeter around it alone for the time it had taken Serathis to redirect two squads to his position.

He looked at me across the distance of the western yard with the steady attention that did not require proximity to communicate its content, and I understood from the angle of his posture and the particular stillness of his expression that he had been aware of my engagement at the eastern breach and had made a deliberate choice to trust me to manage it rather than abandoning his own position to cover mine.

That trust, extended in the middle of a three-front battle without fanfare or declaration, landed somewhere in my chest with more force than almost anything that had happened in the tunnels below.

I sealed the western breach.

The camp went quiet in the gradual, uneven way that combat areas go quiet, the fighting resolving into individual engagements and then into silence, the horns shifting from alarm cadence to the single sustained note that meant the immediate threat had been contained. Talia was already moving through the storage yard with her satchel and two assistants, assessing the wounded with the quick, systematic attention of someone who had been preparing for this before the first horn sounded.

Draevok was near the eastern storage wall when I found him. He had not gone to the healers. He was standing against the stone with his war blade planted point-down in the ground, using it as a support with the studied casualness of a man determined not to look like he needed a support. The cut across his shoulder had not stopped, and the right side of his armor was dark with it, and the favoring I had noticed during the fight had become more pronounced in a way that suggested the impact damage was worse than he had initially allowed.

Kaelor came to stand beside him. Neither of them spoke for a moment, and the silence between them carried the specific texture of two people who have been in combat together recently and have not yet processed what that means for the argument they were having an hour ago.

Draevok looked at the camp around them, at the sealed breaches and the Talia-directed triage and the warriors standing down from combat readiness with the exhausted, functional focus of professionals who had done this before. He looked at me, briefly, with an expression I could not entirely interpret, and then he looked at Kaelor.

"Win the war, Ashhorn," he said. His voice was lower than usual, stripped of its battlefield projection, carrying only the weight of the words themselves. "Then we can hate each other properly."

Something in Kaelor's jaw moved. Not a smile. Something older and more specific, the recognition of a language only spoken between people who have bled in the same direction.

"Get him to Talia," Kaelor said, to the nearest guard, and his tone made it an order rather than a suggestion.

Draevok did not argue. That, more than anything else, told me how badly he was hurt.

I stood in the quieting eastern yard as the last of the battle's noise ebbed into the organized movement of aftermath, and let the Labyrinth's awareness settle back to its deep, patient rhythm beneath my feet. The sealed breaches held. The cult's access was cut. The camp was intact, damaged but intact, and the alliance that Veltheris had spent considerable effort trying to fracture tonight had instead spent the last hour fighting beside each other across three separate points.

It was not reconciliation. It was not trust rebuilt from the rubble of the last several hours. But it was something, and in a world where Veltheris was patient enough to have been working toward this for longer than most of the people in this camp had been alive, something was not nothing.

Torren materialized at my shoulder with the timing of someone who had been waiting for a dramatic moment to pass before inserting himself into it. He was bleeding slightly from a cut above his eyebrow and appeared to consider this a minor inconvenience at best. "For the record," he said, "I was also significantly useful during this portion of the evening."

"You were," I said.

He blinked, visibly startled by the absence of argument. "Oh. Well." A pause. "That's almost worse."

Kaelor came to stand beside me, his warmth registering at my shoulder in the cooling dusk air. He did not speak immediately. He simply stood there, and I stood there, and the camp moved around us in the organized noise of aftermath, and somewhere beneath us the Labyrinth breathed its slow, patient breath through stone that remembered things older than any of us, and whatever Veltheris was planning next, whatever door he was already standing at with his measured voice and his centuries of patience, he had not gotten what he came for tonight.

Not yet.

"He knew what my mother called me," I said, quietly.

Kaelor did not offer comfort. He did not offer assurance that it would be all right, or that the knowing of it meant less than it felt like it meant, because he understood, and had understood since the tunnel, that neither of those things were what I needed.

"Then we make him regret learning it," he said.

The night settled around us, cold and vast and already preparing itself for whatever came next.

# The Heart of the Maze

For the first time since entering Kaelor's world, I was the one everyone followed.

That knowledge sat strangely in my chest as we moved through the outer camp in the gray pre-dawn dark, the seven of us moving in a tight formation with Kaelor at my back and Malakor on my right and the sound of boots on stone behind me that had always, until this moment, belonged to someone else's lead. The sealed breaches were quiet. The camp's wounded were in Talia's care, Draevok was alive and furious about being confined to the healers' tent, and the particular silence that had settled over the encampment was not the silence of peace but the silence of an army that has fought through the night and is now holding its breath waiting for what comes next.

What came next was us.

Kaelor had called it a strike team, which was accurate in the way that calling a wound a scratch is technically accurate. Seven people against the full depth of what Veltheris had built beneath these stones. But seven was what the situation allowed, and at least three of those seven had survived worse by sheer refusal to respect the odds.

The breach point I had sealed last night had not entirely closed. I felt it before I saw it, the way you feel a change in air pressure before a storm arrives, a wrongness in the stone's awareness that radiated upward through my boots with the cold, specific insistence of something that had been forced and had not fully healed. The ground around it was darker than the surrounding stone, stained with the residue of blood-magic that had soaked into the Labyrinth's architecture and left its signature behind.

"Can you find the way?" Kaelor asked. His voice was low, stripped of everything except the question itself.

"Yes," I said.

"Then lead."

Two words. No ceremony, no qualification, no condition attached. He said it with the same absolute certainty he brought to every command, except this one was directed at me rather than issued from me, and the weight of it landed differently than I expected. Not heavy. Something closer to the feeling of a door opening that you had not known was closed.

I went down into the dark first.

The Labyrinth changed almost immediately.

I had been in these tunnels before. I knew the way the stone walls caught torchlight and threw it back in irregular angles, the smell of old earth and deep water and something metallic that had no obvious source, the particular quality of the silence that existed below ordinary sound. But this was different. Within twenty steps of descending into the breach, the passage shifted. Not dramatically, not in a way I could point to and name precisely, but the walls had moved. The angle of the corridor had changed. A door stood open to the left where no door had existed during any of our previous descents, its frame carved from stone so old the markings had been worn to shadows.

Torren noticed it at the same moment I did.

"I continue to find these murder tunnels offensively unsafe," he said quietly, from somewhere behind Malakor.

Serathis made a sound that was not approval.

I moved toward the open door without deliberating, because the Labyrinth's awareness was pulling my attention toward it with the same patient insistence it used when a seal required addressing, and I had learned, in the last several hours, that resisting that pull was considerably less useful than understanding it. The door was meant for me. The corridor beyond it angled downward at a steeper grade than anything I had navigated before, and the walls here were different, smoother, carved with markings that were not decorative but structural, the same architecture I had seen in the ritual chamber's ceiling, repeated in patterns that spiraled inward toward a vanishing point somewhere too far below to see.

"The maze knows her," Malakor said, behind me. He said it with no particular inflection, the observation of someone noting a tactical reality rather than a wonder. But I heard it land differently among the others.

I kept moving. The torches the elite guard carried threw our shadows long and strange against the carved walls, and the deeper we went, the more the torchlight seemed to be supplemented by something else, a faint luminescence coming from the markings themselves, as though the stone were offering its own illumination to someone whose blood it recognized.

Then Veltheris's voice came through the stone.

It was not a sound. That was the first thing I understood, and understanding it did not make it less invasive. It arrived the way the Labyrinth's awareness arrived, threaded through the architecture, present in the stone the way water is present in saturated earth. His voice came from the walls and the floor and the carved ceiling, calm and precise and intimate in a way that made the hair along my arms stand before my mind had finished processing the words.

"She came to me anyway. They always do, when the blood calls loudly enough."

Kaelor's hand found my shoulder from behind, a brief, deliberate pressure. I focused on the feeling of it and kept walking.

"Your mother crossed these halls once, you know." The voice shifted slightly, moving ahead of us as though leading us down a path it had already mapped. "Not willingly. Not the first time. But the Labyrinth has a way of making necessity feel like choice, and she was brilliant enough to understand the difference between the two. She called you vareth because she believed the word was a protection. She was wrong about that, as she was wrong about several things."

My jaw locked. The stone beneath my feet felt colder than it had ten steps ago.

"She thought hiding a key inside a child and calling it love would keep the door locked," Veltheris continued, and his voice carried the unsettling warmth of someone sharing a private sorrow. "It was a remarkable act of desperation. It bought you twenty-five years. That is longer than most keys last."

"Elara." Kaelor's voice was close, meant only for me. "He is reaching for the grief because it costs him nothing to use it."

"I know," I said. My voice came out steadier than the thing happening behind my sternum.

"He is still just a man standing in a tunnel below us."

"A man who has been doing this for centuries."

"So have I." A pause. "Almost."

Something in my chest loosened exactly enough to keep moving.

Veltheris did not speak again immediately. The silence that followed was considered rather than empty, the pause of something that has made its point and is willing to let it settle before adding to it. The tunnel continued its downward angle, and the markings on the walls grew denser, the spiraling patterns overlapping until the stone surfaces were almost entirely covered, and the luminescence from them was strong enough now that Torren had extinguished two of the torches to preserve them.

"He will use you the same way they all have," Veltheris said, when we had descended another two hundred feet. "They always do. The warlord is more honest about wanting you than your uncle was, I will grant him that. But want is not the same as respect, and possession dressed in protection is still possession. You know this. You have always known this."

I felt Kaelor's awareness at my back, steady and constant, and I did not turn around, because turning around was what Veltheris wanted, and because Kaelor had not given me any reason to doubt him tonight, or last night, or in the weeks before that, and because the voice in the stone was specifically calibrated to find the place where I was most likely to break and press against it with the patience of something that has broken things before.

I chose to keep moving. That choice, made deliberately, felt like sealing something.

The outer gate appeared without warning.

One moment the tunnel was a tunnel, stone walls and downward slope and carved markings, and then the corridor widened into a chamber the size of the war council pavilion above, and the gate stood at its far end, and Veltheris was already there.

He was exactly as I had imagined him, which was the worst part. The pale, translucent skin. The too-long fingers marked at every joint with carved ritual lines. The white hair hanging in sparse strands around a face that looked assembled from the idea of a face rather than any lived experience of having one. He stood before the gate with his hands folded in front of him and his head slightly tilted, and when his eyes found me across the chamber, they reflected something that was not the torchlight.

And beside him, small and crumpled and wearing the remnants of nobleman's clothing that had survived considerable mistreatment, stood my uncle.

Valerius looked older. That was the first thing I registered, the way the years had settled into him differently here than they had in the human world, or perhaps it was simply that the last time I had seen him, I had not been looking clearly. He was thinner. His hands shook with the constant, involuntary tremor I had noticed in the war council pavilion when his name had first been spoken as the fey's informant, and his eyes moved between Veltheris and me with the desperate, rapid calculation of a man trying to find an exit in a room that has no exits.

He found my face, and something in his expression shifted toward relief, which was so profoundly misplaced that it made my stomach turn.

"Elara." His voice broke on the second syllable. "Elara, please. I had no choice."

The words were so familiar they had become meaningless. He had been saying them, in different arrangements, since I was eight years old and our village was burning and he had been the one who had told the raiders which house to start with.

"You keep saying that," I said, "like cowardice is a prison."

His face crumpled. Not with shame. With the specific, practiced grief of a man who has used grief as a tool for so long he can no longer distinguish it from the genuine article.

"How touching," Veltheris said. His voice was the same in person as it had been through the stone, soft and measured and utterly unrattled. "A reunion. The Labyrinth does enjoy ceremony."

Kaelor stepped to my left. Serathis moved to the chamber's right edge. Malakor was already reading the room with his black eyes, cataloging Veltheris's position, the gate's structure, the distance between our group and the two figures at the far end, with the unhurried attention of someone who fights best when he has already finished the calculation before the first move.

Torren, behind me, said nothing. That alone told me he understood the weight of what we had walked into.

"Release him," Kaelor said. His voice carried across the chamber without effort, the authority of it absolute and cold.

Veltheris turned his gaze toward Kaelor with the expression of a scholar encountering an interesting but ultimately predictable specimen. "Your instinct is to cut through the problem," he said. "It is a reasonable instinct for a creature built for war. But if you kill the woman's uncle, the ritual activates. The blood-anchor is already placed."

He said it simply, without drama, the way you might note that a bridge has been mined. An obstacle. A fact. Something to be worked around or not, depending on whether you understood the architecture in time.

My attention went to Valerius's left forearm.

The mark was there. I felt it before I could see it, the same signature Veltheris used, the same spiral architecture I had pulled into visibility from Casseth's skin in the pavilion above. But this one was different in scale, deeper, embedded not just beneath the surface but threaded through the blood itself, and the connection it maintained was not to Veltheris but to the gate behind him.

Valerius was not a pawn. He was a mechanism. A living lock-pin woven into the ritual's foundation, and removing him incorrectly would not free him. It would complete the sequence.

"Cowardice is often more useful than devotion," Veltheris said, with something that might have been approval directed at Valerius, or might have simply been an academic observation. "Your uncle came to me believing he was negotiating. He was actually consenting. A useful distinction."

Valerius made a sound that was not quite a word. His eyes found mine again, and the relief had curdled into something more honest, the raw, stripped-back terror of a man who has spent his entire life being clever enough to survive and has finally walked into a room where cleverness was the trap.

"He marked me," Valerius said, and his voice had gone small and thin. "I didn't know. I thought it was a contract seal. He said it was a contract seal."

"It is a contract seal," Veltheris agreed pleasantly. "The contract is simply not with me."

Kaelor's hand was at his war blade. I felt the movement without seeing it, the particular shift in his weight that meant he had made a decision and was waiting only to confirm it was the right one. He was looking at Veltheris with the cold, focused attention of someone who has identified the threat and is already planning how to remove it, and under other circumstances, in a room without a blood-anchored ritual gate waiting to consume everything, I would have trusted that attention completely.

"Don't," I said.

He did not move. But he waited.

"The mark is threaded through his blood," I said, keeping my voice level. "Killing him doesn't close the ritual. It feeds it."

"Then we find another way to close it."

"I know what the other way is."

Veltheris had gone very still at the far end of the chamber. His head tilted slightly further, the attention of something that has expected to wait longer for the calculation to arrive.

"Your mother understood it too," he said, softly. "Eventually."

The grief hit me behind the ribs, sharp and specific and entirely unhelpful. I felt Kaelor's awareness sharpen at my side, reading the shift in my posture without needing to see my face, and I pushed the grief down to somewhere it could not reach my hands or my focus, because I needed both of those intact.

"The ritual requires a blood-anchor to open the gate," I said, mostly to myself, working through it aloud because the Labyrinth's awareness was feeding me the architecture and I needed to hear it spoken to trust that I was reading it correctly. "Valerius's blood is tied to the opening sequence. But the gate also requires a seal-bearer on the other side. Something capable of holding the architecture stable once it activates."

Veltheris watched me with the patient curiosity of a man who has already arrived at the destination and is interested to observe someone else making the journey.

"He doesn't have a seal-bearer," I said. "That's why he needed me here. Not to use my power against the gate. To use it as the counterweight."

"She was always going to understand," Veltheris said, to no one in particular. "It simply required time and proximity."

"What are you saying?" Kaelor's voice was controlled but the control was pressed thin, the sound of a man maintaining discipline over something that would rather break through it.

"I can seal Valerius's connection to the ritual without killing him," I said. "The mark is in his blood, but my power is in the Labyrinth's architecture itself. If I enter the ritual circle, I can sever the anchor from the inside rather than cutting through it."

A beat of silence.

"No." Kaelor's voice was absolute.

"It's the only way to close it without triggering the sequence."

"There is another way."

"Name it."

He did not answer immediately, and the silence that stretched between us carried the weight of a man who is genuinely searching for the answer and has not found it, which was more honest and more painful than refusal would have been.

"You step into that circle," he said, "and you are inside whatever he has built."

"I know."

"Elara."

"I know." I turned to look at him directly, and his molten gold eyes were fixed on my face with an intensity that had nothing restrained about it, all the control stripped back to something raw and specific and entirely unambiguous. "I am not doing this because I have no other option. I am doing this because it is the right move. There is a difference."

Something moved through his expression. Not acceptance. Something more complicated than acceptance, the specific anguish of a person who understands an argument completely and hates every word of it.

"If it goes wrong," he said, quietly.

"Then you pull me out."

"I cannot pull you out of a blood ritual."

"You can try." I held his gaze. "You are very good at doing things that should be impossible."

For a moment, nothing moved in the chamber. Then Kaelor exhaled once, slow and controlled, and the sound of it was the closest thing to surrender I had ever heard from him.

"I will be at the edge of it," he said. "The moment it destabilizes."

"I know."

I turned back toward the gate and Veltheris and the ritual circle inscribed in the stone floor before the gate's threshold, its markings glowing faintly with the same luminescence the tunnel walls had carried, and I walked toward it with my hands loose at my sides and my awareness extended into the Labyrinth's architecture the way Isyra had taught me, reading the structure as I approached it.

Valerius made a broken sound as I came closer. "Elara," he said. "Elara, I'm sorry. I know that means nothing. I know it. But I am sorry."

He looked it. That was the most honest thing about him, perhaps, that his terror was genuine even when his regret was questionable, and standing this close, I could see the mark on his forearm clearly now, the spiral pattern pressing against his skin from the inside, and beneath the architectural signature I could feel the way it was pulling at him, using his fear to feed itself, keeping him compliant through the specific mechanism of showing him what would happen if he stopped being useful.

Veltheris had chosen him well. A coward with something to lose, tied to a ritual through blood and terror, was considerably more reliable than someone who might find courage at the wrong moment.

"You do not deserve mercy," I told Valerius. My voice was quiet, and I meant every word of it, and I also meant what came next. "But I am not making this choice for your sake."

I stepped into the ritual circle.

The Labyrinth's awareness rose to meet me like a tide, vast and patient and overwhelmingly present, flooding through my extended senses with the full force of an architecture that had been waiting for this exact contact for considerably longer than I had been alive. The markings on the circle's floor blazed bright beneath my feet. Veltheris made a sound that was the first thing I had heard from him that was not entirely controlled, a sharp intake of breath, quickly suppressed.

I found the anchor immediately. It was impossible to miss from inside the ritual space, a cord of living magic running from the spiral on Valerius's arm through the circle's architecture and into the gate itself, feeding the opening sequence with a slow, steady pulse. Not dramatic. Mechanical. The Labyrinth did not distinguish between willing sacrifice and unwilling mechanism. It simply used what was connected to it.

I reached toward the anchor's connection point with my awareness, not to sever it, because severing it would release the stored energy into the gate and complete the sequence, but to redirect it. To insert my own connection between the anchor and the gate and act as the seal that Veltheris had planned to force me into being through coercion or capture.

The difference was that I was choosing it.

Veltheris moved for the first time since I had entered the circle, stepping forward from his position near the gate with something urgent and uncontrolled in his movements that I had not seen him display before. "That is not the sequence," he said, and his calm had developed a crack, a hairline fracture through the measured precision, like a surface that has been stable and has suddenly found a flaw.

"No," I agreed. "It's mine."

The anchor's connection to the gate began to separate. Not violently, not with the tearing sensation I had braced for, but slowly, the way ice separates from stone in the first warmth of spring, yielding to a force more patient than the bond holding it. Valerius cried out, a short, sharp sound, and collapsed to his knees as the mark on his forearm flared and then began to fade, the spiral pattern losing definition as the power threaded through it found its connection to the ritual redirected away from him.

"Stop," Veltheris said.

His voice had lost its warmth. What remained was still precise, still controlled, but the academic patience was gone, replaced by something colder and more urgent, the voice of a man who has spent centuries building toward a single moment and is watching it slip sideways.

"Your mother chose the gate over herself," he said. "She understood what the architecture required. You are making the same mistake she made before she understood."

The grief tried again. I felt it, the specific pull of it, the way his words were calibrated to land in the place where I had no armor, because I had never built armor over my mother's memory, had never needed to until he reached into it with his careful hands and used it as a lever.

I did not stop working.

"Your mother hid a key inside a child and called it love," he said, and his voice had gone intimate again, closing the distance between us through sound alone. "Everything you are doing right now is exactly what she did. You are sealing what should be opened. You are choosing the world as it is over the world as it could be. You are making her mistake."

"Maybe," I said. The anchor's connection to the gate was almost entirely severed. Valerius was still on his knees, breathing in ragged, shallow pulls. "Or maybe she was right, and you have spent two centuries failing to understand why."

The anchor broke.

The ritual circle's markings went dark, the blazing light extinguishing from the floor beneath me in a wave, and the gate shuddered, its architecture losing the blood-anchor's feeding pulse, the opening sequence collapsing back on itself without the mechanism to sustain it. Valerius made a sound that was either relief or agony and remained on the ground, breathing.

For three seconds, it felt like the end of something.

Then Veltheris moved toward the gate, and the gate responded to him directly, and I understood, too late, that I had closed the blood-anchor's contribution and had not accounted for the centuries of his own power woven into the architecture from the other side.

He did not need Valerius anymore.

He placed one long-fingered hand against the gate's surface, and the markings on his skin blazed silver-black, and the gate opened.

Not fully. Not with the catastrophic force of a completed ritual. But enough, a crack of impossible dark that breathed cold air from a depth no tunnel should have contained, and the chamber's geometry began to fail around it, walls tilting at angles that had nothing to do with structural damage and everything to do with the Labyrinth's deeper architecture asserting itself through the breach.

Torren swore with considerable creativity from somewhere behind me.

Veltheris stepped through the opening and turned back, and his face wore an expression I had not seen on him before, something almost satisfied, almost serene, the look of a man who has accepted that the path is longer than expected and has decided this does not constitute failure.

"Come home, little junction," he said.

Then the gate's crack widened, and the chamber tore open between us, and the Labyrinth's architecture collapsed sideways into impossible angles, and I heard Kaelor's voice shouting my name from somewhere that was suddenly much further away than it should have been, and I reached for him without thinking, turning toward the sound, and the ground between us was no longer the ground we had crossed to get here.

His hand caught mine. I felt the warmth of his grip, the impossible strength of it, the roughness of his war harness against my wrist as the chamber continued to shift and fracture around us, and for one moment, two seconds at most, we were connected across the chaos, his molten eyes finding mine through the collapsing geometry with the specific, focused intensity of a man refusing to let the world rearrange itself between him and something he will not release.

Then the Labyrinth moved, and the gap between us swallowed the distance, and his hand was gone.

The dark settled around me like stone.

And somewhere below, much further below than any of us had descended, Veltheris's presence moved through the Labyrinth's architecture with the patient, unhurried certainty of something that has been here before and knows exactly where it is going.

He had taken something with him when he fled. I felt the absence of it, a hollow space in the reach of my awareness, as though a thread of my own power had followed him through the gate and had not found its way back.

I was alone in the dark, and the Labyrinth breathed around me, and somewhere above me, on the other side of the collapsed architecture, Kaelor was still there.

I held onto that with both hands and did not let go.

# The Blood-Anchor

Valerius Thorne had betrayed everyone who ever loved him, and somehow the world still demanded Elara save him.

He was on his knees in the dark where the ritual circle had burned itself out, his breathing ragged and shallow, one hand pressed against the forearm where Veltheris's mark had been threaded through his blood like roots through old stone. The spiral was gone now, faded to a bruise-colored shadow beneath his skin, and without it he looked smaller than I had ever seen him. Smaller than my memory of him, smaller than the shadow he had cast over twenty-five years of my life.

The chamber around us was wrong. Not structurally collapsed, not yet, but the geometry had shifted when Veltheris passed through the gate, and the walls now met at angles that my eyes refused to resolve into sense. The carved markings on the stone had gone dark where the ritual's power had drained away, and in their absence the only light came from the faint, persistent luminescence the Labyrinth itself offered, threading pale silver through the floor's seams like light through a crack in a door.

Malakor was at my left, already scanning the chamber with the cold, methodical attention of someone reading a battlefield. Torren had gone very still behind him. Serathis stood near the chamber's far wall with one hand on her war blade, her clouded eye and her good one both fixed on the gate, which had not closed behind Veltheris so much as settled into a new, terrible configuration, its surface no longer a door but something more like a wound.

And Kaelor was not there.

The absence of him hit me before the thought finished forming. I turned, and the space where he had stood was empty, the geometry of the chamber having rearranged itself through that final, catastrophic shift into something that no longer contained him on my side of it. His voice had been there, shouting my name through the collapsing architecture. His hand had caught mine, for two seconds, across the chaos. And then the Labyrinth had moved and the distance between us had become something else entirely.

"He is on the other side of the collapse," Malakor said, reading my expression before I spoke. He said it flatly, without softness, which was more useful than comfort would have been. "The architecture shifted. He is not gone."

"I know he is not gone," I said. My voice was level. I made it level deliberately, the way you press a wound closed before you have time to feel it.

Valerius made a wet, broken sound from the floor.

I looked down at him. The anger was there, banked and hot, but it sat below something steadier now, something that had been forged in the ritual circle when I had chosen to step into it rather than be dragged. He looked up at me with his watery blue eyes and his trembling hands and his ruined nobleman's clothing, and I saw everything he was with a clarity that no longer required grief to process.

A coward who had run from every hard thing and called it pragmatism. A man who had sold his brother's family to save his own skin and spent twenty-five years constructing explanations for why he'd had no other option. A person so accustomed to being the smartest person in the room that he had walked directly into a centuries-old predator's trap because he had mistaken Veltheris's patience for negotiability.

"Please." His voice cracked on the word. "You are still my blood."

"No," I said. "You are only my warning."

He flinched as though I had struck him. I had not. I had simply told him the truth, and the truth, delivered without cruelty and without heat, was apparently more difficult to absorb than a blow.

I crouched down to his level, not to comfort him, but because I needed to see the mark's residue clearly. The spiral was gone, as I had thought, but the connection it had maintained left a signature in his blood the way old fire leaves char in stone, and I needed to know whether any part of Veltheris's architecture remained threaded through him before I decided what to do next.

It did not. The severance had been clean. Painful, clearly, from the way he was breathing, but clean.

"You are free of it," I told him. "The anchor is gone."

"He still has you marked," Valerius said, urgently, his hand reaching toward my wrist. "He said your power was tethered to the gate. He said when you entered the circle, part of you would follow him through it."

"I know."

"Elara, please, you have to understand, I never meant for any of this, I thought I could manage it, I thought I could control the terms, I thought —"

"Stop." I stood, stepping back from his reaching hand without touching it. "I know what you thought. You thought you could negotiate with something that had already decided you were a mechanism. You were wrong. You are alive because I chose to make you a problem I could solve rather than one I could simply remove." I paused. "Do not make me reconsider the math."

His hand dropped. He stayed on the floor.

Serathis made a sound at my back, low and brief, that I had learned to recognize as the closest she came to approval.

"The gate is still open," Malakor said. He had moved closer to it while I dealt with Valerius, close enough that the cold air breathing from its surface was lifting the loose strands of his silver hair. "Not fully. Not the catastrophic breach the ritual was designed to create. But open enough that the Labyrinth's deeper architecture is exposed." He turned to look at me. "He took something from you when he went through."

"Yes."

"Can you feel where he is?"

I extended my awareness the way Isyra had taught me, reading the Labyrinth's architecture the way a healer reads a wound, following the thread of sensation rather than fighting it. The hollow space where Veltheris had pulled at my power was still there, a gap in the reach of my own awareness, but it was not entirely severed. More like a cord pulled taut, the far end of it somewhere below us, somewhere deeper in the Labyrinth's heart, moving with the patient, unhurried certainty of something that has found a path it has walked before.

"Below," I said. "He is going deeper. He does not need the full ritual now. He has a fragment of the sealing power and enough of the gate open to work with."

"Then we follow," Serathis said.

"Kaelor is on the other side of the collapse," I said.

"I am aware." She met my eyes steadily. "He will find the way through. He always does. The question is whether Veltheris reaches the Labyrinth's core before we can stop him."

It was not a comfortable assessment. It was correct.

I looked at the gate. The crack in it had not widened since Veltheris passed through, but it was not stable either, its edges flickering with the slow, irregular pulse of architecture under tension, the way a bridge sways before it decides whether to hold. The geometry around it was still wrong, walls still meeting at angles that defied ordinary spatial logic, and the cold air coming through the gap smelled of stone so deep it had never known sunlight, and something else beneath that, something that had no name I could easily reach for, the smell of the space between things.

Torren appeared beside me, quiet for once, his sharp amber eyes moving between the gate and my face. "I want to note, for the record," he said, "that I have survived several situations that should have killed me by maintaining a policy of not following ancient cult leaders into collapsing magical architecture."

"Noted," I said.

"I am going to follow you anyway," he said. "But I want it known that I find this deeply unreasonable."

Something in my chest loosened, briefly and almost painfully. He meant it as a joke and it landed as something more than that, the specific relief of knowing that the people at your back are choosing to be there rather than simply assigned.

"Valerius," I said, turning to where my uncle still knelt on the stone floor. "You cannot come with us. The Labyrinth will not read you safely now that the anchor mark is gone. Find a way up. Follow the luminescence in the walls toward the upper tunnels." I paused. "Do not make me regret the mercy."

He stared up at me, and I watched the calculations move behind his eyes, the lifelong habit of assessing every situation for advantage, for angle, for exit. Then something in his face changed, something smaller and more honest surfacing through the habitual performance of it, and he nodded once, without speaking, which was the most genuine response I had ever received from him.

I turned back to the gate.

"Malakor," I said. "Can you read the passage structure through the opening?"

"It is not a passage," he said. "It is a fold. The architecture on the other side does not follow standard geometry. We will need to move by feel rather than by sight."

"That is fine," I said. "I have been moving by feel since we entered these tunnels."

He accepted that without comment. Malakor's silences were different from Kaelor's. Where Kaelor's quiet carried weight and heat and the constant awareness of his presence pressing against your senses, Malakor's was simply the absence of unnecessary sound. It was, in its own way, easier to work beside.

The gate's opening was narrower than it looked from a distance. I went through first, because the Labyrinth's awareness oriented around my connection to it and the thread of stolen power below gave me something to follow, and because standing outside it waiting for someone else to test it first would have cost time we did not have.

The cold hit immediately, sharper and more specific than the chamber's ambient chill, and the geometry on the other side resolved itself with the slow, reluctant logic of a dream that knows you are watching it too closely. The walls here were not stone in any ordinary sense. They were older than stone, or stone that had been remade into something else by centuries of the Labyrinth's deepest architecture pressing through it, and the markings carved into them were not the same spiral patterns from the upper tunnels but something older still, the grammar of a language written before the people who built this place had names for what they were doing.

I followed the thread of Veltheris's passage through it and did not look back.

He was waiting.

Not in ambush, not with weapons, not with the theatrical staging of a villain who has prepared a scene. He stood in the center of a space that was neither chamber nor corridor, a place where the Labyrinth's deeper architecture had opened itself into something that breathed, walls moving with the slow, rhythmic expansion of something alive, the stone itself cycling through patterns that were almost organic. He stood in the center of it with his hands folded and his translucent face tilted slightly upward, as though listening to something above ordinary hearing.

When he heard us, he looked down. His eyes found mine across the shifting space, and the expression on his face was not the one I expected. It was not triumph. It was something closer to grief, though grief refracted through a mind that had spent so long rearranging itself away from ordinary feeling that what remained barely resembled the original emotion.

"You followed the tether," he said. "I thought you might."

"Give it back," I said.

"It is not a thing I took," he said. "It followed me. Power recognizes architecture. Your blood knows what this place is, and part of it chose to go where the gate opened." He paused. "You cannot blame a river for finding the sea."

"I am not a river," I said. "And you are not the sea."

His head tilted. "Mercy is merely cruelty delayed," he said, softly. "What you did in the chamber above, freeing your uncle, severing the anchor rather than allowing the ritual to complete, you have not prevented anything. You have moved the consequence further down the path. The Labyrinth will open. The veil between worlds will fail. The only variable remaining is whether you are the one who chooses how."

"She can close it," Malakor said from behind me. He said it simply, without heat. "Let her work."

Veltheris looked at Malakor with the expression of someone encountering a curiosity they have already cataloged and set aside. "A defector," he said. "How familiar. Conscience arrives late, as it always does, wearing the clothing of purpose." He returned his attention to me. "The warlord is not here. You have noticed that. You are trying not to let it change your thinking. You are failing."

He was not wrong about that last part, and the accuracy of it made my jaw tighten.

"What I notice," I said, "is that you are standing in the middle of a space you cannot fully control, holding a fragment of power that does not belong to you, trying to talk me out of the thing you are most afraid I will do." I took a step forward. "You lost your calm back there. In the chamber. When I entered the circle and chose the seal rather than the opening. You made a sound."

His face went very still.

"That was the first time," I said. "In everything I have watched you do, in everything I have heard from the stone walls and the people you have used and the architecture you have spent centuries building, that was the first time something surprised you." I took another step. "You built this ritual around the assumption that I would have to be forced into the circle. That the choice would be taken from me. That is why you needed the blood-anchor, why you needed Valerius, why you needed the coercion of the gate's activation to override my will." The space around us was shifting, the walls cycling through their breathing patterns, and I could feel the Labyrinth's awareness rising to meet me with the same patient tide it had offered in the ritual circle above. "You do not know what to do with someone who walks in willingly."

Something moved through his expression. Fast, and quickly controlled, but there.

"Your mother walked in willingly," he said. "Eventually. After she understood."

"My mother hid a key inside a child and called it love," I said, and my voice did not shake, though the grief tried. "You have been telling me that since we entered these tunnels. You keep returning to it because you believe it will break my focus. It will not. Not because I am not grieving her, but because what she did was right, and you have spent two hundred years failing to understand why, and I am done letting you use her memory as a crowbar."

He was silent. The breathing walls moved around us. The thread of stolen power was close now, wound into the architecture of the space itself, and I could feel the Labyrinth's deep awareness waiting with the patience of something that has always known this moment was coming.

I reached for it.

Not violently. Not with the tearing force of a severance. I reached for the fragment of my own power the way you reach for something you set down in a strange place and finally remember where you left it, with the specific, quiet certainty of recognition rather than reclamation.

Veltheris moved, fast for the first time, his long-fingered hands coming up with the carved ritual scars blazing silver-black, and the architecture of the space lurched sideways as he directed the Labyrinth's deeper power against my reach, throwing the weight of centuries of built intention between my awareness and the fragment.

The collision was not physical. It was architectural, two competing understandings of what the space was for pressing against each other through the medium of the Labyrinth's awareness, and it hit me behind the sternum like a wave, and I went to one knee on the moving stone floor and stayed there, breathing, because the impact had been real even without a body behind it.

"You cannot reclaim it through will alone," Veltheris said. He was still precise, still controlled, but the warmth had left his voice entirely now, and what remained was the cold, stripped urgency of someone who has stopped performing patience because patience has failed. "The power I carry is woven into the gate's architecture. Taking it back would require closing the gate, and closing the gate requires the sacrifice of the anchor that holds the threshold stable." He paused. "There is no clean solution. There is only the one I have been offering you since the beginning."

"Surrender myself to stabilize it," I said, from my knee.

"Become the lock," he said. "Willingly. Permanently. As your mother almost did."

Torren made a sharp, negative sound somewhere behind Malakor. Serathis did not make a sound at all, which told me she was already calculating odds.

I stayed on my knee and felt the Labyrinth breathe around me and thought about what Isyra had told me in the dim light of her sanctuary, about keys and locks and the difference between a door that cannot be opened and a door that simply chooses to remain closed. About my mother, who had understood the architecture well enough to hide a bloodline inside a child and seal it with the specific, stubborn love of someone who believed the world was worth protecting even when it cost everything.

She had not become the lock.

She had become the decision.

And the decision was mine now, and it was not the one Veltheris had built his centuries toward, because he had made the same error he always made, the one I had named to his face in the breathing chamber above. He believed power existed only through control. He had built an entire theology around it, an entire ritual architecture, an entire life. And he had never understood, not once in two centuries of working toward this moment, that the Labyrinth was not a weapon and not a prison and not a mechanism.

It was a boundary.

And boundaries did not require masters. They required choice.

I reached for the fragment again, and this time I did not reach for it as a reclamation. I offered it a way home instead.

The difference was everything.

The power recognized me before Veltheris could redirect his architecture against it, snapping back through the Labyrinth's awareness with the speed of something returning to its source, and the stolen fragment reintegrated with a force that sent a wave of heat through my blood so intense I felt it in my teeth. The gate's architecture shuddered. Veltheris made a sound that was not controlled, a sharp, raw exhale of genuine shock, and the silver-black blazing of his ritual scars flickered and went unsteady for the first time.

I stood.

"You built this to be opened," I said. "I was built to stop this."

He recovered his composure with the speed of someone who has practiced composure the way soldiers practice defense, and his face went smooth and precise again, and his hands steadied. But the crack was there now, visible, a hairline fracture through the certainty, and below it was something I had not expected to find in him.

Rage. And beneath it, calculation already reforming.

Not of death. He had spent too long with death to fear it simply. Fear of irrelevance. Fear that the structure he had built his existence around was wrong, not strategically but fundamentally, and that all the centuries and all the ritual and all the careful, patient work had been built on a premise that the Labyrinth itself did not recognize.

I felt almost sorry for him. Almost.

Then I sealed the gate.

It was not a dramatic event. No explosion of light, no shattering of stone, no theatrical collapse of his carefully constructed architecture into ruin.

The Labyrinth's awareness rose through me the way it always did when I worked with it rather than against it, vast and patient and older than anything I had a name for, and I directed it toward the wound in the gate's surface with the specific, focused intention of someone who knows exactly what a door is for.

The crack sealed. Not slowly, not reluctantly. It closed the way a held breath releases, with the particular ease of something returning to the state it was always meant to maintain.

Veltheris reached for the architecture one final time, his hands blazing, his composure fracturing entirely now, and for a moment the gate shuddered under the competing pressures, and the space around us lurched sideways, and I felt the weight of his centuries pressing against my intention with everything he had built and everything he was.

He was very strong.

He was not stronger than the Labyrinth, so he chose to close.

The gate sealed.

In the silence that followed, Veltheris stood in the center of the breathing space with his hands lowered and his face stripped of everything that had made it readable, and the Labyrinth's awareness moved around him with the slow, implacable attention of something that has noticed an irregularity and is deciding what to do about it.

He understood what was happening before I spoke.

"You cannot imprison me here," he said. His voice was still precise. Still quiet. But something had gone out of it, the specific light of certainty, and what remained was the voice of a man who has finally arrived at an outcome he never modeled.

"I am not imprisoning you," I said. "The Labyrinth is. I am simply agreeing with it."

The walls closed around him, not with violence, not with the dramatic crush of stone on bone, but with the slow, patient inevitability of architecture returning to its intended configuration. The breathing space contracted inward, and Veltheris stood in the center of it, and his expression went through something I could not fully name: grief and fury and the particular, terrible blankness of a mind confronting something it was not built to accept.

Then the Labyrinth folded around him, the deeper architecture closing in layers of shifting stone and living geometry that forced him backward into the collapsing threshold. Veltheris's expression changed. Not fear, not exactly, but fury stripped clean of patience.

"This changes nothing," he said.

Then the Labyrinth sealed between us.

Not a prison. Not a final ending. A containment. A delay.

And something in the architecture told me, with the same ancient certainty it used for everything else, that even the deepest locks eventually open if enough pressure is applied for long enough.

The space went still.

And then the walls began to move in a different way.

"We need to leave," Malakor said. He did not raise his voice. He did not need to. The urgency was in the economy of it, the stripped-down precision of someone reading structural failure. "Now. The architecture is collapsing inward without the gate's tension to hold it."

I was already moving.

The passage back through the fold was narrower than before, the geometry compressing as the Labyrinth's deeper architecture retracted around the sealed space, and we moved through it at speed, Serathis and Malakor ahead and Torren at my back, and the stone was making sounds it had not made on the way down, not cracking but settling, the deep, resonant groan of something very old returning to the shape it had always wanted to hold.

We came through the fold and back into the outer chamber, and it was wrong in every direction, the walls closer than they had been, the geometry still fractured from Veltheris's passage, and the gate's sealed surface behind us was dark and quiet and still.

And on the far side of the chamber, where the geometry had shifted and swallowed the distance between us, Kaelor was there.

He came through the collapsed architecture with the particular, relentless focus of something that has been moving through obstacles without stopping, his war harness scored with dust and something darker, his ivory horns trailing the silver luminescence of the Labyrinth's markings still fading from his passage through its walls. His molten gold eyes found me across the chamber before he had fully cleared the passage, and the expression on his face was not relief and not fury and not the controlled blankness he wore in council.

It was something rawer and more honest than any of those.

He crossed the chamber in four strides and his hands found my face with a gentleness that was almost unbearable from someone his size, cupping my jaw with his rough, warm palms, and he looked at me with that stripped-back intensity, checking me for damage the way you check something you were afraid to lose, and I let him, because my hands had already found his forearms and were holding on with more force than I intended.

"It is done," I said.

"I know." His voice was low and rough around the edges. "I felt the gate close."

"We need to move," Malakor said, from behind us. "The architecture is still contracting."

Kaelor's hands dropped from my face to my wrist, and his grip there was firm and certain, and he turned without releasing me and we moved together toward the passage that led upward, toward the tunnels, toward the fractured light of the camp above, with the Labyrinth settling itself into its sealed configuration around us and the walls moving back toward their proper angles and the carved markings returning to dark as the deep architecture completed the work I had begun.

Behind us, the inner gate was closed. The veil was intact. Veltheris was sealed away, at least for now.

Ahead of us, the tunnel opened upward, and the air tasted of stone and cold and the faint, specific scent of the world above.

I did not look back. There was nothing left behind me worth turning toward, and everything worth moving toward was already in the direction I was going.

Kaelor's grip on my wrist did not loosen, not even when the passage widened enough that we could have separated into single file. I did not try to pull free.

The Labyrinth breathed around us, slow and deep and finally quiet, and we climbed toward the light.

# The Sleeping Maze

The Labyrinth did not take me somewhere else. It took me inward.

One moment I was moving through the tunnel with Malakor and Serathis ahead of me and Torren at my back, the sealed gate cooling behind us like an ember finally spent. The next, the stone beneath my feet shifted with the slow, deliberate purpose of something that had been waiting, and the passage I was walking through folded itself sideways and deposited me somewhere that was not the tunnel and was not the outer chambers and was not any physical place I had a name for.

The others were gone.

I stopped moving and listened, and the silence I heard was not the silence of an empty space. It was the silence of a space that was paying attention.

The walls around me were not stone, not exactly. They were the suggestion of stone, the Labyrinth rendering itself as architecture the way a dream renders a house, structurally plausible but wrong in the details if you looked too carefully. The light came from everywhere and nowhere, the same pale silver threading I had followed through the tunnels below, but diffuse here, ambient, as though the space itself were faintly luminous. The air smelled of cold and old stone and something else beneath both of those, something that had no physical source. It smelled like memory.

I turned in a slow circle and took stock.

No immediate threat. No visible enemy. No passage back the way I had come, because the way I had come no longer existed in any direction I could locate. The Labyrinth had separated me from the others with the casual precision of something that had simply decided the time had come, and arguing with it felt about as useful as arguing with the tide.

"All right," I said, to the empty space and to whatever was listening through it. "What do you want to show me?"

The walls moved.

Not with the violent, geometric lurching of the collapsing architecture below. Slowly, the way water moves when you disturb its surface and wait for the ripples to settle. The corridor ahead of me lengthened and opened, and the light changed quality, warmer and more specific, and I walked forward because standing still had never saved anyone in a place like this, and because the thread of stolen power I had been following since the outer chamber was still present somewhere below my sternum, pointing me forward and down with the patient insistence of a compass that only knew one direction.

The first memory hit me before I recognized it as one.

I was seven years old and the border village was burning and my mother was pulling me through the smoke with one hand and pressing something cold and small into my palm with the other, and her voice was very low and very urgent and she said, *remember this is yours, it has always been yours, do not let anyone tell you otherwise,* and I had not understood what she meant and the smoke had been everywhere and then she was gone, and I had spent eighteen years telling myself I had not understood because I had been seven and frightened, and the truth was I had not wanted to understand because understanding would have required accepting that she had known and chosen anyway.

The corridor released me from the memory the way you release a held breath.

I kept walking.

The second memory was not mine. Or it was mine now, absorbed through the Labyrinth's awareness the way the stone absorbed heat, carrying impressions of things it had witnessed long before I arrived. A woman I recognized from the portrait Mother Isyra had once described to me, raven-haired and lean and standing in a space very like this one, her hands pressed to the walls, her expression set with the particular, costly calm of someone who has made a decision they cannot unmake. My mother, in the Labyrinth's deeper architecture, twenty-six years ago, doing the thing Veltheris had spent centuries trying to force me to replicate.

She had not looked like someone being coerced.

She had looked like someone choosing.

I had to stop walking for a moment after that one. I pressed my own hand to the wall and let the cold of it anchor me, and I breathed, and I let the grief sit where it had always lived, in the space behind my ribs where I kept the things I did not have the luxury of feeling in the middle of a crisis. It was still there. It was not smaller than it had been. But it was mine, and it was not a weapon anyone else could reach for, and that made it bearable.

I walked on.

Veltheris was waiting where the corridor opened into a space that was neither chamber nor corridor, the same breathing architecture I had encountered below but rendered here with more clarity, the walls cycling through their slow organic patterns with the unhurried certainty of something that had been doing this for longer than any of us had been alive. He stood with his hands folded and his translucent face very still, and his eyes found mine with the focused attention of someone who had been expecting me and had spent the waiting time deciding exactly what to say.

He looked, I noticed, slightly less certain than he had below. The fracture I had put in his composure when I reclaimed the stolen power fragment had not entirely sealed itself over. There was something in the set of his jaw, something compressed and carefully managed, that had not been there in the outer chambers. It was not quite what I would have called fear. It was the specific tension of a mind that has encountered a variable it could not fully account for and is still working to incorporate it into its existing model.

"You are still following the tether," he said. "Even here."

Veltheris turned as I entered the inner space, his translucent expression unreadable in the shifting silver light.

For a moment, neither of us spoke.

Then his gaze flicked past me, toward the architecture behind me, and something in his expression sharpened.

“You brought him,” he said.

“Eventually,” I said.

“You continue to mistake attachment for strength.”

“No,” I said. “You continue to mistake isolation for power.”

His mouth tightened almost imperceptibly.

“The threshold is sealed,” I said. “Your ritual failed.”

“For now.”

“Yes,” I said. “For now.”

The Labyrinth shifted around us, breathing slowly, its ancient awareness no longer uncertain but settled.

Veltheris looked at the walls, then back at me, and for the first time I understood that he could feel it too.

The architecture had chosen.

“You think this is victory,” he said.

“I think this is delay,” I said. “And right now, delay is enough.”

Then the wall behind me opened.

Kaelor stepped through.

He looked exhausted, furious, and entirely real.

His eyes found mine first.

“Tell me what to do,” he said.

“Trust me.”

“Always.”

Veltheris’s expression changed—not fear, but something colder.

Calculation.

Then the Labyrinth moved.

Not violently.

Simply decisively.

The deeper architecture folded inward around Veltheris, not crushing, not destroying, but forcing him backward as the threshold's sealed geometry completed itself around him.

“This changes nothing,” he said.

“Probably not,” I said.

The stone closed between us.

Not an ending.

A postponement.

Then the walls began to move in a different way, not the organic breathing of the inner architecture but the settling groan of something very old returning to its resting state, and the cold receded further and the light shifted from silver to the warmer amber of torch-flame, and the corridor that had brought me here reappeared in the wall to my left with the unhurried certainty of a passage that knows it is no longer needed and is offering to close.

"We need to move," Kaelor said, from behind me. His hands were still on my shoulders. He had not moved them during the entire confrontation, and the warmth of them, even through the fabric between his palms and my skin, was a specific and present thing.

"I know," I said.

"Are you hurt?"

I took inventory. My arms ached from the threshold's cold to the elbows, and there was a specific, bone-deep exhaustion settling over me that had nothing to do with physical exertion and everything to do with the sustained effort of directing the Labyrinth's awareness through a sustained confrontation. My hands were shaking slightly. I noticed that without alarm. Shaking was reasonable.

"I am functional," I said.

"That is not what I asked."

I turned, finally, and found him much closer than the distance of his hands on my shoulders had suggested, his gold eyes very steady and his expression carrying that stripped-back quality that appeared when he had stopped performing composure and was simply himself beneath it.

"I will tell you later," I said. "When we are out of here."

Something in his expression shifted, and he nodded once.

The corridor the Labyrinth had opened was narrow and the light within it was amber and moving, and the passage tilted upward almost immediately, angled toward the upper tunnels with the direct efficiency of architecture that has stopped being deliberately obstructive and is now simply trying to complete the transaction. The sounds the stone made around us were different from the sounds it had made during the confrontation, lower and more rhythmic, the deep settling resonance of very old material returning to its preferred configuration.

I went first and Kaelor followed, close enough that I was aware of him without needing to look back, his presence a consistent warmth and weight behind me that I had stopped trying to pretend I did not notice and had simply incorporated into my awareness as a fact, the way you incorporate the sound of breathing in a shared room.

The passage widened as we climbed, and then widened again, and the amber light strengthened, and then the stone beneath my hands changed texture, becoming less worn and more rough-edged, and the air changed quality too, losing the deep, mineral cold of the inner Labyrinth and gaining the specific chill of stone that had contact with the surface world.

We came through into the outer corridor and found Malakor ten feet ahead, standing with his back to the wall with his arms crossed and his black eyes moving over us with the rapid, methodical assessment of someone who has been maintaining position and taking inventory simultaneously. Serathis was beside him, her good eye and her clouded one both fixed on the passage we had come through. Torren was slightly further down the corridor, leaning against the wall with his arms crossed and an expression that was working very hard to appear casual and not entirely succeeding.

"You sealed it," Malakor said. Not a question.

"Yes," I said.

"Veltheris?"

"Contained. Not destroyed. The seal will hold for now."

He absorbed this with the brief, economical nod of someone filing information rather than celebrating it. Serathis said nothing, but the set of her shoulders changed in a way I had learned to read as acknowledgment from someone who did not dispense approval in audible form.

Torren pushed off the wall and fell into step beside me as we moved toward the upper passage.

"I want to be clear," he said, "that I maintained an extremely composed and professional demeanor during the entire period you were both unreachable in whatever that was."

"You were not composed," Serathis said, from behind him.

"I was internally composed," Torren said. "The external expression was tactical anxiety. There is a difference."

The exhaustion was real and heavy and settling deeper as we climbed, and the ache in my arms had extended to my shoulders, and the grief I had been holding in the space behind my ribs was still there, would likely be there for a long time, but it was not crushing, it was simply present, the specific weight of something that had been carried for long enough that you had learned to compensate for it without stopping.

Kaelor moved up beside me when the passage widened enough to permit it, and he did not speak, but his hand found mine in the near-dark of the upper tunnel and his grip was warm and certain and he did not let go, and I did not pull free, and neither of us said anything about it.

The tunnel opened upward and the air changed and the faint, specific scent of the world above reached us, stone and cold and something green beneath both of them, something that had never been underground, and then the passage ended and the camp opened before us and the sky above it was the deep, washed-out grey of very early morning, the hour before color returns to the world, and the torches were still burning at the perimeter and the sentries were still posted and the camp was intact and present and real.

I stood at the tunnel's mouth for a moment and breathed it.

The Labyrinth breathed behind me, slow and deep and finally quiet, the way something breathes when it has completed a long exertion and found rest. The veil-threshold was sealed. The inner gate was closed. Veltheris was contained beyond it, patient and present and alive, and that last part was not comfortable, but it was honest, and I had learned enough in the past weeks to know that honest discomfort was more useful than comfortable illusion.

I looked at Kaelor beside me, at the cut above his brow and the scored harness and the fading rune-glow on his ivory horns, and he was looking at the sky above the camp with an expression I had not seen on him before, something that had the quality of relief so profound it had moved past emotion into something more structural, the specific expression of someone who has been braced for a loss that did not come and is only now beginning to believe it.

He felt me looking and turned, and his gold eyes held mine in the grey pre-dawn light, and neither of us spoke for a moment.

"The veil is sealed," I said. "Veltheris is contained. His ritual is stopped."

"Yes," he said.

"That does not mean he is finished."

"No," he agreed. "It means we have time."

I considered that. Time was not something I had expected to come out of this tunnel with. Time felt, at this particular moment, like a gift of such improbable proportions that I was not entirely sure what to do with it.

"Come," Kaelor said, and his hand, still holding mine, drew me forward out of the tunnel mouth and into the grey morning air of the camp. "The rest can wait until you have eaten something and sat down."

Behind us, the passage sealed itself with the quiet, final click of the Labyrinth completing its configuration, and the stone was smooth and unbroken and solid as though the tunnel had never existed at all.

I did not look back.

Malakor was already moving toward the command tent with the efficient purpose of someone who has a list of immediate priorities and is working through it in order. Serathis fell in beside him. Torren lingered for a moment at the tunnel's former mouth, looking at the smooth stone with an expression that hovered between relief and the specific, skeptical appraisal of someone who has survived enough impossible situations to know that smooth stone does not necessarily mean the problem is solved.

Then he looked at me and Kaelor, at our joined hands, and something crossed his face that was not quite a smile and not quite the sharpness of a comment forming, and he turned and walked toward the camp without saying anything at all.

Which was, from Torren, its own form of acknowledgment.

The morning was coming in from the east, grey lightening toward silver, and somewhere in the camp a fire was burning and the smell of it reached me through the cold air, wood smoke and the faint, warm suggestion of something cooking, and the specific exhaustion of the past hours was settling over me with the full, comprehensive weight of everything I had been holding at bay while there was still something immediate to act on.

I walked into the camp with Kaelor beside me and the Labyrinth sealed behind us, and the veil was intact, and Veltheris was contained, and the war was not over but the immediate catastrophe was not.

And for the first time in longer than I could clearly calculate, the next thing I had to do was not survive something.

It was simply continue.

The distinction was, I was discovering, more significant than it sounded.

# A Crown of Blood and Horns

I came out of the Labyrinth covered in blood, dust, and the impossible proof that I had survived myself. The exit tunnel spat us into the gray pre-dawn light of the encampment, and the sudden openness felt wrong after hours of shifting stone and sealed memory. My legs carried me forward anyway. Behind us the passage sealed with a grinding groan that sent dust drifting across the trampled ground, and I did not look back to watch it vanish.

Kaelor stayed close, one hand resting at the small of my back as though he needed the contact to believe I had made it through. His breathing was steady, but the tension in his frame had not eased. The camp around us moved with the careful rhythm of soldiers who had spent the night braced for worse than they received. Fires burned low. Watchers shifted along the perimeter. A low murmur of voices carried the weight of questions no one had found the courage to ask yet.

I kept walking toward the central clearing where the war council ground had been prepared. My body ached in places I had not noticed while the Labyrinth still held my attention, and the echo of Veltheris's voice lingered behind my thoughts like an unfinished threat. He was sealed. Not dead. The distinction mattered more than I wanted to admit.

The clans had gathered without being summoned. Word traveled faster than orders in a place like this. I saw Serathis first, her iron-brown fur catching the torchlight as she straightened from a low conversation with two of her captains. Malakor stood slightly apart, arms crossed, his dark eyes tracking our approach with the same measured assessment he had given us inside the tunnels. Torren leaned against a supply cart, pretending to clean a blade that already gleamed. Talia hovered near the healer tents, relief plain across her face when she spotted us.

Draevok was the one I had not expected to see upright. A jagged wound ran across his chest beneath hastily applied bandages, and his massive frame swayed slightly with each breath. Blood matted the dark chestnut fur along his ribs. Yet he had come. He met my gaze across the clearing without flinching, and something in his expression had shifted since the last time we stood this close.

Kaelor guided me to the center of the gathered clans. The silence that settled was not hostile. It carried the heavier quality of attention being paid rather than withheld. I stopped when the firelight reached my boots and turned to face them all. My voice felt steadier than the exhaustion in my bones should have allowed.

"The veil is sealed," I said. "Veltheris is contained for now. The immediate threat from the cult has collapsed with him."

A ripple moved through the gathered warriors. Some of them had expected me to claim victory. Others had braced for worse news. I kept my shoulders square and continued before the moment could fracture into argument.

"I did not do it alone," I added. "And I am not offering myself as any kind of savior. I am here because I chose to be. That is all."

Kaelor stepped forward then, his presence drawing every eye without effort. The firelight caught on the silver runes etched into his horns and threw sharp shadows across the broad planes of his chest. He did not raise his voice. He did not need to.

"Elara Thorne stands with the clans by her own will," he said. "She is not a weapon we seized. She is not a prize to be claimed. She is the one who turned the Labyrinth against the one who sought to break it. Anyone who questions her place here questions me."

The declaration landed with the weight of stone settling into place. I watched faces shift through recognition and calculation. Some warriors nodded. Others held their expressions carefully neutral. Draevok pushed away from the support he had been leaning against and took one unsteady step forward. Blood seeped fresh through the bandages at his side.

"She is still dangerous," he said. His voice carried the blunt honesty that had always defined him. "A human carrying that kind of power was never going to be safe. But she used it to close the breach instead of widening it. That counts for something."

He looked at me directly. The acknowledgment cost him. I could see the pride warring with the pragmatism that had kept him alive this long.

"You are still dangerous," I answered.

"So are you," he replied.

"Good. Perhaps you will survive."

A dry sound that might have been a laugh moved through the nearest warriors. The tension did not vanish, but it eased enough for breath to return to the clearing. Serathis spoke next, her tone crisp and military.

"The clans will follow strength," she said. "Today they saw yours. That will carry weight when the next council meets."

Torren pushed off the cart and offered a crooked grin that did not quite reach his eyes. "I would like it recorded that I was brave, useful, and unfairly attractive throughout this entire crisis."

Several warriors snorted. The moment of levity cracked the remaining stiffness, and conversations began to break into smaller groups. Kaelor touched my elbow lightly, a question without words. I nodded. The public moment had served its purpose. The rest could wait until we were no longer the center of every gaze.

Talia approached as we turned toward the fortress path. Her green eyes searched my face with the careful attention of someone who had learned to read wounds that did not always bleed.

"You stayed," she said quietly.

"I chose," I answered.

She smiled, small and genuine, then moved to help the wounded who were being guided toward the healer tents. Malakor fell into step with Kaelor for a brief exchange of low words about perimeter security and messenger birds. Then he peeled away toward the command structure without further comment. The night had taken enough from all of us.

The walk to Kaelor's private chambers passed in near silence. The fortress rose against the lightening sky, its dark stone still warm from the fires that had burned through the long hours of waiting. Guards opened the heavy doors without question. Inside, the air smelled of old leather, iron, and the faint smoke that never quite left these halls. Kaelor led me through the outer chamber and into the smaller room where a low fire already burned in the hearth.

He closed the door behind us. The latch clicked shut. For the first time since the Labyrinth had separated us, there was no immediate threat waiting on the other side. No collapsing stone. No cultists. No voices offering prophecies that demanded blood. The silence that followed felt different from every other silence we had shared.

I turned to face him. His gold eyes held mine with the same steady focus he had shown in the clearing, but something had softened at the edges. The exhaustion was there, carved deep into the lines around his mouth, yet beneath it ran a current of something warmer. Something that had waited through every battle and every political calculation.

"You chose to speak for me out there," I said.

"I chose to speak the truth," he answered. "You are not mine to command. You never were."

The words settled between us with the weight of everything we had refused to name until now. I stepped closer. The scent of him wrapped around me the way it always did, leather and smoke and the darker note that belonged only to him. His horns nearly brushed the ceiling beams. I had to tilt my head to keep his gaze.

"Stay because you choose it," he said. "Not because the maze named us."

"I know."

"Then choose."

"I already have."

His hand rose slowly, giving me every chance to pull away. When his fingers brushed my cheek, the contact sent a low pulse of heat through the weariness in my bones. I leaned into the touch. The calluses on his palm caught against my skin, rough and familiar and real in a way that nothing in the Labyrinth had been.

Kaelor bent his head, and when his mouth met mine, the slow, bruising weight of it shattered what was left of my control. This was not the desperate, hurried heat of the tunnels. It was deliberate, heavy with a possessiveness that made my lungs seize, yet so agonizingly tender it felt like a confession. I opened to him with a quiet gasp, my tongue tangling with his as his hands slid up to frame my face, his thumbs tracing my jawline with a reverence that made me ache. My palms pressed flat against the broad, warm expanse of his chest, tracing the thick ridges of his scars, feeling the furious, heavy thud of his heart beneath my fingers. He groaned deep in his chest—a low, vibration that rattled against my ribs—and pulled me flush against his massive frame until there was no air left between us.

Clothing became an obstacle we both tore away. My fingers fumbled with the heavy buckles of his harness, the leather dropping to the stone floor with a dull thud, followed by the rest of our gear until we stood entirely bare in the flickering hearthlight. My breath hitched at the sheer sight of him—the massive, sculpted lines of his shoulders, the dark fur tapering down his abdomen, and the thick, heavy length of his arousal, fully hard and glistening. He didn't rush. His gold eyes swept over my body, drinking in every inch of my bare skin with an intensity so fierce it felt like a physical touch. When he stepped closer, the heat radiating from him was a wall of pure temptation. There was no fear of what lay beyond the door, no looming shadow of the Labyrinth. We had all the time in the world, and the agonizing slowness of his hands sliding down my hips made my thighs tremble in anticipation.

Kaelor lifted me effortlessly, his large hands locking under my thighs as I wrapped my legs around his waist, my center pressing directly against the hard, burning heat of his stomach. I whimpered at the friction, burying my face in the crook of his neck, inhaling the intoxicating scent of leather, pine, and pure male. He carried me to the wide bed, lowering me back onto the thick, soft furs with a gentleness that contrasted sharply with the raw power of his frame. Before I could miss his weight, he pinned me beneath him, his massive body settling between my thighs. He didn't crush me; instead, he bracketed his weight on his forearms, his chest brushing my sensitive nipples, making me arch off the bed with a soft cry of need.

"Look at me, Elara," he rumbled, his voice raw, scraped back to the bone. I opened my eyes, meeting the molten gold of his gaze as his fingers tangled in mine, pinning our hands beside my head. He pressed the thick, blunt head of his shaft against my soaking cleft, sliding up and down my slick folds until I was slicking his dark skin, begging him with a breathless murmur. He paused, his gaze burning into mine, waiting. "Tell me you want this. Tell me you choose me."

"I choose you," I breathed, arching my hips into his. "I want you, Kaelor. Now."

He let out a low, feral growl and pushed forward, entering me in one long, agonizingly deep stroke that stretched me to my absolute limit. I gasped, my head tossing back against the furs as the sheer, thick fullness of him filled me completely, stretching my walls until every nerve ending screamed with a pleasure so intense it bordered on pain. He stayed still for a long moment, buried deep inside me, letting my body adjust to his massive size while he kissed away the tears of sensory overload at the corners of my eyes.

Then, he began to move. He pulled back almost entirely before driving deep again, the friction of his thick shaft sliding against my swollen, wet walls sending jolts of white-hot lightning straight to my core. I cried out his name, my fingers clawing at the muscles of his back as he built the rhythm, each thrust heavy, hard, and unyielding. The sound of our bodies slating together, wet and loud, filled the quiet room. He angled his hips, his thick pubic bone grinding directly against my sensitive clitoris with every deep, driving plunge. The pleasure was too much, too sharp, a beautiful torment that had me writhing beneath him, my inner muscles squeezing his thick length in tight, desperate pulses that made him grunt, his jaw clenched so hard the muscles jumped.

"You are so tight, Elara," Kaelor growled, his thrusts losing their restraint, becoming harder, faster, driving into me with a primal force that had me completely unraveled. I clung to his shoulders, my legs wrapping tighter around his waist to take him even deeper. The tension inside me coiled to a snapping point, and then I exploded, my vision going dark as a violent, crushing orgasm seized my body, my walls pulsing around him in tight, rhythmic spasms. The feel of my release broke him. With a deep, guttural roar that shook his entire frame, Kaelor gave one final, desperate thrust, burying himself to the absolute root as his thick, hot seed flooded deep inside me, filling me to overflowing. He shuddered violently, holding himself deep within me as the waves of our shared climax slowly washed over us, leaving us tangled and breathing heavily in the quiet warmth of the hearth.

Kaelor shifted only enough to draw me against his chest. One arm remained draped across my waist, possessive without restraint. I rested my head over the steady beat of his heart and listened to it slow. The exhaustion that had pressed against my bones earlier had transformed into something warmer, something closer to peace than I had allowed myself to expect.

"Astrythe will return," I said after a time. My voice came out low against his fur.

"She will," he agreed. "Veltheris remains beyond the seal. Both will test what we built tonight."

"The alliance needs rebuilding."

"It does."

"And I need to understand what my blood can still do."

His hand moved in slow circles along my spine. "We learn together. No prophecy required."

I lifted my head to look at him. The gold of his eyes had softened in the morning light. The scar across one caught the glow and turned it into something almost gentle. He had given me every choice. He had spoken for me in front of the clans without claiming ownership. The bond between us felt chosen in a way that nothing else in my life ever had.

"I do not regret staying," I told him.

"I would not have asked you to remain if you did."

The honesty settled between us like another layer of warmth. Outside the window the sky had begun its slow shift from gray toward the pale gold of sunrise. I could see the distant line of the Iron Mountains rising against the horizon. They no longer looked like a barrier I needed to cross in order to escape. They looked like a destination that might hold something worth defending.

Kaelor pressed a kiss to my temple. The gesture carried none of the urgency that had once defined every touch between us. It was simply presence. Simply chosen. I closed my eyes and let the moment stretch, memorizing the weight of his arm across my waist and the quiet rhythm of his breathing.

When I opened them again, the sun had cleared the peaks. Light spilled across the stone floor of the chamber and touched the discarded harness where it had fallen. The world beyond these walls remained dangerous. Astrythe still ruled the High Fey. Veltheris waited behind the seal, patient and aware. The clans would need time and proof before trust became something reliable rather than political necessity.

None of that changed what we had claimed here. I sat up slowly, the furs sliding down my skin. Kaelor watched me with the same steady attention he had shown since the clearing, waiting for whatever I would do next. I reached for the window ledge and leaned into the morning air. The wind carried the scent of pine and distant smoke and the faint metallic tang of the Labyrinth still sealed beneath the stone.

For the first time in my life, I did not feel hunted by the future. I felt ready to meet it.

# Epilogue: The Second Seal

Peace, I had discovered, was just another kind of tension when you were learning how not to destroy the world.

The training courtyard was cold at this hour, the kind of deep morning cold that settled into the stones overnight and refused to leave until the sun had been up long enough to earn it. My breath misted with each exhale. Sweat cooled fast against the back of my neck. Neither of those things mattered as much as the fact that the sealed gate in the eastern wall was humming again, low and persistent, right at the edge of hearing.

I pressed my palm flat against the stone and waited.

The hum shifted. Moved through the rock like something turning over in its sleep.

"Still there?" Talia asked from behind me.

"Still there." I pulled my hand back. The sensation faded but did not vanish entirely. It never fully vanished anymore. "It's like trying to ignore a sound that no one else can hear."

She appeared at my shoulder, her bronze curls escaping the practical knot she'd wrestled them into, her satchel slung across one hip and already open. She had been arriving at this courtyard every morning for the past six weeks with the focused energy of someone who had decided that helping me understand the Labyrinth's residual pull was exactly as important as cataloging medicinal herbs. Possibly more so.

"Progress," she said cheerfully, pulling a small stoppered vial from her bag. "Fewer accidental magical incidents this week. Last week you collapsed an archway."

"That archway was already unstable."

"It was load-bearing."

I turned to look at her. She offered the vial with the expression of someone presenting a reasonable argument wrapped in a herbal remedy. I took it without protest. Dragon-root, probably. It tasted like wet ash and worked well enough to dull the worst of the headaches that followed a long session of trying to sense the sealed passages beneath the fortress without accidentally waking them.

"The sensitivity is spreading," I said, swallowing the vile stuff in one go. "Farther than just what's beneath us. Yesterday I felt something that wasn't connected to Kaelor's lands at all."

Talia's cheerfulness sharpened into something more careful. "How far?"

"I don't know. Far."

She didn't say anything to that. She wrote something in the small leather journal she kept tucked under her elbow, and the scratch of her pen was the only sound for a moment besides the wind moving through the courtyard's upper stones.

I flexed my fingers, watching the faint silver-gray shimmer that traced my knuckles when the Labyrinth sensitivity flared. It faded within a breath. Two weeks ago, it had lasted several minutes and thrown off enough ambient energy to send three candles flying across Talia's workroom. She had been annoyingly delighted by that particular incident.

We were making progress. Slow, inconvenient, occasionally architectural progress.

The distant pulse came again.

Not beneath my feet this time. Not rising through the stone. It arrived from the north, from beyond the Iron Mountains, from somewhere the Labyrinth had no visible presence that any of us had mapped. It was brief and cold and unmistakably real, and it left a resonance behind it the way a struck bell leaves sound in the air after the metal has gone still.

I straightened. "Talia. Write that down. Exactly this moment."

She was already writing.

---

Kaelor found me at midday, which meant he had finished the morning's council session and chosen to come here instead of summoning me to the war hall. Six weeks ago, that choice would have surprised me. It still carried weight. It simply no longer surprised me.

He moved through the courtyard entrance with the particular controlled silence that had once made my hand reach for a blade on instinct. Now it only made me aware of him in a way that had nothing to do with threat and everything to do with the fact that I had memorized the sound of him crossing a room.

Treacherous, but accurate.

"Draevok asked about you," he said, stopping close enough that the warmth radiating from him reached me despite the cold air between us.

"Asked about me, or asked about my continued existence within the fortress walls?"

"The second one. Phrased diplomatically, which from him constitutes personal growth."

A reluctant smile pulled at my mouth. I crossed my arms against the chill. "What did you tell him?"

"That you remain dangerous." His gold eyes held mine with the steady heat that still had the audacity to affect my breathing, even now. "He seemed satisfied by that."

I had seen Draevok twice since the night we came out of the Labyrinth. The wounds across his chest had healed into new scar tissue, broad and jagged, layering over older ones. He had looked at me the second time with the kind of assessment he might give a blade that had proved itself in a difficult fight. Not warmth. Not welcome. Something more honest than either.

"You remain dangerous," he had said, passing me in the corridor without stopping.

"I assume that was meant as affection," I had answered at his retreating back.

He had not responded. But his pace had slowed, just slightly, before he turned the corner.

I had counted that as progress.

Kaelor's fingers found my jaw, tilting my head up toward him with the casual possessiveness that I had stopped pretending not to want. His thumb traced the line of my cheekbone. The touch was light and certain, sending heat down through my chest in a way that made the cold air irrelevant.

"You felt something this morning," he said. It was not a question.

"You could tell from the council chamber?"

"Talia sent a runner."

I made a mental note to have a conversation with Talia about the difference between helpful reporting and tactical surveillance. She would agree with me cheerfully and continue doing exactly as she pleased.

"North," I said. "Beyond the mountains. A pulse. Same signature as the Labyrinth beneath us, but not connected to anything we know about."

His expression did not shift dramatically. Kaelor's face rarely moved in obvious ways. But the quality of his stillness changed, that particular tightening around the jaw that meant he was filing something into the category of serious rather than theoretical.

"Come inside," he said.

I went.

---

The private chambers were warmer than the courtyard, the fire burning steadily in the hearth, the morning light cutting long angles across the stone floor. He poured water from the stone jug on the table and pushed the cup toward me without ceremony. I drank it, watching him think.

Watching Kaelor think was not an unpleasant occupation. He moved to the window and stood with one hand braced against the frame, his gaze on the mountains, his horns catching the light in a way that traced their runes in silver. The obsidian-and-gold harness had been exchanged for something slightly less ceremonial today, though he still wore the clan sigils at his shoulders. He had been rebuilding authority one council session at a time for six weeks, and the effort showed in the set of his spine.

He had chosen me publicly. That had consequences he had not pretended otherwise about, and he had absorbed every one of them without using me as a reason to justify anything. I respected him for that more than I had words to say cleanly.

"If there is another seal," he said, "Astrythe knew."

"She would have to." I set the cup down. "She has ruled the High Fey long enough to know the architecture of the Labyrinth better than we do. She withdrew after Veltheris failed, but that withdrawal was calculated, not defeated."

"She let him operate," Kaelor said. "The cult served her interests as long as he was useful. When he became a liability—"

"She pulled back and waited." I finished it. "Which means she still has something she wants from the Labyrinth. Something Veltheris's failure didn't give her."

The fire cracked behind me. The pulse from the north had faded, but its echo remained in my awareness the way the dragon-root's bitterness lingered on the tongue.

"Veltheris spoke about seals," I said. "He was obsessed with the idea of the Labyrinth as a system. Barriers between worlds that he believed should never have been constructed." I pressed my fingers against the table, steadying my thoughts. "What if he wasn't wrong about the system itself? What if the Labyrinth is larger than any of us understood, and the gate beneath this fortress was only one entrance?"

Kaelor turned from the window. The look he gave me carried the weight of someone calculating outcomes several moves ahead.

"Other seals," he said. "Other entrances."

"Other Catalysts, possibly."

The word settled between us with the particular gravity of things that cannot be unsaid. I had not spoken it aloud before today. The possibility had lived in the back of my awareness since the night I sealed the breach, since Veltheris had spoken in the Labyrinth's voice about bloodlines and architecture and keys that were never singular.

A knock at the door interrupted the silence.

Torren entered without waiting for permission, which was standard. He was carrying a sealed message cylinder in one hand and looking deeply aggrieved about something, which was also standard.

"Messenger bird from the southern passage," he announced, dropping the cylinder on the table with a clatter. "Arrived about an hour ago. I would have brought it sooner, but Serathis felt the need to brief me on everything that could go wrong if I lost it, and that conversation took time." He paused. "A lot of time. She's very thorough."

"Who sent it?" Kaelor asked.

"Seal's unfamiliar. But the binding marks on the parchment—" Torren tapped the cylinder with one finger. "Those are old. Really old. I would like history to note that I was essential and tragically underappreciated in getting this to you at all, given that Serathis nearly confiscated it for the council archive."

I reached for the cylinder and broke the seal.

The parchment inside was thin, the writing precise and economical in a way that felt less like correspondence and more like carved stone. A single line. No greeting. No signature beyond a mark I recognized: three concentric circles with a broken line through the outermost ring.

Mother Isyra's mark.

I read it aloud.

"The first seal held. The second is waking. What sleeps beneath the Ashwood does not wait for permission. Move quickly, or it will move for you."

Torren was quiet for approximately three seconds, which was a personal record.

"Excellent," he said. "Another apocalypse. We're collecting those now."

"Get Serathis," Kaelor told him. "War hall. Now."

Torren left without further commentary, which told me he understood the weight of what he'd just heard.

---

The war hall convened within the hour. Serathis arrived with two of her senior commanders and an expression that had already absorbed the possibility of catastrophe and begun organizing it into tactical priorities. Malakor stood against the far wall with his arms crossed, his black eyes moving between the message and the map Kaelor had spread across the central table. Talia hovered near the door, her journal open.

"The Ashwood," Serathis said, studying the map. Her scarred finger traced the territory north and east of the Iron Mountains. "That region has been politically neutral for decades. No clan holds it. No High Fey outpost operates there openly." She looked up. "Which means if something has been building beneath it, we would have had no reason to look."

"Veltheris knew," I said. "He spoke about the Labyrinth as though it was everywhere beneath us, not localized. We assumed the gate here was unique. We were wrong."

"If there is a second seal," Malakor said, his voice carrying its usual quiet precision, "and it is waking without a Catalyst present to stabilize it, the breach won't be controlled the way this one was. There's no one there to close it."

"There's me," I said.

The room went still.

Serathis met my gaze without flinching. She was the first to speak. "If there is a second seal, we prepare now. Intelligence before movement. We do not march toward an uncharted Labyrinth gate on the word of one oracle and a pulse you felt in a training yard."

"She is right," Kaelor said.

I did not argue. Serathis was right, and I was not yet so far gone on the need to do something that I would mistake urgency for wisdom.

"Send birds to every contact we have in the northern territories," Kaelor continued. "Malakor, I want scouts moving toward the Ashwood within two days. Quiet. No banners. We need to know what is actually waking before we commit resources."

Malakor nodded once and peeled away from the wall to begin the work.

The discussion continued for another hour, the particulars of intelligence-gathering and defensive repositioning, and the question of whether Astrythe's temporary withdrawal was connected to the second seal or merely coincidental timing. It was not coincidental. Everyone in that room knew it. The High Queen had survived too long through too much to retreat without a reason, and a second Labyrinth gate waking while her armies stood back was a reason that made terrible, elegant sense.

She had not lost. She had simply been waiting for a better board.

---

The battlements at night were cold enough to ache in the bones. I had come up here after the war hall, after the council dispersed, and the work of preparation folded itself into motion throughout the fortress below. Kaelor found me again, as he usually did, with the quiet certainty of someone who had simply decided that finding me was worth the effort.

He stood beside me without speaking for a while. The Iron Mountains rose against the dark sky, their peaks faintly edged by the last light of a moon already dropping toward the horizon. The wind off the high stone smelled of pine and frost and something deeper, something mineral and old that I now recognized as the Labyrinth's passive breath rising through the earth beneath us.

"Do you regret choosing this?" he asked.

His voice was low, private, stripped of the authority he wore in the council chamber. This was the voice he used when there was no audience and no performance required.

I considered the question honestly, which he deserved.

Six weeks of training sessions that left me with splitting headaches and Talia's cheerful notes on my instability. Six weeks of political councils where I was simultaneously too dangerous and not dangerous enough, depending on who was speaking. Six weeks of watching Kaelor navigate the consequences of publicly claiming a human woman with Labyrinth blood as his chosen partner, absorbing the friction without complaint and without apology.

Six weeks of waking up warm, for the first time in years, without needing to check the exits.

"Ask me after the next apocalypse," I said.

A sound moved through him that was not quite a laugh but was closer to one than most people ever heard from him. His arm came around my shoulders, heavy and certain, pulling me against the solid warmth of his side.

"You are impossible," he said.

"And yet." I leaned into him. "Here we are."

His chin dropped to the top of my head. The possessiveness in the gesture was the same kind it had always been with him: not a cage, not a claim over what I owed him, but the physical expression of someone who had chosen a direction and committed to it without reservation. I had spent most of my life treating that kind of certainty as a threat. I was still learning what it felt like when it wasn't.

The second pulse arrived without warning.

It hit like cold water poured down the back of my spine, sharp and unmistakable and coming from the north with a clarity that the morning's faint echo had not carried. My fingers gripped the battlement so hard it hurt. The shimmer traced across my knuckles in silver-gray, brighter than it had been in the courtyard, and this time it did not fade immediately.

Kaelor's arm tightened around me. "Elara."

"I feel it," I said. "The second seal. It's not just waking." I pressed my awareness toward it the way Talia had taught me, carefully, without forcing, the way you coax a flame rather than striking at it. The pulse expanded outward through the Labyrinth's buried network like a signal sent across an impossible distance.

And something answered.

Not the Labyrinth. Not the sealed gate beneath our feet. Something on the other end of that pulse, something that felt ancient and aware and utterly patient, turned its attention toward the source of the resonance it had detected.

Toward me.

The shimmer on my hands flared once, bright enough to throw light across the stone, and then went dark.

I stood very still.

"What answered?" Kaelor asked. His voice was careful.

"I don't know." I uncurled my fingers from the battlement stone. The cold night air pressed against my skin where the warmth of the power had just been. "But it knows I'm here now."

The mountains were silent. The wind moved through the peaks without ceremony. Below us, the fortress lights burned steadily, and somewhere inside, Malakor was already organizing scouts, and Serathis was already drafting contingencies, and Torren was almost certainly stealing something from the supply stores and calling it field research.

The world we had survived remained exactly as dangerous as it had always been.

It had simply become larger.

Kaelor turned us both away from the north, his hand firm at my spine, and we walked back toward the fortress door without rushing. His presence at my side was the same steady fact it had been since the moment he had told me I could leave and I had stayed. It was not armor. It was not a weapon. It was simply the particular gravity of someone who had made a choice and meant it.

I had made the same choice.

Whatever had answered from the darkness beyond the Ashwood, whatever second seal was waking beneath lands none of us had mapped, whatever Astrythe was planning in her withdrawal and

Veltheris was calculating behind his contained silence — none of it had changed that.

It had only given us something new to face.

I pushed open the fortress door. Warmth spilled out across the stone, and the distant pulse from the north faded to its baseline hum at the edge of my awareness, patient and waiting.

It would still be there tomorrow.

So would I.

# About the Author

Aveline Hart writes dark romantasy featuring dangerous magic, impossible choices, monstrous heroes, and fiercely independent heroines. Blood of the Labyrinth is the first installment in an epic romantasy series.

# Acknowledgments

Creating the world of Blood of the Labyrinth has been the greatest challenge and joy of my writing career. I am deeply grateful to my readers for taking a chance on this dark, monstrous journey; your passion keeps my imagination alive.

To my editor, thank you for your sharp eye and for helping me find the heart within the labyrinth. Your guidance was the thread that led me through the dark. To my beta readers, your early reactions and honest feedback were essential in shaping Elara and Kaelor's story.

To my family and friends, thank you for your unwavering patience and for believing in me even when the words wouldn't come. Your support is my foundation. And finally, to everyone who finds solace in stories of monsters and magic—this book is for you. Thank you for proving that the most beautiful things often grow in the darkest places.

With gratitude,

Aveline Hart

www.ingramcontent.com/pod-product-compliance
Lightning Source LLC
La Vergne TN
LVHW090546110826
845146LV00001B/42

* 9 7 9 8 9 9 6 3 5 1 3 0 5 *